J.R. WARD

CLAIMED

·THE LAIR OF THE WOLVEN·

PIATKUS

PIATKUS

First published in the US in 2021 by Pocket Books
An imprint of Simon & Schuster, Inc.
First published in Great Britain in 2021

13 5 7 9 10 8 6 4 2

Copyright © 2021 by Love Conquers All, Inc.

Interior design by Davina Mock-Maniscalco

The moral right of the author has been asserted.

A CIP catalogue record for this book
is available from the British Library.

ISBN 978-0-349-42783-6

Printed and bound in Great Britain by Clays Ltd, Elcograf S.p.A.

Papers used by Piatkus are from well-managed forests
and other responsible sources.

MIX
Paper from
responsible sources
FSC® C104740

Piatkus
An imprint of
Little, Brown Book Group
Carmelite House
50 Victoria Embankment
London EC4Y 0DZ

An Hachette UK Company
www.hachette.co.uk

www.littlebrown.co.uk

J. R. Ward lives in the South with her incredibly supportive husband and her beloved golden retriever. After graduating from law school, she began working in health care in Boston and spent many years as chief of staff for one of the premier academic medical centres in the nation.

Visit J. R. Ward online:

www.jrward.com
www.facebook.com/JRWardBooks
@jrward1

By J. R. Ward

The Black Dagger Brotherhood series:
Dark Lover
Lover Eternal
Lover Revealed
Lover Awakened
Lover Unbound
Lover Enshrined
Lover Avenged
Lover Mine
Lover Unleashed
Lover Reborn
Lover at Last
The King
The Shadows
The Beast
The Chosen
The Thief
The Savior
The Sinner
Lover Unveiled

The Black Dagger Brotherhood:
An Insider's Guide

The Black Dagger Brotherhood World
Dearest Ivie*
Prisoner of Night*
Where Winter Finds You
A Warm Heart in Winter

The Black Dagger Brotherhood:
Prison Camp
The Jackal

Lair of the Wolven
Claimed

The Black Dagger Legacy series:
Blood Kiss
Blood Vow
Blood Fury
Blood Truth

Fallen Angels series:
Covet
Crave
Envy
Rapture
Possession
Immortal

The Bourbon Kings series:
The Bourbon Kings
The Angels' Share
Devil's Cut

The Anne Ashburn Series:
The Wedding From Hell: The
Rehearsal Dinner* & The Reception*
Consumed

Standalone:
An Irresistible Bachelor
An Unforgettable Lady

*(ebook novella)

Dedicated:
To a couple who deserve a future.
No matter how impossible it seems.

CLAIMED

ONE

Town of Walters, est. 1834
Upstate New York

LYDIA SUSI'S DESTINY came for her in the veil, on a random Thursday in the early spring.

As she ran along the wooded trail, two miles into a loop that would take her through the preserve's northeastern acreage, she was measuring the glowing line that topped the contours of the mountains. Soon, the stripe would expand to an aura, and after that, the sun would accept the handoff from the moon, and day would arrive.

Her grandfather had always told her there were two twilights, two gloamings, and if you wanted to find your past, you went into the pines in the evening as the sun went down. If you wanted your future to come to you, you went alone into the forest in the veil, during that sacred transition of night into morning. There, he'd told her, when the distinction between that which ruled the light and that which held domain over the dark was at its narrowest, when the moon and the sun reached for each other before the rotations of their orbits tore them asunder, there was when the mortal could brush up against the infinite and seek answers, direction, guidance.

Of course, that did not mean you got good news. Or what you wanted.

But life was not an à la carte buffet where you could choose everything that went on your plate—another words-of-wisdom from a man who had lived to be 101 years old still smoking a pipe and drinking a glass of sima after his dinner year round.

Why limit spring to just *Vappu*? he'd said.

Lydia had never believed in his superstitions. She was a researcher, a scientist, and the kinds of things that her *isoisä* had gone on about did not fit in with that Ph.D. in biology she'd bought on layaway from the federal government and was still paying off.

So no, she was not out looking for any prognostication from the universe this morning. She was getting her workout done before she headed into her office at the Wolf Study Project. With the way things had been going lately, she was going to blink and it would be seven at night. Short-staffed and underfunded, everything was a fight for resources at WSP, and by the time she locked things up every evening, she was exhausted. So *Carpe Cardio* was her motto and why she was out in this misty darkness—

Lydia let her stride peter to a halt.

Her breath pumped in clouds that captured and held the moonlight, and as a breeze came across the trail, her body did the same with the chill, grabbing it out of the air and bringing it in under her wind-breaker.

As she shivered, she looked behind herself. The trail she was on was the widest one in the preserve, a highway rather than a street, but she couldn't see much into the trees. Pines crowded up close to the shoulders of the packed path, and the fog wafting through the craggy trunks and fluffy boughs obscured the forest even more.

In a quick calculation, she figured she was a good three miles from any other human, two miles from her car at the trailhead's parking area, and a hundred yards from what had caught her attention.

There, up ahead, something was close to the ground, moving.

Fight or flight, Lydia, she thought. *What's it going to be.*

She reached around to the small of her back. There were two cylinders mounted on the strap of her fanny pack, and she left the Mace where it was. Clicking on her flashlight and bringing it forward, she swung the beam in a wide arc—

The eyes flashed over on the left, a set of retinas flaring the light back at her as pinpoints. The stare was about three feet from the ground and the pupils were set close together, as predators' were.

Lydia looked around again.

"I'm not going to bother you," she said. But like the gray wolf spoke English?

The growl was soft. And then came the rustling. The animal was prowling toward her.

"Oh, shit."

Except . . .

Lydia kept the beam down on the fallen pine needles as she, too, walked forward. Something was wrong with the wolf, its gait wobbly and uneven. Yet the spirit of the hunter remained undeterred—and she was identified as its target.

She was about twenty feet away when she got a sense of the fully mature male. He was filled out, at a healthy weight of about a hundred and thirty pounds, and his mottled white, gray, and brown fur was thick and lush, especially at the tail. But his head was hanging at a bad angle, and he was dragging his back paws as he continued to close the distance between them.

It was obvious when the wolf was going to collapse. Though his head remained forward, his body listed to the side, his will staying strong even as his rear legs, and then his forelegs, gave out.

He landed on the soft bed of pine needles on his side, and the struggle was immediate, useless paws batting at thin air and ground cover. As Lydia drew a little closer to him, he snarled, flashing long white fangs, his golden eyes narrowing.

"Shh . . . ," she said as she kneeled down.

Her hand shook as she got out her cell phone. As she called a number from her favorites, she tried to keep her breathing steady.

In the flashlight's beam, she could see the grayness of those gums. The wolf was dying—and she knew why.

"Goddamn it, pick up, pick up—" Her words machine gun'd from her mouth. "Rick? Wake up, I've got another one. On the main trail—what? Yes, it's the same—enough with the talking, get your ass out of bed. I'm on the loop, about two miles into the—huh? Yes, bring everything, and *hurry*."

She cut the connection as her voice gave out.

Letting herself fall back to a sit, she stared into those beautiful eyes and tried to project love, acceptance, gentleness . . . compassion. And something got through, the majestic male's muzzle relaxing, its paws falling still, his flank rising and falling in a shuddering breath.

Or maybe it was dying right now.

"Help is coming," she said hoarsely to the animal.

◆ ◆ ◆

Richard Marsh, D.V.M., gunned the ATV down the trail, the unmuffled engine echoing around the otherwise still and silent forest. As the tires hit tree roots, he fought with the handlebars, wrenching them to stay on course. With the wind in his face, he had to blink a lot. He should have worn goggles. Or at least not left his contacts in.

Almost ten minutes into the racing scramble, the glow of a flashlight registered through the trees, and he eased up on the throttle. Nailing the brakes, he skidded to a stop and dismounted. His med pack was a duffel large enough to haul a set of golf clubs, and its weight strained his bad shoulder as he hefted it off the cargo platform and started marching into the pines.

He stopped dead. "What the hell are you doing?"

Lydia Susi's long, lean body was stretched out on a bed of pine needles . . . next to a full-grown male gray wolf which probably weighed as much as she did. Which was a wild animal. Which was capable of anything.

"Shh," she said, like she knew he was yelling at her in his head.

Rick cursed. "Move away from the wolf. You are violating every common sense and professional standard— I mean, come on. You *know* better than this—"

"Just shut up and save him."

The woman was no more than two feet away from that muzzle, her eyes locked on the closed lids of the wolf, her running tights and shoes crossed, her windbreaker a loose bag around her upper body. Wolves could run nearly forty miles an hour, but that kind of effort was not going to be necessary to bite her. That thing could just lunge forward and sink all of its forty-two teeth into soft skin—

"He's cyanotic in his gums. It's the same anticoagulant as before," she said.

"You're assuming." Rick put his duffel down and unzipped one side of it. "Now get the hell back—"

"You are *not* tranq'ing him," she hissed as she sat up.

"And you're not a vet. You're also clearly not thinking. Has it occurred to you that that animal could have rabies?"

"He's not foaming at the mouth—" She lowered her voice. "If you tranquilize him, you're going to kill him."

"Oh, okay. So I'll just cozy up like you have and ask him for his consent to treat. He can put his paw print on the forms—"

"Rick, I'm serious! He's dying!"

As she raised her voice again, the wolf twitched and opened its eyes. Rick became an instant focal point, and the animal lifted its head to growl weakly.

"Get away from him," Rick said in a grim voice. "Right now."

"He's not going to hurt me—"

"I'm not treating him until you're out of range."

Rick rose to a stand, the tranq gun in his right hand, his trail boots going absolutely fucking nowhere. Predictably, Lydia kept talking, but when he didn't move . . . she eventually did. As she finally shuffled away from the gray wolf, Rick let out an exhale he hadn't been aware of holding in.

Then again, when it came to the Wolf Study Project's behaviorist, he shouldn't have been surprised by any of his reactions. Lydia had been the outlier he had not been looking for since the day he'd met her.

At least now, things moved fast. As she covered her mouth with both hands and curled her knees up to her chest, he discharged a tranquilizer into the animal's flank. Due to the wolf's low blood pressure, the sedation took longer to have an effect than normally, but soon enough, those golden eyes were closed and going to stay that way.

Hopefully not because Lydia was right and he'd killed the animal.

Rick brought his duffel over with him, and he led with his stethoscope, pressing the metal disk to the chest wall. Moving it around.

"Do you have the vitamin K? You brought the vitamin K, right?"

Lydia's voice was right by him and he jerked back. She had repositioned herself at the wolf's muzzle, lifting that head into her lap, stroking the mottled gray fur of the ruff. For a moment, Rick became lost in the way her fingers soothed through the—

"Can you let me finish my exam first," he said. "Before you start prescribing antidotes?"

"But you have the vitamin K?"

Rick peeled back the jowl. The gray gums, the sluggish, uneven heart rate . . . he knew what was going on, and not only because this was the third wolf they'd found in this condition in the last month.

"I'll do what is medically appropriate"—turning away, he grabbed his penlight—"when I'm ready. And can you please put his head back on the ground. Thanks."

As he returned to the animal, she did what he asked—sort of. She scooted to the side, but stayed bent over, still calming the wolf.

He separated the eyelids and shined the light in. Nonresponsive pupil.

Rick went to click off the little beam when a raindrop landed on the wolf's cheek. As the crystalline droplet coalesced and then slowly trailed off the fine facial fur, he glanced at the sky. Strange, the moon had been showing when he'd come down the trail and was still—

"Oh, Lydia," he said.

When she looked up at him, their faces were close together. So his hand didn't have far to travel.

As he brushed the next tear off her cold cheek, she stopped looking at him. And refocused on the wolf.

"Just don't let him die," she whispered.

Rick felt time slow to a crawl. In the lunar glow that filtered down through the pine boughs, Lydia's face was cast in loving light, the planes and angles that made her who she was visually enhanced by the illumination. Her naturally highlighted hair, which was pulled back into a ponytail, had tendrils that curled by her ears and at her neck. And her lips were a promise of things that kept a man up at night and distracted him during the day.

Rick now also looked away. "Of course I won't let him die."

On so many levels, he was not surprised that this woman was making him promise something he couldn't deliver on. But an inspired heart could make stupid out of anybody.

It also made you pretty frickin' lonely.

But who was counting the benefits of unrequited love.

TWO

ONE HOUR AND forty-five minutes after Lydia found the wolf in the veil, she was on the ATV heading back out into the preserve. The sun had now fully risen over the mountain range, the rays piercing through the pines and making her think of gold coins spilled from God's pocket. Up ahead, the trail was as empty as it had been before, nothing but shadows cast by all that beautiful light—

The engine sputtered without warning, the interruption of the smooth purr the very last thing she needed. Cranking the gas, she was relieved by a surge of speed, but it didn't last. All forward momentum ended as the horsepower choked off and the vehicle's heavy, knobby wheels and complete lack of aerodynamic design dragged her to a standstill.

"Damn it," she muttered as she tapped on the gas gauge.

The red pin didn't budge from the E on the far left.

"Shit." Dismounting, she looked up and down the trail. "*Shit.*"

She resisted the urge to kick one of the big back tires, opting instead to take her frustration out by locking grips on the back grate and leaning her weight into a shove. When the ATV was off on the shoulder, she put it in park and took the keys.

Starting off at a jog, she rounded the corner on the trail, her footfalls steady. About a quarter mile later, she came to the pattern of trunks that marked where she had seen the wolf's eyes in the darkness. She followed her own shoe prints into the trees and stopped when she came to the disturbed place in the pine needles where the wolf had collapsed, and been treated, and finally, been carried out to the ATV.

After a moment of sad helplessness, she kept going, heading farther away from the trail. As she went along, she diverted around the pricker bushes, the rotting stumps, the occasional fallen pine. She followed a gradual decline that took her to the water shed trough that cleaved a descent through the elevation's west-facing flank. When she came to the river way, she looked up the pathway of polished rocks. The spring rains had not started, so the torrent that would rush over them a month from now had yet to get going. Soon, though, there would be so much more than damp sand and mud between the boulders and stones.

Lydia jumped into the puzzle-piece-bed and hopscotched upward, leaping from flat top to flat top, keeping her balance by throwing her arms this way and that, making sure that she avoided the lichen and moss growth that could make her slip.

Overhead, crows circled and called to each other, aviary judges that seemed to be following her and running a commentary. She refused to look and acknowledge their paparazzi presence.

Anthropomorphize much? And to think she considered herself a scientist.

Lydia found the first dead vulture about half a mile up the riverbed. Three days old, going by the state of the remains. A raccoon was the next body. Also by the river's edge, about two hundred yards up.

As the going got steeper, she debated whether to continue the climb because this was real needle-in-a-haystack stuff. Taking a pause to catch her breath, she looked over her shoulder at the valley below. Cradled between the palms of the deep green mountains, a blue lake in the form of a salamander caught the sun—and gave it back. The glinting made her blink even from a distance, but how could anyone begrudge the splendor.

In her soul, she knew it was inevitable that she would end up here. All this natural beauty, all this space . . . all this lack of people.

It was also inevitable that someone with dollar signs in their eyes would fuck it up.

On the other side of the valley, at the exact elevation she was, a half-mile section of evergreens had been cleared by machines and explosives. The ragged, raw earth and exposed granite ledge were an injury to the other mountain, something that would take a decade to patch over and partially heal if left alone. But that wasn't the future. Off to one side, enormous steel I beams extended upward, a forest of man-made trunks that were soon to be thick walls to support heavy ceilings.

The resort was going to sit on that site, a blight on the landscape, and service people who were looking for a "luxury spa experience."

Meditation and wellness brought to you by American Express and the fine folks at Diners Club—

The snap of a stick made her turn around and go for her Mace at the same time. But she instantly recognized the tall, intense man who had come up behind her without making a sound. Until he had wanted his presence to be known.

"Oh, it's you, Sheriff."

Sheriff Thomas Eastwind was forty-ish, with strong features and long black hair that was always kept in a single braid. In his uniform, he was fully armed and in charge even out in the wilderness—then again, he was the boss of Walters. With a staff of three other officers, he enforced the law for not only all of the preserve, but the half dozen little towns between Walters and the Canadian border.

"I found what you're looking for," he said. "This way."

Eastwind turned and cut into the forest—and there was no question that she was going to follow him.

Fortunately, she kept up easily, even though his stride was long and he never misplaced his feet on the rocky, uneven ground.

"Will the wolf survive?" he asked as they wound around pines.

There was no reason to ask how he knew another one had been found. "We'll know more in the next twenty-four hours. At least that's what Rick says."

"Was it one of yours?"

"It was tagged, yes. A male. He was magnificent—*is* magnificent, I mean."

There was no more talking until the sheriff stopped and pointed. "Over there."

The instant Lydia focused on what he'd found, she jumped ahead, shoving boughs out of the way. The bait trap was chained to a sapling, the stainless steel box vented and open at the top. Inside, remnants of meat secured by a wire had dried out.

"Motherfucker," she whispered as she knelt down and tested the links of the chain. "I need to take this with—"

"Come stand behind me."

Looking up, she saw that Eastwind had unholstered his service weapon and was holding it by his thigh.

"Don't shoot me," she said.

"I won't."

Hustling out of the way, she put her arms over her face—which was a little ridiculous—

Pop!

As the bullet hit the chain, there was a clang and a *pfft* of loose dirt, and in the pause afterward, a crow flushed from a branch, squawking as it flew off.

Going back to the trap, Lydia uncoiled the links from the trunk, and hefted the thing up onto her shoulder.

"You know they're killing the wolves on purpose," she said. "To protect people who haven't been bothered by animals that have more right to be here than we do."

"I'll take you back to your headquarters." He pivoted and started to walk off. "My vehicle is this way."

"You can't let them do this." Lydia stayed put. "I know that resort is bringing jobs here, but they're too expensive on the wildlife."

The sheriff just kept going. "I'll get Alonzo to trailer your ATV back."

"They're taking what does not belong to them," she called out in a voice that cracked.

When Eastwind continued to ignore her, she glared across the valley at the construction site. That fucking hotel and its five hundred acres of "serenity and rejuvenation." If she could have blown the place up, she would have lit the fuse and tossed the dynamite right this second.

It was the first time in her life she'd seriously considered murder.

◆   ◆   ◆

The Wolf Study Project's facility was located at the head of the preserve, just off the county road that wound its way around the base of Deer Mountain and the shores of Lake Goodness. The parking lot was just packed dirt with an overlay of gravel, and the building was a modest sprawl along the landscape, one-storied, cedar-shingled, hidden by hemlocks. As Lydia and Eastwind pulled up, there was a Jeep and a sedan in place, plus Lydia's hatchback and a WSP truck that had last worked back when Clinton was president.

"Thanks for the ride," she said as she opened her door.

"You're welcome."

With a grunt, she dragged the bait trap out of the wheel well. As she slung the weight over her shoulder, she went to shut the door—

"Lydia."

She stopped and leaned back into the SUV. "Yes?"

Eastwind's dark eyes were grave. "I don't offer to help you with that only because I know you'll say no."

Looking down, she shook her head. "I need you to take care of our problem across the valley. That's the only thing I need you to do. Stop protecting the powerful, it's unseemly in a man of what I'd always assumed was your kind of honor."

She didn't wait for a response. She just closed things and strode off, not to the front of the building, but to the back clinic entrance. As she stepped through into an open area full of vet supplies and tracking devices, she smelled antiseptic cleaner and blinked in the glare of the fluorescent ceiling panels. Rick's exam rooms, where injured wolves were treated and released, and healthy ones were examined and tagged, were completely isolated from the administration part of things.

"I saw you on the monitor," Rick said as he came out of a room. He stopped in the process of drying his hands. "What is that. And no, you don't know that whatever was in there was—"

"Is he still alive." She held out the trap. "And of course this is what poisoned him—"

"Do we have footage of the wolf taking—"

"Test what's left! Jesus Christ, Rick, I'll get you the video—"

"Shh, keep your voice down."

Lydia looked away. Looked back. "Please. I just . . . is he still alive?"

"Yes, but it's going to be a fight."

Lydia shoved the trap into Rick's hands and went to the open doorway of the exam room. In the center of the tiled space, on a stainless steel table, the wolf was intubated and limp, his side pumping up and down thanks to a machine. An IV ran into a shaved portion of his foreleg and soft beeping tracked a sluggish heart rate.

As she went to the animal, she could sense Rick's eyes on her. But fortunately for him, he didn't say one damn thing about how she needed to be more arm's length with the wolves.

"I'm right here," she said softly as she stroked its shoulder. "You're going to be okay."

Over on a counter, a knobby fleece blanket was clean and folded. Reaching for it, she flipped the soft weight loose of its order and draped it over the lower half of his body. Then she just stood there.

Her eyes roamed around the wolf's lean and powerful body, searching for the answer to whether he lived or died. All she got was the pattern on the blanket, an animated beagle chasing flying bones and water bowls across a faded green field. The smile on the cartoon dog's face struck her as false optimism, something that shouldn't be peddled to children.

But like denying them the years before adult reality hit them was any better?

"I'll test what's in here," Rick said with resignation.

Lydia rubbed one of the wolf's paws and then walked over to the doorway. "Let me know what it is?"

"Sure, I'll give you a call—"

"I'm just in my office." When he frowned, she tilted her head. "What?"

"You're not going home to change?"

Lydia looked down at her running tights. "Who do I have to impress? And it'll take too much time."

Yeah, because fifteen minutes back to the little house she rented was something she should pack an overnight bag and a sandwich for. Leaving, though . . . felt wrong.

"Let me know what you find out?" she repeated.

When she turned away, Rick said, "I will."

At the far end of the clinic area, she pushed through into the administration offices. The executive director's door was closed—no news there. The conference room was empty. Supply closet and printing alcove were, too. But there was fresh coffee brewing in the break room, and out front, Candy McCullough's no-shit-Sherlock voice was rapid firing something about a UPS delivery that hadn't come yet.

It was hard not to feel sorry for whoever had picked up the phone at *What Can Brown Do for You?*

That was the old slogan, though, wasn't it, Lydia thought as she flipped the switch in the doorway of her office.

As the lights flickered on, she frowned.

Something was . . .

Crossing the rough rug, she went to her desk and looked at the landline phone, her computer, her lamp. Her mug full of pens and pencils. Her pad of paper and the two files Candy had left in her inbox.

With a shaky hand, Lydia pushed the lamp out of its strict alignment with the edge of the desk. Then she put it back in place.

"You're nuts," she said as she fell into her office chair.

"I don't see why you gotta get personal." Candy was talking as she swung around the doorjamb. "Was that Eastwind who brought you in?"

"Yes, I had to get something out in the preserve." She rubbed her tired eyes. "He's going to tow the ATV back. It ran out of gas—"

As Candy made a dismissive sound in the back of her throat, Lydia looked up—and lost her train of thought. The sixty-year-old woman was, in her own words, "round as a billiard ball, but not as smooth," and her stocky body was currently squeezed into a pair of khaki slacks and a white turtleneck. Her hand-knit vest had a three-dimensional quality to it, knotty flowers and twisting vines circling her torso, the granny-chic not matching her level stare or Brooklyn accent or her high and tight in the slightest.

"I . . ." Lydia still wasn't sure what she was looking at. "Is your hair pink?"

"Yeah." Candy made a *duh* gesture with her hands. "Where's your coffee? You get your coffee yet?"

"Um, it looks good. The color suits you."

Which was a surprising truth. It also matched some of the knit roses.

"Doris did it. And I'm getting you coffee."

"You don't have to." Lydia leaned to the side and opened the lowest drawer. "I am not tired in the slightest, trust me."

"You're going to need it, trust *me*."

As Candy walked off, Lydia paused. Then shook

her head and outed the Lysol wipes. Popping the lid, she snapped two free and rubbed down the laminated top of the desk, skirting the pads, the pens, the phone, the monitor, the inbox. An itch to clear everything off and do a series of long pulls made her check the doorway and do a quick mental calculation on how long Candy was going to take to come back with the coffee that hadn't been asked for.

When you were acting nutty about cleanliness, an audience was the last thing anybody wanted.

"Okay, you ready?" Candy demanded as she came in and banged a mug down on the drying, hospital-worthy antiseptic.

"No offense, but what—" Actually, the coffee smelled great, and as she palmed it up and took a test sip, she decided Candy was right. She did need this. "What's going on?"

"Well, first of all, you and I are using the boys' bathroom again."

Lydia let her head fall back. "Maybe I shouldn't be drinking anything all day long."

"But that's not the big news. I'm sending the *big* news down to you. It's all gonna make sense when you see it."

"It?" Lydia shot the woman a hard stare. "Please do not tell me you overpowered that UPS driver and duct-taped him to that hand truck you like so much. You cannot hold a human being hostage in exchange for a package. Even if it's a week late."

"Hey, thanks for the good idea. You're an inspired leader. But no, that's not it."

As Candy headed back to the waiting area, Lydia called out, "Just to be clear, I am not ever signing off on hostage taking. You keep a person locked in a closet, it's a felony—"

Cologne.

She smelled . . . cologne. A woodsy, very . . . delicious . . . cologne.

And that was when she heard the footfalls. Heavy. Really heavy. A man's.

Candy reappeared in the doorway, a sly smile on her face. "The applicant is here."

"Applicant?"

"You know, for Trick's replacement?"

"Oh, no, Peter's supposed to interview—"

"I explained that as our executive director's in a meeting, you're going to conduct the preliminaries." Candy eased back. "Lydia Susi, meet—what did you say your name was?"

"Daniel Joseph."

The man who stepped into the open jambs was so tall and so broad, he was like a living, breathing door: He blocked out all light and made it impossible for anyone to come or go.

As Lydia's eyes traveled up, up, up, she saw jeans that did little to hide muscled thighs, and a worn flannel shirt that had been freshly pressed, and a set of shoulders . . .

That made someone think things that should never be part of any job interview.

"Should I come in?" he said in that deep, smooth voice.

The chuckle Candy let out drifted off as the woman left.

The man's face was a double-take and a half, his features put together in such a way that you couldn't help but drink them in, everything balanced, symmetrical, powerful. Sensual, too, thanks to that mouth. And of course, his dark hair was on the long side of a short cut, the ends brushing his neck, and pushed back off his forehead, and curling, thick and shiny, over his ears.

"Or do we go somewhere else?" he asked.

Oh, I've gone somewhere, Lydia thought. *And it's going to get me in trouble with HR.*

As she considered all the internal policies she was breaking—and weren't there some federal laws, too?—she decided that she really should have just rolled over and gone back to sleep when her alarm went off at five a.m. Really and truly.

But thank God for Candy's coffee.

THREE

I—AH, NO." Lydia stood up and extended her hand over the desk. "I mean, please come in. And meet you. Meet me. Please to."

Oh, FFS.

"Thanks," the man said.

It took him two strides to get to her, and his arm was so long, he didn't have to bend at the waist to take her palm. His grip was firm and strong, and the contact lasted a second and a half, maybe two—yet the warmth lingered as they both sat down. At least for her—

Well. What do you know. She'd never realized that chair on the far side of her desk was dollhouse-sized.

She grabbed her mug and decided Candy was right. She didn't need the caffeine for sure, but the coffee gave her something to do with her itchy hands.

"So," she said.

As her mind went blank, she smiled in what felt like a fake way—because it was either that or she giggled: Meeting this man in the eyes created a sixteen-year-old vortex, sucking her back to Justin Bieber crushes and that kid in her math class . . . what was his name?

"Isaac Silverstein."

"What?" the man across from her said.

Crap. "I apologize. I'm just making a mental note to call—it doesn't matter."

God, those eyes of his were the strangest color she'd ever seen. Something that was both fire and hazel. Something that glowed.

"Anyway, Mr.—I'm sorry, what was your last name?"

"Joseph. But call me Daniel."

"Right, well, Daniel, our executive director is very busy." Doing frick-only-knew-what. "But I'll be happy to give you an overview of the position."

He shrugged. "I'm just looking for a job—"

Curling up a hand, he covered his mouth as he coughed. Cleared his throat. Coughed again.

"Oh, no—it's the wipes, isn't it."

She clipped the Lysol's top closed and put the container away. Then she waved her hands over the desktop. When he coughed again, like she'd made it worse, she cursed under her breath.

"I'll open a window."

"It's okay, just allergies."

"I'd prefer the fresh air anyway." She cranked the vertical window behind her desk a crack. "I'm a little weird about keeping things clean."

"Nothing wrong with that."

Turning back around, she rubbed her nose in a show of solidarity even though nothing was tickling or irritated on her face. Then again, her sinuses had probably been fried years ago by that linen-fresh scent.

"I hope that's better."

"Thanks."

"Hey, do you want some coffee? I'd be happy to get you some."

"I try not to touch the stuff." He coughed one last time. "About two years ago, I went on a health kick and got rid of everything. Except cheeseburgers."

"A clean liver. I'm mean, not the organ. Like, your life."

Annnnnnd this was why she studied behavior in other species. 'Cuz she needed tips herself.

"I am now." He linked his hands and leaned forward, the chair letting out a groan at the load shifting. "Look, I'll be honest with you. I'm not here for long, and maybe that takes me out of the running. I'm a drifter and my employment history is going to show that. But it's also going to tell you that I'm reliable, I do good work, and I'm not a lot of trouble."

"How long is not long?"

"I dunno, through the warm season and into the fall. Maybe past the winter, but by next spring, I'll be moving on. If that makes me unattractive, I understand."

Even the ugly stick for a week couldn't get you to homely, she thought.

"Well, we'd certainly rather have someone who'd be willing to stick around, but that's not a deal breaker. And I'm glad you're being up front about it. Tell me, where did you last work?"

"Over in Glens Falls, for an apartment complex. And before that it was up in Maine." He thumbed over his shoulder. "I gave my paperwork to—"

Candy reappeared with a folder, like she'd been listening out in the hall. "His application and his résumé, Ms. Susi."

As Lydia took what was delivered with a glare, the older woman jogged her eyebrows and took her pink-haired peanut gallery back out front.

When they were alone again, Lydia made a show of looking at what she'd been given. High school education. Handyman jobs, at apartment and condo complexes. An elementary school. A mall in Jersey. No big cities. No jobs that lasted longer than eight to ten months, but no gaps in employment, either.

"Looks like you've stayed in the New England area."

"I prefer the cold, so getting me any further south than Pennsylvania is tough. Oh, and yeah, sure, I'll take a drug test and agree to a background check. I have nothing to hide."

He'd handwritten the responses on the application form, everything in neat, block letters.

"So you like cold weather?" she asked.

"Yes, and I need to be outdoors. That's why what

you're looking for is good for me. I can take care of your trails, your buildings, your vehicles. I can handle anything from plumbing to electric to Sheetrock."

"A Dan of all trades."

"You got it. And I'm not afraid of long hours, either."

"You were born in Rochester, huh?"

"Yup. But we moved around a lot. Mom had to take what she could find for work. She was pretty much on her own with me. Small family, you know the drill."

Lydia looked up. There was no emotion showing on his face, but like that would have been appropriate? He was here for a job, not an amateur therapy session.

"I come from a small family, too," she murmured.

"Oh, yeah?"

"Just my granddad and me. We stayed put, though, until he died."

"I'm sorry you lost him. Where'd you grow up? If you don't mind me asking."

"The Pacific Northwest, actually."

"Ah, so that's why you're here. You like the trees and the mountains."

Lydia smiled. "Yup, exactly. I'm an outdoor person, too."

"What do you do here?"

"I'm like the census taker for wolves. I track the pack numbers and locations throughout the preserve, and study patterns of behavior from feeding to breeding. I also work with our vet to monitor health. The gray wolf population all but died out in the Adirondacks and Upstate New York in the late eighteen hundreds, but they were reintroduced here on the preserve in the sixties when the balance of everything tilted."

"Balance?"

"Biological systems are all about equilibrium. You take one piece off the table, everything rebalances in ways that are not always beneficial. The best thing to do is leave nature alone. Humans don't like to do that, though—" She stopped herself. "Sorry, I'm on my soap box."

"Don't apologize. I like your passion."

Lydia cleared her throat. "Do you have any questions for me? About the job?"

He tilted his head to the side. "Yeah, how do you keep tabs on them?"

"Them? Oh, the wolves, you mean. They have GPS chips, just like domesticated dogs, and we have monitoring cameras posted around the preserve. I also get out in the field and use drones from high altitudes. We have two thousand acres here so it's a lot to keep track of."

"That's really interesting."

"You're humoring me."

"I have no sense of humor, actually."

Lydia laughed. "What?"

"No, it's true. I can't tell jokes and I rarely smile."

Closing the folder, she frowned and sat forward. "That's really a shame."

"It is what it is. I have other skills."

"You never laugh? Ever."

"No, not really." He shrugged those powerful shoulders. "It's just a gene I don't have."

"I've never thought of humor as a recessive trait. Were your parents also comedy-challenged?"

His stare got a faraway look as if he were running through his family tree. "Well, there was my Uncle Louie. He was the black sheep of the family, laugh wise."

"How so?"

The man with the strange, beautiful eyes refocused on her. "Knock-knock."

"Who's there?"

"Uncle Louie."

"Uncle Louie who?"

"See? It's not funny."

"Wait, what?" Lydia shook her head and laughed again. "That's not a punch line."

"Which is my point. He tried one, pathetic knock-knock joke and it's a disaster. It has no punch line."

Holding up her palm, she really tried not to smile so much. "But I thought he was the black sheep of your—that would mean he *can* tell a joke."

"No, that's how far down the unfunny hole we are. Even the black sheep can't get far at all. We're just that sad."

As Lydia shook her head, she didn't dare try to hide her smile behind sipping from her coffee mug. She was liable to have something come out of her nose.

"You're funnier than you think you are, Daniel Joseph."

"Will it get me this job? Because if I need to stand up on a stage and—well, do stand-up, I will?"

"I'm not sure how that would help with the nuts and bolts of things."

"Well, have you got anything that's broken I could demonstrate on?"

Try our executive director.

"How much do you know about toilets," she said under her breath.

"Take me to your plumbing, ma'am." He got to his feet. "I'm in."

"Really?"

"If the toilet's broken, you'd call your handyman, right? Rather than waste money on a guy with a wrench decal on his truck. So let me fix it for you."

Lydia stood up, too. "It's in the women's bathroom."

"Show me."

Coming around her desk, she felt a pressure of speech that made no sense—and a tingling in her body that made the kind of sense she didn't want to think about. She also had the desire to flip her hair over her shoulder, which was ridiculous: Considering she was calling a man in to do a job she could probably figure out herself, she was *not* going the ingénue route. Nope.

Pride goeth before the flirting.

"Here we are."

Out in the hall, she pushed a door wide, and got hit in the face with a wall of strawberry: Pink walls, pink stall, pink sink, pink pink. And the air freshener on the counter as well as the hand soap and the lotion followed the Nesquik theme.

As Daniel coughed behind her, she was not surprised. "Candy likes the smell."

"There certainly is a lot of it to go around."

"And here is the patient." She hipped the stall door open. "We've been having trouble with it—well, since nineteen seventy-three if you go by Candy's timeline."

When Daniel came forward, she eased back against the tile wall—and still there wasn't enough room. So she got a brush of his soft shirt on the back of her hand, and more of that cologne in her nose.

Which canceled even the fake Fruity Pebble air freshener.

There was a scrape and a clunk as he removed the back of the toilet and toggled the handle. And Lydia absolutely did not look at the fit of those Levi's in the rear.

Really. She didn't.

"You've got two issues," he said. "One, the stopper

is so old, it's cracked and can't make a good seal. Does this leak a lot?"

"Yes. I hate the waste, and when it gets really bad, I turn the water off underneath."

"Yeah. And the second problem is that the chain arm is shot."

"Do we need to get a new toilet?"

"I wouldn't replace this. These old boys are worth their weight in gold. The new low-flush versions don't work well with old pipe systems because there's not enough water volume to them and this leads to stop-ups due to low pressure. Looking at this building, I'm guessing it was built in the late sixties, early seventies. So in addition to fifty years of buildup, you've got terra-cotta pipes running out to your leaching field."

"Is that bad?"

"Tree roots. Big trouble."

"I feel like you've just diagnosed our plumbing with tuberculosis before the era of antibiotics. Be honest, are we terminal?"

"You got slow drains?"

"Now that you mention it, Rick struggles with that in the clinic." She went over to the sink and ran some water. "How's this look?"

He leaned out of the stall. "Slow."

Daniel ducked back in and there was some sloshing. A clank or two. The sound of a chain. Flushing. A grunt and some water running.

As he came out, he held his hands together and

went to the sink. Using some of Candy's strawberry soap, he washed things vigorously.

"'Scuse me," he muttered.

When he sneezed into the inside of his elbow, she shook her head. "You'd swear we're trying to kill you with fragrance. And God bless you."

"Thank you." He snapped two paper towels out of the dispenser and dried his palms in the same powerful way, clapping his hands. "Here's the plan. I've jury-rigged the toilet, but it's not a long-term solution. I can look online for a set of replacement guts, however, and keep it working well enough."

"What about the rest of the system?"

"Well, that's a larger conversation."

"By the word 'conversation,' do you mean 'expensive.'"

"Yeaaaaaaaah." He tossed the paper towel wad into the trash bin, nailing it perfectly so that the force of impact triggered the pink top to spin in its moorings. "But that's above my pay grade. You're going to need a proper company to auger the pipes—although then you run the risk of cracking a hole in something while you're trying to fix drains that are slow but not broken. It's like what you said, balance."

"So we're okay now?"

"For a while. And as long as you don't put a huge load on the system, you could skate along as you are for a year or two. Sooner or later, those roots will get you, though."

"And what happens then? Do we have to dig up the whole thing?" As he nodded, she shook her head. "I wonder if there's a plumbing deity somewhere out there I can pray to."

"You want me to build you a shrine to Drano?"

"Will you?"

"Lumber, nails, and we can buy bottles of that bald guy in bulk and make an altar. It'll be great."

Lydia stared up at him for a moment. "You know, I feel like you're perfect for this job."

"I'm a can-do kind of man, what can I say."

"I'm going to check your references. But if it were up to me, I'd say you're our prime candidate."

"Thanks, that's good to hear." He held open the door into the hall for her. "You've got my cell phone. You can reach me anytime. I'm staying with a buddy in Glens Falls, so if you need me back, I can be here in about two hours. Unless it's raining."

"You lose the top to your car?" she said as she stepped out of the pink bathroom.

"Motorcycle."

As nineties-era romantic movies shot through her mind, she pictured him in a slo-mo shot with a Whitney Houston soundtrack. "Ah."

There was a pause, and then he did that head tilt thing again. "Well, it was nice to meet you, Ms.— what was the name again?"

"Susi. But call me Lydia."

"Okay. Hope to hear from you, Lydia."

He lifted his hand in goodbye, and then he turned away. And walked away.

As she watched him go, she had a sense of homesickness. Which made no sense. You couldn't miss a stranger, who'd come in for a job, and been in your presence for, like, twenty minutes. Tops.

But he had fixed a toilet.

And he'd smelled terrific.

Down in reception, she listened to his deep voice, and heard Candy's replies, and then the outer door creaked open and squeaked shut.

The speed with which Lydia returned to her office was nothing she wanted to dwell on, and as she went over to the window she'd cracked, she parted the venetian blinds. Out in the spring sunlight, Daniel Joseph was striding across to the parking area, his heavy boots crunching over the gravel.

His motorcycle was matte black and old-school looking, not that she knew a damn thing about Harleys. And as he threw a leg over it and kick-started the engine, she braced herself for a roar—but the thing had a good muffler that quieted the exhaust. Walking the bike backward, he checked over his shoulder, pulled a pivot, and hit the gas.

Again, she prepared herself for an explosion of sound. There wasn't one. Just a deep, throaty growl as he disappeared around the bend of the lane, the steam trail from the twin tailpipes dissipating in the cold fresh morning.

Standing there at the window, staring out into a parking lot that now felt like a deserted wasteland, she tried to remember the last time she'd been on a date. As the year reversal closed in on grad school, she shook her head. Passion had welded her to the wolves, this preserve . . . this fight to protect a native species against humans' bright ideas.

Not a lot of eligible bachelors in Walters—

The knock was sharp on the jamb.

Wheeling around, the blinds clapped as she dropped them. "Rick. Hi, did you do the analysis on the bait already?"

The WSP's vet shook his head. "Not yet. I was starting some new coffee—oh, you got some."

For no good reason, she thought about how that stranger had made such a huge impression and yet Rick, who she'd been working with for just over two years, hadn't been noticed much at all. As a man, that was. He, too, had dark hair, and a nice enough face. Also, his eyes were a fine, warm shade of brown, and although he didn't smile much, either, when he did, his off-kilter front tooth made him look younger . . . and charming. And he was in great shape from running the trails.

"Candy took care of me," she murmured.

"She's good like that. As long as you aren't a deliveryman."

"True." Lydia looked down at her mug. Looked back up. "When did you say you were testing that bait?"

"I'll get to it." Rick nodded toward the window. "So who was that guy?"

"Just someone interviewing for Trick's job."

"Looks more like a bouncer."

For a moment, Rick stayed where he was, staring across the room at her. And then he said something about his coffee being ready and left.

Lydia pulled over the folder with Daniel Joseph's application in it. As she reread what he'd written, lingering on the precisely constructed letters and the periods that were dropped like pins on a map, she wondered about the information beyond what he'd filled out.

Family. Background. Beliefs.

Girlfriends.

Wife.

"I really have to get a life," she muttered.

FOUR

F UCK!"

Xhex, beloved *shellan* of the Black Dagger Brother John Matthew, shot upright in bed and grabbed the center of her chest. Yanking at what was covering her, she tore her way down past the duvet and the sheets, and when she came to her naked skin, she clawed at her—

Big, broad hands captured hers, and as she blinked, she didn't see her mate. She saw a man, a human, in a white lab coat, taking control of her body, pushing her down, so he could put a hypodermic needle in her—

The scream that came out of her shattered the dim quiet of their bedroom, and her panic took over. She fought hard, kicking with her feet, bucking her body, twisting under the iron bars locked on her wrists. Baring her fangs, she struck at the forearm, at the bare bicep, at anything that came close, blood flowing into her mouth, onto her naked breasts.

She was going to lose this battle. She always lost. No matter how hard she tried to fight, sooner or later, she was overpowered and at the mercy of the white coats, of the experiments, of the torture.

A raw sob broke free of her throat. "N*ooooooooo*—"

The whistle was high pitched and ascending, an audible flare that rose in volume and octave until it owned the air around her, surrounding her and penetrating through the incendiary terror.

Xhex paused her battle, her hoarse breath still tearing up and down her throat. "John?" she said in a whisper.

That whistle repeated in precisely the same cadence and pitch, a slow ascension that went from low to high. And that was when the veil lifted from her eyes and she could see properly the male facing her.

John Matthew was exactly as he always was, from his dark hair to his blue eyes, his strong face and his wide shoulders.

"Mother*fucker*," she moaned. "Oh, God, what have I done to you . . ."

He was bleeding from bites all over his arms, the drips staining the sheets red, the horror from the nightmare being replaced with the horror that she had hurt him. Again.

"I'll get a towel—I'll get some towels—"

As she went to pull away, he tugged at her wrists. Then he mouthed, *I'm fine. I'm okay.*

"No, no, no, no . . ."

This time, when she tried to take her hands back, he let her go—and she fell out of the bed, landing in a heap on the rug. Before he could help her, she thrashed her legs around and jumped up to her feet. As she lurched for the bathroom, one of her ankles was killing her. She must have knocked it on the mattress frame.

Like she fucking cared.

Their bathroom was across the way, and she felt like it took a hundred miles of flat-out running to get to it—and as she stubbed her toe on the lip of the marble floor, she caught the door and slammed it shut by mistake.

The light in the shower's bright white expanse had been left on, so as she went to the sinks, its illumination flooded from behind her—and turned her into a ghost with substance, nothing but a black outline of a figure.

Her hands were shaking so badly that cranking the faucets was like brain surgery, and when she finally got the water running, she didn't wait for the warmth to come up the pipes. She cupped her palms and splashed her face.

The fact that the dark wine taste of her mate's blood was still in her mouth shamed her to the point of nausea—and just in case, she glanced over to the alcove where the toilet was.

Yeah, she could make it. If she had to.

Her legs felt better.

More with the water. *Splash. Splash. Splash.*

Every time she closed her eyes, she was back in that

lab, and not in a memory kind of way. As in, she was actually there, in her body, trapped and being worked on by humans.

The cool water was good, but the fact that she shut her lids every time she made the round with her palms was making things worse. She needed to re-ground in *this* reality.

In the real reality, that was. *Splash. Splash. Splash.*

As she finally turned off the water, the dripping into the basin was a soft sound, almost a chiming, and she threw out a hand and patted around, hoping to run into a towel. When she felt some softness, she pulled it over and pushed her face into the terry cloth folds. Then she swept them up and over her nearly shaved head, rubbing, as if that would somehow scrub away the remnants of the trauma.

That was when she heard the voices. Out in the bedroom.

Goddamn it.

See, this was the good news and the bad news about living in the mansion with the Brotherhood. You were never alone when you were in the house . . . but you were never alone when you were in the house.

Taking the towel with her, she went to the closed door and leaned into the wooden panels.

"—sure you're both okay."

That was Qhuinn, which made sense. Qhuinn and Blay's bedroom was next door—oh, *shit*. Off in the distance, she could hear the high-pitched howl of a young who had been roused from what had been blissful sleep in its crib.

Great. She draws blood on her *hellren*, wakes up the neighbors, and scares the shit out of an infant.

There was some silence as John signed whatever response he had. And then Qhuinn was murmuring things about getting help for days like this. Days when Xhex woke up in a fit from a recurrent nightmare that hadn't been happening anymore.

Until recently.

Now the fucking thing was like the worst houseguest you could have—rude, noisy, and never leaving.

There was another stretch of silence as John communicated with his hands what he could not share with his voice. Then Qhuinn spoke some more. Another silence, briefer now. Then the other Brother was taking his leave.

As the door into the Hall of Statues was shut, Xhex sagged. Then re-braced herself and stepped out of the bathroom.

"Here," she said briskly. "I'll clean up what I did."

John Matthew was . . . well, pretty fucking resplendent in their now messy, bloody bed. His naked torso was padded with muscle, from his shoulders to his arms to his ribbed stomach—and as she approached him, her eyes lingered on the star-shaped scar that marked his pectoral.

The sign of the Brotherhood. Something a male received when he joined.

Yet John Matthew had had his since birth.

Sitting down, she took his hands and carefully wiped where she had bitten him. He was in such incredible shape, and so well fed from taking her vein on the regular, that she could practically watch the marks of her fangs and front teeth sealing themselves up.

"I'm so sorry," she said when she could trust her voice.

And even then, it was a croak of syllables more than actual words.

"I'm fucking sorry."

John shook his head. Then took his hands back and signed, *Don't be. I don't care about—*

"You should. You should care—you're being terrorized in your own fucking bed."

Xhex, what can I do to help?

She folded and refolded the towel in her lap. "Wear chain mail? I'd suggest tying me up—but that's what got me into trouble in the first place."

In that lab, she added to herself.

Her mate was signing more things, supportive things, things that broke her in half. How this male stayed with her, she had no clue. He was better than her on so many levels.

"Yes," she said. "I'll deal with this. Somehow."

Yeah, because the subconscious was easily controlled. Which was why people only ever did shit they were fully in charge of.

No problem.

"I am sorry," she whispered.

Ordinarily, in her job as head of security for various clubs, and in her life, as a half-breed *symphath*, she was a hardass, capable of staring down drunk humans who were out of their mind on Molly and wouldn't have recognized even God Himself standing in front of them.

But in this bedroom, behind their closed door . . .

John Matthew stopped signing and just held out his battered arms. There was no censure in his face or his eyes, nothing but love and acceptance.

Well—and worry.

Xhex wanted to be strong. But as she collapsed into her *hellren's* arms, she didn't have a choice.

I'll make it up to him, she vowed.

Somehow, sometime . . . she'd figure out a way to be normal.

FIVE

BACK AT THE Wolf Study Project's headquarters, at just before six p.m., Lydia looked up from a dismal financial spreadsheet. "He's still not here. Like, not at all?"

Candy pulled on her puffy down coat. "Nope, and before you ask, no, I didn't put our executive director in a closet. My kidnap fantasies stop at UPS men."

Sitting back in her chair, Lydia did some math. Peter Wynne hadn't been in the office for a week and a half now. Unbelievable.

"Hey," she said. "I heard the vacuum going. Are the cleaners here early? They're supposed to come in Saturday mornings."

"They don't come in on Saturdays anymore."

"So five-thirty tonight works better?" Lydia frowned when there was no response. "What aren't you telling me. Did they quit?"

"No, they didn't quit." Candy walked forward and put an envelope on the desk. "Here's your paycheck."

"What happened to the cleaners?" As Candy

fussed with something in her purse, Lydia put her pen down. "You're kidding me."

Candy lifted her palms like it was a holdup. "Hey, I happen to like vacuuming. And don't get me started on Windex. I'm *obsessed*."

"That's not your job—wait, who's going to take care of cleaning the clinic?" As Candy just lifted a brow, Lydia swallowed twelve kinds of curses. "No, Rick is not cleaning the—he needs to take care of my wolf. The wolf, I mean."

"He said he didn't mind."

"Goddamn it." Lydia shoved her chair back and marched around her desk. "I've frickin' had it—"

Candy snagged her arm. "Where are you going? Peter's not here anyway, and what's it going to get you to yell at his closed door?"

Lydia stared off into the hallway, not seeing the framed maps of the preserve or the black-and-white photographs of gray wolves. Instead, the piss-poor financials she'd been reviewing were like a neon sign mounted directly in front of her face.

"We're going to need to trim some expenses," she announced. "We can't afford to fill Trick's position—"

"We can't afford not to fill it. Eastwind brought the ATV back, and he says it has a leak in the gas tank. There are three bridges on the main trail that need fixing or our insurance company is going to cancel our policy—the letter is in your inbox. The equipment building has a hole in the roof, and you and I both know how well our bathroom is functioning. I don't mind sharing facilities with Rick, but that insurance policy is going to be a big problem."

"Maybe I can fix those bridges."

"Sure. In all your free time." Candy shrugged. "Look, we can all pitch in with the cleaning as a team, but Trick did stuff out in the preserve that none of us are equipped to do. And the fundraiser is coming up. We'll get the money we need, eventually. Well . . . somehow, we'll get it."

"Tell me the truth, Candy." Lydia shifted her eyes to the older woman. "When did the cleaners stop coming in?"

"A month ago."

Lydia threw up her hands. "Why didn't you let me know—"

"You're not the executive director. That's why. You aren't responsible for the way this place runs."

"Did you tell Peter?"

"Yes."

"And he did nothing?"

"Well, look at the time. I gotta go." Candy gave a rough pat on Lydia's shoulder. "It's going to be okay—that's what I've learned. We may work for the wolves, but we're cats at heart. This place and everyone under its roof has nine lives. Now will you please leave before midnight for once? You're turning into a vampire."

As the woman took off, Lydia rubbed her aching eyes—

With an abrupt surge, she hustled out to the reception area with its rustic chairs and year-old copies of *Outdoors* magazine. "Wait, Candy?"

The receptionist paused at the door, the overhead fixture making her pink hair fluoresce like it was under a black light. "Yeah?"

"Why do you not like Sheriff Eastwind?"

Candy did a double take. Then shook her head. "What makes you ask that?"

"You never call him Sheriff. Or by his first name. It's always Eastwind."

"That is his name."

"It's the tone, too."

When Lydia held the other woman's stare, Candy glanced away to her neat desk. Then her eyes returned. "He and I go way back, that's all. You know how small towns are. Now, will you please shut your office down and get home, already? Tomorrow is coming like a freight train, and like my dad always said, it's going to be carrying more of the crap we dealt with today."

The door clapped shut behind her.

Lydia looked around at the log-cabin-style space, seeing the worn carpet, the frayed arms on the chairs, the stain in the corner of the ceiling. She thought of the trails—and the fact that as the weather got more hospitable they would be filled with hikers, dogs, kids. Then she moved on to the ATV. The equipment building.

The toilet.

Heading back to her office, she picked up the envelope and opened it. Her wages for the previous two weeks were just over fifteen hundred dollars. $1,538.41. After withholding and her health insurance, she netted nine hundred and change. It had always felt like a lot to her.

Lydia ripped up the check, put the confetti back in the envelope, and tossed everything into the wastepaper basket. Then she went to the stack of files in her out-box. After she found what she was looking for, she made a note on a Post-it, got her coat, and grabbed her bag. Turning off all the lights, she set the security alarm out in front and locked up. Her beater was parked under a pine tree, and as she got in, she glanced at the building. Twenty-four months was a short blink in the course of an entire lifespan. But she felt like she'd been at the WSP forever.

And there was nowhere else she could imagine herself. For so many reasons.

At least that wolf was still alive, she thought as she drove off. Rick had checked in as he'd left and told her he was going to come back throughout the night to take vitals and make sure he was okay.

So there was that.

When she was on the county road, she took out her cell phone and broke the law by making a call and putting the unit up to her ear. Hands-free was great, unless you were in a fifteen-year-old car that didn't have Bluetooth. Then it wasn't an option, no matter what the rules were—

"Yes?"

The sound of the male voice was such a surprise, Lydia jumped. She'd been prepared for voice mail.

"Ah, hello, Peter." *Remember me, one of your employees?* "How are you?"

"Lydia, look, I'm busy right now. What do you need?"

For you to do your damn job, Peter.

"We expected to see you today. At the project." When there was silence, she said, "Hello?"

Should I give you the address in case you forgot where you work?

"Yeah, sorry. I'll be in tomorrow. We can talk about whatever it is—"

"I need your authorization on a couple of things. It's not going to wait until tomorrow."

"I can't do this right now—"

"Actually, yes, you can. And if you don't, I know where you live, and I'm going to show up at your front door and pound on it until you answer—"

"What do you need," he snapped.

The conversation lasted all of five minutes, and Lydia felt no better as she hung up. Which was hardly a news flash. She couldn't say the WSP's executive director had directed much or been very executive in the last month.

Even though she had other calls to make, she let her cell phone fall into her lap and just drove alone.

Along, rather. In the headlights, the asphalt stripe that tracked the Moth River's winding course around the foot of Deer Mountain reminded her of the opening scenes of *The Shining*. Not that the pavement was in as good condition as she remembered the film's being—here, there were seams in the pavement everywhere, like worms trying to cross the road, the hot and cold of the seasons demanding flexibility out of that which was by its nature more fixed than conditions required.

The town of Walters was just a gas station, a bank, a combined grocery store/diner, a firehouse, and a post office. Orbiting around the tiny retail center were about thirty or forty homes on parcels of land that had been in the families since the French trappers had come down from Canada during the Revolutionary War.

As Lydia contemplated all the empty in her refrigerator, she decided to pull into the IGA's parking lot. Before she got out, she took the Post-it from her bag and punched the ten-number sequence into her phone. She waited to hit send until she entered the grocery half of the building.

She loved Susan, the cashier. She really did.

"Oh, hi!" came the greeting behind the counter. "How's things at work? What's going on with you—"

Lydia smiled. Waved. Pointed at her phone in an exaggerated way. "Call."

Susan nodded and made all kinds of it's-okay with her hands. "You just talk, I'll wait."

Susan was pushing sixty, and still full of beans, a wind-up toy with plenty of strength left in her pull string. Sporting an elaborately coiffed platinum-blond hairdo and a full face of makeup, she was like a starlet waiting for a movie director who had never shown up—but she hadn't just been sitting around. Married to the fire chief, they had raised five sons in Walters, and like so many, she and her husband were lifers here in the valley, never gonna retire, never gonna move, as they said. Plus she had a committed side-hustle. In addition to running the grocery store, she was both the oral historian and chief newscaster of the area. Which was a wonderful service, covering both the past and the present. Of everybody.

No, really. It was great.

As a second ring came across the connection, Lydia walked back to the shallow meat counter and then glanced around at the seven aisles of short shelves. The selection for everything was small, high calorie'd, and uninspired, especially as it was all she'd been choosing from for the last two years. As a fourth ring burbled in her ear, she gave up pretending she was any kind of cook and rerouted to the entry into the diner part of things. She was out of gas tonight, and the idea of cooking anything, even a can of Campbell's soup, was overwhelming.

And that was before she stepped through the swinging glass door and the smell of chicken pot pie hit her.

"Oh, sweet Jesus," she muttered. "That's what I'm talking about—"

"Hello?" came a male voice into her ear.

Lydia stopped. God, the sound of that man was like jumper cables hooked to her butt. "Ah, hi, Daniel Joseph? This is Lydia Susi from the Wolf—"

"Oh, yeah, hi. How are you doing?"

In the pause that followed, Lydia frowned as the music coming across the connection registered. It was an old Eagles song. And the weird thing was that "Take It to the Limit" was also . . . overhead for her as well.

"Lydia? Ms. Susi?"

"Are you . . ." She glanced to the booths that were against the wall. Then turned to the counter where the stools were. "Oh. Hi."

Down at the far end of the lineup of truckers and townspeople, Daniel Joseph was parked on a stool and taking up three spaces. And as his eyes swung over and crossed the distance of a dozen half-eaten plates of beef stew and chicken parm, she lifted her hand. He did the same.

"I guess we should hang up," she said into her phone.

"Sure."

Ending the call, she walked forward, nodding at the familiar faces, the husbands and wives. The widowers. In the back of her mind, she noted there wasn't a person under fifty, evidence that the town was hanging on by a generational thread that was fraying year to year. The sad reality was that the world was getting more digital every day, and the economics were tough this far from any population center. Young people, who were starting out or raising families, needed good paying jobs in urban centers.

"Hi." She slipped her phone into her bag. "I thought you were going back to Glens Falls."

"So did I. My bike broke down so I'm here overnight. You want to sit?"

As he went to move his leather jacket to the stool on the other side of him, she shook her head. "Oh, no. I'm just picking up to go. Where's your bike?"

"Some guy named Paul is fixing it as we speak. Or he will when the part gets here in the morning."

"Oh, you went to Paul Gagnon's."

He lifted what looked like a Coke and took a sip. The straw that had come with the glass had been taken out and put on the counter next to his knife/fork/spoon roll.

"That's the one. So you wanted to speak to me?"

Lydia cleared her throat. "You've got the job if you want it."

"Really?" The slow, small smile was positively devastating. "That's great. Thanks."

As Lydia had to glance away, she pretended like she was acknowledging the trucker sitting in the booth behind him—even though the guy was facing away from her and she didn't know him from a hole in the wall.

But it was either faking a salutation or feeling like something on a hot plate, fresh out of the diner's kitchen.

"When do you want me to start?"

She shook herself back to attention. "Do you go by Dan or Daniel? And as soon as possible."

"Good. I'll start tomorrow. And I'm Daniel, not Dan."

"Tomorrow? Really? But don't you need to go get your things from where you—"

"I'm here for the night anyway and tomorrow is Friday. I'll work the day and head back to Glens Falls when I'm done. What time do you want me?"

"Well, Trick used to come in at eight-thirty and leave at four-thirty."

"Those are my hours, then."

"Great. I'll see you tomorrow. And we'll process your paperwork first thing so we can get you on payroll."

Daniel tilted his head in that way he did. "What is that?"

"Um . . . it's how you get paid? Have you always been under the table?"

"No, your necklace."

Lydia looked down at the worn gold charm that hung at the V of her fleece—and realized she was still in her running tights. Her running shoes. Her sports bra.

As she swallowed a curse, she thought, hey, at least it wasn't a news flash to him. She'd had the stuff on during his interview.

"Oh, it's nothing special." She shrugged. "Just a St. Christopher medal."

"You're Catholic? Sorry, if that's personal."

"It's not, and it was my grandfather's. He was Catholic. I don't know what I am. Anyway, I'll see you in the morning."

"Yeah, sure."

As she turned away, he said, "What about your dinner?"

"Huh?" She looked across the counter at the server coming out of the kitchen. "Oh, right. Hey, Bessie—"

"I've got it coming up, Lydia. Your usual."

Bessie was also sixty and had a perm that had been taken right out of a style book in 1985, but unlike fading beauty queen Susan, she had the vibe of a gym teacher. Or maybe someone who taught karate to army sergeants. After she delivered a hamburger and a plate of fries to Daniel, she wiped her hands on her apron and nodded like she'd taken a blood oath to bring out Lydia's order.

No matter what the obstacles or what it cost her.

"I didn't know I had a usual," Lydia murmured. But like she was going to argue?

She liked her arms and legs just where they were, thank you very much—she'd never been sure whether Bessie's commitment to her job crossed counter lines. Like, if you messed up as one of her customers, did she mop the floor with you?

"You want to sit while you wait?" Daniel asked.

"No, I'm good." She looked up at the billboard of menu items that was bolted to the wall over the soft drink machines, the ice cream coolers, the pie display. "But thanks."

Out of the corner of her eye, she watched as he unrolled his paper napkin, tucked it in his lap, and picked up the burger with fingers that were precisely arranged on the bun. He was methodical about biting and chewing, neat and tidy. Fastidious with the napkin, too, nothing dripping in spite of the fact that there was ketchup involved and things were done medium rare.

He wiped his mouth. "How do you have a usual and not know what it is?"

"Diner amnesia, evidently. On the other hand, it's going to be a surprise—which at least in theory, I'm going to like."

"An entree ordered by your subconscious. Cool."

A moment later, Bessie punched out of the kitchen's flap door with a steaming plate.

"Here ya go, chicken pot pie, nice and hot." She put the food next to Daniel Joseph's burger and grabbed a silverware roll out from under the counter. "You want your Diet Coke, too?"

"Ah . . ." Lydia cleared her throat.

"Looks like we're having dinner together," the WSP's new groundskeeper said. "Didn't this just work out, huh."

SIX

BACK TWO YEARS ago, on the first day Lydia had arrived at her new job, Candy had been in charge of her orientation—and not only about the nonprofit. There had been plenty to learn about living in Walters. And the one piece of advice that had held especially true? Everybody in the zip code was related. If not by blood, then by marriage.

So you never said anything bad about anyone because you were talking to their relative. As Candy had said, just like you wouldn't throw poop at a fan, you didn't want to run down another person 'cuz the crap would come back on you.

Such a way with metaphors—and there was a corollary to the woman's Zip It Rule of Walters, New York.

Standing over the plate of steaming food, Lydia glanced up at the server. Bessie was married to Susan, the grocer's, husband's brother. Which meant that not only did the women work in the same building and take their breaks together, they also rode into and from work as a twosome.

"I'm so sorry, Bessie, but I have to get home. Would you please put that amazing dinner in a to-go?"

"Oh, yeah. Sure. I just thought you'd come to eat with this nice young man—"

"Thanks so much." Lydia smiled. "And you're right, I guess I do order a lot of chicken pot pie."

As Bessie marched back through the flap doors to the kitchen proper, there was an awkward moment. On her side of things.

Daniel just went back to his hamburger. "So I'm guessing word gets around here quick, huh," he said between mouthfuls.

"Oh, that's not the reason I'm not . . ." She glanced at the kitchen's flap doors. "Okay, fine. So much getting around in this town. You have *no* idea."

"And we wouldn't want your husband jealous."

"He wouldn't be—I mean, I don't have one." Since when did she get so tongue-tied all the time? "And what about your wife."

"No wife, no girlfriend. Drifter, remember?"

"I remember."

Bessie came back out again, a paper bag in her hand. "Here you go."

"And here's fifteen. Keep the change."

"Thanks, Lydia. You're a big-city tipper, you know that?"

"If that's my claim to fame, I'll take it." She smiled at Daniel in what she hoped was a professional way. Because Bessie's eyes were bouncing back and forth between them like the woman was reading all kinds of things into all kinds of facial expressions. "I'll see you tomorrow, Daniel. At work."

Daniel glanced over and lifted a casual hand. "I'll be there on time. Even if I have to walk."

"So where are you staying? Pine Lodge?"

"Yup. That's the place."

Lydia frowned. "That's two miles away."

"And God gave me two legs, one mile each."

"I like that attitude."

"Paul said he'll bring the bike over when it's ready. To the Project."

Lydia opened her mouth to offer him a ride in the morning. But a quick glance at Bessie—who was still enthralled—cut that impulse off. Besides, the Pine Lodge was run by Candy's sister and brother-in-law, who were Susan and Bessie's first cousins by marriage.

Too complicated.

"Have a good night," she said before walking off.

"You, too."

As she headed for the diner's exit, she told herself not to look back at him. To treat him as she would Candy. Or Rick. As just a fellow employee of the WSP.

Just as her hand pushed the bar, she—

Looked back.

Daniel Joseph had ducked his head and turned it toward his half-finished Coke. To anybody else in the place, he was just another man filling his empty belly before he headed back out into the spring chill. But his eyes ... those glowing eyes ...

Were on Lydia.

The instant their stares met, he looked away. So did she.

But as she stepped back into the night, things had gotten a whole lot more tropical, in spite of whatever a thermometer might say.

"Damn it," she muttered.

Under the start-as-you-mean-to-go-on theory, she was going to be completely obsessed by that man in a week and a half.

"Not what's going to happen," she announced as she crossed the damp pavement.

Back in her car, she put her food in the passenger seat and tried to ignore the fact that the chicken pot pie was the first warm passenger she'd had in her hatchback since ... well, when?

Funny how meeting a stranger was what it took to make her feel lonely.

Starting her engine, she reversed out and headed down the county road again. She'd been renting a little house by the stream since she'd come to town, and by now, she figured her car could drive the short distance home itself. Keeping one hand on the steering wheel, she fiddled with the radio dial with the other, restlessly going back and forth through the four fuzzy stations. She needed distraction. Noise. A news report, a song with a good beat—hell, she'd take a commercial for a gutter cleaning company or a used car lot.

When she hooked into one of the Canadian broadcasts, she sat back in her seat and tried to decipher the French—

Flashing blue lights from the other side of the two-lane road blinded her.

There were three cop car worths. No, four. And there was also a boxy van and an ambulance.

She hit the brakes as she passed by Sheriff Eastwind's SUV, and with a wrench of the wheel, she cut across the lanes to pull in behind his vehicle. Getting out, she covered her eyes with her hand to cut the blue strobing.

A tall figure in a New York State trooper uniform strode over to her. "Ma'am, I'm going to ask you to get back in your car—"

"What happened?"

"—and continue on your way."

She looked into the tree line. Flashlights were flaring as a group came back toward the road through the forest.

The trooper stepped in and blocked the view. "Ma'am, you're going to leave now, either in my car or your own. What's it going to be?"

"Who got hurt on the mountain?" She glanced at

the man. "I work at the Wolf Study Project up the road from here, and this is our land, part of our preserve."

"What's your name, ma'am?"

Before she could answer, the members of law enforcement broke free of the trees—with a black body bag that was strung like a hammock between the grips of two officers. Something about the way it sagged in the middle made her sick to her stomach.

"I'll handle this," someone said.

As the state policeman nodded and stepped back, she was not surprised to see it was Eastwind.

"What's going on," she demanded to him.

The sheriff took her elbow and started to walk toward her car. But Lydia threw out her anchor and pointed at the remains as they were brought over to the back of the box van instead of the ambulance.

"Who is in there."

In the blue flares, Eastwind's face was a mask of composure. Not that he ever gave much away. "This is an active investigation, Ms. Susi—"

"Don't you Ms. Susi me. I have a right to know—"

"When we are prepared to make a statement—"

"This is *our* land." She nodded at the No Trespassing sign that had been nailed to a thick trunk. "I want to know what happened on it."

Eastwind looked over as the body bag was loaded into the coroner's vehicle. "It was a hiker. We don't have an ID yet."

She made the sign of the cross over her chest. "Accident or health-related? And how long have they been up on the mountain?"

There was a pause. And that answered the first question, didn't it.

"Tell me," she demanded.

"He was attacked by an animal. That's all I'm going to say." Eastwind leaned in and looked her right in the eye. "And I expect you to keep this to yourself."

"Where was he found?"

"That's all I'm—"

As the double doors of the van were slammed shut, she snapped, "*Where*."

"North Granite Ridge. Another hiker found him and called it in. Remains are two days old, and now, if you'll excuse me."

The sheriff walked off to the other officers, and Lydia looked back at where the remains had been marched out of the forest.

After a moment, she went to her car and got in. As her dinner grew cold and she forgot about her hunger, she headed back to the office. When she arrived on-site, she didn't bother going over to the parking area. She pulled directly up to the WSP's front entrance.

Getting out, she had the key ready as she approached the door—but when she went to put it in the lock, she glared up at the roof line. Night had solidly arrived since she'd left and the motion-activated light was supposed to come on.

The fact that it didn't was just one more thing to add to the broken list. At least they had a new groundskeeper, right?

As she got her phone and triggered its flashlight, she hoped it was just a blown bulb, instead of an electrical problem.

Stepping inside, she canned the security system and went directly down to her desk. Turning on the lamp beside her computer, she signed in and accessed the mountain's camera feed program. There were nearly a hundred units mounted in trees in the preserve—which sounded like a lot until you considered how many acres there were.

But there was one on North Granite Ridge.

Closing her eyes, she rubbed her St. Christopher medal between her thumb and forefinger as she waited for that specific feed to load. The recordings were kept live for one week before they were put into permanent storage on the cloud—so it wasn't going to matter how many days or nights ago the attack happened. Although Eastwind had said forty-eight hours.

When the image was set three days prior, Lydia tilted her monitor and sat closer to the desk. The view of camera #046 was of a clearing that ran laterally north to south, nothing but scrubby brush marking the rock ledge. The lens unit was mounted about fifteen feet from the ground, and there were four stations for the wide-angle to lock into. Back on Monday, the position had been on the second one . . . and it provided about a thirty-foot field of vision ahead of its station.

The default program moved the camera through its stations every seventy-two hours on a coordinated schedule with the other feeds—unless it was manually overridden. So there was a good chance the attack wasn't caught. Especially if it occurred behind the tree or in and among the other pines that crowded up tight to the clearing.

Hitting the play button, she continued to rub the pendant her grandfather had given her. "Show me . . . show me . . ."

The only thing that moved was the spooling time counter down on the lower right hand of the feed, the date static, the seconds running by, the minutes waiting on the sidelines for their cue, the hours going nowhere soon. She increased the speed, watching the angle of the patchy sunlight shift over the landscape, the lazy flight paths of vultures more like the quick dive bombs of barn sparrows, the clouds marching across the screen, the greenery twitching like it was itchy. When night came, things went shades of green. And then the dawn brought the standard color back.

Deep inside herself, in the place that she refused to dwell, much less acknowledge, Lydia knew what she was going to see, knew it sure as she could recognize her own reflection. Cold sweat bloomed across her chest under her clothes, and beneath the desk, the heel of one of her running shoes beat out a quick tapping—

As soon as the man dressed in camo shot into the camera field, she cut the fast forward, everything resuming in real time. She took a good look at him— and couldn't tell much. He had a pack on his back, hunter-like clothes, and a brimmed hat that was pulled down low on his face. Moving along, he seemed confident and aware as he scanned the environs—

The attack came from on the left, the wolf leaping forward with such stealth that the man didn't even glance in the direction of the predator. One moment, the hiker was upright, the next he had a hundred-pound female gray wolf locked on his throat. The impact of the animal's body knocked the human off his feet, and the wolf didn't release. Even as the man punched at the head and snout, and then kicked, and tried to roll, there was no movement from the jaw. No shift of the bite, either.

Lydia hit pause and sat back, covering her face with her hands. As she squeezed her eyes shut, she saw only the wolf, with the distinctive silver stripe down its back, and its lithe body, and its dagger-like teeth.

Even as she told herself to get a grip, it was a while before she could resume the footage, and she locked her stare on the time counter, keeping track of the killing in her peripheral vision. Which was still too much information: During the takedown, the wolf struck only once and made it count, the pounds per square inch on that vital airway choking the man out. When the resistance of the prey weakened and those arms stopped flailing, there was a single reposition, a split second of release so that the animal could go for right in front, compressing the jugular vein as well as the windpipe.

As the human went totally limp, the teeth stayed where they were.

For a solid minute and a half longer.

The savagery that followed was something Lydia turned away from. There was no sound associated with the feed. No smells, either. But it was as if the ripping and tearing, the copper bloom of the blood, the consumption of meat and gristle, was happening on the desktop.

The total elapsed time of the attack was only about twelve minutes, and when it was over, the wolf stepped off from the ravaged, glistening corpse. The red stain that marked its muzzle and the fur of its chest was something out of a horror movie.

The predator looked around. And even glanced up at the camera.

Then it trotted off, light and quick on its paws.

The body lay there in the sunlight, like a gruesome beachgoer, and the behaviorist in her analyzed exactly how much meat was still on the corpse. Lots of it.

Taking the man down had been for sport, not on account of hunger. And the wolf had worked alone.

With a shaking hand, Lydia stopped the footage. And then without conscious awareness, she bent to the side, opened the lower drawer, and took out her Lysol wipes. Snapping one free, she ran the damp cloth around the monitor's base. As the fresh linen scent tingled in her nose, she blinked fast.

Clean. She needed to clean things up. If she could only . . .

Stopping herself, she looked down at the wipe. It was warm now, and as she turned her palm over, the thing was the color of her skin, like it was transparent.

The debate went on in her head for about five minutes, and when she came to her decision, she threw out the wipe, put the container away, and thought of her grandfather. He would not approve of what she was about to do. But he would have approved of her reason why.

Her minor in college had been IT.

And it took her no time at all to locate the right editing program on the web, load it, and cut what she needed to of the footage. After that, she went back days earlier in the feed, to when the camera had been in position four. Reviewing the requisite twenty minutes, at the proper time, she made sure there were no giveaways, no telltales that would compromise things, like a downed tree or rainy weather when it should have been partially cloudy. After lucking out with the intangibles, she copied a day and a half's worth of footage, and spliced it into the feed so it replaced the attack. Then she went back into the program that controlled the orientation of the cameras and manually manipulated the direction that lens #046 was pointed in, locking it into position four.

The good news was that though there was a regular schedule, that schedule was regularly random. Depending on the movement of the packs, she was constantly changing the orientation of the cameras all over the preserve so nothing would seem unusual about the override.

The last thing she did was not just remove the editing program from her computer, but go deep into the hard drive and cover her tracks. But that wasn't going to be enough. CPUs could be forensically examined, and just as corpses on the autopsy table gave up their secrets, even if you deleted something, the scar would remain to be found.

The Dell was almost ten years old. Well past the end of its useful life.

The virus she found on the dark web and infected the unit with instructed the computer to turn off its cooling fan. And then to make sure there wasn't a fire hazard, she went down to the break room and located some tin pans that Candy had washed and saved after Thanksgiving leftovers had been brought in months ago.

Lydia put the computer in one of them and made sure it was set away from the edges of the desk.

The bad news about working at the WSP was that

money was always tight. The good news, at least in her current situation? There was very little new high-tech or state-of-the-art anything in place. So the chances of an old PC burning out overnight?

Sorry, Officer. That's just what happened. But at least we have the footage from the preserve, right? Oh, wait, it shows nothing. What a shame.

Signing out of her computer, she just stared at the monitor. That kind of bloody, violent attack just validated what the hotel was acting on. And given that Eastwind was clearly reluctant to do anything, she was going to have to take charge . . . and God knew she would do anything—*anything*—to protect the animals that could not speak for themselves.

No matter what it cost her personally. Or what it brought up from her past.

Yes, it was obvious that an animal attack had occurred. But no one needed footage like that getting leaked and ending up on the Internet—and God knew, that was where everything went these days. Something like those twelve minutes would be used to further scare people off wolves and threaten their reintroduction into this part of the United States.

Predators were a necessary part of the ecosystem.

As far as she was concerned, humans were the ones the planet could use less of, considering all the damage they did.

On that note, she got up from her desk, and walked down to the clinical area. Turning on the light, she went to where the wolf was crated. He did not lift his head, but his groggy eyes opened the instant he scented her. At least he was no longer ventilated.

"Hi," she said as she crouched down. "It's me again."

◆ ◆ ◆

Daniel Joseph was used to being a ghost. He was good at it. He had to be. It was a question of both purpose and survival.

So as he tracked Lydia Susi's progression through the Wolf Study Project's facility, he made no sound. He also triggered no security lights, although there was a totally non-metaphysical reason for that: He'd unscrewed them the night before when he'd come down off the mountain and checked the place out.

And as a bonus, there were no security cameras on-site, which had been good news.

He was only going to be seen by that woman, or anyone else, on his terms and when he wanted to be. And not at all if he chose.

For example, ordinarily, he would not eat out in public. But when it was necessary, appearances had to be created and then maintained. So he had had food among the townsfolk to establish the impression that he was just like the rest of them. Nothing special. Nothing to be noted.

Blending in.

As he moved down the side of the building, the darkness of the night was his shield, his body's ability to be utterly silent while in motion making him a whisper in the shadows, just like the cold air, just like the mountain mist . . . just like the moonlight that had emerged from the clouds to seek the earth from its perch high, high in the heavens.

He had watched the woman through the slats that covered her window as she worked at her desk, typing into her keyboard, staring at images of a wolf attack on her screen. She had been clearly upset by the carnage, and then she had done some work, flipping through screens, using her mouse, moving things around. After that, she'd left her office and returned with a large tin container that she put under her desk. Finally, she had up and left, turning off the lights.

Her path through the single-story building was marked with darkened rooms or hallways that abruptly filled with light, and he imagined her flipping switches that she didn't need to pat around to find. She was heading for the back, and as he came up to a high-set slot window, he hefted himself off the ground on the sill and peered in.

She was going into a room on the opposite side of the building, and the door closed automatically behind her.

Waiting in the night was something that came naturally to him, and as he dropped back down, his body settled into a stable stance that varied only as his chest rose and fell evenly.

If she were in there for half an hour, an hour, the rest of the night? Didn't matter to him—

He saw the headlights first. A pair coming down the lane toward the building.

Turning to face the dark siding of the building, he put his back to the arrival and linked his hands together. The car's beams traveled over his black leather jacket and his black hat and his dark blue jeans—and kept right on going, the vehicle stopping next to the rear entrance.

Which was only about ten feet from where Daniel was.

As a man got out and shut his door with his hip, Daniel cranked his head to the side for a better look. The car was an older Jeep, one that he'd seen parked with the others during the day. The guy who had driven it had glasses that were unremarkable, clothes that were unremarkable, an unremarkable haircut.

Abruptly, the man stared down the side of the building, but not because he had noticed who was watching him. He focused on the woman's old car.

When he pivoted back, there was an air of poignant sadness about him, his shoulders slumped in defeat, his eyes going to ground and staying there. It was a while before he moved toward the door, as if he had to brace himself to see the woman inside—

The rear exit to the building burst open.

"Oh, it's you," a female voice said. "Are you coming to check on him?"

From his close perch, Daniel witnessed a mask come across the man's face, everything tightening up, composure substituting for true detachment.

"Tell me you didn't try to take his vitals," was the annoyed response.

"Of course I did. Right after I performed brain surgery on him."

As the woman stepped forward, the light streaming out of the building caught half her face, half her body—and all of Daniel's attention. She was both average and unusually attractive, a troubling combination: With her sun-streaked hair pulled back in a ponytail, and her blue running tights and red and black shoes, she looked as if she could be any woman in her late twenties who kept herself in a good shape, but wasn't fussy about coordinating her outfits.

There was something about her, though, something intangible and really fucking annoying, that made Daniel look twice. Every time he saw her.

The vet crossed his arms and frowned. "What are you doing here?"

"I had to come back for something in my office—"

"So you've moved your desk into my clinic? Christ, Lydia, I told you I'd check on him—"

"I didn't come back for the wolf, k? I'm going through the budget for next quarter and forgot a report Candy had prepared for me. While I was here, I thought I'd make sure he was all right—and call you if he wasn't. That's it."

There was a pause. "I just wish you'd trust me."

No, Daniel thought. *You just wish she loved you.*

On her side, the woman seemed not only to not reciprocate, but be unaware of his feelings.

"Come on, Rick. You know me. If I'm under this roof, like I'm not going to peek in on him?"

Rick looked away. Looked back. "I'm sorry I jumped down your throat."

"Forgiven, forgotten. But if you're going to check on him, I want to come in with you."

"Remind me again when you went to vet school?" the man muttered with resignation.

"What can I say, night school is a wonderful thing."

As the two entered the building, there was the *clap* of a screen door shutting and then a *thump* as something more solid was closed.

Daniel pulled himself back up on the slot window's sill.

Through the glass, he watched as the woman and the man proceeded through that door she'd gone into before.

Dropping back down, he was just going to wait for them to come back.

And then he would see what he felt like doing to them—

Off in the distance, the howl of a wolf echoed through night, weaving through the pine trees, traveling as if on wings from the throat of the predator to Daniel's ears.

He opened his soul to the haunting song.

It was his absolute favorite sound in the world.

SEVEN

THE FOLLOWING MORNING, Lydia was the first person in the WSP's building. As she opened the front door, the burnt smell was unmistakable, but not pronounced, and she quickly put in the code to the alarm. Rushing back to her office, she flipped the lights on and went around to her chair.

Down on the floor under her desk, in the tin, her computer tower was showing no signs of life even though it was plugged in and had been left on.

The sharp smell of melted plastic and metal made her rub her nose.

Sitting down on the carpet, she closed her gritty, red-rimmed eyes. She'd been so worried that a fire would break out and spread through the whole facility that after she and Rick had left, she'd come right back. Tucking her car behind the equipment garage, she'd settled in for the dawn. Her L.L.Bean sleeping bag had kept her toasty enough, but her back hadn't appreciated her driver's seat as a bed.

And then there had been the constant monitoring.

She'd expected at any moment for there to be a Hollywood-worthy explosion, orange and yellow flames breaking out everywhere, her wolf's tenuous life in danger, her bursting in to save him the only reason he survived.

When the veil had finally arrived and then dawn had come, she'd pulled out from her hidey-hole and gone back home for a quick shower, an old banana, and a slice of toast that had made her realize her chicken pot pie was still in the damn car.

What a waste—

The cough came from her doorway and she snapped to attention. Tilting to the side, she looked around her desk.

And flushed like she'd spontaneously become sunburned.

"Oh, it's you," she said. "Good morning."

Daniel Joseph covered his mouth with his fist and coughed again. Then he waved his hand around. "Everything okay in here?"

"My, ah . . ." She slid up into her chair and pointed under her desk. "My computer held a barbecue last night and ate itself."

Daniel came around with a fluidity that seemed at odds with his size and strength, and as he knelt down and drew out the tin, she took a moment to breathe in deep. Yup, same cologne. And while she was trying not to sniff too much, he let out another cough as he yanked the electrical cord free of the back.

"I promise you," she said, "my office doesn't always smell bad. I make no guarantees about our strawberry-fields-forever bathroom, however."

"It's okay." He pulled out the tray. "And I'm not a computer expert, but this thing is dead."

"It's been on its last legs for a long time. I put it in the tin a while ago because I was afraid—"

He looked up. "Of exactly what happened."

"—of exactly what happened." She flushed as their eyes met. "Snap."

He sat back on his heels, balancing his arm on the desktop. "Hey, can you explain the snap thing to me? Like, what's with the snap."

"Well, two people—"

"—say the same thing—"

"—say the same thing—"

"—at the same time," he finished. "Snap."

"Yup."

"And that's it."

"Now that you mention it, it's like your cousin Louie's punch line. Falls flat and doesn't make a lot of sense."

He smiled ever so slightly. "Uncle Louie."

"Sorry. Uncle. Not cousin."

And justlikethat, time slowed. Then stopped altogether.

As Lydia stared into those incendiary hazel eyes of his, she had a thought in the back of her head that he was so big, their faces were on the same level even though he was down on one knee. She also knew . . . that if he leaned forward, and she did the same . . .

Their lips would meet.

Pull out of this right now, she told herself.

And yet she stayed right where she was—and so did he. Which made her wonder if he was thinking the same thing she was.

"How can I help?" he said in a husky voice.

Lydia shook her head. "I'm sorry, what—oh, with the computer. Ah, I'm good. It's fine. I mean, it's not fine. It's lawn sculpture—but I'll get another one to use."

As her voice drifted off, she reflected that people really didn't meet each other's stares very often, did they. At least not like this.

"That's a really ugly lawn."

"Huh?" She tried to catch up with their conversation. "Oh, right. I made a joke. But don't worry, it wasn't that funny."

"I wouldn't know." And yet he smiled as he got to his feet. "So where do you want me to start?"

Talk about a loaded question. And now that Daniel was back on the vertical, it was impossible not to have her eyes travel up his body. He had on dark blue jeans again, and another flannel shirt, and the same loose black leather jacket he'd put next to him on the seat in the diner the night before. Yet everything seemed like a revelation. No, a revolution . . . in men's fashion.

Okay, she was losing it.

"How's your bike doing?" she blurted.

"Good, I guess. I'm waiting for Paul to call and bring it over."

"So you really did walk to work."

"Sure did."

Lydia frowned. "Paul isn't waiting for a UPS delivery of that part he needs, by any chance?"

"He said one of his buddies was passing through and was bringing it."

"Good, you've got half a chance." Lydia held up her forefinger. "A piece of advice. Don't ask Candy about deliveries. You'll barely make it out of the conversation alive—at this point, I think UPS avoids us because they're scared of her."

"Good tip, thanks."

"And as for starting, the security lights are out," she said. "In the front of the building and all down the side. Let me take you to the equipment building where the bulbs are. There's also a leak in the roof out there I'd like you to take a look at? Then later today, we'll go over the map of the trails, and I'll show you where the broken bridges are. I was out in the preserve earlier this week taking an inventory. Oh, and the ATV has a leak in the fuel tank—or at least that's what the sheriff said when he towed it back yesterday?"

"I'll handle everything."

She got to her feet. "You know, I really like your attitude."

As well as the size of your shoulders, she thought to herself.

As she came around the desk, she tripped on the toe of her trail shoe—and Daniel caught her arm as her weight lurched forward.

"You okay?" he said as their eyes met once again.

"Oh, I'm fine." God, he smelled good. "Thanks—"

A head of short pink hair whipped around into the doorway. And stopped dead.

Lydia yanked back. "Hi, Candy—"

"Well, I was going to ask what was on fire—"

"Daniel Joseph is going to be joining us as our groundskeeper, starting today." Lydia tried to smile while also shooting don't-you-dare-finish-that-fire-comment signals. "Peter hired him last night."

"Did he? From his Barcalounger at home?" The woman lifted an eyebrow. "Multitasking with a bowl of popcorn on his lap while he surfs Netflix. Wow. So what was burning in here?"

Okay, wow. Candy was *so* going to need a refresher on office decorum.

"My computer spontaneously combusted," Lydia muttered.

"Well, Mr. Wynne's is free. Take his. 'Cuz guess what?"

"What?"

"He's not coming in again. I just got a message on my voice mail." The woman turned away. "I'm starting coffee if anybody needs it."

＊ ＊ ＊

Two hours later, the sun was warm on Daniel's back as he hammered nails on the equipment building's cedar roof. The structure was big enough to house a family of four, and even had a galley kitchen and shower. It was also a museum and an archaeological dig and a hardware store: There were jelly jars full of every nail or screw that Daniel had ever seen. Tools that ranged from the generic, like hammers and screwdrivers, to the obscure—and possibly medical, as far as he could tell. There was also a mother lode of two-by-fours, plywood sheets, concrete blocks, random tree trunks, a set of stairs, three mystery trunks that he had yet to open, and the carcass of a Chevy big block that seemed to be used as a cup holder.

Everything had a coating of dust on it, but nothing didn't work.

Well, except for the hollowed-out car engine, and again, even that was functional, its piston holes plugged with Slurpee plastic cups that were stained red.

So yup, he'd found the roll of tar paper he'd needed to patch the hole in the roof, along with the necessary hammer and nail combo, and three spare shingles to replace the ones that had been storm damaged—

The movement registered over to the left and he stopped in mid-swing, his keen eyes tracking the intrusion into his visual field.

On the far side of the office building, a figure

emerged out into the sunlight, crossing to the shallow porch's balustrade and staring through the trees to the valley's distant lake.

His body knew who it was before his eyes informed him it was Lydia Susi.

And that was a problem.

Just like that moment they'd had at her desk. And the one from the night before. And the instant he'd first met her.

As his thoughts devolved into a crystal clear image of her sitting in her office chair and looking up his body, he was unaware of lowering the hammer. The good news was that his mind moved on from that once-over she'd given him. The bad news was that he merely traded that for a preoccupation with the woman herself as she leaned into the railing and continued to focus on the far-off.

The view was obscured—or at least, hers was. His was just fine, considering he didn't care about the lake down below or the mountains on the other side of the valley. Nope, the woman was enough of a landscape for him, everything from her profile to her shoulders and back to the curve of her ass and her long legs more than enough for his eyes to linger on. And he decided it was a shame she'd traded her running tights in for loose trail pants with pockets on the sides.

Yet her mood was also something to take note of. Even as the warm breeze toyed with the blond wisps around her face, and birds chirped sweetly beside her, she was a study in conflict: She was clearly arm wrestling something or someone in her head. And he wondered if it was herself.

She'd lied about putting the computer in the tin days before. He'd watched her do that last night.

Kind of ironic that he'd been spying on her while she'd obviously been setting up her tower to self-destruct overnight.

Putting the hammer down, he hand-and-foot'd it down the roof slope and jumped off over the gutter, landing on the ground with a bounce. As he walked to the main building, he jacked up his jeans and ran a hand through his hair. His boots were heavy, but he made sure they were silent as he hit the damp gravel, and when he transitioned onto the grass, he lowered his head so that as he passed in front of the windows of the waiting room, that receptionist with the pink hair would think he was busy with something important.

Not a lie.

Lydia wanted him. Physically, that was. And he was going to have to use that to his advantage.

But he also wanted her. So he was going to have to be careful—and in this, they were a pair. He, too, was wrestling with himself.

Snap.

As he stepped up onto the porch, he continued to

be quiet because he wanted her to remain focused—because he wanted to study her for a bit longer. He also felt the need to be in control—of both of them.

"See something out of place?" he said when he was ready.

His target wheeled around and put her hand to the base of her throat. "I didn't hear you."

"Sorry I snuck up on you."

"It's okay." She looked back out at the view. "I'm just jumpy."

He stayed silent, giving her the space to tell him something, anything, because he was curious to see what she'd come up with for conversation.

When she just seemed to get lost in the lake view again, he gave her a nudge: "Is it what was in the newspaper this morning?"

She pivoted to him and looked up through the dappling sunlight, her brown eyes catching the golden illumination so that her irises were the color of whiskey.

How fitting, he thought remotely. A man could get drunk on them.

Not him, though. He might catch a buzz, but there'd be no under the influence, much less intoxication, for Daniel Joseph.

"I saw it in the break room," he murmured. "The front page of the newspaper. I read the article on the hiker who was found not far from here."

"It was a good four miles into the preserve."

"Like I said, it's around the block. Compared to the Canadian border."

"You're not in any danger working here, if that's what you're worried about."

"I'm not scared."

She considered him for a moment and pushed a loose curl out of her face. "Maybe you should be. Wolves are wild animals. Their rules are their own."

"Let me amend that statement. Fear is a creation of the mind. It's an internal fiction." He put his palms up. "If you refuse to believe in it, it's fire without oxygen. A spark without kindling."

Her eyes returned to the view of the water and the mountain opposite them. "You haven't met true evil yet. And I commend you for your luck."

"You're not looking at the lake, are you. It's that thing on the mountain, the building site."

"Abomination," she muttered. "An absolute eyesore."

Daniel joined her at the rail. "So that's where the hotel is going, huh."

"Not if I can stop it." A harsh laugh came out of her. "And I can't."

"So that's your evil."

"They're taking things they don't have a right to—and before you throw out something like, hey, they own that property, they can build whatever they want on it, I'll stop you right there. They're poisoning my wolves on my property, which is more than illegal."

"Murder of animals in the first degree?"

Angry eyes swung his way. "You think this is funny."

"I have no sense of humor, remember? And I'm not expressing an opinion, I'm just trying to clarify yours. I don't get involved in business that isn't my own."

"Well, sometimes you have to get involved because it's the only way you can sleep at night." She cleared her throat. "Or I suppose you can go through life not connected to anything, floating above it all as you skip from place to place. I'd argue that kind of insulation doesn't keep you warm, it keeps you numb. But what do I know, right."

The sliding glass door opened behind them, the pink-haired receptionist leaning out. "Lydia, the executive director is here and he wants to see you in his office."

"Peter's on-site?" Shock registered on his woman's face. "I thought he wasn't coming in."

Not that she was his, Daniel pointed out to himself.

"Surprise, surprise. And he wants a royal audience with you, you lucky dog."

Lydia ducked her head and went inside. As she slid the glass door closed, he thought she would look back. She didn't.

Left on his own, Daniel narrowed his eyes on the construction site across the valley.

If only she knew the truth, he thought with a hard smile. The wolves were more than just his business to get involved in.

But he needed to keep that to himself for the duration of his stay. Especially from the likes of her.

EIGHT

LYDIA WALKED INTO Peter Wynne's open doorway. Knocking on the jamb, she waited until the man looked up from his phone.

In the lull, she studied the crown of his sandyblond hair. He kept it short-and-straight and in a rigid side part, swooping the strands over the top where things were getting thin even though he was only in his late thirties. Likewise, the rest of him seemed to be prematurely aging, his navy-blue blazer and gray flannel slacks, his button-down and club tie, not the kind of thing men of his generation wore.

It was like someone had dropped him in the present from a Men's Wearhouse ad, ca. 1987—

With a curse, he slammed his cell phone facedown and looked up through his steel-rimmed glasses—only to do a double take like he'd been slapped.

"Jesus! Don't sneak up on me like that."

She put her hands up. "I'm sorry, but you asked to see me."

"No, I didn't."

Oh, Candy. "Well, since I'm here, I need your signature on the new employment contract—"

"Just sign for me."

Lydia frowned. "My signature isn't authorized for—"

"My name. Sign it." He waved her off and went back to his phone. "Now, if you'll excuse me, I'm busy."

Lydia glanced behind herself. Then shut them in together. He was texting fast, his fingers flying over the screen.

When he looked up again, he frowned as if he were confused. As if he might have lost track of time—or forgotten that he'd dismissed her.

"What now?"

"Are you okay?" she asked. "I know we don't know each other outside of work, but something is clearly going on."

Peter Wynne took a deep breath, in the way somebody did when they wanted to be left alone and had the sense that screaming at the top of their lungs was going to have the opposite effect.

"I'm fine." His eyes went back to his phone. "I'm just busy getting ready for the board meeting next month."

"So you've seen the financials?"

When he just started texting again, she went across to his desk, planted her hands, and leaned in. "The last time you were in here for a full day was a month ago. I don't need the details, I don't require an explanation—

what I'm looking for from you is either a resignation or a recommittal to this organization. You're the executive director—"

Now, the curse was exhausted. "I really don't have time for this right now—"

"It's not about what you need. It's about everything that can't happen around here unless you step aside or get your shit together. This organization has to have a leader and you're the one we've got on our letterhead. Something has to change, and I'm giving you an opportunity to make the choice before I make it for you."

"You can't fire me."

"The board can. And they don't know how absent you've been because I've been doing your job. That can change with a phone call."

Peter put his phone facedown again. As he sat back in his chair, there was a creaking noise. "Fine, I'll sign the paperwork for the employment contract, if you bring it now. And then I have to go."

Lydia stared at the man. He had lost weight, and it had been a while since he'd had a haircut. One side of his collar hadn't been buttoned and there was a stain on his tie.

"Jesus Christ," he snapped. "What is your problem."

"You're scared," she heard herself say. "What's happening, Peter."

"Get out. Right now." He raised his voice. "I'm

serious, Lydia. You and I have never had a problem before, but if you don't lay off, we're going to have a big one."

Slowly straightening, she shook her head. "I'm going to go to the board. Just so you and I are clear. This can't go on."

"You're right about that," he muttered as he checked his phone and got to his feet.

"So you want me to go and have you fired?"

"I don't have time to argue with you. Sign the shit for me—and get out of my way."

The man came around his desk and barged past her, his shoulder knocking into hers. And that was when she smelled him. He hadn't showered in days.

Opening his door, he walked off. Out in reception, Candy said something to him, but there was no response. Or one that was too mumbled to track—

The phone over on Peter's desk rang and Lydia jumped. When the thing rang a second time, she reached across and snagged the receiver.

"Hello?" she said.

There was a period of silence. "Hello?" she repeated.

Click.

Hanging up, she went out front to the windows in the waiting room. As Candy glanced over from a spreadsheet of names, a white Mercedes SUV Lydia had never seen before tore out of the parking lot, kicking up gravel.

"I'm going to miss him," Candy muttered. "Like the black flies in June."

Lydia looked across. Then cleared her throat. "Did you just put a call through to Peter's phone?"

"Yeah. It was from his ass, requesting he relocate his head back to where it belongs. Things are crowded down there, and very dark—"

"I'm serious. Did a call come in for him?"

Candy frowned. "No, but he's got his own direct line."

With a feeling of foreboding, Lydia went back into the man's office. Glancing around, she took note of the three diplomas on the wall. The arrangement of office equipment on the desk. The lineup of book spines on the shelves. The coat rack that had a cardigan slowly distorting from having been hung on a hook by its collar tag.

"Why did you really come in today," she murmured as she stared at his chair. "What were you looking for . . ."

"What're you doing?" Candy asked from the doorway.

Lydia answered absently. "I'm going to be in here for a little while. I don't want anybody coming in."

"Rick's the only other person around."

"Even Rick."

Candy's expression froze. "What's going on, Lydia?"

"I'm going to find out."

◆　◆　◆

As the sun was getting low in the sky, Daniel finally put the hammer back where he'd found it in the equipment building. Which was randomly on a workbench that had lived a very hard life. Any more hunks out of its top and only God would know what it was.

When he turned around, he stopped. "I didn't hear you."

The woman who had been on his mind all afternoon was standing in the open garage bay, the sun streaming in from behind her. Like she was glowing.

"I guess two can play at the stealth game." Lydia glanced down at the concrete floor. "Anyway, I came to—"

"Can I ask you something?"

She seemed to hesitate before she looked up again. "Sure. Don't know if I can answer whatever it is, but I'll give it a shot."

"Does the sunlight always find you?"

Her head pulled back a little, as if he'd surprised her. "I'm sorry—what?"

Reaching across to the workbench, he grabbed a red chamois cloth. The thing was stained, but not as badly as all the others. As he wiped his palms, he took his time with the job.

"Just wondering." He shrugged. "Out on the porch, and now, here? Seems as though the sun likes you."

He didn't glance back over because he wanted her to hold the moment in, and he knew if he made eye contact, she'd be compelled to brush it off. Change the subject. Move along.

"I'm not sure what to say to that," she whispered.

"You don't have to say anything."

"It was a question."

"More like a rhetorical, really." Now he looked at her. "Sorry if I've made things awkward."

"You haven't."

"You're lying." He shrugged again. "But it looks like I'm the one who owes you an apology. I'm crossing all kinds of boundaries here, aren't I. I'm not a scumbag, I promise."

"I know you're not."

"No, you don't. But I'll prove it to you." He let half his mouth lift in a smile. "I guess I'm not used to this."

"To what."

He lowered his lids. "Do you really want me to answer that."

She cleared her throat and put her hands on her hips. "No, I think it's probably better for us that you don't. Anyway, I came out here to say I'm sorry for the way I was out on the porch. I have no right to make any insinuations about you or your life. I let my frustration get the best of me, and not only was it unfair, it was unprofessional. So yeah, I'm sorry."

"Don't worry about it."

"No, I really—"

"I can't even remember what you said, to be honest."

He put the rag back down. "I'm not much for short-term memories—and yup, that probably is part of the drifter thing."

"I don't judge you," she said with earnest eyes.

Man, he could stand to be looked at like that for a while. By her, specifically.

"It's fine if you do judge me. Don't take this the wrong way, but I don't really care what people think of me." As a strange feeling vibrated into his chest, he pointed overhead. "So about the roof. Sorry the repair out here took me so long. After I fixed the obvious damage from that tree falling, I found a bunch of loose shingles on the north side—probably because that's where the storms come from. Things should be stable going forward. The light bulbs are changed on the main building, and I'll be back on Monday to start the bridge work. Weather's going to be nice—what."

"Hmm?" she said with distraction.

"You're frowning."

"Am?" she asked. "I mean, am I? I was actually just so relieved that you've made some progress on anything around here. It all just seems so . . . insurmountable at the moment. Even a new bulb is a miracle to me."

Her hands shook a little as she raised them to her face. Pressing them into her eyes, she looked like she was trying to gouge things out.

"Long day?" he said softly.

"They're all that way lately."

"And why's that?"

"It's just how things have been." Her eyes went to the main building. "You know, it makes me think about something my grandfather always said. Reality is like a coin. It has a front and a back, and you can only see one side at a time."

"What exactly's unclear to you?"

"Oh, it doesn't matter." She swiped her hand as if to bat her words away. "So do you have a place to stay here in town yet? You know, for when you return."

"I've got a couple of leads."

"Have you met Shirley? Down at Walters Realty? If you need a reference, I'll be happy to give you one."

"Even though I'm just skating through life?"

She flushed. "I thought you didn't remember."

He shrugged again. "I don't want to remember what you said. How about that."

"I did insult you, then."

"No, you linger. And I don't like things that linger."

As her eyebrows went up, he found himself feeling the same kind of surprised.

"I didn't just say that," he muttered.

"Didn't you?"

"Nope." He shook his head as he stared across at her. "I did not."

Lydia looked away. Looked back. "Daniel Joseph, never Danny, I suspect still waters run deep with you."

"Can I ask you something else?"

"Sure. Hit me."

"What's the actual policy on employees at the Wolf Study having dinner together?" He put his hands forward. "I'm not asking about you. I want to know if I can take Candy out. I think she's single and I'm feeling lucky next week."

Lydia started to smile. "You'll have to talk to HR about that."

"Who's HR?"

"I guess I am. Considering our executive director is a little distracted right now."

Daniel took a step forward, simply because his body wanted to be closer to her. "So, Ms. HR. Can I have dinner with you or not."

The flush that hit her face looked nice, the color accenting her cheeks . . . the column of her throat . . . her lips.

"I thought this was about Candy?"

"I lied because I was trying not to be obvious. That way, if it wasn't allowed, I wouldn't have egg on my face with you."

"And yet you blew your cover."

"What can I say, I'm not a good liar." He pushed his hand through his hair. "So what do you think. Just dinner. Nothing else—and it can be in a public place, too. You know, in case I'm a masher."

"Are you a masher?"

"No, I'm not." He thumbed out toward his motorcycle. "I have my anti-Masher ID in my wallet over there."

"I didn't know there was a governmental agency that dealt with masher clearance."

"There are all kinds of federal nooks-and-crannies agencies like that."

"Ah. The more you know." She nodded toward his bike. "So Paul took care of you, huh?"

"Yup. And you think about dinner, although not this weekend, of course. I've got to go get my things, not that I have much."

"Minimalism is underappreciated." She laughed. "I'm funny."

"I wouldn't know." He leaned in. "But I'll take your word for it."

Her eyes went lower—to his mouth—and then popped right back up to meet his stare. "Daniel . . ."

He put his palm out. "Wait, I know what you're going to say."

"And what's that."

"You're not looking for complications." Daniel shrugged. "But see, that's the good thing about drifters. We're not looking for anything serious, either."

"Then why even start with dinner?"

"Considering that your background is in biology, I'm surprised I have to explain how the human body works. You know, food intake, the conversion of fats, carbs, and proteins into energy? It's kind of necessary for life." As she gave him a look, he said, "You want me to get a whiteboard and a marker? Maybe some diagrams would help—"

"Okay, see, you've already lied to me once."

"Oh?"

"You do have a sense of humor."

As someone came out of the rear of the building, they both looked toward the parking area. That vet, Rick, pushed a pair of glasses up higher on his hawkish nose. When he noticed that he was being watched, he did a double take and slowed his stride.

Then he lowered his head and went on to his car.

"I have to go catch Rick, hold on."

With a lithe stride, she jogged out and intercepted the Jeep's reversing. Leaning in as the driver's side window was lowered, she went into some kind of back-and-forth with the man. And then she nodded and stepped back, giving the guy a little wave.

That man is totally in love with her, Daniel thought.

It was the way the car didn't move as she came back to the groundskeeping building. How when the driver finally hit the gas, he departed with speed. How Daniel was willing to bet the vet's eyes were locked on the rear view as he went down the lane.

"I'm going to head back to my office," she said. "Are you leaving soon?"

"Yeah, I'd like to get a head start on the trip back to Glens Falls."

"Okay. Well, I'll see you on Monday. Be safe."

"I always am."

She turned away. Turned back. "I can't have dinner with you, I'm sorry. It just wouldn't . . . it wouldn't look right. I'm not your boss, but we're a small organization and . . . you know."

"I totally understand," he murmured. "You're a professional and I respect that."

With a nod, as if they'd come to a negotiated position as intractable as a brick wall, she lifted her hand to him and murmured a goodbye.

Daniel watched her go. And was certain Rick had been given the same message at some point. It explained the yearning on his face.

If Daniel had been a different kind of man, he'd have understood how the guy felt.

Good thing they had nothing in common.

NINE

BACK INSIDE THE main building, Lydia went up to Candy, who was pulling on her coat. "Hey, did Daniel fill out his paperwork to get paid?"

"Sure did. I put everything in the system."

"Oh, good."

"You want to see what he put down?" Candy raised an eyebrow. "In a purely professional capacity, of course."

"It's none of my business—"

"He's twenty-eight. His mailing address is in Glens Falls. No emergency contact listed and no next of kin. There are four fours in his social security number—not sure what that means, but it's my favorite number so I'm taking that as a good sign. Oh, and I checked the bank. You haven't cashed your paycheck even though you went into town on your lunch break. So I'm guessing that's how we're affording him?"

Lydia opened her mouth. Closed it.

The woman hiked her heavy purse up on her shoulder. "That's not right. You've got bills, too."

"Maybe I just didn't make it to the bank."

"Sure. And this pink hair is convincing anybody I'm not in AARP."

Lydia had to smile. Today's sweater was lavender with a string of butterflies around the collar and cuffs. Under the woman's parka, it was like spring trying to break out from under winter's weight. A metaphor made of wool.

"Is that why you colored your luscious locks?" Lydia asked.

"Luscious? Really?" Candy shrugged and got a faraway look on her face. "And I don't know, sometimes . . . you just don't want to look like yourself. Even if it's only for a couple of days and for a stupid reason. Considering I'm about to go home alone to feed my cat and decide which Stouffer's to put in the microwave, you can understand why I might want a change."

"Oh, Candy—"

A sharp forefinger was lifted. Then she cupped her ear. "Did I ask for sympathy? I don't think so. I am quite happy with my choices. I don't have to do someone else's laundry, I always know what is and is not in my refrigerator, and I control my remote. There are women all across America who wish they were me."

"I was offering no sympathy, I swear. I think independence is really important."

"Good. But you're still going to have to pay me back."

"For what?"

"Putting you down as our groundskeeper's emergency contact—oh, don't give me that look. First of all, I'm not doing it as a matchmaker, and second, it's policy. Everybody has to have one and I would have listed Peter, but like he's around? So there you go. Now I'm off the clock and not talking about work until Monday at eight-thirty a.m.—well, maybe eight-forty-five if I get stuck behind Miser's tractor again."

"Candy. I don't believe you're not matchmaking."

"No work talk 'til Monday—"

"You pulled a numerology on his social security—"

"Just making an observation."

"You said it was a good sign."

She shrugged. "I can't help you. Until Monday morning, I'm not talking shop and you two are shop."

"Which is why we can't be dating—"

"Aha!" That forefinger made another appearance. "I *knew* you liked him."

"Wait, what—I don't like him. I mean other than as a human being."

Candy laughed. "I saw the way you looked at him. And so did he."

Lydia opened her mouth. Closed it. Felt like she was on a sinking ship—or maybe one that was already at the bottom of the ocean.

"I don't know what to say to that." She kept going fast before Candy explained and she heard waaaaay too much about everything everybody had noticed. "But I do want to ask you if you have the guest list? For the fundraiser at the end of next month? I was going to get the invitations stuffed and addressed over the weekend, and yes, I know you're off the clock— but think of how much easier your job will be if I take care of all of that for you."

"Well." Candy pursed her pink lips. "You're really pushing my buttons here, aren't you. I just clocked out, but you're going to save me work. Hmm."

"Is there really a choice?"

Candy went back around to her desk and picked up a folder. "If you wait until Monday, I'll help you. You do it before then, you're on your own. This is the master list. Five hundred names."

"I accept this responsibility with full knowledge of the obstacles I will face."

As Lydia went to take the list, Candy held it out of reach. "Do you have Band-Aids?"

"For what?"

"You have no idea from the paper cuts. And don't lick. Use this." She opened her top drawer and tossed over a glue stick. Then she transferred ownership of the folder. "*Seinfeld* was funny and all, but carcinogens are real, and yes, I used vegetable dye on my hair. Don't get judgy—actually, take two sticks, in case you run out. Now, the envelopes are in the supply room, on top of the boxes of invitations. I haven't printed the labels, but they're on the email that I sent to the board for final review. You're cc'd on it. The labels are the Averys we always use for the board packets."

"You've got everything all arranged."

"The fundraiser's coming up fast and we need the money. I can do Peter's parts the night of if he can't, just to make sure we bring some cash home. We'll slap that sad-ass cardigan on me and I'll do my hair the color of middle-aged desperation."

"I thought he was a blond?"

"He is. A lame one."

Lydia had to laugh. "Have a good weekend."

"You, too." Candy went over to the door. Pausing, she glanced back. "Listen, if he asks you out, say yes."

"Peter?" Lydia recoiled. "Never—"

"Our new groundskeeper." In a lower voice, the woman said, "The truth is, no one wants to be me, and you already have way too much in common with my life at a way younger age than I was when I took my foot off the gas and put it on the brakes. Say yes, Lydia. You won't regret it."

Before there could be any argument—or more HR tossed into a heck-no—Candy beat feet out the door and shut things tight.

Under normal circumstances, and for obvious reasons, Lydia would have followed up on the conversation all the way out to the parking lot. But after a night spent in her car, and Peter's crap, and the reality that Candy could talk circles around God himself, a decision to bail seemed pretty close to a survival reflex.

Doubling back, Lydia went down to the executive director's office and sat behind the desk. Signing into his computer, she loaded her email onto his browser, opened Candy's label missive, and got the file front and center. In the printing room, she set up the Averys in the Xerox machine, and then back again at Peter's desk, she hit the go button.

Out across the hall, the soft clicking and shuffling as the printer went to work was a peaceful, industrious sound, and she used it for background music as she began an infiltration into Peter Wynne's computer. Even though she had asked for privacy earlier, that had been to go through the drawers, file cabinet, and shelves. She'd saved the IT stuff for after hours because, considering what she'd done the night before, she was not in a big hurry for anybody to know just how good she was with a keyboard.

She looked at everything on the hard drive: All the files, anything he'd ever deleted, his web search history, what was on his calendar going back five years.

As she dove in, she felt like she had a catcher's mitt, and she was ready for the handoff, the answer.

And she knew what it was going to be.

She just had this sixth sense . . .

About an hour later, after the sun had set and the label-printing job had long finished, a knocking sound reverberated down from the front of the building.

Then there was a silence. And then the demanding sound resumed.

Getting to her feet, she zipped her pullover up to her throat. And wished it were bulletproof.

Not that she was being paranoid or anything.

Nah.

As she headed out to reception, she felt like there were shadows everywhere in the building, even though there were lights on all around. And as she glanced out the windows across the waiting area, the motion-activated security lights that glowed should have been reassuring. But weren't.

She couldn't see who was out there. And there were no lights in the parking lot.

If it was Candy coming back because she'd forgotten something or if Peter had decided to show up, they'd have keys. And Rick would have entered from the rear if he'd returned to check on the wolf who was still barely alive.

Closing in on the front door, she debated pretending she wasn't inside, but how was that going to work with her car right there?

"Ms. Susi?" came a deep voice from the outside.

Lydia jumped forward and opened things. "Sheriff?"

Eastwind took his hat off and gave her a little bow. In his uniform, and with his serious expression, she had a thought that he was going to handcuff her and put her in the back of his SUV. After that? *Orange Is the New Black*. For like, ten years. Or more?

"I ran into Candy at the diner," he said, "and she told me you'd probably still be here. Mind if I come in?"

"Please." She made room by stepping back. "How are you?"

More importantly, how am I? A felon or . . . ?

"Good, thanks. You're working late."

"There are only five of us at the WSP." Well, four who showed up for work. "So some days go into the evening."

"I know all about that." He glanced over to Candy's desk. Looked down the hall to Lydia's office. Checked out the waiting area. "So I'd like to ask you for some help. And just so we're clear, I'm not coming with a warrant or anything."

"Sure. What do you need?"

"Your preserve has cameras mounted in places, correct?"

Bingo, she thought. "We do, yes."

"And how long do you keep the feeds?"

"Forever." As he seemed surprised, she nodded. "It's not like surveillance video for businesses or public places. We need the data for our research purposes. Everything's kept on the cloud."

Eastwind shook his head. "Where I come from, clouds rain. Block the sun. Block the moon. I am not meant for this era."

She smiled, even though her heart rate was high. "There are advantages to technology. And this is about the hiker, right?"

"Yes, it is."

"I'd be happy to give you a copy of the coverage we have for North Granite Ridge. You want me to go back, like, three days? Four?"

"Four would be good. We're not exactly sure when the attack happened."

"It may not be a wolf, you know." When he made a noncommittal murmur, she tried to shrug casually. "I'll send you the files right away. All I need is an email address, and I'll get you a Dropbox."

"Drop box?"

"It's a way of sharing big files."

"Oh. That'd be great."

Out on the mountain, the man was in charge. Here indoors? He was awkward in a way that would have seemed endearing—if it weren't for the fact they were talking about footage she'd obstructively justice'd.

"I will warn you," she said. "Our cameras are limited. They can only scan part of any location, and they move through a system of positions. It's possible we have nothing on video."

"It's still more than we have to go on now."

"Okay, well, I'm just here printing address labels so I can grab the footage before I leave." She got a pad and took a pen out of Candy's holder. "What's your email?"

"Here, take this card." He reached into his back pocket. "It's on the bottom."

Lydia took what he offered. "So . . . have you ID'd the hiker yet?"

"No, not yet. We will, though."

"And you didn't find a car? At the trailheads, or something?"

"Not yet, no."

"So how'd he get on the property? Hikers have to start somewhere on the trails. Unless he walked across the valley from another site—like the hotel's."

"This is an active investigation so I cannot comment."

She put her hands on her hips. "Did you ask the hotel about his picture? What did they say?"

"Come on, Ms. Susi, you know what my response is going to be to that—"

"What was in his pack."

"Excuse me?" Those dark eyes narrowed.

Shit. Maybe she'd given herself away.

"Well, if he's a hiker, he probably had a pack, right? Any chance there were hunks of poisoned meat in it?" When the sheriff just stared at her, she shook her head. "That hotel chain is not part of our community. Why are you protecting them? And please don't active-investigation me again. I'm not buying it."

The sheriff inclined his head. Then he put his hat back on. "Thank you for your help. I look forward to receiving the files."

As the man turned away, Lydia said, "How far is it going to go. How far are you going to let it go."

The sheriff left in silence, and he closed the door quietly.

"Goddamn it," Lydia muttered.

Turning around, she went back through the facility, passing by Peter's office. Out in the clinic section, she pushed open the door to the exam room. As her breath stopped, she hugged herself.

The wolf was on his side, an oxygen mask at the end of his muzzle, his flank rising and falling.

She lingered in the doorway, feeling raw rage.

When she stepped back out, she was careful to make sure that the door didn't make a sound as it closed. And then she marched back to her office and went to her cell phone. Looking up what she needed on the web, she put a call in and waited as the ringing started—

"WNDK news desk. How can I help you," a terse male voice said.

TEN

A H, THE GOD-AWFUL *overhang of a bad day's sleep*, Xhex thought as she stood, back-flatted and headachy, against the far wall of the club.

Fuck that, it was more like a number of days.

All around her, humans were deliberately cutting their ties to reality, using drugs, alcohol, and orgasms with strangers, to extinguish the burn of their regular lives. Whether they were working shit jobs or for people they hated . . . or in relationships that sucked . . . or worried about a sick parent . . . or whatever it was they were bitched about, here, they could surf free of all that weighed them down.

As a *symphath*, she knew the particulars of what they were avoiding. Okay, fine, not names and birthdates, but the emotions were all there for her consumption, the evil side of her feeding off the toxic feelings that drove the humans, defined them . . . and ultimately threatened to destroy them.

Although, hey, maybe there were people here celebrating something, a graduation, a promotion, a new apartment or coupledom. But the good feelings were no nourishment for her so she self-selected out the happy-joy-joys.

And went for the traffic accidents.

Then again, maybe it was because of how things were going in her own life. Fuck knew she was close to cracking open.

"Misery loves company," she muttered as her earpiece continued to burble with reports.

Blasphemy was a new club, part of Trez Latimer's portfolio of emporiums that served up all kinds of legal and maaaaybe-not-so-legal products for consumption. He owned four now, and each had a different vibe. This one, in spite of its name, did not have an anti-religious theme, although it was painted black and red, and there were a lot of Gothic details. The clientele was very steampunk, which by her taste, was sooo much better than the Botoxed, lip-injected glamour bullshit.

But no one asked her.

Just as well.

Her eyes did their scan-thing automatically, her instincts weeding through the crowd on the dance floor, at the bar, down in the back by the bathrooms, ever searching for blowups about to happen, and drugs that were being done too obviously, and actual penetration being engaged in.

You could snog all you want. But you couldn't—

"Alex?"

At the sound of the male voice, she turned her head. T'Marcus Jones was a human who was built like a heavyweight boxer, and even though he was a new hire, it was not hard to respect the crap out of him. He was level-headed, nonreactive, and he had enough muscle on him that, if he had to engage, he was going to win. Even if shit went to a ground game.

Oh, and Alex Hess was the human name she'd always used around Caldwell.

"What's up?" she said.

"We've got a guy smoking in the back hall." T'Marcus nodded toward the bathrooms. "I went down and asked him to leave—"

The human man winced and rubbed his forehead like his frontal lobe had been stabbed with an ice pick.

"It's okay," she told him. "You take my station. I'll deal with it."

T'Marcus pegged her with a hard eye. "I don't let you down. I don't—"

"I know. You're fine."

She left him to be in charge of the floor—testament to how much she already trusted the man—and proceeded down to the corridor in question. Passing the woman's bathroom, her keen ears picked up on a whole lot of moaning. The men's bathroom, on the other side, was quiet, and not likely to stay that way.

The shallow hall hung a louie, but she smelled the Turkish tobacco even before she came to the corner.

And somehow, even though she knew who it was, it was still an uncomfortable shock to see Vishous way down by the emergency exit. The Brother was in a lean, one shitkicker planted against the wall, his leather-clad body strung like a powerful bow.

"You know," she said as she walked up to him, "there are laws."

V's icy diamond eyes shifted over to her and he stroked his goatee with his black-gloved hand. "Are there? Tell me everything."

"In the state of New York, you're not allowed to smoke in public places—"

He gestured his hand-rolled forward. "This bothering you?"

"No."

"Then that's the only law I'm following. New York State can go fuck itself."

"I'm not sure whether that's anatomically possible. Given that it's a piece of land." Xhex planted herself across the way from him. "So what brings you here?"

"How're ya."

Not a question. But come on, like she was going to answer that truthfully. "Great. You?"

"I'm perfect." He exhaled. "No, I think I'm better than that."

"It's good to know your ego remains unscathed."

Annnnnnnnnnnnnnnnd that was when he went silent. V just smoked and stared at the lit tip of what he'd rolled, likely right after First Meal, given the time.

"Spit it out," she muttered. "And if this is some kind of hardass intervention, you'll have better luck talking to an inanimate object."

"Intervention? Nah. I'd be the last person to get in the way of self-destruction."

She wasn't so sure about that. Under his crunchy exterior . . . well, there was a straight-up killer, true. But he had his own set of loyalties, all of which were centered on the people in that mansion she lived in.

"So you just needed a place to smoke?" She motioned around. "There's a big-ass city out there, full of park benches—"

"I dreamed of you," he cut in harshly. "During the day."

Xhex's breath caught in her throat. "Oh, fucking hell."

There were a whole host of things a person didn't want to hear: Your mate is missing in the field. That limb is not going to grow back. Lassiter has the remote.

And right up there with that happy list? Vishous, son of the Bloodletter, telling you he's had a dream with your name on it.

Just as she only tracked the addicts, the desperates, and the malcontents in the clubs, he only ever saw bad news. Very bad news.

In the future.

"What," she gritted out. "Fucking tell me, whatever it is."

It was a long while before the Brother answered—
and his nearly white, navy-rimmed eyes shifted to her
own before he spoke. As fear speared right into her
chest, his one-word reply hit the airwaves—and she
felt even worse.

"Wolven," was all he said.

ELEVEN

TWO DAYS LATER, on Sunday morning back in Walters, Lydia found the footsteps in the dirt outside her rental house.

The two-story, two-bedroom, one-and-a-half bath was barely more than a shotgun, even though the only things on either side of it were a shallow lawn and a whole lot of trees. Given the town it was in, it went without saying that her nearest neighbors were a quarter mile away and her driveway was a hundred yards long.

As she stepped out onto the porch, she had her running shoes on, her windbreaker zipped up, and her earbuds in. At ten a.m., the air was still and cold, and overhead, the sky was a clear, but weak, blue. The sunlight was warm on her face, however, and that felt good.

It also felt calming—which considering the gymnastics her brain had been going through since Friday night was exactly what she needed. Even if it was the kind of thing that didn't last.

After she locked up, she stretched her calves on the stairs, and enjoyed contemplating, for a moment, the simple problem of choosing left or right when she got to the end of her driveway. Right would take her out along the rural road for about a half mile before she could cut into a trail and do some intervals on the mountain's incline. With a left, she'd head into town, going by the post office, the supermarket/diner, and the bank, which would be closed. The decision seemed obvious as there was more traffic on the road—relatively speaking—but she didn't want to go into the preserve.

She didn't trust herself not to end up at the hotel site—

At first, she wasn't sure what got her attention. But as she glanced around, she had the same sense she'd gotten when she'd been sure someone had moved something in her office.

Her out-of-place alarm was never wrong.

And that was when she saw the footprints going around the porch. The depressions in the damp earth were barely noticeable, but sunlight was as always the great revealer, the subtle shadows thrown by the indentations forming a pattern that was unmistakable.

Stepping off onto the scrubby, brown grass, she got down on her haunches. The prints were big, and oddly, they had no tread to them. They were smooth and box shaped—and they went around to the living room window. Went around the whole first floor of the house.

As she tracked them, she was careful not to interfere with the trail, and she took pictures on her phone. By the back door, she fired up her Samsung's flashlight and tried to see if whoever it had been had come up on the shallow landing and left any dirt or residue.

Hard to tell.

Returning to the front, she went inside and checked all of the windows. Everything was locked, the old brass fixtures cranked into place, and all the glass panes were intact—although given how small the place was and how quiet the nights were, she would have heard something breaking or getting smashed.

A cold numbness went through her.

There had been some rain on Saturday afternoon. Given the clarity of the markings and how deep they were, it seemed like the ground had to have been damp . . . so she guessed they'd been made sometime during the night.

Back in the kitchen, she looked over the uncluttered counters. The stove, with her grandfather's teapot and the skillet she'd bought a year ago sitting on cold burners. The table, with the two chairs, the single place mat, and the napkin holder—as well as her laptop, which was worth maybe six or seven hundred dollars.

That Lenovo was the only portable thing of value she had. Well, there was the TV that had come with the house, and that was also where she'd last seen it.

One by one, she opened all the cabinets. The drawers. The door into the little pantry.

Struck by a driving paranoia, she went to the living room and lifted the cushions off the sofa. Picked up the remotes and put them back down again. Measured the distance from the rug's edge to the kick pleat on the old armchair. Checked the shade on the lamp.

Then she pivoted to the stairs.

Had someone come in the house while she'd been asleep? She didn't have an alarm, security cameras, or motion detectors. And locks could be picked, even dead bolts.

As she went up the pine-planked steps, she avoided the one that creaked even though there was nobody else in the house. There couldn't be anyone else—and there hadn't been. Otherwise they'd have hurt her or stolen something, not that she had much of real value.

When she got to the top landing, she looked through the open door of the single full bathroom. The sunlight reassured her, but only because the magical-thinking part of her brain told her that nothing bad could happen on a sunny spring day.

Bad things happened at night.

When you were asleep alone in a house.

They did not happen in broad daylight. No matter what was in the dirt outside those windows.

The guest bedroom—not that she'd ever had guests—was across from her own and she went there first, not sure what she expected to find. An indentation on the pillow? A depression on the handmade quilt? Water glass on the bed stand?

Like she'd had a houseguest she'd somehow missed. Nothing.

She checked the hall closet that was cedar lined and where she kept the extra sheets and her sweaters in the summer. Nothing out of place, but like anybody was going to take a Martha Stewart queen-sized anything?

Swallowing dread, she turned to her own bedroom doorway. There was no way someone had come into her room. NFW.

Over at her bed, she smoothed the comforter, which she'd put back to rights as soon as she'd gotten up. She checked under both her pillows. On her little side table, she checked that her old alarm clock, the radio one she'd had in college and still used, remained at a perfect right angle to the corner.

Nothing out of place.

She checked the drawers of her bureau and the shallow closet with her one-note wardrobe of practical, casual clothes. She even looked under the bed.

Just before she walked out, she glanced over her shoulder.

Across the way, there was a window seat full of throw pillows where, in theory, you could sit bathed in the morning light on a Sunday, and get cozy with the paper or a book, and sip chamomile tea in your robe and fuzzy socks. Maybe a fluffy gray cat with green eyes would curl up at your feet, and if you got a draft, you could pull a handmade quilt over your legs.

She had seen the vision clear as day the second she'd walked into the room. It was the reason she'd picked the house.

Of course, none of that Instagram-delusion had happened: She didn't relax. She rarely read. She hated tea and didn't have a cat. But the fantasy persisted anyway.

Out in the hall, she rubbed her face and did some mental math. Nothing breached and nothing stolen. So there had been another purpose to those obvious tracks—like a message to her that she was being watched. And she knew why it had been sent.

On Friday night, she'd spent two hours on the phone talking to the television producer at WNDK, and then she'd sent him photographs of the bait trap, the meat, and the printouts from when Rick had tested what poison had been used. She'd debated sharing a picture of the wolf—and in the end, she had forwarded the man one image and told him that they could use it, but under no circumstances take footage of the animal or disturb him in any way themselves.

A team was going to come and interview her in the office.

The hotel construction site was operational on weekends. She was willing to bet the producer went there. And the station had certainly called the corporate headquarters for a statement.

Lydia was aware that she had flimsy evidence to go on, nothing but the timeline of the work beginning on the site, and the traps being put out, and the three wolves getting poisoned. So there was a possibility that the hotel chain's lawyers were going to get on the story and kill the whole thing under the libel laws.

They were good at killing things.

Did she call Eastwind? she wondered as she went downstairs.

Peering out through the panel of glass next to the front door, she looked over her driveway. She could just barely see the county road out in the distance.

The house was in what the locals considered the "busy part" of town. Which was to say the traffic in and out of Walters's center, such as it was, passed by—but there were no streetlights up at the asphalt. No lights down the gravel drive. Just one front bulb fixture and one at the back door, neither of which were motion-activated, neither of which were turned on regularly.

Although that was changing, effective immediately.

Given how dark it got? Anyone could have parked just off the county road on her driveway and walked down and around her house—

Her car. Damn it, her car was parked in the open air because there was no garage, and she hadn't locked it. She never did.

"That's another thing that's changing tonight," she muttered as she went out and walked across the grass.

Looking in through the driver's side, she expected to see the seats stabbed and the glove compartment open like a wound.

Nope.

Reaching for the handle, she snatched her hand back and pulled her sleeve over her fingers and palm. When she went to open things, she had a thought a bomb was going to explode. Which was nuts—

The handle made a little noise as she lifted it and she jumped.

"Relax," she muttered as she pulled the door wide.

No *boom!* Nothing out of place, even as she looked in the backseat. And when she went into the glove box, she checked the paperwork. Everything was as she'd left it.

She went around and checked the trunk.

No ticking box. No random human head. No threatening note made out of mismatched letters cut from the pages of a magazine.

Closing her car up, she leaned back against the quarter panel and crossed her arms over her chest. As she stared at her house, she was glad she'd gone to BU and gotten into the habit of always locking her doors. Boston was a big city and crime happened anywhere there were lots of people.

Crime also crept into isolated places.

Her eyes returned to the footprints beneath the windows of her living room. Good thing she always had a deadly weapon with her—

As her phone went off in her pocket, she jumped with a shout. Then she took the thing out. It was a 518 area code, and she had a thought that it was Daniel.

"Hello?" She waited for a response, expecting it to be him. Wanting it to be him. "Hello . . . ?"

When he didn't return the greeting, and a telemarketer didn't click in and tell her that she was due a refund from Amazon or had a repayment option on her college loans, she hung up. Memorizing the number, she went onto the web and typed it into a reverse search—

A text banner came through on the top of her screen.

From the number.

Opening it—

She looked up. Looked around.

As a shiver went through her, she refocused on the image. It was of her, leaning back against her car, looking at her phone in the sunlight.

Her heart skipped and then pounded.

With shaking hands, she put her phone away. Her mouth was dry so she swallowed a couple of times. Then she took a deep breath.

Striding forward, she zeroed in on where the picture had to have been taken from, given its angle. Ten feet into the stalk, she broke out into a jog. Then a run. As her windbreaker flapped and her ears burned from the wind, her eyes locked on a thicket of trees.

Her mind stopped considering the dangers as her body took over.

All she knew was that she was not going to be pushed around.

Even if it killed her.

TWELVE

"So HOW WAS your weekend?"

As Candy's voice registered, Lydia jerked and
looked up from behind Peter Wynne's computer. Even
though Lydia was in the WSP building and supposedly at work, it was still a shock to see the other
woman. Then again, she felt like she'd been gone
a very long time, proof that emotions, if they were
strong enough, could take you on a vacation.

Of course in her case, it had been a bad one, the
equivalent of a Princess Cruise with Norwalk virus as
a cabin mate.

"Hello?" Candy prompted.

Lydia shook herself to attention and focused
properly. "Oh, hey—wow, look at your hair."

"Blond again." Running a hand full of rings over
the short length, the woman shrugged. "You know
what Dolly Parton says."

"Working nine to five?"

"It takes a lot of money to look this cheap." Candy
laughed at her own joke. "Anyway, I saw the folder

you left on my desk. You got all the invitations done. Amazing."

"I'm going to take them to the post office on my lunch break."

"Sounds good. And hey, you look comfy in here."

"Do I?" Lydia glanced around at the wood paneling and the diplomas. "I don't feel comfy."

"Well, I can help you with that."

"You're going to bring me a Barcalounger?"

"Not a bad idea. But let's start with coffee, shall we?"

As Candy headed for the break room, Lydia called out, "Were you a pusher in an earlier life?"

"Are you turning down caffeine?" came the response.

"No," Lydia muttered as she rubbed her eyes.

She'd been up all night, the sense that things were moving in the shadows around her bedroom or that people were peering in her windows and watching her making it impossible to sleep. And even though she'd been two years in that house, she'd never realized how loud it was until every single creak, groan and whistle of the wind had shot through her entire body. It was like she'd been a tuning fork for the soundtrack of a horror movie.

Speaking of which, where was that motorcycle? Even with a good muffler, she would have heard the Harley. Maybe Daniel Joseph had had second thoughts about the job.

Or maybe, as a drifter, he had just drifted away, "not here for long" being a mere forty-eight hours on the job as opposed to a season or two.

Reaching behind her, she cranked the window open, the chirping of the spring birds getting louder, the cool rush tickling her nose.

"Are we here in body, not soul today?" Candy demanded as she came back with two mugs. "All those invitations set you back? You look like crap."

"Why thank you," Lydia said as she took what was given to her.

"It wasn't a compliment."

"I was talking about the coffee." Lydia drank in a gulp, and her eyes watered as her tongue and the roof of her mouth got burned. "You want to sit down for a sec?"

"If you fire me, you're going to have to vacuum this place by yourself."

"I'm not firing you."

"Shoot, I could have taken an unemployment vacation." Candy parked it and pulled her forest-themed sweater into place. "Maybe gotten that face-lift I've always wanted. So what's up, fearless leader."

As the joking title sunk in, Lydia thought about the way she'd rushed into the woods the morning before, determined to kick the shit out of someone who could very well have shot her in the head for all she knew.

Nothing had been inside the line of trees, though.

And there had been no evidence of someone having stood there and taken her picture—no disturbance in the pine needles, no sound of anybody retreating on foot or in a car, bike, or ATV. Had they just disappeared?

When she'd walked back to her house, her whole body had been shaking. Fearless leader? Not even close.

"What made you ditch the pink hair?" she murmured. Because she really didn't want to open any cans of worms. Not until she dead-bottomed the mug.

And all she had were worm cans.

Candy shrugged. "The pink was stupid. It's just that simple. Now give me details on your Saturday and Sunday. I can tell you didn't go to the hairdresser's. You look like you've been pulled through a rose bush backwards."

"You know, you do not have a way with words, Candy."

"Really? You could have fooled me. So . . . ?"

"No."

"No. What?"

"I did not see Daniel Joseph. He was out of town, and I told you on Friday, I'm not dating anyone from work. I'm not dating anybody."

Ever, she added to herself.

"Well, that's a damn shame." Candy adjusted her hoop earring. "I'd give it a whirl if I weren't a hundred and twenty-six years old. So what do you really want to talk to me about?"

Lydia sipped from her mug again, but was more careful with the hot stuff. "I, ah, I want to know if Peter's received anything here that seemed . . . odd."

"What, like, takeout all the way from Plattsburgh?" As Lydia shot a level stare across the desk, Candy rolled her eyes. "FYI, you have to actually *be* in a place to get any kind of delivery. Unless it's me and UPS. I swear, if that driver ever shows his face here, I'm going to—"

"Anything, Candy. A package, an envelope. Something addressed to him that you opened and it turned out to be personal?"

"Not that I'm aware of." Candy glanced over her shoulder like she was checking to make sure they were alone. Then she sat forward and did the unthinkable. She lowered her voice to a whisper. "What have you found out in here?"

"Not a damn thing." Lydia shook her head. "He's either up to no good, but a total mastermind . . . or he's just lost interest in this job and doesn't care what happens."

"Somehow, I'm guessing it's the latter. No offense, but I've never thought Petey-boy was the brightest brake light in the parking garage." Candy got to her feet. "And speaking of jobs, C.P. Phalen's assistant wants to know if you're in the office today."

Lydia sat up straight. "The new board chair?"

"That's the one."

"What does he want with me? Are you sure he's not looking for Peter?"

"Oh, no. It's you. Your name was the one the woman asked about."

Lydia frowned. "Why didn't you tell me this immediately?"

"I figured you'd need the coffee in your bloodstream first. And anyway, there's no hurry. The great and glorious C.P. Phalen won't be here for . . ." The woman checked her watch. "Another forty-five minutes or so."

"*What?*"

"Hey, at least you're not in running tights today."

"That was only once last week," Lydia muttered with distraction. "Well, fine, a couple times this month."

"With your legs, you can get away with it. And good thing I brought some donuts in with me—"

"Maybe they're firing Peter."

"They'll have to find him first."

"My wolf is still alive," Lydia blurted. "Did I tell you that? He made it through the weekend."

"I'm glad." There was a pause. "You know, I'm not much for giving advice. But rich people don't like when the rest of us try to trim their feathers. You need to be careful. They're used to getting what they want and stopping what they don't like."

"C.P. Phalen is on the damn board. He should be on our side."

"He's not the rich people I'm talking about. Those hotel people are bastards."

"Have you heard anything in town about them harassing folks? Like people showing up in places they shouldn't?"

"Not that I know of." Candy went to the door. "Thanks for doing those invitations."

Before the woman left, Lydia said, "If they fire me, you'll make sure Rick takes care of my wolf?"

Candy glanced back. "That's his job, honey. And he might be a nerd, but he's a good man. Actually, you should go out with him."

"Weren't you trying to set me up with Daniel Joseph?"

"Any available man."

"I'm not looking for a port in a storm, Candy. Isn't that the saying? Any available port in the—"

The low growl of a powerful engine percolated through the partially opened window.

"Speak of a port," Candy said with a grin. "Or is he the storm?"

"This isn't a romance novel, you know."

"More's the pity. And I'll let you know when good ol' C.P. gets here. For all the money those board members give, they sure never darken our doors."

"I've only heard their voices over speakerphone."

"Why are the board meetings always closed door and off-site?"

"I don't know. Only Peter's ever met any of them in person."

"Well, I thought they were just something he made up to give himself more power and authority around this joint. Because, you know, this is such a big, important organization. And yes, I'll vacuum out there before the big man comes."

Candy walked off. Returned. "Did I come across as bitter as I sounded?"

Lydia gave the woman a *meh*. "On the bright side, at least you've let all that out before our board chair gets here."

"I like your perspective. I'll send Daniel down to you, so you can park your boat in his slip—or no, wait, it should be the other way around. Unless you're kinky." Candy rubbed one of her penciled-in eyebrows. "I'm really over the line today, aren't I. I normalize my hair and all the anti-establishment is coming out my mouth. Not much of an improvement."

"Maybe meet in the middle and streak in the pink. That way you only curse on your off hours?"

"Yeah, but what if I only curse during work?"

"This conversation is above my pay grade."

"As long as you keep ripping up your checks, technically everything is." Candy leaned on the jamb and did a *tsk-tsk*. "I emptied your trash and found the pieces."

"They were still in the envelope."

"Ah, so I was right. FYI, don't confess before you know how much the other party knows—oh, hello, Daniel. She's right in here, and I'll leave you two to your docks and ropes. Inside joke, too hard to explain. She has a ten o'clock coming, by the way. Toodles."

As Candy took off, Lydia put her head in her hands. "Hi," she said without looking up.

"Hey." There was a pause. "So it looks like you got an office upgrade."

"It's not permanent. I'm just here for the computer—"

"Are you okay?"

I think I might be getting fired, she answered to herself.

"Of course," she said. "How was your weekend?"

"Uneventful. And by that, I mean my motorcycle is still running. You?"

"Nothing special." Assuming she was living a true-crime documentary. "I thought you and I could get the map of the preserve out and I could show you where the bridges are that need to be fixed. We can do that before my meeting?"

Because if she was going to get canned, she could at least make sure the hikers were safe.

Some of the hikers, that was.

◆ ◆ ◆

Daniel stepped into the office and frowned at the woman behind the desk. As her proper name drifted through his consciousness, he tried to keep her as just "woman." It didn't work. Then again, it hadn't worked over the weekend, either.

For so many reasons.

"Lydia, are you okay?" he asked again.

"Absolutely." She gave him a passing smile and picked up something off the corner of the desk. "So here's the map."

As she flattened the folds, he watched her hair fall forward. She hadn't pulled it back this morning and he liked the way the dull overhead light somehow brought out its various colors.

"So there's the main trail that goes around the bowl, as we call it." Her finger traced a brown line marked with intermittent yellow stars in an arc around the lake. "Although there are smaller trails spidering all over our western face, we really have to keep after this main one—particularly where it's intersected by the two rivers that flow down from the summit, as well as the big branching stream that splits off here." She tapped the map in various places. "The three bridges are marked as you can see and they all need some shoring up. We've got loose boards, and some rot on the handrails. I also want you to assess the structural integrity of the supports? When it comes to repairing them, I know there's some lumber in the shed—and if you could use what we have first, that would be great, even if it doesn't look perfect. We're kind of into pinching pennies around here—"

"You look like hell. You didn't sleep last night, did you."

Lydia glanced up sharply. "I . . . ah, of course I did. Like a baby."

"So what'd the other guy look like?"

She shook her head as if he were speaking in a foreign language. "I'm sorry, what?"

"In that bar fight you won. That has to be the explanation for those dark circles."

She laughed in a short burst that didn't fool him. "Oh, my opponent faced complete ruination. Busted nose. Lost a tooth or two. They had to stitch him up."

"Good, I like a woman who can fight with her hands." As Lydia's eyes flared, he tacked on, "It means they take care of themselves. Drifter, remember? Less to protect, less complications I have."

"Now there's an online profile full of character recommendation." She smiled a little more honestly. "Can we get back to the bridges?"

"Sure. You were telling me about how you want to use what we have first?"

"Yup, that'd be great if you can." She pushed her hair out of her face. "And then there are other places that need to be addressed. Some of the inclines have steps that need to be cleared and their rope tethers will have to be tested. But the bridges are the first thing."

"When does the traffic on the trails start building?"

"Soon. The spring rains will keep some of them away, and then we have black fly season."

"That's a thing?"

"They're the size of donkeys around here. They've been known to carry small children off the mountain."

"Really. And I thought that was just an Internet hoax."

"Oh, my God." She put her hand over her heart. "I think you made a funny."

"Did I?" He smiled slowly. "You know, I was giving it a shot."

"You're coming along. By the end of your time here, your middle name will be Henny Youngman."

"Who's that?"

"The master of the one-liner. Look him up." She got serious. "Do you have Mace?"

"What for?"

Her look was all about the well-duh. "There are wild animals out there."

"No matter what the front page of the newspaper says, you don't need to worry about me. I promise."

For no good reason, he found he couldn't look away from her eyes. Maybe it was the way she was staring up at him, so worried. So concerned about his welfare.

Daniel was not used to that. And he didn't want to be.

She smiled again. "Because your fists are registered as lethal weapons or something?"

"Let's just say I can handle myself."

"All right, tough guy. But be careful, okay? And you have a phone. You can always call me?"

She was so earnest, as if she would ride out on a warrior horse and save him, even though he was nothing to her. Even though she didn't know just how well he could take care of any threat made against him. Even though . . . he could see himself being the one to save her.

"You like rescuing things, don't you?" he murmured.

After a moment, she slowly shook her head. "No, I don't. It's . . . horrible. It can break your heart into a thousand pieces, and the only guarantee you have is that you will always be failing because you can't rescue everything."

"Why do that to yourself, then," he said remotely.

"You make it sound like I have a choice." She took a deep breath. "So yes, I can understand the appeal of being a lone wolf like you."

"Funny choice of words."

"Is it?" Then she shook her head. "It's my choice of language, what can I see. I mean, say."

"The woman who studies the wolves."

"That's me. And speaking of work—remember how the ATV's been leaking fuel?" She leaned to the side and picked up her purse. "Here, you can use my car to get the lumber and tools out to where you need them. It's nothing fancy, but it's got four-wheel drive so it can handle the trail—and no, you can't use your bike even to go look. Let's not disturb the wildlife more than we have to. And that little key on my ring opens the Master Locks on the gates."

As she tossed him her bundle of lock-ups and turn-ons, he caught them in one hand. "Do you want me to try to fix the four-wheeler first? Maybe it's a loose line connection. Duct tape is a powerful force in this world, I promise you that."

"Sure. But keep my keys for the gates or if it looks like a long job—"

Outside in the reception area, someone came in through the front door, and Lydia looked past him.

Perfume? he thought as he glanced over his shoulder, too.

Off in the distance, Candy said a few soft words, and then a creaking came down the hallway.

When the older receptionist, who didn't have pink hair anymore, came into view, her face showed no expression. At all. "C.P. Phalen is here to see you."

As Candy stepped back and walked away, her eyes dropped to the carpet and stayed there—as a six-foot-tall woman with a sculpted cap of white hair and a sleek black suit stepped into the doorway.

"Ms. Susi," she said in a smooth, even tone. "I'd like to have a word with you. Alone."

Daniel looked at Lydia. "I'll go get to work on the trails. And I'll bring this map back when I'm done."

He wasn't surprised when Lydia just nodded and murmured a thank-you to him. Passing the white-haired woman, he looked her right in the eye as a test.

She ignored him.

Which was good. That was what he wanted.

Out by the waiting area, the receptionist was back at her desk, and on the phone.

"—certainly did *not* deliver it. No, I was on with you people yesterday getting the ring-a-round. You're going to put me on with a supervisor or I'm getting in my car and driving to—where are your headquarters?"

As Daniel folded up the map and put it in his back pocket, he found himself hoping, for the sake of whoever the manager was, that there were a lot of miles—or maybe an ocean—between that woman and whatever building she was looking for.

"No, the package has not, and did not, come," she snapped, "and as I told you, the signature image you sent me was illegible. Everyone here would sign their name properly so I don't know where you took it or who you thought—"

Daniel went out the front entrance and looked to the left. Over in the parking area, a black Audi A8L looked like a hi-tech defense missile next to some horse and buggies.

He didn't go check out the ATV. That could wait.

Lydia's hatchback was unlocked, and he had to put

the driver's seat way back to fit in behind the wheel. Cranking the key, the Matchbox engine flared to ane-mic life, and as he backed out, he glanced over his shoulder to make sure he didn't hit the building.

He didn't need the map. He knew the mountain by heart.

Proceeding to the main trailhead, he pulled into the parking area and went to the gate, unlocking it with Lydia's little key. Easing her car through, he re-locked everything and then went forward at just a couple of miles an hour over idle. The going was bumpy, the roots of the trees clawing out of the ground, the trail extending to what felt like oblivion given his snail's pace—

The scraping noise was so loud he pumped the brakes.

When he tried to ease forward again, the resistance of something critical to functioning staying caught on an immovable object made him growl.

Killing the engine, he got out, fired up his penlight, and laid flat on his back on the packed, damp dirt. Squeezing himself under the car, he assessed the—

Nope, not a root. A rock. That had been hidden under some pine needles.

It was the kind of thing that if he hadn't been thinking about Lydia, he would have seen a mile away and steered around. As it was, there was such a fucking metaphor going on that he refused to ac-knowledge any part of—

Daniel stopped the beam as it passed by a nook in the suspension.

"Or is it a cranny," he muttered to himself. "And what the fuck is that."

The black box was about the size of a pack of cigarettes. Nothing beeping or blinking on it. Magnetic anchor.

Clearly not a bomb 'cuz he'd have been blown sky high. Or Lydia would have.

Nope, it was a tracker.

Someone was keeping tabs on her.

THIRTEEN

BEFORE LYDIA HAD the opportunity to invite
C.P. Phalen into Peter Wynne's office, the tall
woman took the initiative, stepping forward and shutting the door. The implied authority was somehow
not a surprise: It was clear she was used to taking control and being in charge, and for a split second, Lydia
considered offering the woman Peter's chair. His desk.
Her own house.

Oh, wait, that was a rental.

"I'm going to sit here, Lydia, if you don't mind."

The woman was wearing a black double-breasted
jacket, pencil-leg slacks, and high heels—looking like
someone who was walking on Fifth Avenue in Manhattan and heading for a designer's runway. As opposed to grabbing a chair on the far side of a tinky
desk and firing somebody who no doubt made less
than her butler.

Lydia cleared her throat. "So this is a surprise, Ms.
Phalen."

In so many ways. Although why should it matter

that the assumed "he" had turned out to be a very definite "she?"

"Is it really?" The smile was cool—and condescending because of what the woman was wearing, and the way she crossed her legs at the knee. "You didn't expect that a high-level employee of this non-profit going to the media with accusations against a national hotel chain wouldn't be cause for a visit from me?"

Lydia glanced down at her own hands. She linked them. Unlinked them. "I don't regret what I did."

"I think that's clear given what you told that TV station. But you've created a problem for me."

"If you're chair of the board"—Lydia pegged the woman with a hard eye—"then you should want to protect the animals on our preserve, especially the ones in the name of the very organization you're heading."

"Are you always this blunt?"

"If the subject really matters to me, yes." Lydia got to her feet. "And before you fire me, I want to show you something. Come with me. Please."

C.P. Phalen's expression stayed exactly as it was, nothing shifting or showing on all that Tilda Swinton. And her body didn't move, either. Lydia had the feeling it was because the woman was not used to being surprised—or commanded around—and an inferior had just done both to her. But Lydia wasn't apologizing for any of that crap, either.

Just as the tension was becoming unbearable, at least for her, Ms. Phalen got to her feet. Her stilettoes, rather.

Damn, she was so tall. Well over six feet.

"Lead on. But don't waste my time."

Lydia nodded. "I won't."

Taking the woman down to the steel door of the clinical area, Lydia pushed the way open. Rick was on a stool at the counter, working on a disassembled tracker—and when he looked up, he did a double take.

"This is our board chair, C.P. Phalen. Ms. Phalen, this is Rick Marsh, our vet. I'm sure you've heard his name before."

"Of course I have." The statuesque woman walked forward and extended her ring-less, watch-less, bracelet-less arm to him. "Mr. Marsh, it's good to finally meet you in person. You do fantastic work here."

Rick shook what was offered to him, but still appeared to be confused.

Welcome to the club, Lydia thought.

"Ma'am," he said.

"Please, call me C.P." The woman glanced around at the medical equipment and the supplies in the tiled area, her thick, silver hair shining under the bright ceiling lights. "It's hard to believe I haven't visited here in person yet."

Is it really, Lydia thought, suddenly sick of everything about the Project: The board that didn't allow staff to attend their meetings, Peter flaking off all the time, the lack of resources, that fucking hotel chain.

"You should come more often." Rick's smile was tight, but then he tended to be reserved with people he didn't know. "And I'm glad you're here now."

"How's he doing?" Lydia asked him.

"Hanging in."

"We're going to see him now."

Without giving Rick a chance to answer, she pushed through the closed door to the exam room— and momentarily forgot everything but the wolf. He was still sedated, lying on his side with a mask around his muzzle, and she glanced to the monitors. She didn't know much, but she could see he had a regular heartbeat and fairly decent blood pressure.

"You want to know why I'm rude and pushy?" she said roughly. "Why I called the media? *This* is why. Corrington Hotels did this to him, and he isn't the only one. I've tried to get local law enforcement to take it seriously, I've tried to talk to our so-called executive director about it, I've tried to scour the preserve myself, looking for those poisoned traps—"

As her voice cracked, she kicked her own ass and pulled it back together. "And still this happened. I was the one who found him, and if I'd been any later, he would have died. Hell, he still might die. So if you want to get on me? Fine. But no, I don't have any regrets and I will do anything I can to stop this senseless killing of wildlife."

The sound of those high heels coming across the tile was quiet, and as the woman stopped in front of the cage, she lowered her head. Then closed her eyes.

Something about the unexpected reverence gave Lydia the space to become emotional, a wave of heat hitting her face and bringing tears to her eyes. But again, she refused to let herself lose it. Action was required, and if the board thought they were going to silence her by giving her a pink slip? They were all wrong—

"I didn't come to fire you," came the soft voice.

Lydia frowned and turned to the woman. "You didn't?"

C.P. Phalen shook her head, but didn't look over. She stayed focused on the wolf.

And then abruptly a pair of very hard gray eyes locked on Lydia.

"I want to know what you do," the woman said in a grim tone. "Everything."

◆ ◆ ◆

A little after eleven-thirty, Daniel returned to the WSP's main building in Lydia's car. As he pulled into the parking area, the Audi was gone, and when he got out and stretched his stiff back, some instinct made him walk around to the porch that overlooked the view. Sure enough, Lydia was at the railing once again, staring across the lake to the scar in the opposite mountain.

As he coughed to get her attention, she startled,

putting her hand to her throat. "Oh, hi. Jeez, you never make a sound."

"Habit, I guess."

"You mean you like to sneak up on people?"

"No." He went over to stand next to her, but fuck the view. He only wanted to look at the woman who was haunting him like a ghost for no good goddamned reason. "It's just handy to not draw attention to yourself sometimes."

"Sounds sneaky."

"You want me to take up the ukulele, maybe? The trombone?"

Her eyes, those lovely whiskey-colored eyes, wrinkled at the corners as she smiled. "You would do that?"

"Sure, I'd suck at either one, but I'm game."

"Just to keep this job," she said.

"Yeah, paychecks are nice, you know? And on that note, I didn't wreck your car."

"I didn't think you would." She looked back out at the trees, her profile tense, her hair now pulled back in a rubber band like its strands had been annoying her. "So how are the bridges?"

I like it down here better, he thought.

"I was only able to check out two of them," he said, "and they're not great. But at least I know how to fix them so you can get one more season out of 'em without a big spend. I am going to get the ATV working, however, so I can haul the lumber out. It's too much for your hatchback."

"Do we have enough wood in the shed?"

"We'll see."

As he went silent, he waited for her to say something. But she just refocused on the view, a study in someone with too much on their mind.

"Okay, out with it," he demanded. "Were you fired?"

Lydia's eyes returned to his. "What makes you ask that?"

"Come on, a woman like that strides in like she owns the place, driving a car that's worth more than this facility? She's either a headhunter trying to raid someone or a higher-up dropping the hammer."

"Well, she didn't fire me." Lydia shrugged. "And she's not as bad as I thought she was."

"You want to tell me what's going on?" When she went back to the view again, he said, "You can be honest with me."

There was a long period of silence. After which he was compelled to say, "You know what's great about drifters?"

Lydia murmured, "You never have to worry about being a hoarder?"

"Well, that's true. But we also know how to handle ourselves—and others. So how can I help you?"

"I thought you didn't get involved in business that wasn't your own," she said.

"I'm an employee here. You're an employee. This is my business."

She turned around and stared at the sliding door

that led back into the building. On the far side of the glass, the receptionist was talking on the phone. Hanging up. Taking notes on a pad. Getting into her email and composing something.

"I have to mail a bunch of invitations," Lydia said absently. "Like five hundred. Can you help me take them to the post office?"

"Yeah. Sure."

"Let's go," she said remotely. "Do you have my keys still?"

He took the ring out of his pocket and dangled them. "Right here."

Lydia seemed to set her shoulders. "Great. You can drive."

FOURTEEN

S O HAVE YOU found a place to crash?"

As Lydia tossed the question out, she was shooting for casual in everything she did, everything she said: Even though her body was trembling, she clicked her seatbelt and arranged herself in her hatchback's passenger seat in what she hoped seemed like a laid-back sprawl. And though her voice was threatening to break octave and pull a tension-filled soprano, she tethered it to normal range. No pressure of speech was allowed, either, so she slowed her words, evened her tone.

It was like taking a belt sander to her affect.

Meanwhile, on the driver's side, Daniel Joseph was overflowing everything, and the heft of him was comforting.

"Nah, I don't have a place yet." He backed out and turned them around. "But something'll turn up. It always does."

She looked over with a frown. "So you're staying at the Pine Lodge until you—"

"I'm not sure where I'm going to be. That place is expensive, although running water is nice."

"Tonight you'll stay there, though."

"Yeah. Sure."

Up at the county road, he hit the blinker to go left. "No," she said. "Let's go the other way."

"But the post office is by the bank, right?"

"If you could head in the other direction, that would be great. I just need to go check on something first."

"Okay. Whatever you say."

They waited for a pickup truck to pass by, and then he hit the gas, Lydia's beater letting out a wheeze as it was called on to get over the hump of asphalt with so much more load than it usually carried.

On the proper road, coasting along at forty-five, he glanced over. "So are we going to your house? It's not far from here."

"How do you know where I live?" she said.

Not that it was a state secret. Lots of people knew where she lived.

Unfortunately.

"I ate at the diner, remember?" Daniel rolled his eyes. "That night you almost had chicken pot pie with me. After you left, I got your life story. Where you live, that you've been single since you moved here two years ago, that you're very serious and haven't left for a vacation or even a weekend away. Well, there were two trips to Plattsburgh for that root canal, though. Oh, and you're very serious. Did I say that already?"

She propped her elbow on the window and rubbed an aching head. "Bessie told you all that?"

"Well, to be fair, I got most of it from the supermarket side when I bought a Coke and a bag of Doritos to snack on after you interviewed me. I was waiting to get a copy of your dental records with my receipt, but I think her Xerox was broken."

"How did I come up?" Lydia groaned. "Wait, let me guess. I'm the only single woman in forty miles of mountain terrain and you're not wearing a wedding ring."

"Pretty much. It all started when she wanted to know why I was in town and I told her."

"Susan is such a talker." Lydia glanced over. "And I guess I have no secrets from you now, huh."

Daniel lowered his lids. "I wouldn't say that."

As Lydia's breath caught, images of naked skin and horizontal bodies and fur rugs in front of fireplaces turned everything into a modern-day *Bridgerton*. Not at all helpful, but something to put on pause and save for later.

When he refocused on the road, she did the same and touched her lips. They were tingling as if he'd kissed her.

"Sorry," he said.

"For?"

"What's going through my head right now. You don't want me to go into it, but I'm thinking you know what it is."

Refocusing out the side window, Lydia murmured, "Candy thinks I should go out with you."

"I knew she was a woman of rare intelligence. Unless of course, she came at it like you have no other options. I would still take advantage of that logic, I'd just not admire her as much."

Lydia had to laugh. But it didn't last. "You're right, by the way. I did almost get fired today."

He frowned. "So you're suspended or something?"

"No."

"What was that woman here for, then? And by the way, I'm not sure she should be anywhere near anything dog-like."

"Why's that?"

"She's Cruella de Vil." As Lydia laughed in a burst, he actually smiled. "Come on, you know she has a coat made of something god-awful in her closet."

"Can I just point out that I think you have comedy-dysmorphia."

"What can I say . . ." His hooded eyes met her own. "You inspire me."

As Lydia's face flushed, she pulled the seatbelt free of her chest and sat up in the seat. "Okay, the turn's coming—here, right here."

He jerked the wheel and hit the brakes, shooting them onto a paved driveway that was shaded by an allée of maple trees. Or would have been shaded if everything still wasn't bare. As things were, there was a sinister cast to the skeletal trees, the barren lawn, the dead leaves that whispered across the lane.

"Where are we going?" Daniel said as the car drifted forward at an idle.

"I need to . . ." See what the hell Peter Wynne was doing. "Look, I want to know if my executive director is home."

"He's the one I was supposed to be interviewed by, right? So how long's he been missing?"

"Let's just see if he's here." She glanced over. "And I guess I should have told you."

"What, that we were going to ride up on a murder scene? Yeah, that might be a disclosure worth making in the future. You know, something to keep in mind."

"It's not a murder scene," she murmured as she sat forward and put her hands on the dash.

He gave the car some gas. "You sure about that?"

No. "Yes, of course. People don't get murdered in Walters."

"Tell that to the hiker who's all over the newspaper."

"That was *not* a murder."

"Assault with a dangerous wolf, then."

"That's not funny."

"Then why are you smiling."

She rubbed her mouth back into a straight line. "Why are we arguing about this?"

As the paired-up maples passed by, they were like deciduous sentries guarding a driveway that seemed rarely used, and she braced herself for . . . well, she didn't know what. But her sixth sense was ringing a bell's choir worth of alarm, and her skin was prickling with anxiety.

And she was really glad Daniel was with her.

Around a final turn, Peter Wynne's converted barn came into view. The two-story structure had bright red planks and brilliant white trim, the whole thing looking like it had been taken out of a cardboard box, fresh from the toy store, and set on what should have been an Astroturf lawn with plastic models of horses, dogs, and feral mouse-chasers. That brand-new Mercedes SUV that Lydia hadn't recognized was parked off to the side, and assuming it was a new acquisition of Peter's, the shiny status symbol seemed just his style—although on his paycheck, she wondered how he could afford it considering all the renovations he'd been doing to the property.

Maybe he had family money. Which would explain all those Brooks Brothers blazers and wool slacks.

"Nice place," Daniel said as they pulled around the circle in front and he put the car in park. "Belongs in a magazine."

"I just want to see . . ." She opened her door and got out. "Whether he's home."

Daniel cut the engine and got out as well. "That car didn't drive here itself. Unless your boy's got visitors."

"He is definitely not mine," she muttered.

As she went up to the varnished oak door, she glanced back. Daniel was surveying the acreage, his body relaxed, his hands in his pockets, his expression alert, but disinterested. And that was when she noticed the downed tree limbs. The leaves crowded around the bases of the overgrown bushes under the windows. The fact that there were three newspapers in their plastic bags sticking out of the mailbox's slot.

Turning back to the door, she lifted the brass knocker and let the heavy weight fall once. Twice. A third time.

Inside, she could hear the sound reverberating.

"No answer?" Daniel said as he came up behind her.

She shook her head. "But that car . . ."

"Let's walk around back."

Before she could answer, he was off, heading over to the SUV and glancing into the front seat. Then he continued on to check out the facade of the detached garage.

Lydia had a thought that they were trespassing. That they should call the sheriff, if she really believed something was wrong. But she wanted answers more than she was worried about the law, and besides, she didn't trust the law.

Going down the barn's short side, she came to the rear and wasn't surprised at the build-out. A porch had been added, and it extended the full length of the structure—and vertically, there was a new second-story expanse overlooking the view of the rolling lawn and far-off line of trees.

"Business in the front, party in the back," Daniel

remarked as he went over to a door marked with wind chimes.

"Those chimes should be moving." She joined him under the overhang. "I can feel the wind."

"Bad angle for the breeze, then." He curled up a fist and bang-bang-bang'd on the jamb. "Hello?"

His voice was deep and loud, the kind of thing that would get the attention of anybody inside. And maybe a couple of people across the valley.

As he did another round of fisti-knocks, Lydia went to the first of the windows. Cupping her hands, she leaned into the glass. The sitting area was arranged around a flat-screen TV that had been left on, the white slipcovered furniture balanced by red rugs and black-and-white photographs of nature scenes on wood-paneled walls. It was like a stage set for a hometown Christmas love story.

Except it was a mess. Newspapers were everywhere. There were half-filled mugs littering the coffee table, and plates with crumbs on the floor, and even a bowl with something congealing in it on the arm of the sofa.

"Jesus," she said. "Peter's ordinarily a neat freak."

"I'm going in."

"Wait, what?" She lunged and grabbed Daniel's sleeve. "We can't."

"Why not? We're knocking on the man's door with his car parked right out there." Daniel nodded around the corner. "And it's why we came. Isn't it."

"Maybe we should just call the sheriff."

"Okay, so get your phone out."

Lydia hesitated. Looked down the lineup of long windows.

"This is why you asked me to come," Daniel murmured. "You want to break in and I'm the kind of guy who doesn't hesitate with locks. Even when they aren't my own."

She lifted her chin. "I asked you because of the invitations. They weigh a lot."

"Then why aren't we at the post office." He tilted toward her. "And you don't trust the law enforcement around here, do you."

"I don't trust anyone."

He nodded. "I knew you were smart. And either you call the sheriff now, or I'm taking care of the breaking part of our entering."

"That's trespassing."

"No. Really? Draw me a diagram." He stepped back. "You decide on the count of three or I make the choice for us."

"The doors are locked—"

"One."

"Seriously, Peter could be in there—"

"Then why hasn't he answered. Two."

"And he's the type that will call the sheriff—"

"Or you can. Three."

When she just stared at him . . . and then gave him

a nod, he took off his jacket. Wrapped up his fist with the sleeve.

"Wait, what are you—"

With one decisive punch, he broke the lower right pane in the door's window, the glass square popping free of its puttied confines, the crash on the other side loud as a curse in church as it shattered on the varnished pine floor.

Reaching in, Daniel did something to some kind of dead bolt or knob, and then he opened things up.

As he held the door wide, he said in a calm voice, "Do you want to go in first or shall I."

Lydia blinked. And then rubbed her eyes.

You know, just on the outside chance this was a really weird dream and there was a possibility she would wake up.

When she dropped her hands to find that, yup, he'd actually opened Peter Wynne's door, she tried to imagine calling Eastwind and his buddies in those state police outfits. Once they walked into the house? She was never going to get any answers.

Hell, once the law stepped onto the property, they were going to make her leave—after they asked her a whole bunch of questions she didn't want to answer.

"Ladies first," she said gruffly.

◆　◆　◆

Daniel was surprised that Lydia took the lead. He'd expected her to let him be the tip of the proverbial spear. But there were benefits to her going ahead.

He was able to take his gun out and keep it by his thigh without explaining anything to her—

"Oh, *God* . . ." She recoiled and put her elbow up to her face, vampire style. "That *smell*."

The stench hit him next and even he reared back. "Yeah, we got us some old sweaty trash right there."

"Why is it so hot in here?" She waved a hand in front of herself. "It's like eighty degrees."

"Fire's been left on."

"Peter?" she called out. "Hello?"

The whole first floor was open, the kitchen over to the left, the seating area that had been frat-boy'd with all the dirty dishes and trash to the right. As Lydia wandered across to the gas-fed stone hearth, he checked out the sink, which was full of more plates and mugs. On the brand-new Viking stove, there was a pot on a burner with something vaguely meat-ish in it—at least he was thinking it was beef. The shit was so desecrated and left-for-dead that he wasn't sure exactly what kind of protein it had been.

"Long time, no clean," he muttered.

All of the countertops were smudged with grease and grime . . . broken eggshells were scattered right on the trash bin lid . . . and something spotted the floor by the bottom of the refrigerator.

"What happened to him?" Lydia said as she picked a flapped-out magazine off the floor, put it to rights, and placed it on a side table.

Glancing around at what else he could see of the house's interior, it was clear that not only had everything been renovated, it had all been professionally decorated, too, the red and white color scheme carried into the dining room and the family room out front. The vibe was fake rustic, the honey-colored pine floors glowing with fresh varnish, the exposed beams and pine wall paneling gleaming, the smell of new carpets and still-curing-paint a pleasant undertone to the rank nasty of the garbage.

Someone had written an awful lot of checks to get this homey look.

And they'd done it recently.

"Something was burned in here," Lydia said from the hearth.

Daniel tucked his gun and went over to her. As he passed by the sofas, he noted that they were almost entirely deconstructed, not just throw pillows cast around and out of place, but the cushions themselves.

The place was a stage set gone amok.

Lydia knelt down, opened the fireplace's glass doors, and started pulling little fragments of charred white paper out of the blue and yellow flames.

With a burst forward, he snagged her wrist. "You want to get burned?"

"We need to know what it is—"

"Let it go." He rubbed her fingers. "Whatever it was, it's gone."

Lydia cursed. Then tilted her head. "What is that?"

"It's just the corners of paper—"

"No, that sound."

As she stood up and looked toward the front of the barn, he tried to listen harder. "I don't hear anything."

"Dripping." She started out for the dining room. "Something is dripping."

Daniel didn't hear it until they turned the corner. And then it was obvious. *Drip . . . drip . . . drip . . .*

Together, they went past a long, cottage-rough table with white upholstered chairs and a white runner, and a white, knobby rug under the setup.

"Guess they don't like red wine around here," he muttered. "On the bright side, if anybody was murdered over the entree, you'd know it."

"Unless they were strangled."

"Good point."

Out by the front door, Lydia stopped short and stared up the wooden staircase. "It's a river . . ."

Sure enough, water was on the descent from the landing above in a lazy flow that had pooled at the base of the staircase and then disappeared into the nearest floor vent on a drool.

"We need to go up there," Lydia said.

The fucker is dead, Daniel thought. So no, ladies were not going first this time.

Charging ahead, he hit the stairs and took things two at a time, his boots splashing through the flow, disturbing the current. At the top, the second floor was all open space, but there was a sliding pine door that was shut tight straight ahead. From beneath it, seeping through the gap at the floorboards, water was pumping out.

Daniel glanced to the right. A walk-in closet with glass doors showed off all kinds of compartments with neat-as-a-pin clothes hanging on matching hangers. And across the loft, the king-sized bed was flush against the opposite wall—but the white duvet and sheets were stained. Not with blood, though. They just looked grungy, all wrinkled and washed-last-month.

No reason to get his gun out.

"I got a bad feeling about this," Lydia whispered by his side.

So did he, not that he was going to say that.

Pulling his sleeve down over his hand, he pushed the panels aside . . .

"What . . . the *fuck*," Lydia breathed.

FIFTEEN

As Lydia pushed Daniel's heavy shoulder out of the way, she got a better look at everything that made no sense in Peter Wynne's bathroom: The silver faucets of the white tub were running in a torrent while its drain was stopped up, the overflow valve in the fixture no match for the volume pouring free. Likewise, both of the sinks at the white marble counter were cranked on, the basins turned into infinity pools that spilled onto the tiled floor. And the shower was on full force, the rain head in the center of the marble alcove rushing onto a drain blocked with a wad of white towel.

The resulting flood had picked up the white bath mats and floated them forward on a pond that was churning, the soggy squares jamming at the lip of the marble floor at the doorjamb. Meanwhile, on the walls, all the mirrors and the window were streaked with condensation and two framed photographs were dripping at the corners.

This had started out hot, she thought. The dense, humid air was cold now, though. How long had it all been running?

More important, why had someone done this?

Glancing around again, she saw a toothbrush was still set upright in a white holder between the twin sinks, and monogrammed towels were hanging on rods, and the toilet and bidet had their lids down.

Lydia breathed in deep, but she wasn't sure what she expected to smell.

That was a lie.

Blood . . . she was looking for the copper bouquet of blood—but she was not a search and rescue dog. All she got was some vague kind of chlorine tinge from the water having been treated.

"Someone's covered it up," she said grimly.

She didn't feel the need to define "it" out loud. But she knew Peter Wynne was dead, and she had a feeling that he'd been killed in here.

Wheeling away, she stumbled—and saw the glass door to a walk-in closet. The order inside, compared to the chaos elsewhere in the house, was eerie. Like a car radio playing after a crash.

But not everything was tidy in there. As she entered the shallow room, over in the corner on the white carpet, there was a twisted pile of monogrammed PJs, as if the wearer had had night sweats and been disgusted by his lack of sleep. There were also undershirts mixed in that were stained with what looked like food. Boxer shorts. Socks.

She went back out. Daniel was over by the bed, bending down, looking under the mattress without touching anything.

"Do we turn off the water?" she asked as she glanced to the second-floor windows.

The back of the property was on a gentle slope to a man-made pond—or at least she assumed it was man-made given its cement-and-stone shoreline. The trees had been trimmed back, and just into the edge of the forest, she could see the remnants of an old horse pen and shelter.

"Let's check the rest of the house," Daniel said. "But no, we don't touch a damn thing."

They went down the river of stairs together and took a right into a library that yielded nothing in particular. Out the far side, there was a hall that led back to the main area.

"What do we do?" she said as they reemerged into the family room. "I mean, I know we should call the—"

From out of the corner of her eye, the muted TV screen registered. It had been tuned to the Plattsburgh affiliate and a newscaster was looking into the camera—with an image of the WSP's headquarters floating by his head.

"Where's the remote." She looked around. "Where's the—"

Daniel went over to the flat-screen. "I've got it."

He covered his knuckle with his sleeve and upped the volume on the side of the TV itself.

"—reporting on a developing story. A source at the Wolf Study Project has accused the developers of the five-hundred-acre McBridge property on Bread Loaf Mountain of poisoning wildlife. The Corrington Hotel chain, well known for its luxury sites around the world, is building a resort on the land, having received zoning approval just two months ago. Concerns about the neighboring preserve and its population of wolves with regard to the safety of visitors to the spa and retreat have been noted in internal memos obtained by WNDK. Tune in for the full story from the award-winning Live at Five team—"

With a curse, Lydia stared out at the backyard. Then she frowned as she tried to see those structures inside the tree line.

"We need to go back and look there."

"Look where?"

"There," she said, pointing to the forest—

Somewhere in the house, a phone started ringing, the electronic *brrrrrring*'ing echoing around empty rooms, cutting through the dripping coming from the front hall.

"We need to leave," Daniel said.

He was standing over the red couch, his arms crossed on his big chest, his head shaking back and forth as he focused on the television. Then his eyes locked on hers.

"We really have to go now, Lydia. We can talk about next steps in the car, but . . . we've got to get out of here. *Now*."

She wanted to argue—but for no good reason. He was right. Hell, they never should have come in.

"Okay."

They left without another word, filing out of the back door he'd broken in through. After he closed things tight, he took her arm and rushed her to her car—and the way he was looking around made the nape of her neck tingle. Or maybe it was doing that anyway. At the hatchback, she went to the driver's side out of habit, and he didn't seem to care who was behind the wheel. As she fell into her seat with a thump, she was twelve feet from the dashboard, so she reached between her legs, yanked up the bar, and shoved things forward manually.

He handed her the keys. She started the engine.

Her heart was pounding so hard that she could swear he heard it, too, and she found herself compulsively swallowing even though her mouth was dry.

Hitting the gas, the tires skidded on the gravel, and then she was whipping around the circular drive and careening her little POS down the allée of maples. Up at the lip of the county road, she didn't bother putting her blinker on. She just gunned it and shot out into all the absolutely-no-traffic.

"Slow down," he said. "You're going to wreck us."

Lydia let off on the pedal and glanced over to

find him braced against the window and the dash. "Sorry."

"It's okay—"

"Wait, that van coming toward us." She leaned forward. "Is that the news crew?"

Sure enough, over in the opposite lane, a white van with a satellite dish mounted on its roof was going like a bat out of hell. As it passed by, the NBC logo was a splash of color. WNDK.

"They're going to Peter's." She checked the rear view. "I swear they're going to Peter's—"

As the vehicle went around the curve in the road, she pounded the brakes and did a U-ie. Stomping on the gas, the engine whirred under the hood.

"We're not going back there," Daniel said as he braced himself again.

"I have to know if they're going to Peter's."

"Don't be crazy. We just broke into the damn house. You want to explain to them, on camera, how we walked around? And didn't call the police?"

"We have a sheriff in this town," she muttered. "Not police."

Before Daniel could go any further, she yanked the wheel to the right and shot them onto a rough dirt road that was one car wide. Holding on to the steering wheel so her head didn't bang on the roof, she fought against the bumps as Daniel threw out his hands and grabbed on to the door and the console. For the third time.

"Where the—*hell* are we—going?" he gritted as they rattled around.

"This parallels Peter's property," she said over the din. "We'll be able to see—"

"Jesus—Lydia. We're going—to get caught."

"They won't—know we're here."

"If we're close enough—to see them, they're close enough to—see us."

She forced herself to lay off on the speed. Besides, she didn't want to leave parts of her car behind. Like the whole engine or maybe an axle.

"They won't be looking into the woods," she said as things leveled into a boat-like swaying. "They're going to be all about what's happening in that house."

"And when they call the cops to search the property?"

"We'll be gone by then. They'll never know we were anywhere."

"You sure about that?" he muttered. "'Cuz I left my molars behind on this goat path, and dental records are admissible in court."

◆ ◆ ◆

Wild. Goose. Chase.

When Lydia finally stopped the car, Daniel looked past her to where that barn of Wynne's should be— and saw nothing but undergrowth and tree trunks. The property they'd been on wasn't visible at all.

As she got out, he wanted to pull her back into

the car and talk sense into her. They were courting trouble of the badge variety here, and whereas that wasn't going to bother him, she was going to run into problems she couldn't solve for herself. And while it was true that he wasn't interested in taking care of anyone else, sometimes his golden rule got a little tarnish.

Well, not sometimes. Just in the case of Lydia Susi. With her, he found himself sucked in. Kept in. Locked in.

Goddamn it.

Daniel got out, too, and before he could start air-mailing her a second dose of get-real, she pointed into the trees.

"This way," she said as she headed off without him.

The dirt path she set them on was to humans as that bumpy lane was to vehicles, a single-file cramper that challenged the width of his shoulders. Up ahead of him, she ducked and held back the branches that cut across their way, her body lithe and assured, flexible and strong. The air was cool and damp, smelling of the earth and growing things.

And Eau d'Bad Fucking Idea.

Then again, he was the one who had pushed the issue of popping that glass pane. The difference, he argued with himself, was that he wasn't pulling a revisit to the scene of their minor crime.

Minor, that was, compared to whatever had been done to the barn's owner.

That waterfall bathroom was a cover-up to a murder if he'd ever seen one.

"Just a little further," she whispered after they'd gone a good three hundred yards or so.

As she rerouted once again, the craggy bushes thinned out some and she drew him over to a thick oak. At first, he wasn't sure what she was doing—but then he saw the two-by-fours hammered into the trunk. The camouflaged deer stand was mounted about twenty feet from the ground, and she started up the ladder like she was a cat, climbing without a pause.

He followed tight behind her.

And tried not to look at what . . . was directly above his head. 'Cuz not only was eyeing her backside indiscreet and arguably a letch-move, it sure as shit was inappropriate considering they were about to spy on people.

Not a time to get the sex on.

Up top, the stand was about ten feet long and five feet wide, with walls that were tall enough to cover even his bulky crouch. And what do you know, the view was perfect, the tops of the pines breaking and providing a clear shot . . . to the back of that renovated barn.

Where there was plenty going on: A man in casual clothes with a video camera up on his shoulder was standing at the back door next to a woman in a polished-looking red skirt and blazer. Both were leaning in to inspect the open doorway.

I closed that, Daniel thought. That door had been closed when he and Lydia had left.

The WNDK folks started talking to each other intensely. Then the woman took out her cell phone.

"They're calling the police," he said.

"Sheriff," Lydia murmured.

"Can we go back to the car now?" When she shook her head, he leaned in closer to her. "We don't want to be up here when the *sheriff* comes."

"This isn't part of Peter's property. This is Bessie Farlan's husband's tract of land. We have every right to be here."

"Do you like living on the edge?"

"No," she said. "I hate it."

Daniel sat back on his ass, and double-checked that what was under him was, in fact, as strong as it seemed to be. Fortunately, everything appeared to be holding. Then again, it had probably been calibrated to hold two beer-gutted shotgun slingers and their twelve packs of high-test Budweiser.

"I really think we've seen enough," he said.

"They've called Eastwind," she muttered as she focused through a break in the boards. "And he's going to do nothing. Goddamn him, I do not understand why he's protecting Corrington."

"Lydia, I know I'm sounding like a broken record here—"

"Fine," she hissed as if to herself. "I'll just do the damn legwork. I'll find the evidence—or whatever the hell it takes. But I'm not going to stand by and let those people—"

"*Lydia.*"

"—ruin this land. I don't care what they do to me or how they try to scare me—"

Daniel frowned as he plugged in to what she was saying. "Wait, what? Have they done something to you?"

As she continued to mutter while staring at the barn, he tapped her on the shoulder. When she finally looked away from the newscaster and cameraman, he took Lydia's hand to make sure she paid attention.

"What did they do to you." He put his palm up as she opened her mouth. "No, you don't fucking lie to me. You brought me into this. You don't get to start editing the story now."

Her eyes went back to the barn, her brows down, her lips in a tight line. As a breeze came up, her ponytail was swept in his direction and he caught a whiff of her shampoo.

"You can trust me," he said softly.

Her laugh was short. "Weren't you the one who just told me not to trust anybody?"

"I wasn't referring to myself."

"Well, I still haven't checked your references." This was spoken absently. Like it was a mental note that had just popped up as a reminder on her proverbial brain screen. "I don't know you."

"You wanted me to come with you for a reason.

That had nothing to do with the gross weight of those invitations."

When she crossed her arms over her chest and didn't respond, he took out his phone. Going into his contacts, he called up a number, hit send, and held the cell out to her.

"Here," he prompted when she just stared at the thing.

"Who did you call?"

"Take it. It's for you."

Her hand was shaking as she reached forward, and he had a thought that he was pushing her too hard. And then he decided no. She could take it. She might be scared, but she wasn't running.

Lydia put the phone up to her ear, her brows drawing together again. "Um . . . hello? Ah, yes." She shot him a glare that was all about the this-is-not-the-time. "I—ah, sorry. Did you have an employee by the name of Daniel Joseph—oh? Oh, good. Well, my name is Lydia Susi and he's applied for a job with the nonprofit I work for. You're listed as a reference for him—oh? Oh. Really?"

As she went back to staring out the gap between the boards, there was a series of pauses. Then some more affirmatory commentary from her.

After which she hung up just as out at the barn, the newscaster put her phone up to her ear.

"What did they say?" Daniel asked.

"They loved you." She glanced at him. "They said

you went above and beyond, even in small things. They said they'd rehire you in a second. Congratulations."

He took the phone from her. As he went into his contacts again, she spoke up. "You already have the job. We don't need to—"

"This is not about the job." He hit send and then pushed the phone back at her. "Go on. Take it—"

"Daniel."

"Or are you going to talk to me about what happened to you. Your choice."

She batted the cell away. "We're up in a tree—"

"I know where we are. Talk to them or talk to me."

"Are you always this pushy?"

"Are you always this hard-headed?"

As they glared at each other, Lydia took the phone, ended the call, and put the cell in her own pocket. "You get it back when you stop dialing."

Daniel blinked. And then had to laugh softly. "Did you just put me in a time out?"

"Yes, I did. Now be a good boy and give me a little more time up here. Or no dessert."

Lydia returned to the crack in the boards—and he couldn't help it. His eyes traced over her shoulders and down the curve of her spine.

Dessert sounded great, he thought.

And the fact that he wanted her on his double entendre menu was a cliché. Then again, he was pretty sure she could say anything in any situation and he'd be able to find a horizontal inference.

A lick of time. Let's touch base. Play your cards right.

Even single words weren't safe from his dumb handle's bright ideas.

Potato, for example.

Damn, he was a sick fuck.

Focusing on her profile, he felt a twist in his gut that had nothing to do with anything hot and bothered.

"What did they do to you, Lydia," he said grimly.

SIXTEEN

BEFORE LYDIA COULD respond to Daniel's stark demand, she had an eerie sense of warning tickle its way across her nape.

Twisting around, she found a different gap in the boards that let her look out away from the barn. As she tried to identify what had gotten her attention, her heart rate tripled. Just as she was getting frustrated with herself—

A man was coming through the trees, heading right for the deer stand. Dressed in a black, military-style uniform, he had a black ball cap that was pulled down low to hide his face, and all kinds of weapons holstered on his hips and strapped to his back.

"Oh . . . God," she whispered.

Next to her, Daniel had noticed as well and was rolling to the side so he could look out another knothole.

Closer. Closer. So that now, she could hear the soft footfalls on the damp ground. As Lydia's nose started to itch, she rubbed it. Rubbed it again. If she sneezed—

The man was thirty feet away. Twenty. Ten.

And he stopped.

Squeezing her eyes shut, she trembled and clamped a hand on her mouth. Questions like who he was and who he worked for were so much less important than whether or not he was going to take one of those guns he had on and fill the stand full of lead.

Her heart pounded so hard that it was a roar in her ears, and she prayed, *prayed* that—

The footfalls started up again . . . and began to fade.

She couldn't help it. She had to see. Hoping like hell she didn't hit the one loose board on the base or the sides, she turned herself around and watched the man, soldier, whatever, march away from them.

"Stay here," Daniel whispered.

With a quick hand, she fisted his jacket. "Where are you going—"

"He's looking for your car."

Lydia shook her head. "There's no way he knows we're here. This acreage doesn't have cameras—"

"Stay here." He pegged her with hard eyes. "I will come back for you."

"Daniel—"

"Watch the barn. Stay here."

In spite of his size, Daniel made no noise as he stood up and threw a leg over the stand's wall. Instead of going down the ladder, he hung off the side and then dropped down to the ground, staying hidden by the oak's thick trunk. With absolutely no sound at all, he stalked off, falling into the path of the other man.

She lasted . . . maybe a minute and a half.

Yes, Daniel was big and strong. But maybe she could help or . . . she didn't know.

Surveying the forest, she made sure there was no one else coming. Then she extricated herself out of the stand and descended the trunk ladder. As she stepped off onto the pine needles and leaves, she didn't follow the men. She triangulated an approach to where Daniel was going to intersect the soldier, weaving her way through the pines, a light jog taking her forward—

Through the trees, she saw the soldier still striding through the forest.

But his forward progress didn't last long.

The attack was so fast, so overpowering, that she gasped. Daniel Joseph somehow stole up behind the uniformed figure and leaped on the other man's back as if he were spring-loaded. With his body nearly parallel to the ground, his heavy arms shot around and locked into place—then he wrenched his target off the ground, using momentum to his advantage to slam the other man facedown. There wasn't a second of recovery time. Before the other guy could react, Daniel put his knee at the lower back and his forearm on the nape, and the soldier—or whatever the hell he was—became completely incapacitated.

Daniel leaned down and said something in the man's ear—

And then he ripped off the hat, grabbed a fistful of

hair, and yanked the skull up. Wrapping his free arm around the man's neck, he gripped his own wrist— and began to pull back. Pull back hard.

So that the crook of Daniel's elbow locked in like a vise on the soldier's windpipe.

"What are you doing?" Lydia said as she jumped forward.

Running across to him, she didn't care who else heard her. "Stop—*stop!*"

Daniel didn't look over. Didn't appear to have even heard her. He stared straight ahead, the veins popping out in his neck, his forehead, no doubt his whole body. He wasn't even breathing.

Just like his victim.

The soldier underneath him was gaping, his face ruddy as he strained for air, his black-gloved fingers clawing at the iron bar that was crushing his airway.

"Stop it," Lydia hollered. "You're going to kill him!"

She grabbed for Daniel's arm and started yanking. But it was like trying to disengage something that was bolted on. Nothing moved.

Digging her heels in, she leaned back and grunted. "Let him go—"

The clicking noise the other man made was terrible. So was the flapping as he beat with decreasing strength against his killer.

"No, *no!*"

Lydia's feet slipped out from under her and she dropped to her knees, even though it gave her less leverage, especially as she slid on the pine needles. As she strained, tears squeezed out onto her cheeks, and she had a detached thought along the lines of how could this be happening? How had she gone from meeting with C.P. Phalen to fighting against Daniel's superhuman strength as he killed—

All at once it was over, Daniel releasing his hold and slipping his arm free of Lydia's grip at the same time, the dead man going limp and falling face-first into the ground, Lydia flying backward and landing hard on her ass.

"You killed him!" She scrambled forward and shoved at Daniel. "What did you do!"

"Shh—"

As she hit at him, slapping his head and shoulders, he caught her wrists and held her off. "He's alive— Jesus, Lydia, will you relax—"

"He's dead—"

"No, he's *not.*" Daniel pushed her back and rolled the man over. "See for yourself. He's fucking breathing."

Lydia wiped her forearm across her eyes. The man—soldier, whatever—was . . . actually, yes, his chest was going up and down. Slowly, but evenly— and his color was still florid from the struggle.

"You tried to kill him," she moaned.

"No, I wanted to render him unconscious." Daniel pointed off in the direction of where she'd parked the hatchback. "Go back and get in your car. He knows where you are—he's after you."

"What?"

"He's here for you."

Lydia shook her head to clear it. "Wait, how do you know I was being stalked?"

"I don't have time to explain." With a vicious yank, he ripped open the front of the black jacket. "And no, I'm not going to kill anybody—I just want to give you a chance to get away."

With that, he began to pull weapons off the man: Two handguns. A lethal-looking silver-bladed knife. Clips of bullets.

Lydia's eyes bulged. "This is over for me." She patted around her pockets for her cell phone. "I'm calling the sheriff—"

"Call the National Guard, I don't care." Daniel moved down and patted the pockets of the legs. "Just do it from your fucking car as you drive away from here. Go! Before he wakes up."

As Lydia took out Daniel's phone instead of her own, she checked on the man. He was still breathing.

"I don't know who this is." Daniel moved down the calves and removed another knife from the left ankle. "But he's dangerous as hell, unless you're unfamiliar with what all this metal I'm taking off of him is used for. And if you don't want me to kill him, you need to get away, *now*."

"Come with me," she blurted. "We can call together—"

"No, I have to stay here and make sure he doesn't follow you." Daniel shook his head. "I don't know what you did or who you called or—shit, anything else. The one thing I'm clear on is that he knows where you are—"

Lydia stood up. "Just leave him here. Let's go—"

"There's a tracker. On the bottom of your car." As Lydia recoiled, Daniel glanced around again. "I found it this morning when I got stuck out on the trail. It's a magnetic-mounted GPS tracker behind the chassis on the driver's side. That's why I think whoever this is is after you. I think he's following the signal your car is letting out—and yes, I was going to tell you. Now give me my phone back and go. Get safe. *Please*."

Lydia pictured the footprints underneath her windows.

So that was what they'd done while they were on the property, she thought. They hadn't gotten inside; they'd tagged her car.

"You need to come with me," she asked roughly.

"No, I have to stay here. If he wakes up, we've both got a problem, don't we. Just give me my phone and I'll be fine. I'm always fine."

Lydia tossed his cell over and then palmed her own. "I'll call the sheriff to come get you."

"I don't care what the fuck you do. Just as long as it's from your car and it's moving. Go—before he regains consciousness. Which is going to be in another minute, maybe less."

Lydia started to pant, as if she had already begun to run off. "Hold him here. And I'll go to the sheriff—"

"Don't tell him we went into that barn. Don't get me involved with that."

"Eastwind will be at Peter's now. He's who will answer the call the newscaster made."

"Well, good for them both—like I care? Just please fucking leave. Go!"

"I'm calling the police," she said as she turned away.

"You have a sheriff, remember," he tossed back.

On that note, she started to bolt over the springy ground cover. She glanced back only once. Daniel was staring at her as he knelt beside the soldier, a grave expression on his face. Like maybe he was wondering what the fuck he'd gotten himself involved in.

Join the club, she thought.

◆ ◆ ◆

Daniel watched Lydia run off, her footfalls drifting into silence along with the soft rustle of her loose windbreaker. Her car was about five hundred yards away, too far for him to catch the sound of her engine turning over.

So he gave it four minutes. And as he waited, he picked up one of the guns he'd taken from the guard. There was a full magazine in it.

When a groan rose up from the incapacitated man, Daniel sifted through the various weapons and ammo on the ground. Extracting a cylinder from the pile, he attached the hollow tube to the muzzle of the auto-loader by screwing it on.

Double-checking that Lydia hadn't changed her mind and come back, he listened. Looked around again.

Then he put the suppressor to the other man's forehead and discharged a single bullet right into the frontal lobe of the brain. No sound from the gun, but the body jerked, the extremities rising for a beat and landing back down in a flop.

Daniel collected all of the weapons, pocketing them. Then he rolled the man over and patted down the back. No ID, no kidding. Cell phone, however, in a rear pocket of the combat pants.

Whoever it was looked more military than law enforcement with all the equipment and the no badge'ing—and that was why Daniel was sure it was a private guard of some sort. But working for who?

Getting to his feet, he tucked the ball cap into his pocket, grabbed a hold under the armpits, and hefted the body up into a fireman's hold. With careful feet, he made his way deeper into the forest, away from the execution site.

Daniel had no particular plan of where to hide the remains. So he did what he always did. He relied on his environment to provide him with the solution to his needs. And sure enough, as if the forest was happy to lend a hand, a shallow cave appeared and he muscled the body into the dark, dank confines. He was careful not to disturb anything more than absolutely necessary, moving as if he were in the middle of a crime scene.

Ha-ha.

Hey, maybe Lydia was right about his sense of humor.

Nah.

Taking out his cell, he triggered the flashlight. Damp stone walls gleamed, but the dirt on the ground ate up the illumination.

The soldier's knife was just what he needed.

As Daniel bent over the man's face, he put his cell in between his teeth so the beam was where he needed it. Then he peeled open the right eye with his thumb and forefinger. The silver blade had a surgical tip to it, and inserting that pointy-pointy into the far corner—

He popped the orb free of its socket, the optic nerve a mess of delicate wiring in the back.

After he repeated the removal on the other side, he took out the bandana in his ass pocket and wrapped his little prize up. Then he killed his light and backed out of the cave in a crouch, straightening when he was sure he was free of the overhang.

Glancing around again, he put the bundle into his jacket and strode off.

As he returned to where the execution had gone down, there was a disturbance in the ground cover, obvious even if you weren't looking for anything. It went without saying that there would be some blood, too.

He looked at the gray sky. "Come on, rain. I could use a little backup, if you don't mind."

Kneeling down, he dug through the leaves and needles, going into the dirt. It took some sifting with his bare hands . . . but he found the bullet. Thanks to a granite shelf about ten inches down, the lead slug hadn't penetrated very deep.

There was nothing he could do about the strike mark on the stone but cover it up.

At least he wasn't worried about local law enforcement. Small towns like these didn't have bloodhound professionals who were going to deconstruct an area the size of this clearing just on the outside chance they found something.

Especially when they had two eyewitnesses who said a man had been choked out, instead of killed.

With one last look, and a few kicks with his boot, he turned away and headed for the path, the lane . . . the county road that had pavement.

The sense that he was being followed wasn't a news flash. He was used to his deeds staying tight on his heel.

But the fact that he cared what Lydia Susi thought about him was a real goddamn inconvenience.

SEVENTEEN

A S LYDIA RAN up to her car, her heart was
going triple time and her eyes were bouncing
all around, the trees seeming to move as she herky-
jerked her head left and right. But nothing came out
at her, no one dressed in black, no one armed, no
one . . .

Not Daniel, either.

What if that other man woke up? What if they
were fighting now, and Daniel was being overpowered
because the element of surprise no longer worked to
his advantage—

As a wave of dizzy panic shorted out her brain,
she forced herself to palm her keys and get into the
hatchback. Cranking the engine, she had a thought
that she should find whatever the hell had been put
on her undercarriage, but the mental image of those
guns Daniel had taken off that soldier cured her of
the impulse.

Back to the county road. Get help. Save Daniel.

Yanking the gear shift into reverse, she twisted

around and backed out down the little lane, its twin tracks of raw dirt like a set of train tracks and good thing. She needed the help to stay on course.

It was forever before she emerged into the open air, twelve years if it was a moment. And when she got to the asphalt, she barely looked for traffic. She just backed right out into the middle of the road, spun the steering wheel, and took off. She needed to get far enough away to dial the sheriff—

As her phone rang, she jumped and fumbled with it. "Hello—"

"I'm okay. I'm all right—"

"Daniel!" She hit the brakes for no good reason. "Where are you?"

"I'm coming through the woods on a southwesterly tack. I have no idea how long it's going to take me to get out to the road."

"Where's the soldier? Or whatever he was?"

"I tied him up with a zip cord he had. I just left him there and ran."

"Thank God." She closed her eyes briefly. "I'm looking for a place to pull over—"

"Get where no one can see you and I'll tell you where the tracker is. You need to take it off and throw it away first. You're still in danger until you do that—"

At that very moment, one of the trailheads into the preserve appeared. It was the route that led up the "ugly side of things" as the locals put it, so there was no one parked in the small, shaded area.

"I'm here," she said as she pulled in. "I'm stopping, I mean."

"Good."

"Are you sure you're okay?" She put the gear shift in park. "Are you—"

"I'm just having a nice jog in the woods. Enjoying the view. You know, touristy stuff."

She closed her eyes again. "Where am I going under this car?"

"Driver's side. It's right behind the front wheel. You'll see it with your phone light."

"Okay."

Getting out, she dropped to the ground and shimmied under. There was heat coming off the engine block, transmitted through the metal of the frame, and the smell of oil and dirt made her sneeze.

"You still there?" she said as she put Daniel on speaker and turned on the light.

"Yup." His voice was tinny. "Where are you?"

"Under the car."

"Where are you stopped?"

"Burning Tree Trailhead. The parking lot. There's no one else here."

"Okay, turn your head a little right. It's—"

"I got it."

The black whatever-the-hell was larger than she'd

thought, about the size of her palm, and as she moved her light around, it was like something out of a 007 movie.

"Is there any chance I take it off and it explodes?" she said.

There was a pause. "Yeah, that might happen. I don't know."

Lydia cursed. "Remind me not to ask you for my risks of cancer."

"Nah, you're good with the cancer. You eat right, exercise. Although what are your genetics like?"

"I'm a total mutt," she muttered as she got a grip on the device. "Okay, am I counting down or just doing it?"

"Just do it."

"Great time to live the Nike slogan."

Closing her eyes, she took a deep breath—

"Shit!" she said as she ripped it free.

"Lydia? *Lydia!*"

"Oh, God, it's blinking." She turned the thing over in her hand. "What the hell is it?"

"Throw it! Throw it as far as you can—just fucking throw that thing into the woods."

In a scramble that left her banging her head as she came out from under the car, she jumped up, hauled back, and put every ounce of strength into a Lamar Jackson, pitching the device into the trees.

"Lydia?" came Daniel's voice. "Did you—"

"Yes, I threw it."

"Get out of there."

She didn't waste a second: In the car. Not even a seatbelt. Slamming in reverse and skidding on the dirt as she k-turned and took off.

"You okay?" Daniel said.

With a shaking hand, she put the phone up to her ear even though he was still on speaker. "I'm not. No. I'm not. Where are you?"

"Still in the woods."

"Are you safe?"

There was a pause, during which all she heard was the sound of him running and breathing. "You don't have to save me, Lydia. I told you, I'm always fine."

Out on the county road, she just drove in whatever direction her car was pointed in. Every time she blinked, she caught snapshots that dismantled her composure further: the bathroom at Peter Wynne's, the soldier walking under the deer stand . . . and then what Daniel had done to protect them both.

The newscasters had called Eastwind already. She just knew it. Who else could they go to?

"Lydia?"

"I don't know where I'm going," she mumbled.

"Then just keep driving."

"How can you say that?"

"Because that's all you need to do. Don't hit anything and just let yourself go."

She blinked. Blinked again.

When something hit her windshield, she jumped.

It was just rain, though, a dappling of fat drops that landed like miniature fists on the glass.

"It's raining," she said into the phone that was still on speaker.

Lydia had some thought that she was scared to end the call, as if their connection over the phone was what was keeping him safe, keeping him alive. Keeping her the same.

"What are we going to do?" she whispered as she started the wipers.

"You're just driving right now, Lydia. That's all you need to think about. You've got to give that adrenaline a chance to work its way out of you before you make any sense."

"Peter is dead."

There was another pause, with nothing but Daniel's footfalls coming through the connection. "Yeah, he probably is."

"Do you think that man in the uniform did it?"

"I don't know. Can you tell me why anyone would want to hurt your boss?"

Lydia thought about those papers that had been burned up in the fireplace. "No, but I'm going to find out."

◆ ◆ ◆

As Daniel jogged along through the trees, he kept the phone up to his ear. On the other end, he could hear the whirring of Lydia's car and what he thought was the slap of windshield wipers.

Right on schedule, he thought as he glanced up to the rain.

The oaks and maples were all bare-limbed, providing no cover, and pines had never made good umbrellas. This was all good news for him.

"Lydia?" he said as he slowed to a walk.

"Hmm?"

Glancing behind himself, he got a whole lot of coast-was-clear. With any luck, that would last— because backup for that now-dead boy-in-black would be a problem.

"What did they do to you?" he asked. "What happened."

He wasn't surprised that Lydia took her time answering. And then she shocked him by telling him what he knew in his gut was the truth.

"Someone came and looked in all my windows Saturday night. That was when they must have put that tracker under my car. And then . . . they took a picture of me as I was standing outside of the house, just after I'd noticed the footprints and was checking them out."

Fuck.

"Who do you think it was?" he asked.

"The hotel. It all happened after I called the media."

"Is there anything you haven't told me, Lydia?"

"No, that's it. I swear on my grandfather."

Daniel stopped. Turned around. Waited. He trusted his instincts in the woods more than anything, but he was distracted—and that was how you got yourself killed. Which that guard had learned the rigor mortis way.

"Do you have a lawn?" he said as he refocused and kept walking.

"A lawn—you mean at my house? Yes."

"Is it pretty big? Like what we saw at your executive director's?"

"I guess. Why are you—"

"You mind if I put my tent on the far corner of your property? I don't have the money to stay at that Pine Lodge place for very long, and I promise I won't go inside your house unless you ask me in or need me. But that way, I have a place to crash and you're not alone— and there's a shower in the groundskeeping building so no, I don't need to borrow your bathroom."

In response, there was only whirring coming across the connection. And that thumping slap.

"Why would you do that?" she said with exhaustion.

"I need a place to crash."

"You weren't going to stay at Pine Lodge, were you. You were just going to tent up on the mountain."

"Camping outdoors is a drifter's paradise." He checked over his shoulder once again. "And whether that's on an elevation or a flat lawn, it works both ways."

"There are wolves all around this area."

"And here I thought the *W* in WSP stood for worms. And hey, I would be safer in your yard, right?" He gave her time to reply. "Lydia, I know you don't know me, but lock me out. Turn every dead bolt in the place. You'll be safe in your house, and if someone else comes and walks around—I can hold them down while you call for help. Something I've already proven I can do."

There was a long pause. "I'm scared."

"I know you are. So let me help—and no one needs to know. It would just be between you and me."

"I have to go," she said remotely. "I'm calling the sheriff now."

"Good. Let's take the law back to that guard. He wasn't going anywhere fast when I left him where I dropped him."

"I want to come pick you up."

"I can see the road through the trees from where I am. I'll be walking on the shoulder."

He ended the call and put the phone away. By now, the rain was falling steadily, and if he was lucky, any blood would be gone by the time they got back. If not?

Well, there were wolves in those woods, weren't there.

EIGHTEEN

A S LYDIA HEADED back toward town, she
called Eastwind's number—and wasn't surprised that she got voice mail. Immediately redialing,
she hoped she'd see Daniel Joseph walking along the
shoulder—and when her second call wasn't answered,
she cursed. A third try had her passing by Peter
Wynne's and the lane that had taken them to the deer
stand—thank God!

There Daniel was, a powerful figure striding along
the opposite side of the country road with his back to
her. Just as she was checking to go across to get him,
the sheriff answered his cell phone.

"Eastwind."

She let out a breath that she was unaware of holding. "Sheriff . . . this is Lydia from the WSP. I need
your help. I have to see you—"

"I'm out on a call right now, but I can—"

"You're at Peter Wynne's. I know."

The sheriff's voice dropped in volume. "As a matter
of fact I am."

Hitting the directional signal, Lydia cut over the outgoing lane and pulled in front of Daniel's path. As he approached, her eyes obsessively inspected him in the rear view mirror—but there were no arterial wounds that she could see. No limping, either. No contusions on his handsome face.

"I need to talk to you," she said to Eastwind. "Right now."

"I can come to you when I'm finished here—"

"No, it has to be right now. Farlan's Lane. Meet me about a quarter mile in from the entrance. I have something . . . you need to see. Delegate what you're doing to Anthony or Phil. I need you *now*."

Daniel tried to open the door. When it was locked, she fumbled with switches and buttons like she'd never been in the hatchback before.

"All right," the sheriff said. "I'll see you there in five minutes. But I don't have a lot of time."

Lydia found the unlock button and hit it, a punching sound released inside the car. As she ended the call, she looked over.

Daniel squeezed himself into the passenger seat. Shut his door while he brushed his rain-wet hair back. And then he looked over casually, as if they'd done nothing more strenuous or unusual than drop those invitations at the post office: No bizarre investigation of Peter Wynne's mysteriously empty and waterlogged house. No spying on the reporter and the cameraman. No strange soldier stalking under that deer stand and Daniel—

"Hi," he said. In a very chill, how's-your-day-going tone of voice.

The trembling came over her in a wave, her body vibrating in the seat so badly, she hung on to the wheel. "We have to go back to the deer stand. Eastwind—the sheriff—is meeting us there."

"Okay, good. You all right to drive?"

"No, I'm not."

The rain was lashing now, the wipers not keeping up with the deluge. And as they slapped back and forth, she stared out the windshield.

"One step at a time," he said quietly. "Cut the impossible into pieces."

"How are you so calm?"

"Just turn us around."

As a truck came toward them and then passed by, she screwed the twelve thousandth k-turn, and just threw them into reverse. Twisting around and grabbing on to his headrest, she piloted them backward to Farlan's Lane.

The little cut into the forest came quicker than she expected, and as she took them off onto the twin dirt tracks into the trees, she glanced up at the yellow-and-brown road sign. So official for what her grandfather would have called a goat path.

"What are you going to say when he asks why you didn't call him at Peter's?" Daniel asked. "You should be prepared."

Looking over, she asked a question she feared the answer to. "Have you been in jail?"

"You've seen my background check."

"That's not a no."

"I can't forge my record." He drummed his fingers on the console like he was frustrated, but she wasn't sure whether it was with her or himself. "When I was young, I had some issues. Just petty shit. Juvenile detention. Nothing as an adult."

She nodded and bumped them along. "You just seem like you've done this before. With the law, I mean."

And breaking into a house.

And flattening some guy to the ground.

"Don't mistake detachment for familiarity."

They fell silent as she went farther and farther into the property. Overhead, the bare tree branches and spindly pine boughs did little to cut the rainfall so she kept her wipers on. Some distance in, she stopped about where she thought they'd halted the first time. Turning the car off, she popped the hood and got out. As she leaned over the warm engine, Daniel joined her on the other side.

"We need to—"

"If you want to make it look as if we stalled," he murmured, extending his arm down, "we'll just do this."

He pulled out a set of tubing.

"You read my mind," she muttered as a big set of headlights bumped up and down toward them. "Here he comes. I think I'll leave the hood up."

As Daniel just nodded, she pushed her damp hair back. "I'm not used to any of this. And I *hate* lying."

"I know you do," he said.

The Walters Township sheriff's SUV had front beams that were the new, icy kind, and in the forest, on a cloudy day, they were blinding. Eastwind killed the sting as he cut his engine, and he put his hat on as he got out. The thing had a plastic covering in place, like a shower cap, but the rest of him got as wet as Lydia and Daniel were becoming.

"Hi, Sheriff." Lydia lifted a hand as she shivered. "Thanks for meeting us."

The sheriff touched the brim of his waterproofed hat and dipped his head. "So what's this about? Looks like you need a tow truck more than me."

"It's not about the car." Lydia rushed through her words. "Someone's been following me. They were on my property Saturday night." She motioned toward Daniel. "He and I were going to the post office when I noticed this suspicious car behind me. I pulled ahead and came down here because I figured I'd lose them. When my car died on me, Daniel and I took into the trees. We found a deer stand and decided to hide up there while we called for help—and that's how we knew you were at Peter's. We could see the barn from the stand and it was obvious something was wrong."

"And no one came down here after you?"

"Actually, they did." She glanced at Daniel. "Somehow the man followed me. Us. On foot to the deer stand."

Eastwind focused on Daniel, his brown eyes shrewd. "And you are?"

"Daniel Joseph," came the reply. "The Wolf Study Project's new groundskeeper. I was just helping her with some invitations because the boxes were so heavy."

"Can either of you describe this man?"

Lydia spoke up. "He was like a soldier. Dressed in all black. He looked . . . professional."

"And where is he now?"

Lydia stared at Daniel. "He's back in the woods. Where Daniel . . . handled him."

"I wanted to protect her." Daniel shrugged. "I disarmed him and subdued him so she could get away. Then I left myself and ran for the county road."

"When I got back to the car," Lydia said, "I tried to figure out what I could do to fix it. But I don't know anything about cars. I was so scared. That's when I called you."

So many holes. Her story felt like a hot mess, held together not with truths or facts, but a sloppy knit of bullshit. But what else could she do? She didn't trust Eastwind, either.

"Let's go back to him." She nodded at the woods. "I'll take you to him."

"By all means," Eastwind murmured. "Show me everything."

+ + +

"He was here . . . we left him, here."

Lydia frowned and kneeled down where the leaves and pine needles had been roughed up. In the midst of the otherwise undisturbed ground cover, the struggle between Daniel and that man in the black uniform had left obvious marks, raw dirt exposed and gouged by the heels and toes of both their sets of boots as well as the soldier's body.

But the other half of that fight was nowhere to be seen.

Oh, God, she thought. He was out there. Somewhere.

And given that she had rushed over to try to stop what she'd thought was a murder—the man had seen her and he knew she had seen his face.

She pointed in the direction of the deer stand. "We were way over there, but this was where Daniel jumped him."

Eastwind glanced around. Then focused on Daniel. "And you say you disarmed him?"

"I did. I didn't take the weapons, though." Daniel opened his leather jacket, flashing his pockets, the waistband of his jeans. "I wish I had, though."

"What was he carrying?"

"An autoloader. A knife. Bullets."

"And how badly did you hurt him?" the sheriff asked.

"I just choked him out." He looked at Lydia. "I only wanted her to be able to get away so as soon as he was unconscious, I stopped. When I figured she was far enough ahead, I zip-tied him with his own stuff and ran for the county road."

"Did you guys see his face?" Eastwind took out his phone as it vibrated, but sent whoever was calling to voice mail. "Could you ID him if you had to?"

"I saw his face," Lydia said. "I absolutely can identify him."

Eastwind put his hand up like he was stopping an argument before one started. "Not that I'm doubting you, but what makes you think he was a threat to you?"

"Other than all the weapons?" Daniel muttered dryly. "And the fact that he followed us in here?"

"Well, there are no weapons here. And no one around." The sheriff looked at Lydia. "So I'm asking, what gave you the impression you were being stalked?"

"The footprints under my windows at home." She took out her phone. Went through her pictures. "Here. Look at them."

Eastwind took her cell and did some scrolling. With a pinch, he closed in on one of the images. "When did this happen?"

"Saturday night, I think. I found them Sunday morning."

His brown eyes lifted from the screen. "Why didn't you call me?"

"I wasn't sure how significant it was. But I know now, and that's why I made you come here even though you were busy—"

"There was also a GPS tracker on her car."

As Daniel spoke up, Eastwind's brows flared. "I beg your pardon?"

Daniel nodded. "I found it this morning when I took her car into the trail to work on the bridges. I got stuck on a rock, and as I went to check on the damage to the undercarriage, that's when I saw it. I wasn't sure exactly what the device was, until that man followed us in here."

"This acreage is huge. How did he know where you two were in some deer stand?"

"He didn't," Daniel countered. "He was looking for her randomly and got lucky. And he's *still* out there looking for her."

"I was the one who talked to the media," Lydia said. "I know you've seen the news, or been contacted yourself by WNDK. I did call them about Corrington, and if that hotel can poison wolves, they can do worse. Peter Wynne—well, something's happened to him, hasn't it. And I don't care if my story doesn't make sense to you because I know what I've seen and I know who was behind my car and then looking for us in these trees."

Eastwind gave her her phone back. "I wish you'd called me on Sunday."

"Me too, but I didn't want to overreact. After this, though . . ." She toed at the pine needles. "I don't want whatever was done to Peter Wynne to happen to me."

"How do you know anything was done to him?"

"You didn't want to leave his house." She crossed her arms over her chest. "There's a news truck over there and two other sheriff's cars. Considering there are four officers in your department, including yourself, you've called in every one of them except the guy off duty this afternoon."

"Where's this GPS locator?" Eastwind glanced at Daniel. "Let me guess, you took it off and threw it away."

"Damn right I did. When we got up to the road, I threw it in the back of a truck."

"You're a sharpshooter, then."

"Not at all." Daniel shrugged. "They stopped to ask if we needed a lift. I tossed it in the open bed."

"So you were willing to possibly endanger someone else?"

"They're looking for her. They don't care about anyone else."

"And let me guess," Eastwind said to Lydia. "Neither of you know who was driving that truck. Or got its license plate."

Lydia slowly shook her head. "No, we didn't."

"Can you even tell me what color it was," the sheriff drawled.

Like he wasn't buying a goddamn word they were speaking.

NINETEEN

T HAT NIGHT, BACK down in Caldwell at the Brotherhood mansion's dining room table, Xhex finally figured out what the hell was going on with her nightmares. She hadn't been looking for the revelation. Ever since V had dropped his vision bullshit on her, she had filed both that happy little exchange and her piranha wake-up calls in the giant black hole in her brain entitled: Not Fucking Now, Not Fucking Ever.

Destiny, however, was like poison ivy. Once it brushed up against you, it was tenacious, irritating— and the kind of thing that did not go away on its own.

So there she was, sitting next to John Matthew at First Meal, blithely pushing some eggs around on her plate and hoping like hell he didn't notice how much she wasn't eating ... when she happened to look across the enormous table.

Darius, who had built the mansion long before the Brothers had even had a thought of living under one roof together, had created a dining room big enough to fit a city and the table he'd commissioned held its own in the cavernous space. All of the fighters, their mates, their children—and various special guests—could be accommodated down its flanks.

And God knew Fritz was a more-the-merrier kind of butler. If that male could feed a thousand every night right after the sun went down? Happy *doggen*.

The din of conversation could get to be a little intense, though, all the Brothers talking over each other as a matter of practice, the dick swinging and ball busting clearly part of their job description. And she looked up only because Rhage started to laugh at something Butch had said to Lassiter . . . and no matter what mood she was in, Hollywood throwing his model-perfect head back and belly-chuckling it until he turned beet red and had to wipe his eyes with his damask napkin was something worth witnessing.

It was like a corgi puppy trying to bite a tennis ball. Worth the eyeball time.

While she was watching Rhage yuck it up, something in her peripheral vision registered, a little cognitive bell getting rung.

Turning her head, she was surprised at the hi-how-ya that her instincts were floating. Nate, adopted son of Murhder and Sarah, was minding his own business. In fact, he had retracted from his rather large size, his shoulders curved in, his chin down, his elbows tight to his torso—like he desperately didn't want to get noticed.

She knew why.

In spite of the fact that the kid had *every* right to be sitting in his chair—and even though Nate was only a "kid" by virtue of having recently gone through his transition—he was awkward and overwhelmed.

Then again, it had only been three or four months since he'd been out of the same kind of lab Xhex herself had been held in.

These were early nights and days for him. And it was going to be a long, long time before his brain rewired itself and his sensory perceptions toned down.

That was the thing when you were experimented on: Your body was not your own. While you were getting pumped full of diseases and drugs, and dealing with the haywire reactions to things you did not consent to, your brain was forced to reconcile it all with your emotions. For her, she'd disconnected through rage, and when she'd had her chance to get free, she'd taken it. On her terms.

But Nate had been a young. And they'd killed his *mahmen*—

As if he sensed her stare, his eyes lifted to her. Her first instinct was to look the fuck away, but no. She owed him more than that. He was a survivor, just like she was, and there was a good chance, if she avoided him, he was going to dub in something like she felt sorry for him. Or she was blaming him for having been too weak to get out.

Xhex smiled as much as she could—which was not much. And then she lifted her hand in a casual wave.

He flushed, like he could read her mind and knew she was managing him. But after a moment, he lifted his own palm.

They both looked away at the same time.

The tap on her knee brought her head to her *hellren*. "You finished already?" she asked John Matthew.

Her male shook his head. Then he signed, *You want to take a walk?*

How the fuck did he know her so well? Then again, they had been together for what seemed like an eternity.

"Yeah," she said softly, "I would."

The two of them got up together, and they left their plates—because if you picked anything off the table and tried to take it into the kitchen, you were going to have to look into Fritz's hangdog face, his heart broken, his eyes watering with self-condemnation at the utter failure in his duty to clear.

Rhage had tried it once with a napkin, and the entire household had ended up with a case of the guilts from the *doggen*'s unrelenting self-flagellation.

As she and her mate went down the table to the archway into the foyer, they nodded and smiled at people. John Matthew clapped Blay and Qhuinn on the shoulders. She studiously ignored V's heavy-lidded eyes.

Nope, sorry, V, she thought.

The next thing she knew, they were in the study, but they kept going. Opening up one of the French doors, she held it wide for John Matthew, and then they were outside on the barren terrace. Although it was spring, they were in way upstate New York—and on a mountain. So no lawn furniture, and the pool was battened down, and the formal garden's flower beds and fruit trees remained insulated for winter.

John Matthew closed the doors behind them, and he hung back, letting her walk around. Sometime later, maybe it was five minutes, maybe it was ten . . . maybe it was twelve hours . . . she stopped and looked at the night sky.

"They say there are aliens all the time up here." When he whistled in an ascension, she glanced over her shoulder. "No, really. People upstate see them regularly. The thought is that it's, like, secret shit from Plattsburgh."

John Matthew pursed his lips in a *well, huh* kind of way.

"Yeah. Not everything that flashes across the heavens is a shooting star."

She mostly kept the bitterness out of her voice, even though she could give a shit about whether humans were taking pictures of aliens or weather balloons. For fuck's sake, she was a vampire. Like ET didn't actually exist?

"I figured out why I'm having the dreams." The

words were spoken quick, like maybe she could duck the whole fucking thing if she spit the syllables out fast enough. "Nate."

John Matthew nodded. And signed, *I should have made the connection.*

"Me, too. But yeah, he's the reason I'm having the nightmares. What he went through is bringing it all back. You know."

She hated the weakness, the emotion, the fact that under her surface were pain and suffering she had not volunteered for and couldn't seem to lose. Then again she'd been sold by her own family into that lab, in retribution for a violation they could not forgive.

Murhder had been a former lover of hers. And it was because of that relationship that her own blood had taught her a lesson. Or thought they had—

John Matthew whistled, and when she glanced at him, he signed, *But Vishous's vision wasn't about the lab. It was about wolven.*

"I'm not going to worry about his prognostication crap. For all we know, he had Arby's at one a.m. and his smokehouse brisket didn't sit well with him."

So what are you thinking?

"I'm not." She cursed when it was clear he wasn't buying her lie. "Oh, come on. Is my *symphath* rubbing off on you?"

John Matthew just shrugged. And as he stared at her, she looked down his huge body. He was dressed in black, his skintight T-shirt and his leathers as dark as the shadows he would stalk along in the field as he protected the vampire race from its new enemy.

"I love you," she said roughly.

Her *hellren* mouthed a curse. Then signed, *Fuck, you're thinking of going to the Colony, aren't you.*

TWENTY

Darkness abounded, dense and fraught with shadow.
O'erwhelming the land as it claimed the souls of the
unjust. The earth a vast grave o'er which the dead
roamed, searching, searching for all that they had lost . . .

As NIGHT FELL in Walters, Lydia was sitting at her kitchen table with a mug of Campbell's tomato soup between her palms, the old poem rattling through her head in her grandfather's voice, in her grandfather's language. The fragments were all that remained in her memory of the full piece, as if the words were fabric that had disintegrated with age.

"Stop it, stop it, stop it . . ."

As she spoke out loud, she took another sip from the lip of the mug. She tasted nothing, couldn't have said whether it was hot enough, didn't know if she had made it with water or milk.

Lies were a sickness, her grandfather had always said. And too many of them could be terminal.

The weight on her chest sure as hell felt like a disease.

Glancing to the window beside the little table,

everything outside was dark—and not dark in the way things had been in Boston. Not city-dark. Walters was country-dark, like where she had grown up outside of Seattle, no ambient anything throwing off a glow, no soft, urban-diffused illumination to reassure a person who was jumpy and unhappy that all was not lost. All was not a void that you could fall into.

Especially if you were a sinner. Or if you lied.

"Forgive me, Grandfather," she whispered.

She put the mug down, finding the normally comforting smell revolting. And as she glanced at the level to see how much she'd actually taken in, the sight of the heavy, viscous red soup was worse.

It reminded her of blood.

Bolting up, she took her sad-sack dinner to the sink and looked away as she rinsed out the mug.

The kitchen had been renovated last in the late eighties, the cabinets a *Home Improvement*-era mauve, the linoleum floor a pink and blue color scheme that matched. The appliances were black and coordinated with nothing. The sink was stainless steel and matte from use and cleaning.

But none of that was what she dwelled on, and not because she'd gotten used to the Candy-style decor: There was a window over the sink. Another by the table. A third in the door that opened to the detached garage and the backyard.

Her hands shook as she rushed around and pulled the flimsy curtains shut. Then she hustled out of the kitchen, and zeroed in on the stout front door and its dead bolt. As she turned the brass grip and pulled, the catch of the lock in its sturdy metal cage made a clapping sound.

Putting her other hand on top of the first, she bent her knees and leaned all of her weight back. Then she pulled again.

"It's locked."

Even as she told herself the obvious, she didn't believe it. And as she straightened, she wanted to test things again and again, like she could maybe make it all stronger by the repeated challenges.

Spinning around, she fell back against the wood panels and hugged herself.

The house was so small that aside from the kitchen and the parlor she'd just raced through, there was only one other room on the first floor: A study with a desk, a random bean bag chair, and a side table that she'd put her wireless printer on. Given that the home office was on the far side of the stairs, there was absolutely no light carried in from the kitchen.

Stepping over its threshold, she approached the window that faced the backyard with her heart in her throat and her body on a live wire.

Flattening her back against the wall, she took a couple of breaths. Then peered around to look through the wavy antique panes. Like she was taking cover from a shoot-out.

She expected a face to be there, a stranger with evil eyes in a black uniform, returned to do what he'd failed to accomplish in the trees.

Nothing. And as she continued to look out across the scraggly yard, reality seemed to shift on her, the past moving forward and overtaking the present. She had always felt like such a fraud among others, and maybe that was why the lies had been so easy to construct and say out loud to Eastwind. But that didn't mean any part of it sat well with her.

Disturbed, she was back in the kitchen before she knew it, before she was aware of choosing to move or picking a place to go.

At the back door, she watched from a distance as her hand reached out for the shiny brass knob. Like the one on the front door, the thing was original to the house, old and tarnished except for where palms buffed and polished it through use.

Her intention was to test the dead bolt, just like she had the one in front. And then retest how sturdy it was when her brain refused to accept what her eyes were seeing.

Instead, her right hand went to the bolt and released the mechanism. Then her left turned the knob and opened the door.

Stepping out onto the back stoop, she breathed deep and smelled the remnants of the rain that had fallen all afternoon long. The scent of earth and growing things, of wet cedar shingles and puddles on the driveway's pavement, was yet another announcement of spring's arrival. But the temperature was still cold.

Or maybe that was her insides. She felt frozen under her skin.

Across the yard, just into the tree line, the tent Daniel had set up was nearly impossible to see: If she hadn't been looking for it, even her keen eyesight wouldn't have noticed the ever so subtle thickening in the shadows' density.

There was no light to give Daniel's presence away. No fire, either.

He must be so cold—

From out of the tent, a tall figure emerged, the full height of the man extending far above the black nylon roofline.

Aware that she could be seen, she lifted a hand.

Daniel came toward her, striding over the scruffy grass. When he stopped in front of her, he was close enough so that she could see his eyes. His five-o'clock shadow. Every wave of his on-the-long-side hair.

"You okay?"

"Not really," she said. "You?"

"I'm good. Just chilling."

"How did you know I was out here?"

"Chilling is not sleeping. And I made sure that I can see your house through a little screened flap."

She moved her hair over her shoulder and rubbed her upper arms. "Are you warm enough out there?"

"Yup." He patted the windbreaker that covered his pecs. "This thing is insulated."

When she didn't say anything else, he lowered his voice. "You did what you had to, with Eastwood."

"Eastwind," she corrected. "And I don't think he believed us."

"Doesn't matter if he did. It's what he can prove or disprove that's important—and there's no evidence that refutes our story."

She looked away. "I truly believe he's committed to keeping the hotel happy. He wants the jobs, the tax dollars, the traffic. But I still hated lying to him."

"What was your choice?"

Her eyes shot back to him. "The truth."

"If you think your life is complicated now, try being a suspect in Peter Wynne's murder."

"Oh, I wouldn't be."

"Really? Your superior goes missing, and you benefit from his death because you get his job. That would at least make you a person of interest."

"I don't want to be the executive director. I'm a scientist, not an administrator—"

"You're sitting in his office, aren't you? Using his computer, aren't you."

"That doesn't mean I—I couldn't kill anybody."

"You'd be surprised what you can do when you have to."

"Well, I *didn't* kill him. How's that."

Daniel put his hands up. "I'm not accusing you. I'm

just telling you what your sheriff buddy would think if he knew we went into that barn and took a stroll around. At least I didn't see any security cameras inside or out—which was a surprise, by the way, and the only reason we're going to be okay."

Lydia rubbed her eyes. "Are you safe out there?"

"Yup. Don't worry about—"

"—you. Yes, you've told me that before." She nodded over her shoulder toward the tent. "Did you have anything to eat?"

"Doritos and Coke. I had some left over in my saddlebag from when I got the lowdown on your whole life at the grocery store."

With a frown, she dropped her hands. "Aren't you supposed to be on a health kick?"

"You have no idea what I used to eat. And drink. And smoke."

"What was it, rubber tires and cement blocks?"

"Yup, both chewy and dry. A great combination, but at least my cholesterol was okay."

She smiled a little. "And that terrible snack is all you've had?"

"Calories are calories, I'll survive, and the diner opens at six tomorrow morning. I plan on eating three plates of pancakes, as well as bacon and eggs, as soon as I can."

Lydia glanced over her shoulder. "I have food. I went shopping on Saturday."

"Did you eat any of it? I'm thinking you didn't—"

"Let me make you something proper for dinner. Then at least . . ."

"What, I can die on a full stomach on your back lawn?" As her head shot over to him, he winced. "Sorry. Too soon?"

"Too much." She motioned to the open door. "I'm no gourmet chef, but I can do better than Tostitos and Coke."

"It was Doritos. And I am not going to say no."

She turned away.

"You don't have to do this," he said sharply.

"I know," she answered as she looked over her shoulder at him. "But as long as you don't make any more bad jokes about buying the farm on my back forty, I'm happy to feed you. Plus, I need something to occupy the next hour and seventeen minutes."

He frowned and glanced at his watch. "You have something you need to do at nine?"

"You don't go to bed before nine." She stepped into her house. "It's like people who refuse to have a glass of wine before five. It's a tent pole in the day. After nine, I can collapse and try to sleep."

"Do you have the same kind of rigid rule for waking up?"

"Never before four a.m." She motioned with her hand. "Are you coming in?"

He held up both his forefingers. "Wait, are you saying four-fifteen is in play? For wake up?"

"Yup."

Shaking his head, he stepped over the threshold. "Man, I'm surprised you don't go to bed at seven-thirty."

❖ ❖ ❖

"Looks like we were destined to have dinner together, huh."

As Daniel bit into the sandwich Lydia had cobbled together out of the remains of her last three nights of non-eating, she sipped her tea. It was funny how much he filled the house up. Even though he was just in the kitchen, it was as if he were in all the rooms at the same time.

"I think this is linner, actually." When he cocked an eyebrow, she shrugged. "Lunch as dinner. Linner. Because let's face it, it's better than 'dunch.'"

As Daniel's mouth twitched, he lowered his head, like he didn't want the smile to be seen. "Who knew, a whole new meal."

"If you were having your pancakes and eggs and bacon right now, it'd be dinfast."

"Brinner."

"See, you totally get it." She took another draw from her mug. "Is it too damp out there?"

"Tent's waterproof." He wiped his mouth with a napkin he'd taken out of the holder. "And before you ask, I'll be gone at sunrise. There'll be no sign I was ever there—"

"I want to ask you something."

His eyes flashed up at her, but his face remained relaxed. Then again, she had to wonder if he had a speeding semi coming at him whether he'd even twitch. The man had the nervous system of an inanimate object.

And who'd have thought that would be something she'd ever envy.

"Hit me," he said.

"And you can say no."

"I realize this." He took a drink of the milk he'd asked for. "So what have you got for me, Lydia Susi?"

"I want to go to the hotel site."

Daniel paused in mid-chew. "Okay. And do what?"

"I don't know. I just want to see what's there."

"If you got a pair of binoculars, you can do that from your porch at work."

She moved her mug around in circles on the table with her forefinger. "I want to find evidence."

"Of what."

"Anything." She gave up any semblance of calmness, and put her head in her hands. "I don't know what I'm doing."

"If you think trying to fool Eastwind over the deer stand shit was a party, try trespassing over on that hotel property. They'll have security cameras everywhere, and guards, and—"

"I shouldn't have brought it up—"

"Oh, I'm in." As her head lifted, he nodded. "Call me Nancy Drew. But I will say that you need to be

careful how far you take this. And you need to be prepared to get caught—"

"We can go in the veil."

"What's that?" He finished his last bite and wiped
his mouth. "And check me out, I'm learning all kinds
of things tonight. Linner. Dinfast. The veil."

She flushed. "It's the time right before dawn. When
it's mostly dark, but not completely so. That way, we
won't need flashlights to find our way. And if we wear
dark clothing, we'll be even harder to spot."

"Okay. When are we going? What night?"

"I'll come out to you at four-fifteen a.m." It wasn't
like she was going to be sleeping. "We can—shoot. I
don't have my car, do I."

The damn thing had been towed back to Paul's
Garage, and Candy had had to give her a ride home
from work—after Lydia had spent what remained of
the afternoon trying to play normal, and saying nothing about going to Peter's.

As well as everything else that had happened.

"We'll go on my bike." Daniel got up and took
his plate over to the sink. "I'm assuming you plan on
parking somewhere off the property and hiking in?"

"Yes."

As he put a little dishwashing soap on her sponge,
she found herself watching his hands. They were big.
Tanned. Calloused. A working man's hands, nothing
like Rick's or Peter's.

They were . . . sexy hands, actually.

"Well," he prompted. "Have you?"

Lydia shook herself back to attention—but failed to reroute her eyes from the way the water traveled over his fingers while he rinsed the plate.

"I'm sorry?" she murmured.

"I asked if you've ever gone over there before?"

"I've thought about it. But . . . no."

"So we have a plan."

He put the dish in her rack, and the sight of it next to her soup mug seemed intimate. Like two people lying in bed.

"You have my number in your phone," he said. "You can always call me. Meanwhile, I'll be like a junkyard dog, guarding everything out there."

She had to smile at that. "I feel like I'm cursing you with all this."

"You're not. I'm a grown-ass man. If I didn't want to deal with it, I wouldn't be on your property with my tent pitched and sleeping bag unrolled."

"You're very kind."

He leaned back against the lip of the sink and crossed his arms over his massive chest. "I'm not sure that's the word."

"Then what would you suggest?"

"I don't know."

Getting to her feet, she was done pretending she was drinking her lukewarm Earl Grey. "Maybe it'll come to you."

As she tried to head for the sink, he stayed where

he was . . . so she ended up stopping in front of him.

And that was when the change in the air happened.

When he didn't move and neither did she, the world condensed into the charged space between their bodies, a shimmering electricity flaring. Sizzling. Heating.

"Here," he murmured. "Give me that and I'll wash it for you."

Lydia had no idea what he'd said. But when he put out his hand, she placed her mug in his palm—and didn't let it go.

"What else do you want me to do for you?" he asked in a low voice.

"Nothing."

"Liar." But there was no censure in his tone. "Tell me what you want, Lydia. It's just the two of us here. Behind drawn curtains. No eyes upon anything."

Her voice deepened as well, a husky note threading through her words. "You make it sound like if there are no witnesses, the tree makes no sound when it falls."

"Impossible question to answer, isn't it."

"Still hits the ground hard, though."

"I can't disagree with that."

What are you doing? Lydia asked herself as she stared into his eyes.

"Just so you know, Lydia, I don't overthink things." He reached up and tucked a strand of her hair behind her ear. "I take them as they come. Sometimes, that's the only way to be free on this earth."

"I'm not right in the head."

"Who is?" he whispered as he leaned down and put his mouth right by her ear. "Life is short. We need to do what we can to live while we're here."

God, the smell of him.

Lydia breathed in. And then didn't want to exhale. The fact that she wanted something of him inside of her, even if it was only his scent, seemed crazy.

"I'm not like this," she protested.

"Like what?"

"This."

"You're going to have to be more specific." He eased back. "Tell me."

Step away, Lydia, she thought. *You need to step away from this man before you do something stupid.*

Instead, she lifted her hand toward his face. She stopped, though, right before she made contact.

"Where do you want to touch me," he said roughly.

"Now is not the time."

"Sure it is."

God help her . . . but she happened to agree, even though there was no logic to any of it.

With fingers that trembled, she brushed his lower lip, the tips whispering over his mouth—breaching the momentous divide of the space between them, space that was not just air and inches, but time and gravity and life.

On some level, she couldn't believe she was touching him.

"I don't know what I'm doing," she said.

"I want to be your learning curve."

With that, he opened his mouth ... and sucked her forefinger in, his hot, slick tongue circling her flesh as his burning eyes went right into her soul.

Lydia moaned, and there was no hiding the sound. But given the way he was staring at her, she wasn't sure she would have held back even if she could have.

As his mouth slowly retracted, she gasped at the sensation.

And wanted to keep going.

TWENTY-ONE

IN SO MANY ways, Lydia should have known. From the moment Daniel Joseph had appeared in her office doorway, there had been something about him. But she hadn't expected . . . *this*.

"Unless you tell me to go," he said in a husky voice, "I'm going to kiss you."

As Lydia stared up into his face, they both knew what she wanted. What she needed. Still, she kept them on the edge for a heartbeat or two.

"I don't want you to leave."

"Good," he growled.

When he lowered his head, there was a rumble of satisfaction in his chest—and then she wasn't hearing anything. Thinking anything. Worried about anything.

As big and strong as he was, his lips were soft against her own. Gentle, too, as if he knew she wanted to be handled with care—not because she didn't want him, but because she did. Too much. And God, there were more reasons to pull away than get close to him, except there was no denying the chemistry. The connection. The heat.

And the experience was even better than the anticipation.

Aware that she was going to stop this sooner than she wanted, but much later than she should, Lydia lifted her arms and put them on his shoulders. His heavy body was rock-hard under his windbreaker, the muscles roping up to his neck—and that was where her hands went.

She just wanted to see if his hair was as thick and lush as it looked—

It was.

As she dug into the waves, he purred in response, like he was a great cat and she had found his favorite stroking place. And that was when he wrapped an arm around her waist. She did not feel trapped, though. She had the sense, as he continued to stroke her lips softly, that he would let her go immediately.

Not that she was going anywhere anytime the hell soon.

Inch by inch, their bodies came into full contact, her breasts against his chest, the front of her thighs meeting his, their hips brushing. And then the kiss deepened, his tongue licking into her—

Letting out another moan, she tightened her hold on his nape, in his hair, a sense of desperation making her rougher than she should have been—she was holding him to her now, grabbing on to him. But he was going with it. One of his hands traveled from her shoulder to her waist, to her hip, and she moved against his palm, imagining what it would be like to be naked with him touching her.

With those workman hands.

Daniel eased back and stroked her hair away from her face. "You're a good kisser, you know that?"

"Am I?" She smiled like an idiot. "I could have sworn it was you."

"I guess it's us." His eyes roamed her face. And then one side of his lips tilted up. "I'm going to go now."

Lydia exhaled in surprise—but like she was going to sleep with him here on the mauve kitchen floor?

Not a bad idea, actually, she thought as she glanced down.

"Okay," she said. "I understand. We do work together—"

"That's not why I'm leaving."

"So why are you?"

He traced her cheek. Then her jawline. "If I stay, I'm not going to let you get any sleep at all." He stepped back. "You know where to find me, if you need me. And I'll see you after we're allowed to wake up at four-oh-one a.m."

She nodded. "Good night, Daniel."

Turning away, he lifted a hand over his shoulder. When he got to the door, he said, "Don't forget to lock up."

And then he was gone.

Putting her head in her hands, Lydia felt like she was under a heat lamp. Or that she'd swallowed one. And on that note, her clothes felt tight and irritating. And her lips tingled. And her body yearned.

Meanwhile, the solution to all of it was making his way across her lawn. In the dark. In the cold.

As she locked the dead bolt, the urge to call him back was nearly overwhelming.

To make sure she didn't, she went out to the staircase and ascended to the second floor. As luck would have it, her room faced the backyard, and keeping the light off, she stretched out on her bed and curved onto her side. Tucking her arms into her chest and bringing her knees up, she stared out the window.

If it had been daylight, she could have seen him get into his tent—and she imagined him bending down, folding that big body into his flimsy quarters, stretching out on his sleeping bag. And on that horizontal note, she couldn't stop thinking about where they would be if he hadn't stepped away. Or if she had called him back.

The sexual need was painful. And it made all of the reasons not to sleep with him seem flimsy. Cowardly.

Reaching around to the back pocket of her jeans, she took her cell phone out and tucked it into her chest.

It was the closest she was going to get to Daniel Joseph tonight.

Maybe ever, depending on what was out in that forest with him—

The footsteps coming up the stairs were soft and she wrenched around. But then she caught the scent of handmade shaving soap.

"Oh, thank God," she whispered. "And where have you been?"

The smell of her childhood deepened, and she waited as the stairs creaked and then the floorboards of the hall registered a slow progression down to her room.

All around her, the air temperature dropped about ten degrees, and as she shivered, she was aware she was clinically insane.

But then the ghost of her dead grandfather appeared between her doorjambs. As usual, there was little to be made of the face, or even his old-fashioned, formal clothes, yet the whip-lean form and that smell brought tears to her eyes.

It had been a long time since he'd visited her, the last appearance being when she'd been deciding whether or not to take the WSP job.

He came at crossroads, ever since he had passed.

"*Isoisä*," she whispered. "Is he dangerous?"

As usual, there was no response from the apparition. And she was stuck once again not knowing whether he came to reassure her.

Or as a warning.

"Can you stay awhile," she begged. "Please. And I haven't forgotten the rules, I promise."

He didn't remain with her. He never did. Before

her very eyes, the ghost disappeared, as if he had never been.

With a curse, she lay back down, the loneliness she lived with like a tangible weight on her. The apparition was just another reminder that there were two worlds for her, the internal and the external—and whereas that was true for everybody, on a night like tonight? With a man she wanted out on the lawn, and a stalker who could be anywhere?

It all seemed so irreconcilable.

Then again, maybe she'd fallen asleep already, and this, like so many other things, was just a bad dream.

◆ ◆ ◆

As Daniel sauntered across the scruffy grass, he expected to hear his name called out at any second. He could practically hear the husky syllables, the need, the gut-clenching sexual frustration, in Lydia's voice.

Kind of ironic, this satisfaction he took in getting her hot. Because it was also a cudgel for himself.

He couldn't remember feeling this juiced over a woman. Ever. But that couldn't be right. There must have been someone else, lurking in his past, another woman who got through to him like this, eating him alive with his own sex drive.

Pausing, he looked back at the house. The windows on the second floor were black. Was she up in her bed yet . . .

Jesus, why the hell had he left?

"Because you're not a complete asshole, that's why," he said out loud.

There were things she didn't know, things that would change the way she thought about him.

To keep from kicking himself, he took a little stroll around the traps he'd set up. Nothing was out of place, the balanced sticks and precisely arranged pieces of bark on the ground undisturbed.

Inside the tent, he untucked his gun and stretched out, keeping the weapon in his hand. Using his arm under his head as a pillow, he stared up at the nylon roof.

The sounds of the night surrounded him, the hoots of an owl, the tender-foot of a deer on the left, the rustle of a raccoon over the ground, all signals telling him there was nothing within a fair radius of him. And of Lydia.

Closing his eyes, he rearranged his body, crossing his ankles and tightening his grip on his gun.

Funny weapon, a gun. It was handy in so many situations. But it was limited, too. Sometimes it was best to get up close to your enemy. Do things the old-fashioned way.

As the past came a-knockin', he shook his head like his memories were a person looking for a conversation he didn't want to have. The good news? He had a powerful distraction he could offer up to his mind.

Although like all things, it came with its own complications.

When he pictured Lydia staring up at him with those golden eyes of hers, her lips parted, her face flushed with anticipation, his erection reinflated instantly. And demanded attention.

Maybe putting her front and center wasn't the best plan.

Especially with his cock now trapped at a bad angle in his combats—and of course, as he went to rearrange things, the contact of his hand over his fly was enough to make him hiss through his teeth. With a rough jab, he tried to ease the constriction, but the more he pushed at the rock-hard ridge, the more the thing pounded with its own heartbeat.

Resolved to ignore the dumb handle, he repositioned his arm under his head and closed his eyes like he was slamming shut a pair of vaults.

Yeah, nope.

All he could think of was the feel of her under his mouth, the way his arm had fit around her waist, the grip of her hands on his shoulders, in his hair.

He lasted a good five minutes.

After which he was unzipping things, and pushing his hand inside—

"*Fuck.*"

Gritting his teeth, he stroked himself, his memories of that woman like a blowtorch to his blood, the heat raging to the surface, his upper lip curling back. Up and down, harder . . . faster . . . he was rough with his shaft, but like he gave a fuck? He'd have beat the thing with a hammer if it would have gotten him the release he was suddenly panting for—

The razor-sharp image of his finger popping free of her lips made him lose it. He barely had time to snag a T-shirt and cover the head of his arousal before he came—

At the last second, before the orgasm totally over-took him, he had the good sense to release the hold on his gun. Otherwise, with all his straining, he was liable to shoot himself in the fucking foot.

Or somewhere else that wasn't going to grow back.

With a groan and a rolling of his hips, he let him-self go—and as the ejaculations pumped out of him, he didn't stop. It was like Lydia was some kind of erotic stimulant, the memory of her against his body giving him a stamina that couldn't be drained in just one release. In two.

In three.

The entire time, he imagined that he was filling her up, releasing into her, pumping off so that her sex got filled.

And all the while, he knew that it was a fantasy that was going to come true.

God save them both.

TWENTY-TWO

YES, XHEX THOUGHT, *she was going back to the Colony.*

As First Meal was breaking up in the dining room, and members of the Brotherhood household were dispersing, she stepped out of the mansion's grand front entrance with John Matthew right beside her. They were both heavily armed, but they were not going into the field. For one, she wasn't a Brother and she didn't fight for the race like that—and even if she was and she did, mated couples were never allowed to engage together.

"Are you ready?"

When she asked the question, it was directed at herself. And when John Matthew nodded in a decisive way, she felt like he was answering for them both. Taking his hand, she pulled him in close, and he dropped his lips to hers for a lingering kiss.

I am with you, he mouthed as the cold spring wind blew into their faces. *Always.*

"I do not fucking deserve you."

Yes, he signed. *You do*.

At that, they dematerialized, both moving in a scatter of molecules even farther north and west, to the flat planes on the far side of the Adirondack Park mountain range.

She felt like she was going into the mouth of Hell.

The Colony had been established because *symphaths* had not been welcome anywhere near vampires for generations—and for good goddamn reason. Her father's side of her bloodline was a devil-in-no-disguise. Members of the subspecies were sociopaths with special powers, utterly unconcerned and unconnected to pesky little things like morals, empathy, compassion.

And yup, her brother fit right into that toxic soup.

Re-forming next to a pond that looked like an ad for rural living, she found John was already in place, two deadly guns in his hands, his narrowed eyes scanning the bucolic setting.

The fuck it was a place to relax, though. Despite the bench by the weeping willow and the picnic tables by the bike trail, it was no municipal anything—and nothing you wanted to even pass through, much less cop a squat and hang out at.

But this was the point. It was a trap to bring humans in, a bait so that a switch could happen and toys could be gathered: The entrance into the underground labyrinth of the Colony was that shed over there, a mere thirty yards away. There were about a half dozen of these new outposts spread around the four-hundred-acre area, each camouflaged by the same kind of nothing-going-on-here, stay-awhile snow job. In this particular case, the flimsy, nondescript building by the public bathrooms had a set of stairs, and there was a reason there were no locks on anything, no warnings, no discouragement of human exploration.

Those *symphath* fuckers really knew how to build a better mousetrap, didn't they.

John Matthew tapped her on the shoulder, and as she glanced over, he signed, *Rehv is here. He's going to make sure nothing happens.*

Given the concern in his eyes, her knee-jerk response was along the lines of, *I'm not worried.* But she never could hide anything from her *hellren.*

"Rehv's a good guy," was all she could say.

Well, actually, the king of the *symphaths* was so much more complicated than that. Like her, as a half-breed, he had a combination of characteristics from both the vampire side and the dangerous cesspool of their fathers' DNA. But at least she didn't have to take dopamine to constantly keep herself in check. Unlike her, Rehv had to medicate to stay on level—

The shed door opened, and a figure in blood-red robes stepped out, looking like a gospel singer who'd lost his altar spot.

As the wind changed direction, and she caught

Blade's scent, her fangs descended and she unholstered a gun.

The nasty laugh that came across on the breeze made her question this whole thing: The meeting. The quest she seemed to be falling into. The reality that she felt completely out of control. And as her brother closed the distance, he was just what she remembered, tall and powerfully built, his wavy jet-black hair like a flock of crows orbiting around his head.

Either that or an evil halo.

"The prodigal sister returns," he drawled.

"Spare me the bullshit, okay."

"Is that any way to greet your bloodline?" Blade looked at John Matthew. "And who is this? Wait, let me guess, he's your—"

Blade didn't get a chance to finish what was no doubt a doozy of an insult, likely with a sexual innuendo chaser. John Matthew had at the *symphath* in the blink of an eye—one second standing back from the other male, the next grabbing her brother around the throat with a thick forearm and putting one of his muzzles right to her "bloodline's" temple.

In the silence that followed, Xhex thought . . . *Yeeeeeeah, this was among the reasons she'd mated the guy.*

Meanwhile, Blade, a.k.a. Horace to the Colony, didn't blink an eye. He just smiled at her, his fangs long and white.

"So he's bonded, has he," was the response.

"Yup," she said. "And I'm not going to feel bad if he puts a bullet through your frontal lobe. He *will* get a couple really good blow jobs out of it, though."

John Matthew's brows popped. Then he mouthed, *Niiiiiiiiiiiiiiiice.*

Blade wasn't as impressed. "Oh, but then you won't have what you came for, will you. Such a waste of time traveling up here from that gilded cage you live in on that mountain. And consider the dry-cleaning bills—it's windy out here so my gray matter is going to end up on your leather, too . . . sister mine."

"I'm sure there are other ways to find out what I need to know."

"Are there?"

"Always."

"Then tell him to pull the trigger. Right now. Go on."

Xhex ground her molars. "Stop playing games, Blade, it's boring."

"Oh, I think this is quite fun, actually." Blade hummed a couple of bars of the *Jeopardy!* theme. "And I'm happy to tell you what you need to know, but your hubby is going to have to take this piece of metal off my temple."

After a moment, she nodded at John Matthew, and her mate stepped off so fast, Blade had to catch his balance. As he straightened himself, his sanguine robing swung forward, looking like it was alive and trying to lunge at Xhex.

Her brother glanced at John Matthew. "You know I'm named after a vampire killer, don't you."

"He's not going to care," Xhex cut in. "And it's just your nickname."

Blade ignored her. "Cat got your tongue there, big man? Or are you just the strong, silent stud type."

"Tell me about the lab," she demanded. "There's another one, isn't there. And it's somewhere around here."

With a twist of the head, Blade transferred his focus to her. And for an instant—just an instant—she could have sworn that his left eye twitched like he was having some kind of an emotional reaction. He hid that shit quick, though. And she couldn't have guessed what it had been.

"Yes, there is a lab. And it is up and running again."

Behind her own facade of composure, Xhex was aware that her insides had liquefied from terror. But two could play at the all-fine game.

"So where is it." When Blade didn't answer, she stepped up to him. "You're a half-breed, too, 'brother mine.' So don't pretend your guilt isn't showing. It bothered you when they gave me over to the humans—"

"The hell it did—"

"—and it still does." She laughed tightly. "And that's the reason you came out here. It's not because Rehv made you. He can't make you do shit. You still feel bad and you figure if you tell me what you know, it gets you off the hook."

As Blade's eyes narrowed, she shook her head. "FYI, it doesn't bother me that you're a self-serving sonofabitch. It's actually the only reason I'd trust any word out of your goddamn piehole tonight."

"Aren't you a little *symphath*, sister." Except then Blade looked away. And looked back. "And I don't feel any guilt at all."

Xhex put her forefinger to the center of her brother's chest. "I know what's in here. I see you, brother."

When Blade slapped her hand away, John Matthew re-leveled his right-handed weapon directly at the other male's skull.

Blade glanced over at the forty's barrel. "Please. Spare me." Then he refocused on Xhex and stopped with the bullshit. "I don't know the details, but I can tell you where to go to get them. Maybe. There's someone who knows, and if you're a good little girl, they'll talk to you. But that's all on you."

"If you double cross me, the Black Dagger Brotherhood will *ahvenge* my death. You know that, right. And Rehv will not stop them."

In the silence that followed, she wondered whether the male was going to try to bravado something to that. But he didn't. Because he knew it was true.

Blade just crossed his arms over his robes. "You have to go to Deer Mountain. In Walters. I'll have the person meet you on the main trail. I'll arrange everything."

Xhex inclined her head. "Fair enough."

"You'll have to go alone."

"I'm not afraid," she said grimly. "And again, I'd think carefully about what you line up. You fuck with me and the shitstorm that will fall on your head from the Brotherhood will make Armageddon look like a tea party."

On that cheerful note, she and John Matthew dematerialized up, up, and away. To say leaving was a relief was an understatement.

To say she was looking forward to whatever came next . . . was pure insanity.

But sometimes, you had to do shit you didn't want.

So you could sleep at day.

TWENTY-THREE

THE FOLLOWING MORNING, at 4:23 a.m., Lydia stepped out of her back door and looked to the trees. Then she checked around what she could see of the property.

Locking things behind herself, she zipped her keys in the pocket of her windbreaker and pulled the waistband of her running tights up. With her sports bra on and a nylon shirt, she had created an illusion that she was just a runner out for an early morning jog—and also ensured that if she had to beat feet out of a bad situation, she had the right gear on.

That was the thought going through her mind as she—

There might have been no moonlight because of clouds, but the veil had come to the sky, the sacred dawn preamble glowing through the bare-limbed trees and fluffy pine boughs off to the east.

Just as the shimmer registered in Lydia's eyes, at the moment her gaze shifted up and zeroed in on its source, a figure walked out of the trees, Daniel's broad shoulders and strong legs creating a dark shadow in the midst of the mountain's mysterious gleam.

If you want to see your future, she heard in her head, *go into the forest at the veil, and what is your due shall come unto you.*

Daniel stopped halfway up the lawn. "Right on time."

The sound of his voice snapped her out of the spell, freeing her from the lock-in of an ancient proverb she told herself she did not believe in.

Stepping forward, she tried to make like she was as cool and calm as the morning—

"I'd like it noted," he said as she came up to him.

"What noted?"

Daniel tapped the back of his wrist. "My on-time bit." He bowed a little. "And I'd offer you my arm, but it seems forward. So let's just do this."

"Okay, yup. Right—"

Shut up, she told herself.

"Where's your bike?" she asked.

"Right back where I was. I'll show you."

Together, they went into the trees, and she glanced around at where his tent had been. Or at least where she thought it had been. There was no sign he'd spent the night anywhere in the forest.

"Tidy camper," she remarked.

"You better believe it. Harley's over here."

The motorcycle was half-draped with a camouflage tarp that matched the woodland's palette of grays and browns and greens, and Daniel pulled the covering completely off. As he folded it up, he asked her something and she responded, but she didn't track the conversation.

The next thing she knew, he was throwing a leg over the seat and looking across his shoulder at her. As his mouth moved, she heard nothing. It was as if the world had lost its speakers, a stereo with vital components unplugged.

It was the light. It was . . . the veil.

As she stared at him, he had a halo around his head and upper body, and the illumination was so pronounced, she blinked—and then had to put her hands up so her eyes weren't blinded.

"Lydia?"

"The light is so bright."

"What light?"

Feeling like a fool, she forced herself to drop her arms—and frowned. "Oh . . . it's gone now. The illumination's faded."

"You okay? You having a migraine or something?"

No, that wasn't it.

I was wrong about the wolf in the woods the other morning, she thought. *You, Daniel Joseph, are my future.*

"I'm fine," she whispered. "I don't get headaches like that."

"You're lucky." He straightened the bike out of its lean on the kickstand, and jumped on one boot to start the engine, the growling purr shocking even though there was no reason for it to be. "Hop on."

Coming even closer, she tried to balance as she lifted one leg and attempted to get it over the full saddlebags.

"Use me." He put out his arm. "I'll keep you right."

Putting her hand on his bicep, she got herself on the bike, the sloping seat bringing her tight to his backside. As the scent of him flooded her nose, she closed her eyes briefly—

On the back of her lids, all she saw was the profile of him spotlit against the mysterious, brilliant illumination.

As she cursed and popped open her eyes, she rubbed her face.

"You okay back there?" he said. "I don't wear helmets anywhere, by the way. But I'm a licensed driver and you can hold on to me."

When he hit the gas, she jerked back, and instinctively her hands went to his waist. But after that, he was careful with the speed, finding the bumpy way over to the dirt road she'd told him to use, the one that, ironically, took them to McBridge's property— and from there, out to a side lane that intersected with the county main drag.

Once on the asphalt, he gunned the bike, and for a moment, she was able to forget where they were going and what they were going to do. It was just the man, the bike, and the bracing morning air, so clean, so cold, so clear. As they zoomed along, the trees whipped by on either side of the road, and the scents of the forest and the earth entered her blood.

Racing, everything racing. Her heart. Her mind.

Her body.

Turning her head to the side, she rested her cheek on his back. As unsettling as the light show had been, this . . . this felt normal. This felt right.

You know, except for the fact that they were going to trespass on a hotel's property.

But no worries there. It wasn't like they hadn't done some breaking and entering before.

"Shit," she said into the roar of the wind.

◆　◆　◆

Daniel was not a morning person. Never had been. But it was interesting how Lydia had turned him into a crack-of-asser. And as for this little road trip? With her holding on to him and leaning into his back? He was tempted to just keep going.

To like, fucking California.

Too soon, she was straightening and tapping on his shoulder. "The trailhead's up here," she shouted into his ear.

He cut the gas and glided them into a parking area that had a rustic bathroom, a carved sign announcing the trail's name, and not a whole helluva lot more.

Heading around behind the loo, he tucked the motorcycle by the cistern tank. It wasn't a total snow job, more of a less-obvious than truly-hidden. But whatever. Better than leaving the Harley out in the open.

As he cut the engine, Lydia dismounted, and wasn't that a loss of colossal proportions. Forced to follow suit, when all he really wanted to do was have her up against him for so much longer, he got off and pulled his jeans up.

"Lead on," he said as he snagged his key.

With a nod, Lydia took off for the trail, striding fast, throwing out those long legs of hers. He picked up his pace and stayed right with her. After going a good distance, she tugged at his sleeve and drew him into the forest proper. That was when the incline started, the ground underfoot rising, becoming more rocky.

The light from the east gathered in intensity and that shit was bad news.

Actually, this whole thing was a bad idea, but she was the type who would do it without him.

So she was going to do it with him.

Just as Daniel was wondering how they'd know where the hotel property was, a twenty-foot-tall chain-link fence with "No Trespassing" signs presented itself.

"Let me guess," he said as he tossed some ground cover on the links to make sure it wasn't electrified. "We've reached the up-and-over part of our adventure."

She glanced at him. "This fence goes on for five miles. And the only entrance has a guard station."

"Are you going to be okay climbing—" Daniel shook his head. "Or . . . you could just go right ahead there."

Lydia was like a cat, clawing up the fence like she'd been a gymnast in an earlier life. And he started to follow her—when he froze.

"Wait," he said.

When she ignored him, he threw up a hand and snagged her ankle. "Stop."

She looked down at him. "What's wrong."

His head slowly shook of its own volition. And to make it seem like he'd picked up something definitive in the environment, he made a show of looking around.

But it was an internal thing telling him no, they shouldn't go up there.

"Lydia, we can't do this."

"What are you—" She shook his hold free and focused on the top of the fence. "I'm going without you then—"

"No! You can't—"

At that moment, a vehicle's headlights pierced through the dimness of the early morning.

"Get down," he ordered. "Right now."

Lydia let go and he caught her in midair, taking her down to the ground and covering her with his body. As he stopped breathing, and so did she, they both looked to the road on the far side of the fence. The truck that passed by them was white with some kind of logo on the side.

And it wasn't the only one.

The construction vehicles came next, trailers busing in bucket loaders, cranes, diggers. They were like a marching band of earth-moving equipment, and he had to wonder why it was all being brought in this early.

"Are they breaking ground on another place?" Lydia whispered.

The smell of diesel fumes wiped out the earth and pine scents, and the rumbling of the weight vibrated up through the ground.

It must have been fifteen huge hunks of machinery.

After the parade was over, neither he nor Lydia moved. But how did they know there weren't more coming?

"What are they doing here so early?" she asked.

"Let's keep going—but we stay on this side of the fence. Even if we're seen, it's not their business because we're not on their land—"

Daniel looked down at her, intending to continue. But as he stared into her face, the feel of her breasts against his chest and of his thigh in between her legs made him realize that but for all their clothes, he'd be inside of her.

Well, assuming they weren't just chain-links away from all kinds of trespassing fun.

As her eyes locked on his mouth, he shook his head.

"Man," he murmured. "Wrong place, wrong time, huh?"

With a curse, he got up and offered her his hand. As she took it, he helped her to her feet, and enjoyed the sight of her flushed cheeks. Hot as she was, hot as she made him, there was a reserve to her that he liked getting under.

"Fucking pity, really," he said as they started walking.

They'd gone about five hundred yards farther when they came into range of the massive clearing, the bald earth like a mountain case of alopecia. The builders were setting their foundation on a flat ridge that ran in a straight shot about two thirds up the elevation to the summit. Down below, the lake that marked the valley was going to be a great view for all the easterly facing rooms—

"Fuck," he hissed. "What is that?"

Lydia saw what he did at the same moment, and they stopped together: A person was at the chain-link fence, and totally absorbed in what they were doing . . . with a set of bolt cutters.

Whoever they were, they were systematically cutting the links—

"Rick?" Lydia called out. "What the hell are you doing?"

TWENTY-FOUR

LYDIA RECOGNIZED THE gray and black jacket. And as she said Rick's name, the figure with the bolt cutters jerked up from the fence.

The vet's features were recognizable even in the veil and the shock that hit his face was exactly what was going through Lydia's mind.

"What are you doing?" she repeated as she walked forward.

He sat back with a kind of defeat—and that was when she saw the duffel bag. Not his medical bag, but one just as big.

As she stood over him, he didn't say anything, just shook his head.

It was with a sense of disassociation that she knelt down by the duffel. The thing had a set of twin zippers around the top flap, and as she drew them back, the access panel of the bag opened to reveal . . .

"What is this," she said as a chill went down her spine.

And yet she knew.

"Oh, God, Rick. This is a bomb."

The pipes were duct-taped together, sealed at both ends, and connected to an old-model cell phone.

He rose to his feet and dropped the bolt cutters like a zombie. And as he just stared straight ahead through the chain-links to the hotel's property, it was as if all his consciousness had funneled out of his body.

A big set of hands entered Lydia's field of vision.

Daniel gathered the handles of the bag and lifted the weight out of Rick's reach. As Lydia tracked the movement, she realized that there was a gun in Daniel's free hand. Down at his thigh.

So she hadn't imagined that back at Peter Wynne's house.

"I'm sorry," Rick said in a detached voice. "I don't know what I'm doing here."

Somehow, she believed him, and it was strange, how clarity came to a person. Because as Lydia stood up, too, she realized . . . no, she wouldn't do anything to stop the hotel. She wouldn't resort to murder. Sure, in the hyperbolic hypothetical, the vow to kill was a way of giving validation and airspace to her anger, her desire for revenge, her heartbreak.

But when it came to a black duffel bag toting a homemade IED?

No, she would not take things that far.

"Please don't do this," she said to Rick. "I know you're full of rage. I'm the same—"

The laugh that came back at her was harsh and he looked over at her. "You don't know what I feel. And that's always been the problem."

"I don't understand."

"It's you, Lydia." His eyes shifted over to Daniel. "It's always been her."

"Me, what?"

Rick shook his head again and didn't stop staring at Daniel. "Jesus, even in my moment, she still doesn't see me. Be careful, my man. She's unlike any other woman you'll ever meet—and I don't mean that in a good way."

Lydia rubbed her eyes. "Rick, you're talking nonsense here—"

"So what are you going to do?" the man demanded. "Call Eastwind? Turn me in?"

Daniel spoke up. "Don't know why we would. You were just doing a little trimming. Landscaping. This kind of thing. And it's not like you're even on the property."

Rick seemed taken aback. "Why the hell would you protect me? Then again, I'm not much of a rival, am I—"

"Just stop this whole thing." Lydia swiped her palms in front of herself. "Everything. Let's all go home."

"You're an accessory to my crime." As Rick pointed to the cut in the fence, the smile on his face was haunting. "It's probably the only thing we'll do together, isn't it. Kind of ironic."

"You're not thinking right. We're going to go our separate ways now, but we're taking the bag. You need to talk to someone, get some help. I can ask around—"

"For a friend, right," he said. "You'd be asking for a friend."

Lydia put her hand on his shoulder. "Because you are one. Rick, you don't know me. You're not in love with me. If you have feelings, they're based on a fantasy."

Oh, God, she thought as she glanced at Daniel. Words of advice she should take herself.

And how could she not have noticed Rick's obsession? Then again, he had always seemed so professional and intense about his own job. In fact, whenever she had been around, he'd usually been irritated.

Then again, unrequited love could do that . . .

"You don't know the real me," she repeated.

"Yeah, well, you don't know me, either," he shot back. "And there are a lot of things a smart person like you can extrapolate in life, but you can never see into the heart of another. Not really. Not unless they speak of it themselves. So call Eastwind, or don't call him. Get me the number of a therapist because that'll be *so* helpful. Forget this ever happened. I don't really care anymore. Just do *not* presume to know what I'm going through right now, okay? I don't blame you for not wanting me, but I'm not going to be misrepresented."

As he glared at her, she thought about what he'd come here to do.

"Fine." She put her hands on her hips. "Then how about this. Hurting people is not the way to get any woman's attention."

"You hate that hotel."

"But not the innocent construction workers who are working here. You'd injure people who are just earning their living. That's unforgivable on all levels."

Rick shook his head. Then looked away. After a tense silence, he said, "Your wolf has come around, by the way. His levels are fine. I took him off life support at midnight and watched him for three hours. I also fed him and he drank. He's making a full recovery. I would say he can be released in another twenty-four hours."

"That's what we have to focus on. And we'll let the law handle the rest. Okay?"

As Rick didn't respond, she found herself willing him to agree. To renounce his sick plan to pay her some kind of tribute, to get her attention . . . to earn her love.

"Please," she begged. "Let's just let the law handle everything with the hotel."

"That was not how you felt the other morning."

"Well, it's how I feel now."

After a long moment, Rick's head turned toward her. "I'm fucking exhausted. I haven't slept for days. I'm going to go back to my house and take a shower. I'll be waiting for Eastwind there. I know you're going to call him because you always do the right thing. It's one of your very best qualities. You *always* do the right thing."

"Rick . . ."

As he stared at her, his voice broke. "Promise me you'll do the right thing. I can't fake any of this anymore."

Without waiting for a response, the man turned away and started walking. Lydia had a thought that he had no idea where he was going. Maybe that was right, maybe that was wrong.

"Come on," Daniel said. "Let's go back the way we came."

She glanced over her shoulder at the cut in the chain-links. Then she picked up the bolt cutters.

Daniel held the bag open as she put them inside. She was the one who pulled the zippers closed.

As they made their way back to his bike, Lydia was silent until just before they reached the trailhead.

"I need to go talk to Rick," she said.

"I'll destroy all this. Don't worry."

"I have to see what's inside properly."

Daniel set the duffel down and opened things up. As she turned her phone's flashlight on and shined it in, nothing had changed. The bundle of pipes, and the wires, and the cell phone were right where they'd been.

"This is a bomb, right? Are we safe?"

"Yeah, but I unplugged the wires from the detonator." Daniel jogged the bag. "Hear that rattle? There

are nails in those pipes. He didn't intend to hurt people, Lydia. He wanted to kill them."

◆ ◆ ◆

Daniel didn't need to ask where they were going next.
When Lydia called the sheriff and had to leave a message, it was no shocker that she told him to drive to the
man's own house. Conveniently, Eastwind lived on a
farm only four minutes away, and when they came up
to the street it was on, the fact that the gravel drive was
marked with an "Eastwind Lane" sign made it clear the
sheriff and his ancestors had been on the property for
a long time.

The home turned out to be a 1930s-era, two-story
job, the white siding and shiny black accents well-
kept to the point of being suburban. Back behind the
house, there was a barn and a fenced-in meadow, but
no animals were anywhere around.

As the Harley's headlight flashed across the front of
the Colonial, all the windows were dark. Then again,
it was quarter of six in the morning. And before they
could fully come to a stop, Lydia jumped off the seat
and strode to the front door. Grabbing on to the lion's
head knocker, she worked that brass to the beat of
an AC/DC song—and the effort paid off. Moments
later, Eastwind answered, a navy-blue flannel bathrobe
pulled around his trim body, his feet in slippers, his
long hair still braided as if it might never be allowed to
go loose.

Lydia was talking fast, and Eastwind was trying to slow her down, when Daniel decided to bring visual aids to the party—because it was going to make things so much more comprehensible.

Tragically, multi-pipe bombs spoke for themselves in all kinds of situations.

As he stepped forward with the duffel, Eastwind looked over, but not for long, like Daniel was a side issue.

"—bag. Daniel has it—" Lydia glanced over her shoulder. "Oh, good. Will you show him what's inside."

Daniel did the reveal, tilting the thing forward so that the lantern light overhead shined inside.

"Rick's going home." Lydia crossed her arms over her chest like being anywhere near the homemade explosive made her uncomfortable. "We need to go talk to him."

"I'll get dressed and go over there." Eastwind put his hand out. "And I'll accept that duffel bag, thank you."

"Happy to turn it over to anybody," Daniel said as he passed the shit to the sheriff.

"We're going there, too." Lydia put her hand up. "And stop. I've worked with Rick for two years. He's a friend and he's . . . confused. Upset. He's not making sense."

"How did you both know he was on the hotel property?"

Eastwind kept the question casual, but Daniel

wasn't fooled. The man had eyes like the lenses of a camera, and they recorded everything.

"We went for an early morning hike." Lydia shrugged. "When we came up to Corrington's chain-link fence, we didn't want to trespass, so we just went along the outside of it. We found Rick using bolt cutters to get in. They're in the duffel."

"And he just told you he was going home?" the sheriff demanded. "Why didn't you stay with him and call me?"

"He looked beat down. Exhausted—and he knew I was getting in touch with you. He said . . ."

"He said what."

"That I always do the right thing. Look, he was aware that we had to turn him in. And we got the bomb—"

"How do you know he didn't have more of them in his car? At his house?"

Lydia opened her mouth. Closed it. Then she shook her head. "He's not a danger to anybody else. And I'm going to go there now and make sure he's all right. He's—"

"He's in love with her," Daniel cut in. "And he thought instead of a dozen roses, he'd blow up the hotel. That's why she wants to go over there. She feels partially responsible, and from your point of view, I'd want her around. She'll get through to him like no one else can. I saw it myself."

"He knows what he was going to do was wrong." Lydia looked down. "But that's no defense."

"No," Eastwind said. "It's not. And you don't go over there without me. I'll be five minutes to get dressed."

As the sheriff went back into his house, Daniel returned to his bike. Threw a leg over. Waited with a grip on the handlebars.

When he felt Lydia get on behind him, he jump-started the engine. "We're not waiting for him, are we."

"No," Lydia said. "We aren't."

TWENTY-FIVE

RICK'S PLACE WAS not far from the center of town, and as Lydia told Daniel where to go, she thought of all the little moments she'd shared with the WSP's vet: Laughs in the break room with Candy. Tracking the wolf packs through the preserve on camera and out on the mountain. Tagging and releasing the wolves.

Rick had been every bit as committed to their mission as she was, and he'd always seemed to have his head on straight—although now, as she thought about it, he had been tense and more irritable lately. She'd assumed it was because of the financial struggles of the WSP and the way he was being forced to economize on his supplies.

There clearly had been something else going on, and God, she prayed it wasn't only what he felt for her. If it was, then Daniel was right. She did feel responsible, even though she had never encouraged him, never led him on.

With a sad curse to herself, she remembered him

coming through the forest just the other morning, as she had laid by the poisoned male, so disapproving, so competent.

She had never expected them to end up here.

Wherever "here" was.

Although surely, he was going to be arrested.

Rick's cottage, which he owned, not rented, was set back from the road, in a field that bloomed with wildflowers during the spring and summer. There was no garage and his Jeep was parked by the side of the little house. When Daniel pulled up behind that vehicle, Lydia got off, but didn't go right for the door.

Which was open, even though it was cold.

As dread clawed up her spine, Lydia searched the windows with her eyes. All the drapes were pulled— which hadn't been the case ever before. When she'd given him a ride home or had to drop something off, she'd always been able to see inside the place. But maybe it was just because the winter had been so cold and he was trying to lower his heating bills.

"Stay here," she heard herself say.

"If you need me, let me know."

She nodded in a distracted way and went over to the flagstone path. Following the gray and cranberry pattern up to the door, she swallowed hard.

"Rick?" she said loudly. "It's me, can I come in—"

The sound of the gun going off was so loud, it rang in her ears.

"*Rick!*"

As the echo of the *boom!* faded, she rushed inside and skidded on the rug in the parlor. Her breath was loud in her ears, and she looked around in a panic, barely noticing the furniture.

"Oh, my God, oh, my God . . ." She kept repeating the words, a mantra that prevented her from panting and going light-headed.

"Rick?"

Walking forward, she went into the kitchen in the back. No messes, no clutter, no dishes in the sink or things out on the counter. It was too neat, like he'd put everything in order before he'd left—because he hadn't expected to ever come back.

The house was the polar opposite of Peter's—and yet she felt like they were just different sides to an evil coin.

The gunpowder smell reached her nose as she was turning to leave the kitchen. And that was when she saw through a narrow doorway . . . a dark room full of bookshelves. With the drapes all pulled, a computer screen was its only source of illumination, the ghostly blue glow drawing her forward.

Beneath her feet, the floorboards creaked, and as sweat broke out on her forehead, she brushed it away with her sleeve. Her lungs struggled to pump, and with her throat as tight as it was, she had to open her mouth and suck air in.

As soon as she stepped through into the study, she saw the feet sticking out from the far side of the desk.

Rick's running shoes were lax, the treads muddy, the toes out to the sides.

"Rick," she choked as she leaped forward—

The shotgun had been dropped on his chest, as if he had been sitting on the floor when he'd pulled the trigger. And it was obvious he had put the muzzle in his mouth—

Crashing down beside him, she covered her own mouth. Then she wrenched to the side, planted her palms on the rug, and dry heaved.

With eyes squeezing shut, she continued to see the details of the face with horrible clarity, the jaw vaporized, the nose gone, one of the eyes hanging loose.

Her friend, the man she had known and worked beside, the vet she respected and valued, was no more.

And it felt like all her fault—

Warm hands drew her back, and she collapsed into the compassion being offered, sobs racking her torso as she was held against a strong chest. With her head angled away from the horror, and her body supported, she couldn't think of a reason to pull herself together, and as she let out a moan, a low, deep voice spoke to her in soothing syllables.

Although she couldn't follow the words, Daniel's murmuring was the only thing that kept her on the planet.

He was still holding her when Eastwind walked in.

"We haven't touched anything," she heard Daniel

say. "And he pulled the trigger just as she got to the open front door."

Lydia intended to lift her head and speak.

But in the end, she had no voice.

◆ ◆ ◆

Later that day, much later, Lydia walked to work.

After everything that happened, she needed the fresh air, and with her car at Paul's Garage, she had no other option than showing up on the back of Daniel's bike.

Considering Candy was the only person on-site, it probably would have been okay, but she felt like she had to breathe by herself for a while. God, there seemed to be fifty percent less oxygen in the atmosphere than there usually was.

As she went along the side of the county road, she was aching from head to foot, proof, she supposed, of the mind/body connection: She wasn't injured. She hadn't overexercised. She wasn't sick. But her muscles throbbed as if she had been put in a tumble jar, no surface on her left unbattered.

She and Daniel had stayed for a couple of hours at Rick's house, out on his lawn, in the sunshine. She had remained sitting up, her arms balanced on her knees until her elbows had lost feeling and so had her dangling hands. Beside her, Daniel had stretched out flat on the mostly brown grass, his legs crossed at the ankles, one arm under his head. He had been like a dozing dog, lifting his lids at sounds that were outside the bandwidth of chirping birds, occasional cars out on the county road, and dim conversation inside the house.

The two of them had watched the other sheriff's officers come. Had witnessed the coroner arriving in her boxy van. And when it had come time for the black body bag to be removed from the house on a gurney, she and Daniel had gotten to their feet.

It had been incomprehensible that Rick Marsh had been alive just that morning, in the veil. At that fence line. With a bomb in a duffel bag.

But some things shouldn't be easy to make sense of.

Sheriff Eastwind was the only other one who had stayed the whole time. And during one of the lulls, he had taken their statements. Around noontime, she and Daniel had finally left, with him dropping her off at her house before he'd gone into the WSP for a shower.

They hadn't said much. He seemed to understand that she needed space.

Not like it had helped. At all.

Back at her house, she had eaten some cereal and discovered she was ravenously hungry. An old box of Near East's rice pilaf had solved that problem in a calorically dense, nutritionally deficient kind of way. And as she'd sat down to eat, she'd thought of Daniel and his health kick . . .

Coming back to the present, she looked around

at the deep green of the conifers and the gray of the road and the bright yellow dotted line that cleaved the pavement in two. Overhead, the mostly cloudless sky was a resplendent blue, and the glinting yellow sunshine was proof that no matter how long and hard the winter, the spring always came.

As her eyes started to tear up again, she wiped at them.

The good news was that she was coming up to the WSP's driveway, and she could focus on opening the mailbox and taking out whatever was inside. Pulling the black door down, she reached in for the bundle of letters and pouches—and the normalcy of picking up the daily delivery felt all wrong.

She cradled the modest load to her chest as she walked down to the main building.

In the parking area, Candy's car and Daniel's Harley were side by side.

Rick's Jeep would never be under that tree again.

Lydia didn't go to the front of the building. She took the mail to the clinic entrance. It was locked, so she used her key, and she opened the door slowly. Motion-activated ceiling lights came on, flickering to life and illuminating the otherwise dark area. Everything was so neat, so clean, the stainless steel counters gleaming, the cupboards closed up, the glass fronts of the cabinets showing rows of medications, trackers, equipment, supplies. Randomly, she pulled open a few drawers and doors. There was nothing that she didn't expect, just all sorts of sterile syringes in unopened boxes, bandages in their packaging, and plastic-covered surgical instruments in trays.

With a sense of dread, she put the mail down and turned to Rick's office.

Walking over to the open door, she flipped the wall switch on. His desk and chair were mismatched and worn, but everything was spotless and organized, his old computer monitor and keyboard off to one side, his landline phone beside them, the office lamp over in the corner. There were no papers out. No folders. And when she opened one of the drawers . . .

"What the hell?" she muttered as she went to the next one down.

They were all empty. Not even a stray pen, a pad of paper, or a document clip.

As she straightened from the desk, she looked around. There were no personal effects anymore: The pictures of him on various hikes around the country and bike rides were gone. His extra jacket. His WSP branded fleece. His dog calendar. His Hydro Flask and his nylon insulated lunch sack.

Just as with his house, he'd intended to never come back here. He'd cleared the space for the next person to hold the position.

Rick had been on a suicidal mission with that bomb.

Putting her head in her hands, she took a shuddering breath. Then she cleared her throat and went to the exam room the wolf had been in.

The crate was empty, the monitoring equipment put away, the space disinfected and ready for its next use.

With her heart in her throat, she went to a door that was mostly Plexiglas. On the far side of the foggy insert, she could see the transitional pen that was used for recovering wolves about to be re-released into the preserve.

Lydia's wolf was across the way, up on his feet and looking directly at her. By the doorjamb, a clipboard with a log listed notes in Rick's handwriting: When the last feeding had occurred and what had been offered and eaten; how much water had been taken; observations on how alert the animal was.

She ran her fingertips over the printing. Then she touched the Bic pen that was on a string.

The door was locked at the knob, and as she opened things, she could hear Rick's voice in her head yelling at her, telling her that she shouldn't get close to the wolf.

With a sad smile, she ignored the warnings she had heard so often.

As she stepped into the enclosure, she glanced around. The walls were concrete to about three feet high, and on top, they were chain-link to a good ten feet up. Fresh spring air, sweetened by the sun, blew in and around the pen.

The wolf's eyes remained locked on her, glowing and golden. Like the sun, she thought. And though his ears were pricked forward, his hackles were relaxed, his breathing even, and his lithe body loose and un-tensed.

"Hello," she said softly as she sank down.

She was careful to leave the door open behind her just in case she was reading this wrong. But she knew she wasn't.

"You look so much better. I'm going to make you your dinner tonight. Then tomorrow . . . we're going to let you get back to where you belong."

The wolf lowered its head and took a step forward. And then another. One of his ears twitched as if he had an itch on it, and he licked his jowls.

Lydia put her palms out. "You look so much better. You're going to live."

The tears that rolled down her cheeks fell onto the earth as she spoke to him.

The wolf stopped mere inches from her hands, and she reached out to him, touching his shoulders.

"You know who I am, don't you?" she said. "Yes, yes, you do."

He moved his body against her, circling, his ears now easy and loose, his fur both rough and soft as he pushed into the petting she offered him.

"You had a helluva vet," she whispered. "I need you to know that. A helluva vet saved your life."

TWENTY-SIX

LATER, DANIEL WOULD wonder what exactly called him around to the back of the WSP's main building. He'd been out in the equipment building, working on the ATV to get the fuel tank fixed, when something tickled his instincts. He'd brushed off the sensation, as if it were a fly, but there had been no denying the prickling awareness.

No ignoring it, either.

Things made a little more sense as he hit the porch that faced the lake view . . . and looked down to some kind of enclosure.

There, inside a pen, Lydia was crouched by a wolf, her head right next to the animal's, her hands on its body as it circled, circled, circled in front of her. The two were oblivious to the world, in a moment of their own, as tears streamed down her face and dotted the blue jeans she had on.

Daniel's first instinct was to push the wolf out of the way. But not to save her.

It was so he could be the one she was petting.

Instead of giving in to that jealousy, he stayed where he was, as under her spell as the other animal was, that magic Rick had warned about, and that Daniel had experienced himself, blooming in the air as if she were a holy object emanating a benediction.

A wild creature brought to heel in the palm of her open hand.

Daniel was the same.

Except he did not want to be tamed. He could not *afford* to be, even if he'd wanted it.

With a curse, he backed off—and knew it was time to get back to work. Heading over to his bike, he mounted up, cranked the engine over, and tooled down the drive to get off the property. When he came to the county road, he went to the left and gunned the Harley into a proper roar.

The cold air felt good on his face, and the vibration of the handlebars in his hands was so familiar, it calmed him.

See? He was free, after all.

Or at least that's what he told himself. The reality was different. Images from the morning kept hitting his mind's eye with shrapnel-snapshots, the worst being what Lydia had looked like down on the floor with the body.

Daniel was never going to forget taking her in his arms, holding her and staring over her head at what that man had done to himself. With everything Daniel had seen over the course of his life, you'd figure he'd handle the shit better. Instead, it was haunting him.

Although it was more about Lydia.

He didn't want her to see things like that. Ever.

Up ahead, the town center, such as it was, came into view, and as he approached the diner/grocery store, he pulled into the mostly empty parking lot and checked his watch. A little before two p.m.

Fucking hell, he felt like it was three in the morning.

Entering the grocery half of the building, he went to the cashier. As she looked up from the book she was reading, she smiled like she'd pulled a good fish out of what she'd assumed was an empty pond.

"Well, hello there, Daniel." She patted her bottle-blond hair that had been sprayed into place like the top of a soft-serve ice cream cone. "How's a man doing today? I'm Susan, in case you don't remember."

He felt like he needed to say *howdy*. "Afternoon."

"You looking for lottery tickets?"

"No. I'm here for—"

"Because you look like a lucky man."

"Do I?" He only tossed that out because he sensed there was a quota of back-and-forth required before you could buy anything. "I'm not sure I have an opinion one way or the other about my luck."

Liar, he thought to himself.

"Maybe that's why you're lucky," she said.

"How so."

"Luck is like a cat." Susan wagged her forefinger

at him, as if she were correcting a child who should know better. "The more you go after it, the more it eludes you. You can chase what doesn't want you, but you only catch what chooses to be in your palm."

In his mind, he remembered that wolf stroking its fur on Lydia's outstretched hands, her fingers tangling in its thick coat, her beautiful face luminous with the sadness she felt over a man who had probably deserved her love, but hadn't gotten it.

Daniel was willing to bet she was blaming herself, like if she'd felt differently the vet would still be alive. Even though none of it was her fault.

"Or your wallet, as the case may be."

He came back to attention. "What?"

"Your wallet is where you'd want that luck."

"You're right." He pointed behind her, but not to the scratch offs that gleamed with foil details. "I'd like a pack of Marlboro reds."

"Soft or hard?"

"Doesn't matter—actually, make that two? And I need a lighter."

"Does the color matter?"

"I need the reds. Not the light packs—"

"No, on the Bic. I got blue, green, yellow, red—"

"Doesn't matter."

Susan chose a red one and swung back around on her stool. Instead of giving him the forty coffin nails and the flint flicker, she held them against her chest—in a way that made him look at her clothes. She had on a casual sweater that was pink and white, and pale blue jeans, and a tiny little silver watch that seemed too dainty for the rest of her. With her hair all coiffed, she was like someone who was going to a prom, but hadn't changed into their flouncy dress yet.

"Are you sure you want to do this?" she asked.

Daniel blinked. "I'm sorry?"

"Look, I sell a lot of cigarettes to a lot of people. And the ones who have quit and are going back to 'em always buy two packs and a fresh lighter. If you were a constant smoker, you'd have plenty of half-filled Bics in your house, your car, all your pockets. And you'd be buying a carton. Or if you just needed something to tide you over until you got home? You'd only buy one pack and no lighter. But here you are—"

He put out a twenty dollar bill. "Will this cover it?"

"See? This is my point. If you were a regular smoker, you'd know how much they are. And no, it won't."

He took out another twenty. "This will cover it, then."

Susan stared across the counter at him. "And if you were starting out, you'd sneak them from someone else."

But at least she took his cash and gave him the cigarettes.

Daniel left before she could hand him his change.

+ + +

Back at the WSP, Lydia gave the wolf a final stroke down his back and then she told him that she'd return at five to fix him dinner and make sure he was okay—as if he spoke English. Yet as she was reclosing the door, she met his eyes . . . and he knew. He knew she was not leaving him forever.

Then again, wolves were like that.

"Soon," she promised. "You'll be back out there very soon."

Shutting things up tight, she locked the knob—

"Is it true, then?" a quiet voice said.

Lydia closed her eyes for a moment. Then she turned around to Candy. The older woman looked every bit her age, her face drooping, her hands worrying the collar of her button-down. Then the knit cuff of her sweater.

"Yes," Lydia answered. "He's gone."

Candy's composure was immediate, a mask of reserve settling over her features. Yet it was impossible not to reach out and put a hand on that shoulder. But what could Lydia say to make any part of it better?

She cleared her own throat. "I just . . ."

Where could she start? With what happened at the chain-link fence? Or maybe what it was like to go into that study and see Rick's running shoes sticking out behind that desk.

How about the gunpowder smell? The blood?

"I don't know what to say," she sighed with defeat.

"He was a good vet," Candy said.

"That's just what I was telling the wolf."

Candy broke away and went to the Plexiglas window to look into the pen. "Is he going to live?"

"Yes. Thanks to Rick."

"I saw you when you were in there with him. I was out on the porch—" Candy jerked back. "Guess he doesn't like all humans, huh."

The snarl that permeated through the door was a low warning.

"He just doesn't know you." Lydia drew the woman away. "I'm going to release him tomorrow morning."

"How?"

"I'm going to tranquilize him. And then take him out into the preserve on the back of the four-wheeler."

Candy's brows dropped. "How much does he weigh?"

"Around two hundred pounds. He's bigger than your average gray wolf."

"And you can lift that kind of dead weight?"

No, Lydia thought.

"I'll take care of that somehow," she said.

"Maybe you can ask Daniel to help."

"Sure—"

"How are we going to get by?" Candy demanded. "I guess the larger question is, how much longer do you think we're going on? I don't mean to be practical, but I have bills to pay. I need to . . . find another job."

Lydia shook her head. "I don't know."

Candy rubbed her short hair, the bright blond

spikes smoothing out under the friction. "I'm sorry. Maybe I shouldn't be bringing this up so soon after . . . well, you know—"

"No, it's okay. Things only stop for the dead, not the living. We need to figure it all out."

"Where the hell is Peter Wynne?"

"I don't know. And that's the truth."

Candy went over to the pile of mail and started going through the bills. "Well, just so you know, I'll stay for however long I have a check." The woman glanced around the clinic area. "And also, I really liked Rick. He was a good man. I don't know why I feel the need to say that out loud, but I do."

"I couldn't agree more. He was . . . a very good man."

"But Peter?" Candy's stare grew hard. "I wouldn't give you a plug nickel for that piece of shit."

They both fell silent for a moment.

Then Lydia said abruptly, "Can I ask you for a favor? I need to borrow your car."

TWENTY-SEVEN

O N THE WAY back from his nicotine purchase, Daniel went past the WSP's driveway. As he continued on, the turnoff he was looking for was slow in coming—or maybe he just wasn't sure what the fuck he was doing and that made everything seem fuzzy and sluggish.

Farlan's Lane was right where they'd left it, and he didn't cut his speed much as he angled in and picked the right of the two dirt tracks. Heading deep into the trees, he went up to where they'd towed Lydia's car from, with Paul of Paul's Garage having done the drag duty.

You had to wonder whether the guy was going to mention to anybody that shit had just been yanked inside the engine. Probably not. Paul seemed like the live and let live kind.

Of course, if he were asked? Who knew.

Killing the engine, Daniel swung a leg free and took the key with him. As he strode forward, he took one of the packs of Marlboros out. The efficiency with which he stripped the plastic proved that a strong past habit could override the "perishable skill" part of almost anything. And as he popped the top and took out one of the filter-first soldiers, he decided that this wagon fall-off was just a temporary thing.

And it wasn't a slip-up. This was a conscious choice.

So he could un-conscious the choice after all this was over.

Or maybe that was un-choice. Not choice. Whatever.

The fact that Susan the checkout woman had picked a matchy-matchy red for the Bic seemed a declaration of her style philosophy. Meanwhile, on his side of the transaction, all he cared about was the flame—

The coughing fit was immediate after the inhale, and as he put the back of his hand to his mouth, he wondered why it was that he always felt hacking your liver up went better if you had something covering the pie hole part of things. It was like a boxer with a punching bag, he supposed.

You gave things a target, not just bald air.

By the third inhale, the disruption eased off, and he felt a buzzing in his head and under his skin. Halfway through the length, he was back in the swing of things, exhaling great streams of smoke like he was a steam engine, a calming coming over him at the same time he felt an intensifying focus.

Not that he'd been confused.

When he came up to the deer stand, he crushed

the lit stub between his forefinger and thumb, the lick of pain something he enjoyed. Then he put the butt in his back pocket and looked toward Peter Wynne's barn—not that he could see much.

Changing directions, he kept going and found the cave where he'd stashed the body easily enough—and the undisturbed nature of that which he had done his best not to disturb was good news.

"Where the fuck were you yesterday?"

At the sound of the voice, he glanced over his shoulder. And casually put his hand in the pocket he kept his gun hidden in.

"Well, if it isn't Mr. Personality," Daniel drawled.

As he turned around, his oldest friend and ally was looking like he had a hair across his ass. Dressed in loose clothing that covered a variety of guns and ammo, those familiar dark eyes were narrowed under the brim of a hey-there's-nothing-unusual-about-me John Deere hat. Other than the fact that the guy's shoulders were big and his jaw like an I beam, everything about him was cultivated to blend in. Escape notice. Remain undetected among the people who passed him by.

"So where the fuck were you?" came the demand.

"Busy. I'm taking up a new hobby."

"Oh, I know. And her name is Lydia Susi."

Daniel took a step forward. "She's not a part of this."

"She's fucking in the middle of it—"

"She's doing nothing but tracking and ensuring the health of the population. That's it. She's not involved."

The smile that came back at him was a knife edge. "Did you get this from her before or after you fucked her—"

Daniel lunged and locked a grip on the front of his buddy's throat. "You want to rephrase that. While you still have a voice box?"

"So. It. Was. During."

The syllables were choked, but there was no fear reaction. No struggle, either.

There was a reason they got along, damn it.

"She is not who we're looking for." Daniel shoved hard, but his buddy's balance was not lost for long. The recovery was nearly immediate. "It's against her principles."

"Oh, then let's just look elsewhere because your girlfriend has some kind of pabulum tattooed on her forehead."

As Daniel tightened the grip on his gun, he had to tell himself to calm the fuck down. "The WSP has no resources. You know that—"

"*You* are out of control."

"Fuck off—"

A ramrod-straight forefinger came at him like a laser beam. "You have a conflict of interest. You think I don't know you're sleeping—"

"On her property, asshole," Daniel snapped. "I'm not in her house."

"Then it's just a matter of time before you're in her bed. I know how this shit goes."

"Because you're such a frickin' genius. Right. I forgot."

"It happened to me once. I got over-involved and I fucked everything up." His buddy's massive torso tilted forward. "You stay separate or I'm taking over. We don't have the time to, or the interest in, rescuing you from a mess of your own creation—"

"You're not in charge."

"You want her killed?" His buddy shrugged. "You care *that* little about the woman? What do you think is going to happen to her."

"She is *not* who we're after."

"Well, the one thing you and I both know for sure? You can't be two of a kind. She's either guilty or she's innocent—but either way, if you keep involving yourself with her, she'll end up dead."

Daniel looked off into the distance. He'd hidden those weapons from the day before, and damn if he didn't wish he had that suppressor.

"So you want to do this?" he said to his buddy in a bored tone. "Or keep talking at me. Because the latter's making *such* a difference in my life."

"You need to recognize your weaknesses, friend."

"And you need to step the fuck off. You don't like what I'm doing, get me removed. Or try to."

On that note, Daniel brought out his cell phone and triggered the flashlight. Ducking down, he entered the shallow cave—

The body was gone.

Like an idiot, he moved the beam around, you know, just in case he had missed the one-hundred-and-eighty-pound sack of no-longer-breathing on the dirt floor.

He leaned back out. "Did you already take him?"

"Take who?" came the response.

"Motherfucker," Daniel muttered.

◆　◆　◆

Lydia didn't have to go as far as she thought she would. She'd been prepared to drive an hour or more. Instead, her destination took only ten minutes of traveling along the network of county roads around the mountain.

And that was a good thing. Time felt tight, like there was a deadline looming. The trouble was, she didn't know what exactly she was supposed to do, where to go, what to hand in to the proverbial professor.

But it wasn't the first time in her life she'd had to figure stuff out alone.

As she coughed for the hundredth time—and thought of Daniel—she didn't know how Candy could stand being in the car. There was so much fragrance packed into the interior that it was like breathing in Funfetti cake, each inhale a dense pack of fake fruit.

Talk about your nose blind—

And that was when the stone wall started. From out of a turn in the road, a fifteen-foot-tall barrier appeared out of nowhere. The rocks that were stacked and mortared were gray, cream, and a blush pink, and the cement that held it all together was a weathered fog color. She imagined that it was very thick, and knew it had been built very recently. No moss or lichen growth.

After what felt like a mile, the locked gates appeared. They were majestic, all twisted black iron that rose to a curlicue cresting, and they were split in half so they could break apart and allow access.

Pulling Candy's car in, she paused by the keypad/speaker. As she put her window down, she wondered if—

The camera was mounted on the wall, its lens angled down at her. She almost waved.

At least she was sure she was in the right place, she thought as she extended her arm to hit the telephone icon.

Before she made contact with the call button, there was a clanking and then a whirring sound, the gates opening as if she were expected. Which she wasn't. She glanced into the rear view. No one was behind her.

But this is why she had come.

Hitting the gas, she proceeded through the bulwark, pulling onto a freshly paved lane bracketed by twin hedges so high and thick, there was no seeing through them: She was in an evergreen chute with no shoulders, and she hoped there was another way in and out of the estate. A delivery truck came at her now? She was going to have to reverse it or—

Everything opened up about fifty yards on, and the expanse of grass was so large and rolling, it was as if she were on a golf course. And then there was the house. Or . . . more like a castle, an American castle that was made of the same stone as the wall out on the road.

Jesus, the mansion was huge, with three or four stories and a front facade that seemed bigger than all of Walters.

The paved driveway made an ambling turn in front of the house, skirting a covered entrance that looked like it should have a pair of soldiers on either side.

Rolling to a stop, she opened her door—

Off in the distance, there was some noise she didn't immediately recognize, but she lost track of it as she checked out the house's facade. Something was off about the windows. Instead of allowing her to see inside, they mirrored the grounds, displaying the lawn, the drive, the fountain. And it wasn't because drapes were drawn and the afternoon light was playing tricks on things. There was a reflective covering on—

The quartet of Doberman pinschers came bolting around the far corner of the mansion, the four of them silent while on full attack, their ears back, teeth bared, and paws eating up the ground cover.

With not a bark, not a growl, they were like bullets through the air.

Lydia jumped back into the car and slammed the door. The window was down—shit! She fumbled with the keys, dropping them then stabbing the wrong one into the ignition.

Just as the dogs skidded into the driver's side, she stabbed the key home, cranked it, and punched the window button.

They jumped up on the glass pane as it was rising up, their fangs flashing, jaws snapping, drool streaking all around—

Just as a helicopter came over the top of the house. The black raptor with its double rotator blades was big as a bus, and whoever was driving—piloting?—the thing brought it down on the grass right in front of Candy's too-sweet-smelling car. The gusts created were so strong, they kicked up waves of dirt that sprinkled the windshield and caused the dogs to close their eyes even as they kept attacking.

Before the blades slowed even a little, a set of stairs unhinged from the smooth body and lowered down.

A woman in black with a cap of icy white hair stepped out and strode forward, the gale-force wind seeming to not bother her in the slightest.

All at once the dogs dropped their aggression and loped to C.P. Phalen, circling behind her and falling into formation, two on each side.

Lydia's heart rate started to ease a bit, especially as

the woman made a hand motion, and the Dobermans took off like a flank of fighter jets, shooting back around to the rear of the house.

Where they no doubt resumed chewing on the bones of a newspaper boy. Or DoorDash driver.

The noise from the helicopter was growing quieter, and given that the guard dogs were out of sight, Lydia opened the car door again and got out.

"Unexpected surprise," C.P. Phalen said over the din.

As the wind streaked Lydia's hair into her face, she batted it away. "I needed to see you."

"You came just in time."

So did you, before your dogs peeled Candy's car like a grape, Lydia thought.

C.P. Phalen smiled. "A little later or earlier and I would have missed you."

At the woman's motion, Lydia followed her under the covered area to the ornate entrance. It was not hard to imagine a grand party at the house, expensive cars pulling up under the porte cochere to discharge all manner of tuxedo'd, gown'd fancy types.

The whole setup was intimidating. But Lydia wasn't leaving until she got what she'd come for.

The mansion, like the stone wall, had clearly been built to look old, but there was no attempt to hide the modern keypad by the door. And when C.P. Phalen put her thumb on the screen, there was a muffled shifting and a clank.

"If someone wants to get in here," the woman said

with a sly smile, "they're going to have to cut my finger off and use it as a key."

On that happy note, she opened the massive iron and glass doors, revealing . . . okay, wow. It might as well have been a hotel lobby: The interior floors and walls were all pale marble, polished and gleaming, and so, too, were the double winged stairs straight ahead. Rooms as big as whole houses extended out from both sides of the space, and crystal fixtures sparkled on the ceilings like galaxies.

But there was no furniture, no rugs, no paintings or sculptures. Anywhere.

"Lydia?"

Reaching up to rub the prickle at the base of her neck, she refocused on C.P. Phalen. In spite of the fact that cap of hair had been in a hurricane, the white-and-gray waves had resettled into their proper place, and the black suit remained perfectly pressed, as if it had just come out of a dry cleaner's.

With a suddenly dry mouth, Lydia swallowed and tried to find her voice. "Rick, our vet, is dead. Peter Wynne is missing. I'm pretty sure I'm next—and you're the only powerful person I know."

TWENTY-EIGHT

S O I'VE JUST moved in."

As C.P. Phalen led the way through what Lydia assumed was a dining room, given the long, narrow nature of the space, the woman's heels made sharp sounds that echoed.

"Or rather, I am moving in." She gave Lydia a smile that did not warm her cool gray eyes. "The furniture is arriving tomorrow in trucks."

Lydia had an image of all the construction equipment funneling down to the hotel site. Then she remembered what Rick had looked like, crouched on the ground with the bolt cutters, working his way up the chain-link fence so he could fit through. With his duffel.

"I've been building the house for over two years," C.P. Phalen continued. "I've always lived in cities, but now, I just want the quiet, the privacy, the freedom you don't get in Manhattan. I'm not married and I have no ties to anyone so the choice was mine and mine alone to make."

The woman pushed through a flap door into some kind of staging area with counter space everywhere and all sorts of glass-fronted cabinets for dishes and crystal.

At least Lydia assumed it was for setting up big banquets and dinners. She had no experience with houses like this.

"I'm never going back to the city." The woman laughed a little. "I already have my bedroom set up upstairs. So I'll be sleeping here tonight and forevermore."

"Aren't you afraid?" Lydia asked. "Such a big house, all by yourself."

C.P. Phalen stopped in front of another flap door. In a calm, even voice, she said, "I'm not afraid of anything."

The statement was the kind of thing that was made by teenagers and drunks all over the world, Lydia thought. But something about the way the words were put out there made it seem like any bad guys should be really afraid.

"So I'm not much of a cook," the woman said as she pushed her way through. "But this kitchen isn't for me."

And what a kitchen it was, all stainless steel, like a restaurant's, with an entire bank of ovens, and a mixer the size of a bathtub, and enough burners to cook for an army.

"I can, however, offer you some coffee." As Lydia's feet slowed, the other woman went over to a lonely little K-Cup machine that seemed like a child dropped off on a college campus. "What's your poison?"

Bad joke, Lydia thought. Plus her nerves were shot.

"I'm okay, thanks."

"I like mine plain with just a little bit of sugar." The woman glanced over her shoulder. "Sweet things don't really interest me."

"Can I sit down here?"

Without waiting for a yes, Lydia went across to some kind of prep station, pulled a stool out from a lineup of them, and parked it. Hanging her head, she wondered what the hell she was doing.

"So tell me what you'd like me to do for you," C.P. Phalen said.

Lydia watched as a mug was retrieved and a pod was placed in the machine. A full five-pound-bag of sugar was taken out and then a teaspoon. When the brewing was done, "a little bit of Domino's best" was added and stirred.

"You haven't answered me," the woman said as she leaned back against her cook's counter and cradled her white mug. "What exactly do you want me to do for you?"

"I don't know where else to go."

"That I believe. And I already spoke with the hotel's CEO."

Lydia's brows popped. "You did?"

"Corrington himself took my call. I told him

the next time one of your wolves is found dead or poisoned, I was going to go to the Securities and Exchange Commission with all I know about his company going public last year."

"I'm sorry?"

"Corrington Hotel and Resorts went public and a number of friends of his were allowed to buy in early. Classic insider trading. Of course, he's such an arrogant fuck, he thought it was no big deal. Just another one of Tom Wolfe's masters of the universe—although I suppose a wolf of Wall Street is the more current saying." When Lydia just blinked, the woman laughed a little. "I can see this is not your field of interest, but it is mine. I manage a couple of hedge funds, and although I specialize in pharmaceutical companies, I have my fingers in a lot of pies. Which is how I know what Corrington pulled."

There was a pause, and when Lydia didn't say anything, C.P. Phalen smiled. "Have I lost you entirely, or are you just surprised to have heard me say 'fuck.'"

Lydia cleared her throat. "What was Corrington's response?"

"He denied everything, but took great pains to point out that the hiker that was found a couple of days ago was a prime example of why he needs to protect his guests. I told him to keep that chainlink fence up permanently and then he won't have to worry about wolves on his acreage."

"There's no proof that it was a wolf."

The level stare was so direct Lydia dropped her eyes.

"What else can I do for you?" the woman said.

Lydia took a deep breath. "Do you know of anything that Peter Wynne or the WSP might be involved with that's dangerous? Or illegal?"

"No. Why do you ask this?"

"Peter's been acting strangely." And Rick had been, too, but not for the same reason. "And out of the office all the time."

"Maybe there's something going on in his personal life?"

"I didn't know anything about him," Lydia said. "Other than he just stopped showing up to work, and we've run out of money."

"That's news to me," C.P. Phalen said remotely. "About the money."

"I looked at the financials just two days ago. There's next to nothing in the operating and the payroll accounts. In fact, I ripped up my paycheck so we could afford to replace our groundskeeper. And we let the cleaners go."

As C.P. Phalen's eyes narrowed and a nasty frown set up shop on her otherwise line-less face, Lydia thought . . .

Yup, this was why she'd come.

◆   ◆   ◆

Daniel was back at the WSP before the office closed at five-thirty. As he walked in, Candy looked up from her desk.

"Do you know where she is?" the woman demanded.

"Who? Lydia? No."

"She took my car—with my permission. But I have to get home. I got a cat to feed."

Daniel frowned. "Where did she go?"

"She didn't say."

"Can we call her?" He took out his phone. "I'll just c—"

"I've tried. Three times—"

The sound of tires on the gravel drive had him turning around. Through the windows that faced the front, a familiar Chevy sedan came rolling down the slight decline.

"Thank God," Candy said as she grabbed her coat and purse.

Daniel purposely ignored the breath he released. "All's well that ends well."

As Candy passed him by, she paused. "You're a smoker? I don't think I knew that."

"No, I'm not." Except then he sniffed the sleeve of his windbreaker and could smell it, too. "Okay, fine, I just had a couple."

"If there ever was a day for it, it was today." The woman patted his shoulder. "You take good care of our girl. We need her to not quit. If she goes, I'll have to get a new job. Hell, I probably need to anyway. See you tomorrow, assuming there is one."

Candy stepped out of the door, her voice carrying as she started talking at Lydia before the other woman even got out of the car.

The pair met in the middle, halfway between the parking area and the building, where more words were exchanged, along with a set of keys.

After that, Candy went to her sedan, got in, and drove off.

Lydia stood where she was and watched the woman go, arms crossed over her chest, the setting sun bathing her in gentle light. To get her attention, Daniel knocked on the windowpane—and then regretted it as Lydia wrenched around, fear on her pale face. He lifted his hand in what he hoped was a friendly way. A calm-cool-collected way.

Which was not at all how he was feeling.

If he went with his emotions, he'd be rushing out there and throwing his arms around her. Holding her tight. Not letting her go, maybe forever—

Fuck, Mr. Personality might have a point, he thought.

As she came over to the building, her eyes were on the ground, and the second she stepped inside, she seemed to gather herself, her shoulders straightening, her chin lifting.

"Sorry I was gone so long," she said.

"Guess you owe Candy some gas money, huh."

"I refilled the tank before I came back." She took a deep breath. "You were right, a drive really helps clear the mind."

"I do my best thinking on my bike with an empty road ahead of me."

There was a pause. And then she said in a far-off way, "How do you know when to leave? A place, I mean. A job."

Daniel shrugged. "I don't know. For me, it's kind of an internal clock—or maybe it's more like one of those oven stuffer roasters with the pop-up buttons? Something inside just shifts and I'm done."

As she looked around, her eyes lingered on Candy's desk and then went to the hall that led back to the offices and the clinic entrance.

"Can you help me free the wolf tomorrow?" she asked.

"Absolutely."

"Thanks." She seemed to refocus herself as she brushed her hair back. "I'm just going to go feed him now. You're free to head home. Or . . . off, I mean, wherever you're going, if you're . . ."

"I'll be in my tent again tonight on your back forty."

When she just nodded absently, he wasn't sure she'd even heard. But then she said, "Have you ever had *suomen makaronilaatikko?*"

"No? I'm pretty healthy, though. Little cough now and then, but nothing more than that."

Lydia blinked and then laughed softly. "It's Finnish macaroni and cheese. I have some frozen back home and I was wondering if you'd—"

"Oh, right. Actually, I love solemn macaroni. It's right up my alley, a serious dish for a man who has no sense of humor."

Her smile lasted a little longer and he was glad.

"Okay, well," she nodded over her shoulder, "I'm happy to walk home, if you'd like to go—"

"I'm waiting for you right here. You take your time with your wolf."

Just in case there was an argument, he went over and parked it on the waiting room's sofa, crossing his legs ankle-to-knee. Fortunately, Lydia didn't fight him; she just murmured an I'll-be-quick and strode off.

Daniel rubbed his face and then let his head fall back. The sun was setting, the light fading from the sky, everything starting to go dark. Funny, how some days were long.

And some seemed like a lifetime.

Just as his neck was getting sore, he heard a car pull up to the building. As he straightened and looked out the window, he put his hand into his windbreaker, onto the butt of his gun. It was a UPS truck, boxy and brown with the right logo in the right place in the correct color. A man in a coordinated short-sleeved uniform got out with a box the size of a toaster oven.

Looked legit. But Daniel didn't trust anything.

He kept his hand on his gun as he got up and went

to the door. Opening it, he smiled casually. "That need a signature?"

"Yup," the guy said. "Here ya go."

"Thanks." Daniel scribbled on the electronic reader with his left hand. "Hopefully this is your last stop."

"Two more and I'm off. You have a good night."

"You, too, man."

Stepping back inside, Daniel locked things up and went to the window. The truck did a wide turn and nearly clipped the Harley, but then it was off, moving away down the gravel road.

"Who was that?" Lydia said as she poked her head out of the clinic's door. "I just saw someone's taillights."

"UPS." He held up the box. "And it's addressed to Peter Wynne."

TWENTY-NINE

L YDIA HELD ON to the package all the way back to her house. She kept it between Daniel's body and her own on the bike, one of her arms around his waist, the other keeping the box tight as a football in a receiver's grip.

She forgot to tell him to go the long way to the back of her property, just to make sure no one saw them. But really, after everything that had happened? Who the fuck cared. If Susan and Bessie wanted to carry the news he'd given her a ride home to everyone who ate at the diner or bought a carton of milk and a newspaper, so be it.

Besides, all anyone would be talking about was Rick.

God, how could he be gone? As the question rico-cheted around her mind for the hundredth time, Daniel pulled into her drive and went up to her house—

Had she left that light on?

"What is it?" he said as he cut the engine and she didn't get off.

"I can't remember whether I . . ."

"Your bedroom light was on when we left."

"Are you sure?"

"Yup, but let me go through the house first."

"I'm not staying out here." She dismounted and got her keys from her pocket. "I feel like a sitting duck everywhere I go right now."

"Let me put the bike around back."

She nodded and walked with him as he rolled the Harley out of view from the driveway. Then they entered into her kitchen. As he closed them in, she looked around.

"Everything seems distorted," she said. "Like my whole world has been shifted a quarter of an inch to the left."

"So something's out of place?"

"No." But she double-checked just to be sure. "It only feels like it."

As he spoke to her, she knew he wasn't paying attention. His eyes were sweeping over the windows, the door into the cellar, the rooms beyond—which were dark.

She wished she'd left every light she had on.

"Are you always armed?" she asked as that hand of his stayed in his windbreaker's pocket.

Daniel looked at her. "Would it bother you if I said yes?"

"Considering the day I've had? No. Not at all."

"My weapon is legal and I know how to use it."

"Good." She put the box on the table and then

dead-bolted the door. "I'm coming with you while you check."

"Okay, but stay behind me. Bullets don't have a reverse gear."

Just as she went to follow him, she doubled back and grabbed the box. With him in front, like he was a shield, they went through to the parlor, leaned into the study; then turned to the stairs.

"At least you don't have a flood coming down them," Daniel remarked as they started for the second floor.

"Where the hell do you think Peter is?" she asked, more to herself than to him.

"I don't know if you'll ever find him."

The sound of a rattle coming out of the box made her shake the thing just to double-check it was the source of the noise. It was. Whatever had been shipped to Peter was loose.

Please, God, let it not be bones, she thought.

Daniel made quick work of the two bedrooms and bathrooms, and he went through closets and checked under the beds. There wasn't an attic.

"I'll do the basement when we get back downstairs," he said.

"It has a dead bolt because there's a storm door to the outside." She went over to the window seat and sat down. "I want to open this now. Up here."

Where no one could see them.

He took something out of his back pocket and tossed it across. "Use this."

Lydia caught the Swiss Army knife and flipped the big blade free. "Thank you."

The box was sealed up with clear packing tape—all of its seams, even the ones that didn't have to do with top or bottom flaps, were covered with a double layer. The UPS label had a return address from Lancaster, PA, and a delivery of—

"Wait." She looked up. "This was supposed to go to Peter's home. Not the WSP."

"Maybe he changed it online under delivery preferences. We used to do that at some of the apartment buildings I worked at for equipment that the management office didn't want to deal with."

"It was mailed twelve days ago."

As she turned the box over, so she didn't mess up the label by cutting through it, the contents rattled again, some kind of weight thumping into place.

One quick slice and she was in, popping the flaps.

"What is it?" Daniel asked.

"Just old floppy disks." She took some out. "The kind before USB drives took over everything."

The black plastic squares with their silver slides were branded Memorex and unmarked with labels. They'd been in holders, but the three half containers were as loose as the floppy disks, unable to hold on to their contents.

"What do you know," she said as she set them aside. "Radio Shack is still alive and well."

"You going to see if you can open them up?"

"Maybe." She cleared her throat. "You want to eat?"

"Oh, yes. I'm starved."

They went back down, and as she got out frozen servings of her favorite Finnish comfort food, he unlocked the cellar door and went into the basement. After she turned on the oven and put two carb blocks on a baking sheet, she sat down at the table.

And felt like crying.

Instead of giving in to all that nonsense, she took the gold medallion her grandfather had given her on his death bed and rubbed it back and forth between her fingers.

When Daniel came up the stairs, his weight was so great, the wood steps creaked, and then he was in the open jambs.

"Would you like to stay in the guest room?" she said abruptly.

"Yes," he answered. "I would."

◆ ◆ ◆

Out at his Harley, Daniel lit up a cigarette. He only coughed once, which was progress in a bad direction. But whatever, as soon as shit got handled, he was going to quit again. This was just a vacation, not a permanent relocation, to Nicotineville.

Biting on the filter with his front teeth, he leaned

down and unbuckled his saddlebags. When he straightened, he checked the barren lawn and the rough line of the forest—or what he could see of things as the night sucked the light out of the sky. Still, the silence around him was so pervasive, he was inclined to trust what his ears were telling him: Nobody else was on the property.

At least not right now.

"I didn't know you smoked."

He looked over his shoulder. Then he bunny-eared the cigarette and exhaled. "I un-quit today."

"I can't say as I blame you."

"I won't do it inside, and this is not, like, I'm not forever with this."

"My grandfather smoked a pipe. More fragrant, but not that different." Lydia sat down on the back steps. "Was stopping part of your health kick?"

"That and the drinking. I was never into drugs—but I got a little too fond of Jack Daniel's. That I will never un-quit."

"I'm glad you got things under control there."

"Me, too. Not a road I'm going down again."

Out on the county road, a car approached and kept going, the headlights white, the taillights red.

"I'm sorry you're mixed up in all this." She took her hair out of its tie and rubbed her scalp as if she were trying to relieve a headache. "You came for a job, and now—"

"I have a job."

"Well, technically, that's just an eight-thirty to four-thirty kind of thing. So you're working overtime and not getting paid here."

Daniel exhaled over his shoulder even though the wind would have carried the smoke off anyway. "I'm not staying with you for work. We're . . . friends. I'm here because a friend needs my help."

"Friends."

"Yup." He tapped the cigarette. "Unless you have a better word for it."

"English is my second language. I wouldn't know."

"Wow, you sound like a native speaker to me." He looked around again at the lawn, the drive, the house. "No accent. Good vocabulary. If there were another word, I think you'd know it."

"I guess . . . friends it is."

Daniel nodded, licked his fingertips, and crushed what was glowing orange—

"Ow!" she said as she jumped forward. But she stopped herself before she touched him, falling back into her sit. "Didn't that hurt."

"Pain is in the mind." He tapped the side of his head. "All up here."

"I thought that was fear."

"Pain, fear, anxiety. The mind game is everything in life."

"What about joy, love, happiness? Are they just in the mind, too?"

"Yup, exactly. It's all an illusion, I'm afraid. Made

manifest by a fruit salad of sensory receptors and bundles of neurons firing under your skull."

"Wow, that is remarkably . . ."

"Biological," he pointed out.

"Cynical."

Daniel shrugged and finished undoing his saddle-bags. "It's the truth and you know it. You're a behaviorist. Just because an emotion is felt deeply doesn't mean it's any more powerful than what it actually is—which is ephemeral. Intensity doesn't change its nature, and all feelings fade over time."

There was a length of silence.

"You know"—she looked at the sky—"I might be inclined to see your argument. If I hadn't walked in on a good man just moments after he'd shot himself in the face this morning."

Daniel swung the saddlebags up on his shoulder. "I'm sorry. I don't need to be spouting my shit right now."

"It's okay." She got to her feet. "Besides, you either don't really believe your theory or you're not as good at detachment as you think you are. Otherwise, you wouldn't have taken up your old habit again today, would you."

THIRTY

Y OU'RE ABSOLUTELY RIGHT. The ketchup is everything."

As Daniel Heinz'd his full plate of *suomen makaronilaatikko*, Lydia nodded at her houseguest across her little kitchen table.

"My grandfather always had it with lingonberry sauce, but ketchup works for me. And it freezes beautifully. Just like in *Steel Magnolias*."

"Huh?" he said as he recapped the bottle.

"Yeah, that movie's probably not in your collection. Annelle wants to give Maline's family something that 'freezes beautifully' before the kidney transplant. I always think of that line when I make a big batch of this."

"Classic comfort food."

They fell silent, nothing but forks on plates making any sound. And then he was getting himself another mug of coffee and helping with the almost nonexistent cleanup.

"I can't keep my eyes open." She covered a yawn with the back of her hand. "I need to lie down."

"Let's go upstairs."

He went across and checked the locks, and then as they walked around to the stairwell, he made sure the front dead bolt was engaged—and something about the care he took made her realize how much she'd been doing on her own.

Her legs were wobbly on the ascend, and when she got to the top landing, she said something to him about fresh sheets being on the guest bed, and her needing to take a shower, and that she hoped she didn't snore. Chatter, chatter, chatter.

Then again, he was the first man she'd had in this house.

In any house she'd lived in, actually. Well, apart from her grandfather and he didn't count in this situation.

"You're going to be okay," Daniel murmured. "It's just going to take some time. If you need me, I'm here."

He brushed her cheek, and then he went into the guest room and shut the door halfway.

Down in her bedroom, she undressed over the laundry basket, dumping everything she had on in it, and then she got her robe. When she reemerged into the hallway, she looked both ways like it was a busy intersection, and tiptoed over the bare wood to the loo. Just before she pushed her way in, she told herself not to look over to Daniel's—

But of course she glanced in.

He had put his saddlebags down on the floor on

the far side of the bed, and he was bending over them, getting something out that he tossed behind himself to the comforter. As he straightened and faced the far wall, he unzipped his windbreaker and removed it— and then he peeled off his T-shirt, taking it up and over his head.

His back was . . . spectacular.

He was so muscular, but also lean, as if he were an athlete: From his bulking shoulders to the strong line of his spine, muscles fanned out in a series of peaks and valleys that tapered to a tight waist. And below that? Well, those jeans were hanging low, but not because his butt wasn't—

Daniel glanced over his shoulder.

As she flushed and looked away, he said, "Did you need something?"

"Sorry, I'm just taking a shower," she said.

A freezing cold one.

"Okay."

Shutting herself in the bathroom, Lydia leaned back against the door. All she could see on the insides of her lids was a bumper sticker she'd noticed on a car once: "Save Water, Shower w/a Friend."

"Friends," she reminded herself. And like she could handle anything else given all the damn drama?

The shower filled an alcove and was the only new thing in the house—as if an old Victorian claw-foot'er had bit the farm and required replacing. The glass enclosure with its tub looked great when it was clean, but keeping the soap scum at bay was a bitch. She'd finally resorted to a squeegee and a spray bottle of OxiClean down on the tile floor—

Wow, she was actually trying to distract herself with lame conversation.

In contrast to the cold wash her libido needed, she made sure the water was hot before she stepped in— and oh, God, it felt wonderful. Slumping under the spray, she hung her head and just let the warmth rush over her. When she started to worry about how much was in the hot water tank down in the cellar—you know, in case Daniel wanted one of these miracles— she got to the shampooing and a stiff-brushed wash, as her grandfather had called it. By the time she stepped out onto the bath mat, she was partially revived. No doubt it wouldn't last, but she'd take the improvement for as long as it did.

Back in her robe, she wrapped her hair up in a towel, brushed her teeth, and told herself that she had shaved her legs because it was just time to.

And not because she was thinking about being naked with anybody—

Bullcrap she wasn't thinking that.

Using a hand towel, she cleared the condensation off the mirror over the sink. Her face was drawn and the bags under her eyes were so pronounced, it was like she had hay fever. Not exactly sexy personified, and she had a thought that she needed to step off from this fantasy stuff.

Besides, even if things had been otherwise normal in her life, there were rules: Her grandfather's traditions were a heavy weight on her, as they always had been. And the two times she'd broken them, she couldn't say that the night of so-called passion had been worth the guilt afterward.

Although with Daniel? She had a feeling it would be a more than fair exchange ...

Staring at her reflection, it was as if there were a mist between her and what she was seeing. Had she changed somehow, as a result of what she'd witnessed today? Of what she'd done?

It was like walking into her kitchen, she supposed, and finding that everything seemed off even though on the surface nothing was different.

With hands that shook, she reached up behind her neck and found the clasp to her gold chain. Freeing the claw hook, she removed the medallion her grandfather had given her and put it in the basket that held her hairbrush, her tweezers, her scissors, and her nail files.

She couldn't wear that right now. Not with what she was thinking about Daniel.

But as soon as morning came, she was going to put it back on.

Funny how you followed the rules you were raised with, even when you were grown. It was as if they were part of the bones that took you to your adult height.

As she went to unlatch the door, her heart sped up,

and the creak of the hinges made her skin prickle—but not in fear. In anticipation.

In spite of the "friends" label.

And everything else.

Taking a deep breath, she opened things fully and paused—and as she stood there on the threshold, she realized that her convictions to stay away from the man hadn't lasted any time at all. *Poof!* Gone.

She should have known when she took the pendant off.

Lydia stepped out into the hall.

As her eyes returned to the guest room's doorway, she prepared an explanation, a justification, a reason that felt concrete and not irresponsible, for the fact that she wanted him. And not in the future. Not in a fantasy. But now.

"Daniel?" she said softly as she walked over.

Across the way, he had stretched out on top of the queen-sized bed, his body so long, he'd had to angle himself to keep his feet on the mattress. He'd doubled up on the pillows, his head propped on a stack, his arms clasped over his abdominals. With his eyes closed, he looked dead.

Like he was in a coffin.

Staying quiet, Lydia tiptoed to the base of the bed. When he was awake, he was so vital, so masculine, so strong, that anything less than that vibrancy was . . . not something her brain could make sense of: He seemed exhausted to the point of a coma.

She pictured him out in that tent in the woods.

And was glad he had a roof over his head and was dry and warm.

"Good night, Daniel," she whispered.

◆   ◆   ◆.

Lydia sat up in her bed in a rush, heart hammering in her chest, her gasp echoing in her silent room. Fumbling for the lamp on her side table, she turned the light on—and then blinked when she blinded herself.

Slipping her legs out from the sheets, she put her bare feet on the floor and tilted forward. As her eyes stopped stinging, she listened for footfalls. Talk. Lights out on the lawn. Cars—

The groan was soft and far off, but it got her right to the vertical. Scurrying to her door, she ripped it open and leaned out.

That was when she heard the sound again. A low release of pain. From the guest room.

Rushing down the hall, the light from overhead shined into the space and fell on the bed, on Daniel: On top of the duvet, he was churning, his legs sawing as if he were running in his sleep, his head going back and forth on the pillows, one hand gripping the covers in a fist so tight that it shook. With his mouth open, his chest was pumping up and down—

"Daniel?" she said. Then louder, "*Daniel*—"

Just as she had done, he shot upright, but as his eyes met hers, he did not see her; there was no recognition in his stare as his lids peeled wide and his face stretched with terror.

"Daniel." She went around to him. "Daniel, it's okay, you're all—"

"I can't breathe." His hand let go of the comforter and went to the front of his chest. As he twisted the T-shirt he'd changed into, his face turned to her, his opaque stare finally locking on her even as he seemed not to know who she was. "I . . ."

"You're breathing."

"I am?"

"Yes, here." She put her hand on top of his own. "See? You're inhaling and exhaling. You're okay."

"Am I?"

"I promise you. Let's breathe together."

Now his eyes clung to hers, as if she were the only thing keeping him on the planet, as if gravity had decided to forget about him and he was in danger of floating away without her.

"I can't breathe . . . ," he choked.

With no warning, he caved into her, his full body weight crashing against her torso. He was so big, she scrambled to hold on to him as he lurched forward— and she had to get up on the bed or she was going to drop him. Instantly, his heavy arm came around her and he pulled her closer. Then he curled up in the fetal position. The shaking that came over him was so intense, it rattled the headboard against the wall.

Repositioning herself, she tucked his head into

her neck and stroked his thick hair. "Shh . . . I've got you. You need to just let it go, let it out. Whatever it is you're holding in, just let it go . . ."

"I can't," he croaked.

"Yes, you can," she whispered. "Give it to me. Let it go and give it to me."

The moan that came out of him was like a piece of his soul had broken off the whole, and now, abandoned and lost, it was crying out in the darkness of fate to find its way back.

"Give it to me, Daniel. I'm strong enough for your burden. I can carry whatever you need me to. Give the burden to me—"

"I can't breathe."

"You're breathing—"

"I can't breatheIcantbreatheIcant—she's not breathing. Oh, God, she's not breathing . . ."

"Tell me."

There was a period where he didn't speak, nothing but his sawing inhales filling the entire house, the whole world. And then, when he at last talked to her, his syllables had pounding hooves, his words trampling over the distance between his past, where he was alone, and the present, which they were both in.

"She's in the water. She's fallen from the bridge into the river. Her head's under the surface. It's dark out, I can't see where she is . . . the current is fast . . . the water is muddy . . . I can't see—I'm jumping. I'm jumping. I'm hitting the cold water. It's hard as stone

and it's . . . in my mouth and my nose. I'm choking . . .
I'm swimming. I'm calling her name . . ."

He was breathing even harder now. "Mom . . .
Mom . . . *Mom* . . . where are you?"

Lydia squeezed her eyes shut.

"I can see her . . . her head is bobbing . . . I'm swimming to her. Mom! Mom, I'm coming for you . . . oh,
God, my arms are tired, but I'm swimming as fast as I
can—*Mom!*"

Lydia stroked his hair and murmured her empathy
as the story rolled out. It was all she could do, even if it
wasn't good enough. Nothing would be good enough.

"She's not . . . oh, Jesus . . . she's not . . ."

As he seemed to get stuck, she whispered, "She's
not what, Daniel."

"She's facedown. She's not . . . she's floating facedown in the river . . ." He let out a groan of pain. "I've
got her, I've turned her over . . . I'm pulling her toward
the shore, I'm swimming against the current . . . Mom,
I've got you . . . I'm trying to get you . . . help . . . *help* . . .
I can't hold her . . . I'm trying . . . to . . . *Mom!*"

Abruptly, the shaking stopped.

And she was not surprised as he jerked against
her—and then pulled away.

"What are you—Lydia?" he said. "Are you okay?"

THIRTY-ONE

Y OU WERE DREAMING," Lydia said in a thin, worried voice. "I came in . . . because you were dreaming and you called out."

In the light streaming past a partially open door, Daniel tried to get his bearings: The body against his own was very feminine, and there was the smell of fresh shampoo in his nose. The room he was in was a bedroom he wasn't familiar with—but he knew who was with him. Lydia was beside him.

Which was not good news.

One look at the shock on her face and he thought, *Fuck.* What story had come out of him? What had he told her in his sleep?

There were things she couldn't know about him. When you lived in two worlds, and straddled the in-compatible . . . you had to watch what came out of your mouth. Even in your fucking sleep.

Maybe especially in your sleep.

Daniel moved away from her, rolling onto his back and bringing his legs up. He'd kept his jeans on, and he pushed his palms into his thighs and moved the denim off his hips.

"Sorry I woke you with my noise." He tried to keep his voice light, casual. "I talk in my sleep sometimes. I should have warned you—in the future, just ignore me."

Stop talking so fast, he told himself.

As she pushed her hair out of her face and sat up higher also, he had a thought that this is what she'd look like after he made love to her. Well, except for the expression on her face.

Which was more like after someone had been in a car accident. Or maybe the victim of a robbery.

"You weren't talking, Daniel." She cleared her throat. "At least not at the beginning."

"Sorry." *Goddamn it*. "So, ah, what was I babbling on about."

"It was your mom."

Daniel's breath caught. "What about her."

"She was . . . in the water."

All at once, his lungs froze in his rib cage and his torso became a slab of granite. But he told himself it was good. It was better than so many other options that could really have complicated things.

Rubbing his chest—you know, just so that he could separate being in that cold river from where he actually was on this totally-dry-land mattress—he shook his head.

"Wow. Been a while since I've gone there."

"I just wanted to . . . help you," she said. "That's why I came in."

"I appreciate it, but like I told you, if it happens again, just ignore me." He forced his mouth into a smile. "And listen, if you want, I can go back out into the woods—"

"No."

"Okay."

Annnnnnnd then it was cue the awkward silence. Lydia was obviously too polite, too respectful, to pry, and he didn't want to ever go back there under any circumstances ever again. But he felt like he owed her an explanation. Or a context. Or . . .

"So . . ." The words would not come out of his mouth. "How 'bout those Mets?"

When she didn't crack a smile and just stared down the bed, the sadness in her was so tangible, it changed the temperature in the room.

"You don't need to worry about me," he said—and almost kept the roughness out of his voice.

"I should go."

And yet leaving seemed to be for her the same thing as him telling her she should head back to her room: An intention that had no energy behind it.

Daniel cracked his knuckles one by one. And when he'd finished with the thumb on his left hand, he took a deep breath—and felt like he was breathing in nothing at all.

"My mom jumped, okay? Off a bridge, into the

Ohio River." He shook his head. "It was no big deal, all right? People jump off of bridges all the time."

Her dumbfounded expression was totally understandable, but he wasn't going to take the words back.

"How can you say that—"

"Because I have to believe it or it's all my fault." When she looked up at him sharply, he looked away from her just as fast. "I was not expected, okay? My birth was not a happy event because I was not . . . what she wanted. Frankly, I don't blame her. Didn't blame her. Whatever."

"Oh, Daniel—"

"No, don't be all sorry for me. It is what it is."

Rubbing his tired eyes, he wondered how long they had to stay in his cesspool—

"What happened that night?" she asked softly.

Daniel frowned. "How did you know it was night?"

"You said so. You said you couldn't see anything."

"Yeah." Sensations of drowning, of cold water in his face, in his mouth, down in his lungs, threatened to drag him back into the past. And he kept talking just to try to pull himself out of the memories. "She, ah, she was drunk and behind the wheel. She stopped in the middle of the four-laner bridge. When she got out . . . I thought it was just to run. You know, leave me and the car, just get the fuck out. But she, ah, she headed for the railing. She didn't hesitate. I mean, she just grabbed on and swung her legs out to the side. I remember she got one of them caught—so she kind of fell sideways? She must have hit the water on her side. I don't know."

"Oh, Daniel. I'm so sorry. To see that—"

"I was an idiot, of course. I ran to where she'd jumped. But like I could do anything up on the bridge? And then there was the fact that the current was going under where I was—she was already being swept away. When I finally figured that out, I hustled across the highway and looked into the water. The moon was out, and there were lights all over the bridge. I saw her surface right below me so I jumped in." He shook his head again. "Man, that water was freezing and hard. I got the wind knocked out of me—but not because I hit bad. I went in feet first. It was just a stun because it was so cold."

He wrapped his arms around himself. "As soon as I got my breath back, I tried to find her. I couldn't see shit. Water was splashing into my face and the waves made it impossible to look around and I was being carried away from the bridge lights. But there were these docks up ahead. Piers. They had lots of gas lanterns—and somehow, I saw her head bob. I swam like a motherfucker. I swam as hard as I could. And then I got to her . . ."

The physical sensations came back in a fresh wave of agony, the cold, the coughing, the weakness in his body. His mind had been screaming and he would have let it out, but he hadn't been able to spare the oxygen.

Every time he blinked, he saw the wet hair fanned around his mother's head and her back bobbing up and down.

"I rolled her over so she could breathe. But it had taken me a long time to get to her. A lifetime." He coughed a little. "And then I started swimming. I thought if I could get her to shore . . ."

"Someone would help you."

"Yeah." He pictured those piers, the big lantern lights, the parking lot that had been empty. "But I lost hold of her body. I was going down myself . . . swimming with one arm—and it was so cold."

Snapping out of it, he shrugged. "In the end, I saved myself. They found her the next day after she'd gone over the Falls of the Ohio. Fifteen miles down the river."

As he fell silent, Lydia brushed the tears from her eyes. "I am so sorry."

"It just is." He glanced at her. "I can't go back and change anything. She made her choice and I couldn't save her and that's where I need to leave it. Enough with the emotion, you know? Feelings don't change shit."

"How old were you?" she said softly.

"Fourteen."

When Lydia closed her eyes and cursed, he shrugged. "Look, the honest truth is that no matter how old I was, I wasn't going to save her. It didn't matter how tall I was, how strong I was, what I weighed, you know? A fall into cold water from that height, when the person was already drunk, and maybe high? Add in a bad landing and there you have it."

"You were a child."

He laughed harshly. "Children are five. I was two years away from a learner's permit."

Lydia put her head in her hands. "What happened to you afterward? Where did you go?"

"I was put into the foster system, but I didn't stick around for long. I dropped out of high school when I was sixteen and went off on my own. Eventually, I found a few people like me, so I wasn't totally alone. It is what it is."

"What about your father?"

Daniel flattened his mouth. "I don't talk about him. Ever. Sorry."

As he eyed the open doorway and measured the distance to bolt out of the room, he didn't really have anywhere to go. And that was the ball buster. Everywhere he went, there he was.

And besides, Lydia still needed protecting.

"So that's my story," he concluded.

"Now I know why you think about emotions the way you do. And why you move around."

As a wave of exhaustion hit him hard, he closed his eyes and swayed. "Man, I'm tired."

"You could lay down."

"I think I'm going to have to."

And that was how he ended up giving her a pillow and taking one for himself. "Come here."

As he settled on his back and put his arm out, she didn't hesitate. She brought herself right against him, her head resting on his pec.

"Let's try and get some sleep." He could hear the mumbling in his voice and didn't try to hide it. Why bother. "Tomorrow's a new day."

Without any preamble, his lids slammed down over his eyes, and his consciousness got sucked away from his will to stay alert. God, even if the house had been on fire, he couldn't have fought the sleep.

Daniel was all but dead as he lay beside . . .

. . . the one and only human being he had ever told that story to.

THIRTY-TWO

TOWARD THE END of the night, Xhex went alone to Deer Mountain.

Leaving her motorcycle at one of the trailheads, she double-checked that her weapons were in place and then stepped onto what appeared to be a main trail. The beaten pathway was wide enough to accommodate a car, and relatively smooth, the occasional gnarled root the only hazard there was.

God, she hoped Blade wasn't setting her up. But he'd told her he had a contact who knew about the labs—and would be waiting for her on the main trail.

As she walked along, she kept her hands on the guns that were holstered at her hips. Breathing deeply, she smelled fresh pine and clean dirt, and although she'd never really given a shit about the mother-nature, tree-hugger side of things, she had to admit . . .

It wasn't half bad.

But she was far from relaxed. Even *sympaths* knew better than to trust *sympaths*.

She'd gone about a quarter mile, maybe more,

when her phone vibrated inside her leather jacket. Taking it out, she smiled a little.

"I'm fine," she said as she answered the call. "Really."

Over the speakerphone, on the other end, Blay's voice was warm. "Well, your boy here worries."

"I know you do, John. But you're out in the field tonight, and besides, you know what Blade said."

There was a pause, and then Blay muttered, "He's not real impressed with your brother."

"I don't blame you." Her eyes scanned left to right as she spoke. "But this person meets me alone or not at all."

Another silence. Then Blay asked, "He wants to know if you're being careful."

"I'm taking no chances. And the GPS locater around my neck is on—"

She stopped. Turned around. Sniffed the air that was traveling toward her, moving right across her face.

"Really. You two *really* want to play this game."

There was a pause. And then both males dematerialized directly before her. She put her hands on her hips.

"Did you think I wasn't going to notice you? Given that I'm downwind of your location?"

John Matthew smiled in a sheepish way and signed, *I thought we were playing this cool.*

"Me, too," Blay murmured.

The pair of them had hopeful expressions on their faces, as if they were trying to appeal to her better nature—which was a joke because she didn't really have one.

Well, except when it came to . . . well, the two fighters who stood in front of her.

"So you're off rotation tonight?" she demanded.

With a nod, John Matthew said, *And it was the original schedule. We didn't weasel out of anything.*

"Fuckers," she bitched as she took two steps forward and rose up to kiss her mate.

Then she punched Blay in the shoulder. "Okay, you come if you're going to, but you split off from me right now. My brother told me I had to do this alone and I'm not fucking this up because you two have protection issues. Are we clear? You stay back and out of sight, and make sure you don't give yourselves away—which you did on purpose, didn't you. Because you hate lying."

This she directed to her mate, and he nodded like a dog who was asked if he wanted to go walkies.

He was kind of cute, really—as long as you ignored the width of his shoulders and all the weapons on his body. Then he looked like what he was, a trained killer who knew all kinds of tricks with all sorts of metal things that went click, click, bang, bang. At his side, Blay was the same. With his red hair cut in a high-and-tight, and his head-to-toe black leather, he was another page out of the don't-fuck-with-us playbook.

She shook her head. "You're going to scare the shit out of whoever this is."

Unless they're an enemy, John pointed out. *In which case, we're where we need to be and we'll do what we have to.*

"I'm not going to argue," she said. "But we part ways now, and unless things go south, I can't see you until I'm back at my bike."

There was no reason to bring up the reality that they may have already compromised her. And at least the contact she was here to meet didn't know where she'd entered the mountain's preserve. There were a lot of ways into the massive acreage.

Maybe they were still okay.

Please be safe, John Matthew signed.

"Always."

When she leaned in again for his mouth, he dropped his head down. As their lips met, she kept it brief.

And then after Blay gave her a formal bow, as was his way, the pair of them ghosted off, leaving nothing but thin air in their wakes.

Xhex turned and started walking again.

There was a timeless quality to the night, minutes passing like hours, with the inverse also being true, an hour going by at the blink of an eye. And yes, she would have dematerialized as well, but she wasn't sure who she was going to see. Or exactly where on the trail they were going to meet.

Sometimes, it was best to keep your true nature to yourself. Even among people who couldn't necessarily hurt you.

And especially among people who might.

It was unclear to her exactly how far she'd gone when she felt herself being watched. But she ascribed it to the creatures of the night who moved around to stay out of her way: wolves, deer, owls, raccoons. The farther into the preserve she went, the more she was forced to cede to the curiosity of the native animal populations.

And she didn't mind it exactly.

Not when she was so clearly the apex predator—

It was at that moment when someone stepped into the trail up ahead.

Xhex stopped where she was. As a shiver went through her, it had nothing to do with air temperature. Something was . . . very off . . . about the creature that had placed itself in her path.

You have come to the mountain in search of your past.

"Hello," Xhex said with annoyance. "Are you—"

And yet you do not know your true quest, child.

Okaaaaaaaaaaaay. Like she needed this smoke and mirrors, touchy-feely malarkey.

Yes, I am who you seek.

The entity came forward through the pines, but not on foot. It floated, traveling like it was on a hover board over the uneven ground, the shimmering robes swirling around.

The face that it chose to show her was that of a white-haired old woman, its features heavily lined, the eyes nearly sightless from under heavy lids, its wrinkled forehead echoing its sagging jowls. But only a fool would have been snowed. Enormous metaphysical power emanated from the being, to the point where the energy supercharged the air around it, tiny sparks crackling in the darkness.

That was what shimmered, not the fabric of the robing that covered its "body."

"Listen," Xhex said, "my name is—"

Your name is not important here on the mountain. Ask your question, and I will reply.

Xhex glanced behind herself, wondering if—

They are not far from you, child. They've been with you the whole way.

Ripping back around, Xhex opened her mouth. Closed it. "I'm here to ask about the labs. Whether they've started up again, and if so, where I can find them."

That is not your question.

"Yeah, no offense, I'm pretty sure it is."

That is not your question.

"Look, I'm thinking this was a mistake. You know, a trick played on both of us." *Fucking Blade.* "I just want to know where the other laboratory is—"

You're standing on the laboratory.

"I beg your pardon." Xhex mostly kept the fuck-you out of her voice. "Actually, I think I'll go now—"

They've experimented on the wolves who make this mountain their home.

Xhex narrowed her eyes. "What have they been doing to the . . . wolves."

They are looking for forever. It is in the nature of human mortals to seek that which is not their due. To them, it is progress. Power. And in their desperation to succeed, they are cruel. Even those who would not usually seek to inflict pain become monsters to the innocent.

"Fucking hell," Xhex muttered.

And that was when she realized the problem with the entity. Whatever it was . . . had no grid. Which meant Xhex was at a disadvantage she was unaccustomed to.

Ask your question, child.

The being came farther forward, closing in. And yet Xhex was unafraid. In fact, it was as if she fell into a trance, hypnotized by that aura.

You are safe here. Ask your question.

Xhex blinked. Under her skull, her brain constructed another sentence to the tune of *I gotta go.* That was not what came out of her mouth, however.

"Will I ever be free of what was done to me?" she whispered.

The entity reached out its glowing hand, stopping just short of stroking Xhex's face—and yet she felt the contact, a soft, compassionate brush of her skin.

There is a path before you, my child. It will be long and dangerous, and the resolution of your quest is not clear at this time. But if you do not start . . . you will never, ever finish.

Xhex thought of all the days she had woken up in terror, clawing at her mate, screaming inside her skin, her soul.

"It's supposed to all be behind me," she choked out. "It was years ago. The scars are all healed, I've dealt with it."

The energy is trapped just beneath your flesh. Unless it is released, once and for all, you will never be at peace.

Abruptly, she thought of the things in her life she was in the middle of: Setting up the new club. Working with Trez on the others. Her relationship with John Matthew. Her place at that dining table with her . . . family.

And then there was her *mahmen*, precious Autumn.

"I don't have the time to deal with this right now, okay?" She pictured Mary, the household's therapist. "I'll tell you what, I'll talk to someone. I'll just—you know, sit down and have a little chat. All right? It'll be—"

You have a disease of the soul. If you do not cure it now, it will destroy you.

"I don't want to do this."

You must, child. Or you will die by inches . . . and take all you love down with you.

"You said you don't know the ending." Why in the hell was she talking like this? Like this . . . thing . . . knew anything about her? "You said—"

To start is to have a chance. To stay where you are is a death sentence.

With that, the entity disappeared from in front of

her. But it didn't completely leave. Up ahead on the trail, it re-formed.

It was no longer an old woman.

It was a majestic silver wolf.

The entity turned away, loped away.

Xhex stood where she was, unable to move. It was as if she had become suspended in a pocket of existence that was neither here nor there, a gap in the space/time continuum. And shit, she couldn't feel her body, didn't know whether she was warm or cold, standing or lying down—

John Matthew materialized right in front of her. As his presence registered, she jumped back with a shout.

Xhex? Xhex are you okay? he signed.

Forcing herself to come back from . . . wherever the hell she'd been . . . she focused on her mate's eyes.

"Yeah, yeah, I'm fine." She rubbed her face. "How are you?"

He gave her a strange look. *I'm fine.*

"Okay. Good. So, yeah."

Are you going to keep going? Or do you think nobody's coming?

She frowned. "What are you talking about? Didn't you see the . . ."

As he just stared at her with worried inquiry, she cleared her throat. "No," she said. "I don't think anybody's coming. This was just a wild goose chase. My brother, true to his *symphath* roots, was toying with me."

John Matthew shook his head. *What an asshole.*

"Yeah, he's that in a nutshell."

As she turned away, her beloved *hellren* put his arm around her, and she did the same to his tight waist. Blay, meanwhile, had waited at a discreet distance, and when they came up to him, he nodded as if to say, *Just respecting your privacy over here.*

Together, the three of them walked back to where she had come from, back to her bike, back to their lives.

Just as the trail took a turn, Xhex looked over her shoulder.

But there was nothing behind her. Only pine trees . . . and the darkness of the still, silent mountain.

And yet she was being stalked.

Sure as if the events that had stained her past had formed arms and legs, they were following her—and closing the distance to kill her.

THIRTY-THREE

AS DAWN ARRIVED, Lydia woke up to a banked fire pressed tight against the back of her. Sometime during the night, she and Daniel had turned on their sides, and with his arm around her waist and his hand entwined in hers, it was as if they had done this for years, the soft snoring above her head a peaceful, familiar sound.

But he was wide awake in one part of his body.

It was impossible not to feel that hard ridge, and it wasn't far from where she found herself desperately wanting it—

With a snuffle, Daniel jerked—and then there was no more snoring.

Lydia stared over at the open doorway and wondered what she should do. Did she slip out, all time-to-go-to-work, I'm-not-sexually-frustrated, no-really-I'm-fine? Or did she do what she wanted?

Which involved rolling over in his arms, and bringing him even closer.

As well as other things, of the no-clothes variety.

Daniel solved the issue by easing away from her, and then there was movement on the mattress as he stretched—and okay, wow, a lot of popping and crackling in his joints.

Lydia decided to quit with the possum routine. "You ready for breakfast?" She glanced over her shoulder, seeing his long legs in those jeans and his black-socked feet. "I don't have much, but whatever is in my kitchen is yours."

"I'm going to take a shower," he said. "Then I'll help you with it."

"Okay, sure." *Yeah, truly. Totally sure fine.* "That'd be great."

But come on, there was no reason for her to be crushed. You can't be denied something that you hadn't been offered, she reminded herself.

"It's early," he said as he got off the bed on the other side.

His shoulders shifted as he did something at the front of his hips, and then he bent over to his saddle-bags. Pulling out a little black bag, he nodded at her and headed for the exit.

And then it happened.

In the doorway, he said casually, "You could just rest there. If you want."

At that, he disappeared into the bathroom, shutting the door, turning the shower on.

Was he suggesting—

Before she could answer that for herself, she

scrambled off the bed and silently fleet-footed it down the hall. In her room, she opened all kinds of drawers: Bedside. Bureau.

"Shit . . . shit. *Shit.*"

In the closet, hanging on the back of the door, she had her two alternate purses. Which were both black with shoulder straps, but whatever, she was not going to worry about her fashion ruts right now. Pawing her way into the bags, she pulled out appointment cards from that endodontist, a pair of sunglasses she thought she'd lost, the extra house key, deconstructed tissues—

The Rolaids were a relief. Kind of.

Fruit flavored, not mint.

The trouble was, there was no gum to be found anywhere. Which was what happened when some-one who did not chew gum went looking for it. And with him in the bathroom with her toothbrush? She couldn't get anywhere near the Colgate she wished she could use.

Ripping open the tinfoil roll, she took the first one, which was kind of pink, and tossed it into her dry mouth. As she crunched the tablet between her molars, the thing turned to plaster dust that powder-coated the inside of everything.

"Damn it . . ."

Smacking her tongue like a dog with peanut butter, she shot over to her bedside table. Her water glass was half-full from the night before, and she gave the level a quick lint-screen before tossing things back, swishing her mouth out, and swallowing.

It was the best she could do.

She was rushing back down the hall when the shower turned off. Given the amount of surface area the man had to soap up, he'd clearly given himself the express wash, and thank God she'd moved as fast as she had. Throwing herself in between the sheets, her heart was pounding and she was flushed—as well as feeling stupid that she'd made a big deal out of morning breath. But she didn't have a ton of experience with the whole sex thing, and she was not bringing a green cloud that could melt paint off a car door to the party—

Now, the sink was running. He was at the sink. And under the familiar scent of her own shampoo, she could swear she smelled shaving cream.

She hadn't minded his five-o'clock shadow. Then again, she'd have taken him any way he came—

Blushing at her own stupid-ass joke, Lydia put her hands to her hot face. Under her skin, her blood was rushing in a way that had absolutely nothing to do with her Hail Mary breath mint expedition. And it did not slow down as the bathroom door opened, and a roll of steam curled free into the cooler air.

Daniel stepped out. In a towel. That barely fit around his waist, and not because he was overweight in the burger-and-beer sense. Oh, God . . . his hair was damp and curling at the ends, and his torso was rippling with muscle, and his legs strong and sure.

He paused in the guest room doorway. As their eyes met, she took a deep breath.

And pulled the covers back to welcome him.

Daniel came to her, his beautiful body moving fluidly, powerfully.

"I'm still dripping," he murmured.

"That's okay with me."

With that, she held her arms out, and he didn't hesitate. He laid down beside her and pulled the covers into place over them. And then they were melding, her breasts pressing into his bare chest through her T-shirt and his hips coming up against hers. When he rolled her onto her back and propped himself up on his elbows, his hair dripped onto her face.

Lydia pushed it back, stroked it back. "I want you."

"And I ache for you."

As he moved his hips onto her, she spread her legs to make him room, and his weight was delicious, pressing her into the mattress. Running her hands over his shoulders and down his heavy arms, his skin was warm and smooth, the muscles underneath rigid and powerful. Looking up at him, she thought he was magnificent, more animal than man—especially as his glowing eyes bored into her own.

"Lydia . . . ," he whispered as he dropped his mouth to hers.

She moaned as the kiss swept over her, and then she tilted her head to the side, opening herself up to him even more. As she arched into him and breathed deep, she couldn't believe it was happening, that *this* was happening . . . the nakedness, the raw grind of hunger, the fact that she wasn't going to stop.

And neither was he.

Lydia was absolutely going to see this to its full culmination—because in the back of her mind, a rock-solid belief had coalesced out of the ether of present thought and short-term memory: They were running out of time. The two of them, Daniel and herself, had a clock ticking and the numbers were speeding to the zero hour.

How she knew this, she didn't have a clue—

Oh, wait. Maybe it was because people were dying and/or disappearing all around her.

On that note, she slipped her hands down under the covers and found the towel. The tuck that had kept the thing in place had loosened, and as she shifted her hands onto its damp softness, she wanted him fully naked.

So she took it off. As she pulled the barrier to the side, he lifted his hips to help—and then he was against the soft folds of her PJ bottoms, his arousal a hard brand on her inner thigh. Instantly, the kissing got more involved, his tongue seeking hers, probing, licking. Dear Lord, he was like a drug that made reality disappear, nothing but sensation grounding her—and she was so fine with that.

God, she was done thinking. It was just such a relief to give in, give up, let go, in this sacred, private space.

And when she felt his hand drift down onto her breast, she surged up to him. "More . . ."

She was the one who pulled up her T-shirt—and then took that thing off like it was tearing up her skin. And as the cool air hit her nipples, they peaked and he let out a growl.

"Don't hold back," she said. "I want it all."

As he lowered himself down to her breasts, his muscles surged under his skin, his arms flaring out in a bow as he suspended his talented mouth over her collarbones, her sternum . . . the underside of both. The kisses were soft, just a little tickling of his lips, but she felt everything and relished the exquisite tease of it all.

Finally, he nuzzled at her, then . . . licked at one of her tips.

Calling out his name, she speared her fingers into his thick hair, torqued under him, and pitched her head back. In response, he latched on to her nipple, sucking for a time before rolling it with his tongue and flicking at it. The pleasure felt too much for her to hold in. Writhing against him, she swept her hands down to the small of his back and then she wrapped her legs around him.

So that her core was where his erection hit.

Now he was the one growling, and as if he couldn't control his pelvis, he started pumping against her—

All at once, he stopped everything. Pushed himself off her. Held himself over her.

His eyes were closed and he was breathing through his open mouth. Looking down between their bodies, she saw his massive arousal, poised, ready . . . straining.

"Daniel?" she asked.

For a moment, she was worried he was going to put an end to it all. Had she done something wrong—

"I got to slow the fuck down," he panted. "Fuck . . . Lydia . . ."

As he moved to the side, his sex brushed against her hip—and he hissed and bit his lower lip hard enough to nearly draw blood.

"Don't stop," she begged.

His lids popped open. "Oh, I'm not going to. Hell no."

With that, he lowered his mouth to her breast again—but he didn't stay there. He started going down her body. First, it was off to the side, on her ribs. Then it was across her stomach . . . and on to the curve of her hip.

At first, she wasn't sure what he was doing—but then she closed her eyes and bowed up.

Because she realized *exactly* what he was doing.

His thumbs hitched the waistband of her PJs and she lifted her hips as he pulled down the loose plaid flannel. And then they were both naked. Thank God.

Daniel continued on, his mouth kissing a path to her waist, to her hip . . . and going lower still. When his palms caressed her thighs, she bent up her knees and opened herself.

"Lydia," he moaned as he drew his tongue along her lower abdomen.

Now she writhed, her peaked breasts undulating toward the ceiling.

"I can't wait anymore," she gasped.

Well, didn't he follow direction well.

His mouth swooped between her legs, pressing a kiss to the top of her sex before he swirled into her with his tongue. With a growl, he became a whirlwind at her core, sucking her in, lapping at her, penetrating her with his fingers at the same time.

As she looked down her body and got an eyeful of his dark head between her thighs, the sight of him coupled with the hot, wet sensations pitched her into a release that shot through her like a thunderbolt, her pelvis thrusting forward, her spine arching again, every cell in her body blowing apart.

Daniel rode it all through with her, keeping the orgasm going, his two fingers inside of her finding a rhythm that brought her to the brink again just as the first release was subsiding.

He was a master of pleasure. He was power and control. He was, in a strange and undefinable way, taking not just her sex, but her soul. She was . . .

Claimed.

◆　◆　◆

Daniel had been prepared for hot. He got surface of the sun.

He'd been ready for getting into it. He was desperate.

He'd been psyched for a release. He was hit by a frickin' tsunami.

As he worshipped Lydia's core with his mouth, he was lost in the feel and taste of her. The noises she was making. The way her nipples and breasts bounced as she jerked and thrashed her way through the pleasure he gave her. And when he eased back a little and watched his slick, glossy fingers go in and out of her—

His voice exploded out of his throat. "*Fuck!*"

All at once, his arousal went haywire on him, the orgasm he had been holding back, the pain in his balls, the urgent need to release, getting away from him. Like a teenager, he pumped into the towel that was wadded up under his hips, ejaculating—

"Damn it," he hissed.

Lydia lifted her head and looked over her tight-tipped breasts at him. "What?"

Looking up from her glistening sex, he closed his eyes. And then he spoke a line he'd never thought would come out of his mouth.

"This never happens to me."

"I don't understand—"

When he sat up with the towel in his lap, she looked down at him. Looked back up.

"I swear, this has never happened to me before," he muttered.

"Did you—"

"I mean, I'll be ready to go again." He stared at her through lowered lids. "That is *not* going to be a problem with you."

Bringing his fingers to his mouth, he sucked them in, and then deliberately split them with his tongue—and was gratified by the way Lydia gasped with an erotic jerk. Unable to resist, he planted a palm by her waist and held himself over her. Putting his hand back where it had been, he stroked her sex, thumbing the top of it. Then he lowered his head and flicked one of her nipples with his tongue. He worked her slow at first, but that didn't last. Faster and faster, he went—and when she started to come again, he took her mouth.

And swallowed her cries of release.

It almost made up for his lack of self-control.

Almost.

THIRTY-FOUR

O KAY, HE'S ASLEEP now."

As Lydia stared through the Plexiglas door into the transition pen outside the WSP's clinic, she monitored her wolf's slow, easy breathing as he lay on his side with his eyes closed. She'd hated tranquilizing him, but she had to do what was right by the animal. Her feelings couldn't get in the way.

And didn't that truism generalize. Especially after what she and Daniel had done in her guest room about two hours ago.

Her emotions had been in turmoil ever since. After those orgasms? She could feel herself getting attached to him in ways that he wasn't going to want, and she wasn't going to enjoy in the long run.

With a hot flush coming on, she glanced across the exam room. Daniel was looking at her as he leaned against the counter and sink. In fact, it felt like he hadn't stopped looking at her since he'd learned all kinds of things about her body—

"Do you want me to go inside there and pick him

up?" He glanced at the Plexiglas door. "I can take him to the ATV?"

"I think you're strong enough to carry him, right?" She put her palms forward. "And don't worry, he really is out, and we've got a good thirty minutes until he wakes up. You're safe."

"I'm not afraid of him."

Under her breath, she muttered, "You and C.P. Phalen."

"Hmm?"

"Nothing. And yes, let's do that. I'll unlatch the pen gate and we can put him on the back of the ATV to drive him out into the preserve. I'll sit with him."

Daniel nodded and came over. For a moment, their eyes met, and she knew that he was thinking about what they'd done together.

"Lydia," he said softly.

She could only stare up at him. "Yes."

It was an answer, not an inquiry, and he nodded, as if they'd made concrete plans to finish what they'd started.

But God, she was in over her head, wasn't she.

Opening the Plexiglas door, he went over to the wolf, put his arms under the animal, and lifted all that furred weight off the ground like he was merely picking up a newspaper.

Rick would so not have approved, Lydia thought sadly as she stepped out and closed the exam room up.

After she opened the gate, they went around to

the ATV, which was parked by the rear entrance of the building. Daniel had fixed the leak in the fuel tank—or patched it, as he'd explained, so that it was good enough for them to take the thing out into the preserve. And if it died halfway back after they'd freed her wolf? Who cared, they could walk.

"I'll sit on the rear platform," she said as she hopped up onto the carry shelf that was mounted across the back tires.

"You sure? That's a hard seat."

"I'll be fine." She arranged herself and put out her arms. "Lay him across my lap. And go slow."

Daniel leaned down and draped the wolf over her legs. To make sure she was steady, Lydia braced her hiking boot on the corner of the cargo level.

"You guys okay?"

She nodded and stroked the wolf's fur. "Ready. And just go for about a mile, starting at the main trail and taking every right you come to. I want to free him as far as possible from the hotel."

"You got it."

As Daniel mounted behind the handles, the suspension absorbed his weight with a lurch-and-settle. Then the engine came on, the whiff of gas making her nose itch.

"Let's do this," he said.

He eased them forward and onto the WSP's private path to the main trail. When things widened, he picked up speed and avoided the roots that had broken through the dirt track, the subtle swaying of their forward motion hypnotic.

Meanwhile, she held on to her wolf.

With the trees going by and the fresh pine in her nose . . . she was not relaxed in the slightest. Staring out at their wake, she was barely aware of being on the back of the ATV. If it weren't for the fur against her hands, she wouldn't have known where she was.

Fourteen.

Daniel had been fourteen years old when his mother had killed herself. When he had jumped off a bridge to try to save her. When he had lost his hold in the cold water and no doubt barely got out of the river alive.

No wonder he compartmentalized emotion like he did.

Closing her eyes, she went back to being on that bed with him, all naked and totally exposed. He had been an incredible lover, and contrary to what he'd thought, the idea that he'd been so into pleasuring her that he'd lost control himself was pretty much the biggest compliment she'd ever been given.

He hadn't spoken much afterward.

When she'd collapsed in a boneless heap, he had held her to his chest and stroked her hair. And when they'd finally gone their proverbial separate ways, her to take a shower, him to downstairs for food, she'd been floating. He'd made them breakfast. They'd murmured over the eggs. He'd driven them into work early, before Candy had come in.

And everywhere she went, his eyes were always on her. Tracking her.

Not in a creepy way. It was as if he found her . . . captivating. A mystery.

She liked being someone's fascination.

Scratch that . . . she liked being Daniel's.

But what about when he left, when he moved on? He was going to leave a helluva hole to fill.

Assuming she lived that long.

As he pared off at the first branch in the trail, going to the right, just as she'd told him to, she tried to stop thinking like that. Thinking at all.

Focusing on the wolf, she ran her hand over his gray-and-white fur. The currents of air ruffled the stray, longer hairs and teased his tail, and she sent up a word of thanks to Rick—and then added a prayer in her grandfather's tradition.

For the wolf.

And for Daniel.

◆ ◆ ◆

Daniel was pretty good at distances. After taking three right turns, and heading so far into the preserve that even the hotel's shave job on that forested ledge was no longer visible, he eased off the gas and let things roll to a stop.

Over the *putt-putt* of the ATV's idle, he said, "This good?"

"This is perfect," Lydia said.

He cut the engine and left the key in the ignition. Dismounting, he went around and stood off to one side. Lydia was petting the wolf, running her hand in the direction of his fur, over and over again.

She didn't want to say goodbye.

As he watched her, he knew how that felt—and maybe that was why he couldn't stop looking at her. He didn't understand what it was about the woman that had gotten him so deep. Was it her hair? Her eyes? The feel of her body, the taste of her lips?

What was it exactly?

Some kind of magic as far as he could tell. Except it was not enough to keep him here, and in fact, it was something that made leaving an imperative.

But he didn't want to say goodbye, either.

"I should just let him go," she said in a sad way.

"It's gotta be tough," he murmured. "What with Rick having worked on him. Last ties and all that."

Her hair had fallen forward and was blocking his view to her face, so he reached out—as if he had any right to reposition the waves behind her ear. Before he made contact, though, he snatched his hand back.

"You mind if I step away and smoke?" he asked. "I'll stay downwind."

"No, that's fine. I just want to have a little more time."

Daniel nodded, even though she wasn't looking at him.

Walking off a short distance, he leaned back against a tree and took out the open pack. As he flipped the top, he was surprised to find so many of the Marlboros gone. When had he been smoking so much? Whatever. Lighting up, he coughed into his fist and then stared out to the valley. The northernmost tip of the lake was gleaming in the sunshine and the unseasonable warmth seemed like a peace offering from the weather, a way of making up for the brutal, long winter.

God, he was tired. And that fucking nightmare, just what he didn't need—

"I think he's coming around," Lydia said. "We better lay him down and move away. We can watch him to make sure he fully revives, from a distance. Rick always . . ." Her voice caught and she cleared her throat. "When Rick and I used to do this, we made sure that the wolves were safe, but not interfered with. He wouldn't . . . well, he never approved of me getting so close."

Daniel glanced at the lit Marlboro. For some reason, it was down nearly to the quick, like he'd been puffing for a good ten minutes.

His sense of time was really fucked, wasn't it.

"You took amazing care of him," he said as he killed the butt with his fingertips and put it in his back pocket. "That's all that matters."

As he went over to her, she said, "Rick's standards

were higher than mine—or maybe my heart is just too in it. I should be more professional."

Studying her, Daniel thought, *I want to hold this memory forever. Of this woman and her wolf, both so fierce, so fragile.*

"You're beautiful," he said hoarsely.

Her shy eyes lifted to his. "My hair's a mess."

"Don't change, Lydia. Keep your heart just as it is. Will you promise me that?"

She blinked as if he were speaking in a foreign language. Then she tilted her head. "You sound so ominous."

"Here, I'll get him off of you."

As he bent down to get his arms under the animal, the smell of Lydia, of her shampoo, her clothing detergent, her skin . . . was enough to burrow into his brain and knock out his higher reasoning. Forcing himself to remember what the hell he was doing, he picked up the wolf and straightened.

"Where do you want me to lay him?" he asked.

And she was right about the animal coming around. Those closed eyelids were not so closed anymore, and there was resistance in the legs and in the neck that hadn't been there when they'd done this back at the pen.

"Over here," she said. "In this patch of sunlight."

Lydia walked up a little incline and then dropped into a crouch in front of a soft bed of pine needles that was glowing with golden illumination.

As Daniel went to her and put the wolf down, the sun bathed the animal in a pool of beautiful light.

"He'll be warm here," he said.

"That's the idea."

They stood up at the same time. Then she put her hands on her hips and stared down.

"Come on," Daniel murmured. "He's really waking up."

On that note, the wolf's eyes locked on Daniel and those jowls twitched like innate aggression was also coming back online—and the predator didn't like what he was looking at. Yet there was nothing like that sent Lydia's way. It was almost as if the animal was protecting her.

Yeah, well, back off, fuzz ball, I got that job, Daniel thought to himself.

Although for how much longer?

He put his hands up and took a step back from the wolf. "Relax, I'm not going to hurt her."

"I'm not sure he speaks English."

Daniel found his stare returning to the woman who was haunting him, even as he was standing right next to her.

"Well," he said roughly, "I mean it just the same."

THIRTY-FIVE

I PROMISE, I'LL BRING it back in one piece."

As Lydia stood over Candy's desk, she smiled at the other woman like everything was fine. Like life hadn't gone haywire. Like she wasn't lost in familiar surroundings.

"You look like shit," the woman said.

"Are we back at this again?" Lydia pushed her hair off her face. "We talked about not using that kind of language."

"Did we? I can't recall. Fine, poo-poo. Is that better? Or do you want me to go with 'doody.'" Candy motioned around the empty waiting area. "God knows I wouldn't want to offend alllllll these people in here. I mean, we got a standing-room-only full of church-goers. These hankies start flying and we're at Six Flags without the rides."

Lydia dropped her head. "You're trying to be funny."

"Is it working?"

"Yes."

"Oh, good. I mean, you look *so* much better now." The woman held out something. "God, will you mop up here before you get me started?"

"I'm sorry?"

A Kleenex box was jogged in front of Lydia with impatience. "Clean your puss up, girl. We'll have none of that crying stuff."

Flushing, Lydia snapped a tissue free. "Sorry, I'm sorry." She pressed her eyes with the soft cotton—God, she hadn't even realized she'd teared up. "I'm fine. Really."

"Good. So am I." The Kleenex disappeared and was replaced with car keys. "We're both fine. Don't hit anything."

"I won't."

On the way to the door, Lydia had a feeling that some other things were said. Nothing was tracking, though—which considering she'd just promised not to run into anything with Candy's car was probably something she needed to address before she clicked that seatbelt in place.

Outside, she took a deep breath. Then she walked over to the parking area. As she got in behind the wheel, she took a moment to feel how impossible it seemed that Rick was never, ever going to bring his Jeep into work again. Ever.

At the end of the day, so much in life was malleable. Death, however, was the hard stop, the existential rigor mortis that never departed the remains, everything frozen in whatever position it had been in: No more cars to be driven. No more clothes to be worn. No money used or earned, no food consumed in the fridge or wet washing put in the dryer.

She'd learned that sad truth from her grandfather's passing, especially when she'd packed up their little house and had to give away all his clothes.

Because really, why was she keeping any of them without him?

Trying to get out of her mourning spiral, she was extra careful as she backed out, making sure that she gave Daniel's Harley plenty of space—you know, in the event her eyes were not judging distances accurately.

Before she put things in drive and gave the engine some gas, she glanced at the bike. The saddlebags weren't on it.

Because they were still on the floor, in the far corner of her guest room.

And she was glad they were there.

It meant he was still in Walters. Still in her house.

What he'd said when they'd freed the wolf, about not hurting her, had been . . . a lovely sentiment. Yet instead of the words warming her heart, they'd chilled her to the bone. She felt like death was stalking her house and she knew she was safer with Daniel in it— plus there were other, sexual reasons she wanted him there.

He was an illusion, though.

Although was anyone mortal really any more than that?

Lydia drove off over the gravel. When she got to the county road, she went right and headed down to the highway. The nearest biggish town was about thirty miles north, and she covered that distance by going up only two exits. That was the deal in this part of up-state. Lot of distance between everything.

The high school she was looking for was not far from the highway. No doubt it had been purposely lo-cated just off the interstate so that the kids from Wal-ters and the other small satellite towns could funnel in from all four compass points efficiently. As she pulled into the parking lot, there were cars in the spaces—the teachers and staff, and maybe the seniors, too, lining up their sedans, trucks, and minivans, in orderly rows off to the side of the building's single-storied sprawl. Meanwhile, out in the back, bleachers framed a playing field that was ringed by a red and green track.

The sprawl was right out of the John Hughes lexicon.

She found a vacancy about four rows from the en-trance, and after she pulled in, she grabbed her bag and got out of Candy's sweet-scented smell-mobile. Her purse was heavier than usual, and as she slung it up onto her shoulder, her neck felt the strain.

Striding to the entrance, she jogged up and crossed beneath an overhang that read LINCOLN HIGH SCHOOL in white letters. On the far side of a bank of glass doors, there was a lobby filled with glass-fronted cabinets crammed with trophies, ribbons, and photographs from earlier eras.

The front office was right there, and as Lydia walked in, the receptionist looked up from her desk. "Oh, hi. Are you—"

"Yes, I'm the one who called."

"I'm glad we have what you need." The woman pointed to a clipboard that had a pen tied on it by a string. "If you could sign in, I'll tell you where to go."

Lydia glanced down—and was struck by the fact that it was the same brand of clipboard that hung by the Plexiglas door to the transition pen. And between one blink and the next, she saw Rick's notes on her wolf. When he had eaten last and what. When he had taken a drink and how much.

"You okay?"

She shook herself back to attention. "Oh, sorry. Yes, of course."

Lydia filled in her name under the column marked "Visitor." Then did the same where you were supposed to put the date and time. Under "Reason For Visit," she put "Library."

"Okay," the receptionist said, "you want to go out of here and take a . . ."

The woman was very animated, all smiles and hand motions, as if she enjoyed telling people where to go in the school. Absently, Lydia noted that she was just on the cusp of middle-aged, youth still glowing in her face and in her eyes, even though her clothes were a little old-looking for her.

"Great, thank you," Lydia murmured.

As she stepped back out into the lobby, she had no idea where to go. Hadn't the receptionist told her to take a left?

Fortunately, there were signs mounted at all the corners and intersections of the halls, and there were even arrows that led to where she needed to go. And what do you know, the library was just what she expected: Glass-fronted, with rows of stacks and a sitting area with magazines and periodicals, it was another throwback to an earlier time, before iEverything and computers made life virtual, even if people were face to face.

Ahhh, the dry, inky smell of books.

The checkout desk was over to the right, and as she stepped up to the counter, a man in a navy-blue button-down and a bow tie with gold stars on it smiled at her.

"Are you the lady looking for the old computers?"

"Word travels fast." She smiled back to be pleasant. "And I really appreciate this."

"We get the odd request from time to time and we're happy to be a resource. Come with me." The man walked off into the stacks, striding faster than she'd expected or his belly seemed to suggest he'd be capable of sustaining. "The students only use the new

PCs, of course. But you never know, and that's why we keep everything."

There was a set of stairs by an elevator, and the man took the former, traveling down the shallow, rubber-treaded steps at a good clip and whipping around a single landing. Down below, in the basement, there were more stacks, as well as an old-fashioned micro-fiche machine and—

"Here she is." He patted a smudged, cream-bodied monitor that was the size of a small stove. "She still works. Of course, it'll depend on what kind of program your files require."

Lydia inspected the tower that was under the wooden desk. "I, ah . . . I don't really know a lot about computers. I just have these old floppies and I'd like to see if I can still print out my fifth-grade book reports."

"So you think it's Word files?"

"Is this hooked up to the Internet?"

"As a matter of fact, yes. Remember dial-up? Well, this thing used cable even back then. It was state of the art when it was gifted by one of our alums—so you can hop on the web if you need to. Here, I'll get you started."

He leaned over and hit a button and there was a whirring sound. "We're open access, so you don't need a password to sign on or access the Internet. There are age-restricted sites, though."

"You don't need to worry about that with me."

"I didn't think so." He smiled again. "I'm upstairs if you need help. I'm no Bill Gates, but I know my way around this machine a little. Just holler up and I'll hear you."

Lydia smiled back at him and sat down. And then she waited until he was gone before she got one of the floppies out of her purse.

Her heart skipped a beat as she leaned down to the tower and put the disk into the slot. Before she pushed it home, she reached around and found the cable wire that was plugged into the back, the one that, just as the man had said, connected the computer to the Internet. After she unclipped and pulled it out, she finished the job with the floppy, the insertion smooth, a little click locking it in place.

The monitor was ancient, the graphics rudimentary. But the rounded screen delivered information to her eyes just fine: The disk was not password protected. And the file directory was . . . full.

The listings were just numbers and letters, no words that made any sense. And the dates were from twenty-five years ago, assuming she was reading them correctly.

She opened the first in the list—

Lydia jerked her head back. Then she leaned forward, so far forward, she knocked into the keyboard.

It was . . . a page from a document. Not the first page, but something in the middle, going by the number in the lower corner, and the footnote that had some kind of code on it. Plus the paragraphs were referring to a "subject" which was not defined. And the "subject's" response to . . .

The gasp she let out was so loud, she slapped her hand over her mouth and looked around in case the checkout man had heard it.

When he didn't come down the stairs, she refocused on the screen. As her eyes went from left to right, left to right, words stuck out like screams in the dark: "Non-Hodgkin's lymphoma." "Melanoma." "Osteosarcoma." "Glioblastoma." She didn't need her biology degree to know they were all cancers, and very bad ones.

And these vicious, deadly cells had been "introduced to the subject." To test "the subject's immune response to the diseases."

And that was the end of the page.

With a shaking hand, she moved the mouse and closed the file to open another one. It was also a page from the middle of a report. A different page number. Same footer ID. And now she was noticing that the image was actually a photograph of an old-fashioned Xerox copy, the letters fuzzy, black dots speckling the margins randomly, everything tilted a little like the original hadn't been put squarely on the copier's bed.

This second page also picked up in mid-sentence, but now she got details. The subject was—female. A female who weighed a hundred and twenty-four pounds. Subject was considered healthy, with various scans and test results being listed: Chest X-ray. Internal ultrasound. EKG. Notations on blood pressure, heart rate—

Lydia read the next paragraph in a whisper. "CBC reveals abnormalities that are so extensive it is impossible to assess what is normal for the species."

So they were working on an animal? she thought.

That made no sense. Why were they infecting an animal with human diseases?

She closed out and opened the next file.

And that was when she saw a word that made no sense at all. She was so sure she had it wrong, she had to read it twice. A third time.

Vampire.

THIRTY-SIX

WHEN LYDIA FINISHED skimming the fifteen files on the disk, she bent down to the tower, ejected the Memorex, and put the floppy back in her bag. Then she just sat there with her purse in her lap and her arms wrapped around the contents of Peter Wynne's UPS package.

On so many levels, her brain rejected everything she had read, but the document fragments were what they were: Some company had created a program for testing human diseases on another species, a humanoid species that was so closely related to *Homo sapiens* that there were vast overlaps in anatomy—and vast differences, too.

"Oh, God."

She passed her hand over her face, and considered throwing up in the black trash can next to the little wooden desk.

"I have to go," she said into thin air.

Getting to her feet, she knocked over the chair, and when she went to right it, the other disks poured

out of her bag. She was picking them up off the linoleum and stashing them as fast as she could when the
checkout man with the galaxy bowtie came down the
stairs.

"You okay there?" he asked.

"Oh, I'm fine." She held her purse between both
hands so he wouldn't notice how badly she was shaking. "And I'm all done here."

"Was it fun to read your old work?"

"What?"

"Your old book reports."

Lydia released her breath. "Oh, yes, of course. Such
a trip down memory lane."

"We're all getting so much older. Me more than
you, obviously. But life is a terminal disease, you know.
None of us get out of this alive."

"True, true." Well, wasn't that a cheerful thought.
"Ah—"

"So did you want a printer?"

"I'm sorry, what—oh, right. No, I think I'm going
to wait. It was enough just to know I have the files."

"Sounds good. You can always come back."

Lydia followed in his wake back to the stairs and up
to the first floor, making sure there was plenty of distance between their casual conversation and the roaring
storm in her head.

The next thing she knew, she was out by the
visitors' office. The woman who had checked her in
was turned away, the phone held to her ear by her

shoulder as she typed on a computer. Not wanting to disturb her, not knowing if she even had to tell someone she was leaving, Lydia walked toward the front doors—

Bells rang, shrill and loud, all around her.

Students now. A rushing tidal wave of them, talking, walking, heading out to a lineup of cars that had formed in front of the school.

To avoid getting trampled, she moved over against the glass cases. To avoid making eye contact, she turned to the awards and the trophies. With her thoughts so scrambled, she could make sense of none of it: Not what was in front of her, both shiny and dusty, not what was behind her, so chaotic and frenzied—

At first, the photograph didn't register outside of the fact that it was black and white, and had been taken out on the bleachers. The girls who were the subjects had been arranged on the rows in a triangular fashion, and their matching uniform shorts and muscle shirts were in what she guessed were the school's red and blue colors. But it wasn't a recent image. Their hairstyles had the trademark Farrah Fawcett wings of the seventies.

"Girls' Varsity Track," read the printing on the frame. "1979–80. NY State Champions."

And then there were the names of the team members, first initial followed by the last—

C. McCullough.

Lydia frowned. "Candy?" she said into the din around her.

Bending closer, she searched the faces of the girls, and sure enough, a younger version of Candy was in the second row from the bottom, all the way on the left by the coach—

"Wait, what . . . ?"

The man standing by the team, wearing slacks and a colored shirt with the school emblem on it, was big, but trim, with a straight, no-nonsense jawline and black hair that was cut short. Going by the planes and angles of his face, he was somewhere in his forties.

"Eastwind," she breathed as she read the line, "T. Eastwind."

Somehow, in some impossible way, Sheriff Eastwind was in a photograph forty years ago . . .

. . . looking exactly as he had when she'd seen him the day before.

◆ ◆ ◆

"You are *not* going to believe this."

As Lydia came through the WSP's front door, Candy was already focused on her and talking, like they'd been in a conversation the entire time she'd been gone.

"What?" Lydia asked with exhaustion.

"Here you go."

The envelope that was held out over the reception desk had nothing written on it and wasn't sealed. Lydia traded car keys for the thing.

"Thanks for the loaner," she said. "I topped up the gas. And listen, I got a message from Paul saying mine will be ready tomorrow—"

She stopped as she pulled her paycheck out. "What's this?"

"I think it's self-explanatory?" Candy sat back. "I called the bank to try and see where we were because the electrical bill is due—and surprise! We have fifty thousand in the bank."

C.P. Phalen, Lydia thought.

"That's amazing," she said.

"So you can buy yourself dinner tonight. And maybe for someone else, too."

"I don't know what you're talking about."

"Okay." Candy smirked. "But Bessie's husband saw you on the back of a certain motorcycle this morning coming in here early. So unless our groundskeeper is running a side hustle as an Uber driver . . ."

Lydia shook her head. "I just caught a ride into work with him because we had to release my wolf. And would you rather come in at eight in the morning with me?"

"Nope." Candy put her hands up. "I start at eight-thirty."

"Exactly."

"But tell me something, where is he staying?"

Lydia didn't hesitate because she'd been waiting for someone to ask her this: "Out in the woods on the preserve. He showers in Trick's stall in the equipment building."

"Well, there you go. I guess the mystery's solved."

As Candy just stared across the desk, it was clear the woman wasn't buying the story, but whatever, nothing to be done about that.

And then Lydia frowned at her check. "Wait, who should sign this? There's no signature on the bottom."

"You have to."

"But I can't sign my own check, can I?"

"Okay, fine. I'll just go out into the woods and find a wolf to do it. But don't worry, I'll make sure the paw print is of age."

"How about I start with looking at our bylaws."

"All right, and when that tells you nothing, we'll put the wolf plan in play."

Lydia laughed a little and started to walk away. Then she looked back. "So I went to Lincoln High just now."

Candy frowned. "What for?"

"Just needed to use the library. You used to be on the varsity track team."

The woman laughed. "Oh, my God, you saw that picture. Makes my pink hair seem not so scary right? I had feathered hair for days back then. That was right after my parents moved us out of Brooklyn. As you've noticed, I kept the accent as a parting gift from my borough."

"You were a seventies queen, for sure." Lydia hesitated. "And your coach. That was Sheriff Eastwind's father, right? They look . . . like twins."

Candy's face did not change its expression. And her voice didn't alter. And . . . nothing really was off about the woman. But the air became charged around her.

"Yeah, that's right. He's the spitting image of his dad."

There was a long moment. And then Candy's brows lifted. "Is there something else?"

As Lydia's temples started to ache, she rubbed one of them. "No, nothing. I just thought the resemblance is uncanny."

With a shrug, Candy turned back to her monitor. "Sometimes that happens. Not that I know personally. My fur baby doesn't look a damn thing like me."

THIRTY-SEVEN

OUT IN THE preserve, Daniel took a break from the hammering. The temperature was around sixty degrees, which would have been fine for physical effort. The sky was cloudless, though, so the sun was baking him like a ham.

Fortunately, he didn't have to go far for relief.

The last of the three bridges was the one in the worst condition, but it spanned a cool mountain stream that was running. Hopping down onto the stones, he bent over and splashed his face and neck. As he righted his head, the cool water dripped onto his chest and was absorbed by his T-shirt.

To get at the bridge's problems, he'd had to deconstruct the whole thing, taking the handrails off as well as all the planks. The three base supports were the issue, the stream having eaten away at their undersides to rot the wood span. The good news was that there was enough left intact on the ends at the shores so all he needed to do was run supporting two-by-fours across the damage and nail the fuck out of it all. He'd brought six ten-foot lengths with him on the ATV—and with them now bracing the weakened sections, he was confident they'd get one more season out of the thing.

Glancing around, he hopped back up onto the shore and started in with the planks. There were about two dozen of them. He'd be done in a half hour and then he could return to the WSP.

And check on Lydia.

After he removed the old nails from the boards, he laid everything in place and went about resecuring them. Which turned out to be a fucking production. The hammer in his hand felt like it weighed fifty pounds every time he raised it over his shoulder—another example of how powerful the brain was. Courtesy of his mood, the simple movements felt like he was pushing an Army tank uphill, even though nothing had really changed about his life, his situation, his reality.

Well . . . except for Lydia—

"Fuck!" he spat as he nailed his forefinger a good one.

Shaking his hand out, he hissed and looked up—

The flicker came from down on the right, at a lower elevation on the mountain. Narrowing his eyes, he put his hand up as a shield to the sun.

And there it was again, something metal catching the rays.

Going over to the ATV, he took out the binocs

from the glove box on the dash. Training the lenses on where he'd seen the not-found-in-nature winking, he had to scan around before he caught it again.

A hatch. In the earth. Or at least that's what it looked like.

Finally, he thought.

Quickly finishing up with the planks, he locked the tools and his cell phone up on the ATV, took the key, and pulled a camo-covered poncho over himself. With the hood in place, he went off away from the trail, moving fast through the trees, keeping his head down and his feet light.

His gun was in the palm of his hand. Or rather, the gun with the suppressor that he'd lifted off that stalker. Who'd conveniently disappeared.

As he descended, he was aware of everything around him: The breeze in the air, the twinkle of the lake in the distance, the soft pine needles under his boots. No one was following him.

That he was aware of.

Closing in on where the flash had come from, there was a sense of inevitability about his path, as if a chain had wrapped around his chest and was pulling him in to a predetermined location. It had been a long, hard road, and he was finally finished with the searching part of things. And yet with every step he took, he told himself not to get ahead of things. He didn't actually know if this was what he'd come for . . .

yet some sixth sense didn't buy the mediation-of-his-expectations bullshit.

In his gut, he was convinced—

Stopping, he looked behind himself. Looked all around. Then he took cover behind a trunk—although considering he wasn't sure where the threat was coming from, he didn't know whether he'd actually given himself shelter or put a better target on his chest.

When nothing moved and there were no sounds, he decided to keep going, although he was more careful, moving from trunk to trunk like a slo-mo pinball.

The "No Trespassing" signs started up about a hundred yards later. The orange and black warnings were posted in a line extending down the slope of the preserve's mountain, demarking a change in ownership.

No fence, though. No cameras that he could see in the trees. No . . . anything.

He kept going, crossing onto the other land parcel.

Unfortunately, he missed the infrared beam that he tripped with his foot.

◆ ◆ ◆

Lost in thought, Lydia went to her office and sat at her desk. Glancing down at the empty tin she'd put her computer tower in, she was glad that their dumpster had been emptied on time. No way anyone could find the burned-out unit now, and if somebody from law enforcement came looking for it, it wasn't like she could be blamed for throwing out a ruined PC when she wasn't a party to any official investigation.

As she looked at the empty surge protector, she told herself she needed to do something. Instead, she just sat there.

Out in the waiting area, Candy answered the phone and talked to someone. After a couple of sentences, it became clear it was Rick's family calling to report on the where's and when's of the memorial service. A few minutes later, there was the sound of the receiver being set in its cradle, and then creaking floorboards as Candy came down the hall.

The woman started talking before she entered the office. "Okay, so the funeral is going to be next weekend in Rhode Island. They've got some family overseas who want to come home for it." She leaned around the doorjamb. "Are you going to go? Both of us are invited, and we could carpool if you want. It's a—hello?"

"Huh?" Lydia shook her head. "Sorry."

"Listen, maybe you should go home and have a lie-down. You look like you need it."

No, what she needed was to find herself a computer accessory to print out all of those files on each of those floppies to read in private. And then she had to . . .

Do what, go where? she wondered.

"You're right," she mumbled. "I've got to snap the hell out of all of this."

"We'll figure out about the funeral later." Candy disappeared—and came right back. "Oh, and I've got a business question. Are we having the fundraiser next month or not?"

Lydia blinked as she tried to translate the words she damn well knew the meanings of. "Ah . . . that's something to ask the board. It's their people who are coming, not ours. Well, obviously not mine as I don't know anyone."

"Then you need to pick up the phone and find out what's going on. I've got vendors calling and asking questions. Tent setup, caterers, all this kind of stuff. I don't know what to tell them. I mean, I'm on the frontlines of this place, everything comes through me, but I have no authority—"

For some reason, everything about Candy became super clear, from her short shock-blond hair, to the blue eye shadow that matched her blue sweater, to her pink, perma-press slacks.

"What," the woman said. "What's wrong."

Lydia slowly got to her feet.

"I need you to be honest with me, Candy." As the words left her mouth, they were an octave lower than her normal tone. "No more fucking around. What do you know. What are you keeping secret."

The receptionist's eyes narrowed. "You're my boss now. If something was happening in this organization—"

"You open every piece of mail that comes here. Each supply order. All the packages and FedEx envelopes." Lydia stepped around the desk. "You have access to all the bank accounts because you pay the bills and do the bookkeeping. You are the network administrator for our computers, you got us our cell phones, you're my emergency contact at my doctor's."

She continued forward until she was standing over the woman. "Several million dollars is gone from the accounts—that I didn't even know had come in. The package you've been calling UPS about got delivered here—instead of Peter's home address, which was what was on the label. And you weren't all that surprised about Rick's death. So I'll say it again, what the fuck is going on here, Candy."

The receptionist's left brow raised, but other than that, there was no reaction. "You've just accused me of doing my job. Congratulations, Columbo. And how I feel about Rick is none of your business—"

"You know what's been happening under the surface here. You know the truth." Lydia searched the woman's face. "And you killed Peter Wynne. Didn't you."

THIRTY-EIGHT

AS DANIEL CAME up to the metal hatch that
had been installed in the ground, he looked
around. Except for a pair of crows circling overhead,
there was no one anywhere near him.

And now that he was right up on the damned
thing, he could see why it had caught and winked
back the sunlight. A rotten trunk had fallen off its
root bed and skidded down the slope, tearing a swath
of the pine needles off the circular seal—and in the
process, scraping some of the steel clean so it was reflective.

Four feet in diameter. With a wheel crank that was
low to the lid.

"Well, hello there, needle in a haystack."

Tucking his gun, he knelt down, grabbed the
wheel, and gave it a pull. A harder pull. With a curse,
he put all his strength into—

The wheel broke off its crank with a screech and
Daniel fell back, landing on his ass. "*Fuck.*"

He had to get inside. To complete what he'd come to do, he was going to need full access.

Repositioning himself over the seal, he wiped more of the dirt off to get a sense of what he'd need to open the thing. Talk about solid. There were no gaps around the—

The bullet sizzled by his ear and *pfft'd!* into the pine needles behind him.

With a lunge, he threw his body up and over the fallen tree—but because of the rot, most of the trunk was hollow so it offered only visual, instead of tactical, cover. Palming his gun, he hustled down to the base, where things were more solid.

Triangulating the location of the attack, he saw the black uniform behind an outcropping of rocks. About fifty feet away—

"Oh, look at you," he muttered as he recognized the face. "You got your eyes back, didn't you."

It was the guard he'd killed. The one he'd disarmed—

More bullets. Striking wood. Striking ground. Ricocheting off of stone.

Daniel ducked down. What he needed was some backup—

When the count of the bullets got high enough, he jumped up and ran hard, taking advantage of the nanoseconds that reloading required. And just in the nick of time, he back-flatted against one of the few oaks this high up on the mountain.

The guard thought he was still behind the downed trunk, the other man focusing forward as he aimed from behind those boulders.

Daniel leveled his gun and started to pull the—

Pop!

A bullet that was not his own hit the guard in the side of the skull, vaporizing his head, a red cloud with white flecks blowing off in all directions. The decapitated body slumped forward, landing with a thud—and then like the trunk that had revealed the hatch, the still-warm, still-twitching corpse slid forward on the slope until its momentum ended on a facedown.

Or no face, as it were—

Daniel swept his own muzzle around. And pointed it at the tall figure who'd snuck up on the scene.

The Walters Township sheriff was standing on a ridge about thirty feet away, boots planted, hand-cannon service weapon just lowering.

"I think you're safe now," came the dry comment. "At least from me."

With a glance over his shoulder, Daniel made sure he wasn't being rode up on, on the other side. "Am I?"

"I'm the law. I don't murder people."

"You'll excuse me if I don't fall for that."

The sheriff shrugged and strolled forward, putting his weapon away in its holster. But he didn't come at Daniel. He went across and stood over the guard.

Or what was left of the guard.

Daniel kept his gun on the man, tracking him as he leaned down.

"I know what you are, Daniel Joseph," Eastwind murmured. "And I know why you're here."

"You don't know shit about me."

"You're wrong about that." The sheriff shook his head. "No eyes to take this time, I'm afraid. That's what you did with the other one, didn't you. That's what you do."

"I got no clue what you're talking about."

"You killed the other one. I don't know what you did with the body, but you did something. And you took the weapons on him—did you stash them somewhere? I'll bet you did—before you walked out to the county road and Lydia picked you up. You hid them so she wouldn't find out what you'd done."

Daniel stayed quiet. Which was what you did when an opponent was busy sharing exactly how much they knew about you.

"You can't afford for her to know you killed him." Eastwind looked across the distance that separated them. "She has no idea what you are, does she."

"And what have you done to protect her," Daniel demanded. "I'm just curious. I mean, after she told you she was being stalked, that someone had been on her property, that there was a device under her car . . . what. Did. You. Do."

"She can take care of herself."

"She's a woman living alone—"

398   J. R. WARD

The sheriff laughed in a burst. "Your chauvinism is wasted on someone like her."

"And you're neglecting your duties—"

"You have no idea what my duties are."

"Not that confusing, are they? You're supposed to protect and serve, and when it comes to Lydia Susi, you're doing neither."

"Well, I just saved your life."

"Bullshit. I had him."

"Did you?" The sheriff rose up on his feet. "Then you're a gambling man who doesn't recognize the true odds when he sees them."

"I never gamble. I don't have to."

"As you say." Eastwind inclined his head. "At any rate, here's the way we're going to handle this. I'm going to take care of our little issue here, and you're going to forget you ever saw me. You're going to go back to that bridge, get on that four-wheeler, and return to the Wolf Study Project—where you are going to resign. Then you're going to get your things out of Ms. Susi's house and you're going to leave this area and never return."

"You have no right to order me around."

"Yeah, I do. This is my land."

Daniel narrowed his eyes and smiled a little. "You're going to have to answer to a higher power than your zip code badge if you want to get rid of me."

"Not really." Eastwind once again shrugged casually. "If you continue to be around Lydia Susi, you're going to die. And then you're no longer a problem to me."

◆ ◆ ◆

Standing in front of Candy, Lydia shook her head slowly. Then repeated the words she'd spoken.

"You killed him. You killed Peter."

In the silence that followed, the other woman's expression didn't change. Then again, she must have seen a confrontation coming, sooner or later, and prepared herself for it.

"You're way off base with that one," she said in a low voice.

"Am I? I don't think so." Lydia leaned in. "Did you get some of those millions of dollars? And then want more? Was he in your way?"

"I have a three-bedroom house and a cat. What the hell am I going to do with that kind of money."

"You tell me, Candy."

"Why should I bother." The woman wrapped her arms over her chest and set her chin. "You seem to have made up a better life story for me than I could have. The fact that it has absolutely *nothing* in common with anything I've done or even thought about no doubt doesn't bother you. Fiction is just too much fucking fun for people, isn't it. So, yeah, I've got nothing to add to your fantasy, sorry."

Candy looked down the hall, out to the waiting room. "But you are right about one thing. It has been two years since I've had a day off. You want to know why? It's not because I'm committing some kind of embezzlement. It's because this place is all I have, and while that makes me lame, it doesn't make me a criminal—or a murderer—thank you very much. So I'm taking the rest of what's left of today off, and when I come in here tomorrow morning, we're going to forget you ever said this shit to me. Or, if you want, call Eastwind. Have him come over to my house with some handcuffs and cart me off to jail. G'head. Let's see how far that goes, shall we? Anyway, have a good fucking evening. I'll see you tomorrow."

The older woman turned away. Walked away.

In her wake, Lydia stayed where she was as there was a rustling out in the waiting area, like Candy was putting on her coat and collecting her purse. Then the door opened and shut.

Heading back around her desk, Lydia went to the window, separated the blinds, and watched Candy back her car out and drive off down the gravel lane.

I'm never going to see her again, Lydia thought.

Hard to know if the portent was good news or bad.

"Shit," she said in the utter silence of the building.

Collapsing into her chair, she propped her head on her hand and remembered when she had first walked into the WSP. It had been for her interview with Peter, and she could vividly recall stepping out of the winter cold and into the warmth of the waiting room.

Candy had looked up from her desk and started talking, just as the woman always did.

As if they had been carrying on a conversation. For years.

Back then, Peter had been in his office every day, and Rick had been working in the clinic, and she had been full of excitement about her new job.

After so many years of feeling groundless, of being groundless, after her grandfather's death, she had thought, yes, finally.

Roots.

From which to grow.

But now, here she was. Alone—

The door out front opened, and footfalls came down the hallway, slow and heavy.

As she looked up, her breath caught even though she knew who it was. Hell, no doubt it was because she'd recognized the stride: Daniel's face was tanned from his time out on the preserve, and his hair was smooth from having been stroked by the wind as he had raced along the trails. Likewise, his clothes were marked with river mud that had dried into dirt.

She didn't give him a chance to speak.

Lydia sprung up and raced for him, throwing her arms around his neck as she launched herself against his powerful chest.

"Oh, God . . . ," she croaked. "I am so glad you're here."

THIRTY-NINE

I N RESPONSE TO Lydia's hard embrace, Daniel put
his arms around her stiffly. At first. But as she sank
into him and shuddered, he closed his eyes and nes-
tled her in under his chin.

"What happened?" he said, aware that he had a
report he should make of his own.

But could not.

"I just . . . I think it's all hitting me now." She pulled
back. "Everyone is gone. Peter. Rick. Now Candy.
They're all gone—but you're here. Thank God."

As she stared up at him, he intended to speak . . .
except he found that he'd lost his voice. Her eyes were
just so hypnotic, ringed with tears, glowing with emotion. All he wanted to do was protect her from hurt.
From harm.

Sweeping his hand over her hair, he rested his forehead on her own. "Lydia."

Her name was a preamble to words that he ultimately couldn't say: They stayed there in silence for
what seemed an eternity, their bodies creating a col-

lective warmth, their souls melding. Meanwhile, all around them, whirling fates that were only hinted at were like a ring of fire closing in on their future.

On their present.

But they had this moment. And if pricelessness was based on rarity, then this quiet instant was invaluable—because he knew that it wasn't going to happen again.

When he lowered his mouth to hers, he had no conscious thought. He couldn't afford to think. He'd spent the return trip on the ATV reliving the feel of the hatch's cold wheel under his hands. He heard once again that rogue gunshot. He saw the uniformed guard's head blow up.

He remembered the red spray in the air.

As he kissed Lydia, as he licked into her mouth, all of that receded. None of it was with him, anymore. She was the great eraser.

And it was more than the present she took with her. She took his past, too.

Without warning, Daniel threw himself into her, bending her backward until she gripped his shoulders and his strength was the only thing keeping her off the floor. He kissed her harder and harder, and then he kicked the door shut and cleared her desk off with his arm, things hitting the floor, something breaking.

Like either of them cared.

He laid her down on the top, her body thumping against the wood. "I need you," he said. "I have to . . ."

Her answer was a scramble with her hands at her pants as she released the button, yanked at the zipper. When she kicked off her boots, they banged against the side of the desk, and bumped as they hit the floor, and then the jeans were gone—

He tore her panties. Just ripped the cotton right off of her.

He wanted to keep going, get her all naked, take his time.

But that wasn't happening in her damned office.

Daniel did a yanking of his own, and his cock exploded out of his fly. Planting his palm by her shoulder, he leaned over her, grabbed the back of her thigh, and pulled her to the edge of the desk. As her naked ass squeaked on the wood, she cried out and her legs fell open.

He backed off a little and looked down. When he saw her glistening sex, bared to him, hungry for him, he felt his balls tighten.

Oh, no you don't, he told himself. *We're not going that route again.*

Taking hold of himself, he growled, "You're mine."

Gritting his teeth, he stroked the head of his erection up and down her core, and in response, she jerked up, her spine arching, her mouth falling open. With her hair spilled out around her, loose and shining, and the flush on her face, and her gasping and straining for breath, she was life to his numb heart, warmth to his cold soul.

In another time, in another destiny, she would have been the path he walked, the way through his mortal landscape.

But they had met out of sequence—

Daniel thrust inside her and she grabbed on to his shoulders while she called out his name. Dropping his head, he started pumping. He meant to go slowly. He couldn't stop. He was not in control. His body was working independently, slapping into her, clapping against her. As he bent over and fucked her, he was grunting like an animal, totally unhinged, and underneath him, she was taking everything that he had to give her.

He'd gotten it wrong.

She wasn't his. It was the other way around.

She owned him.

◆ ◆ ◆

Underneath her lover, Lydia's body absorbed the powerful thrusting, Daniel's hips swinging at the base of his spine, his erection penetrating her deep and then retreating, penetrating her and ripping back out. It was hard—it was rough. It was raw.

And she wanted the sex to last forever.

That was her thought as a release shattered through her, torqueing her body, making her feel a rush of sensation she had never known before. And just as she flew, Daniel locked against her, his arousal kicking inside of her, making the pleasure crest again—

His mouth found hers, and they were kissing as the orgasms kept going.

And then it was over, as fast as it had begun.

Yet the sex was so intense, she felt like she had been gone for a hundred years as they fell still. In the aftermath, they were both breathing hard, and Daniel collapsed on her, his weight pressing her into the desk. Which could have been a down mattress for all she knew. Or cared.

"Fuck," he muttered against her ear. "I'm sorry. This is not what . . ."

Running her hands through his hair, she wrapped her legs around his hips and crossed her ankles. "What are you apologizing for? I wanted it, too. And don't worry . . . I can't have children. I'm not—there will never be any pregnancy."

He blinked, as if she'd shocked him. "I, ah . . . I should have thought about that."

"As I said, you don't have to." When he pulled up a little and looked awkward, she shook her head. "It's not something to be emotional about. To use a phrase of yours, it is what it is."

"I'm sorry."

She stroked his face, marveling that he was inside her. "Let's not ruin the moment. Come on, let's just . . . be here, where we are."

"Lydia . . . I wish so much was different."

With her forefinger, she smoothed his brows. "At least we have right now. Or . . . had it." As her sadness returned, she cradled his face in her hands. "Let's lock up, and go home?"

"All right."

He kissed her again. And again.

And after that, she tilted her head one way and he tilted his another, and then they were moving in a wave, softer, slower, but no less intensely. This time, the pleasure was like a flame, instead of a bomb burst, but it burned with just as much heat even though there was no urgency.

Holding on to him, she looked at the ceiling above her desk. With every thrust, her head moved back, and with every withdrawal, it righted itself, her visual point shifting to the same rhythm that he made love to her.

Oh, God, was she really doing this in her office? she wondered. Was this actually happening . . . or was it some erotic dream where she'd wake up with her thighs clenched and her breath tight as she pushed her face into her pillow on a groan of frustration—

"Daniel . . . ," she moaned.

Her orgasm was more gentle now, but longer in duration, and his mouth was on hers again as she rode it out.

Squeezing her eyes shut, she felt like crying. Instead, she just held him tighter.

As if he were liable to disappear at any moment.

Like a dream.

FORTY

D ANIEL PUT THE plate down in front of Lydia
and stepped back. "My cooking isn't as good
as yours."

When she looked up at him, her sad smile broke his
heart. "Come on now, this is a gourmet meal to me."

Not even close, he thought. Goddamn, he wished he
could make her some BBQ on a grill, out in the fading
August sun, with tinfoil-wrapped corn, and a big-ass
salad from a garden he took care of. Then homemade strawberry ice cream with hot chocolate sauce
he cooked up in the old-school way with corn syrup
and semisweet morsels. Oh, and he wanted to do all
this in a kitchen they shared, and eat it on the porch
they enjoyed their lazy Sundays on.

"Spaghetti out of a box," he said, "sauce from a jar."

But made with lov—

No, he stopped himself.

"Aren't you eating?" She looked to the sink and the
strainer. "I'll wait while you get your plate."

"I had a big lunch out on the trail."

"A picnic?"

He sat down across from her with one of his Cokes from the vending machine in the WSP's break room. With the amount he was drinking at work, he was going to empty the thing of all its red cans.

"Yup, a picnic. Made up of picnic things." He sat back and stretched. "Anyway, the last of the bridges is fixed. Equipment shed roof is solid. That doctored toilet is good for a little longer. ATV is fixed."

"Your checklist." Lydia twirled her fork around. "Everything done."

As she let the sentence drift, he wondered if she hadn't guessed he was leaving.

Fucking Eastwind. But that sheriff wasn't the reason behind the departure. Bottom line, the most important thing he could do for Lydia was get the fuck out of her life. In the short term, he might be able to keep her safe-ish, but he would have to go sooner rather than later—and he had his own enemies.

"Where is the rest of your family," he asked. "Cousins, uncles, aunts?"

Anybody.

Lydia shrugged. "It was just my grandfather and I. Only children of only children kind of narrow the family tree."

"What happened to your parents?" In response to his question, she just kept looking at her plate, teasing the spaghetti with the tines of her fork. "I'm really not prying."

Bullshit.

"It's okay," she said with a haunted smile. "I just . . . it feels like a different life and it was so long ago. And I guess . . . well, I've always lived in two different worlds, neither one nor the other. Talking about my mother and father feels like trying to reconcile the irreconcilable."

"Tell me," he whispered.

Lydia's smile was lost as she kept poking at her pasta. "Well, my mom left me right after I was born and my dad was never around. If my grandfather hadn't stepped up, I honestly wouldn't be here."

"Wait, what—your mother left you?"

"When I was born." Her eyes flipped to his as if she were checking to see how he was reacting. "I wasn't expected, either. You and I have that in common. And both our mothers left us, didn't they."

"Yeah, they did." Daniel shook his head. "So she just abandoned you at the hospital?"

"It was a home birth. At my grandfather's house. She tried to end the pregnancy . . . so many times." As he cursed softly, she kept going, her words coming faster as if she just wanted to get through the story. "She tried to give herself a home abortion with a coat hanger. Then there were two suicide attempts with pills. The last one . . . she threw herself in front of a car. But I stuck."

Daniel could only blink. "Fucking hell, Lydia."

"I only found it all out because her diary was

in the things she'd packed for the birth at the clinic. But labor happened too fast to get her across town, so after I was born, as soon as the bleeding stopped and she could walk, she got in her car and drove away. That bag was all I had. I slept with it under my bed. When I was ten, I finally opened it. She'd clearly packed with a mind to bolt from the hospital. I read the diary, but I didn't understand it all until a little later, when I was older." She laughed awkwardly. "The only picture I have of her was the one on her driver's license—she didn't even take her wallet, and I was glad I got it."

"Is she still alive?"

"I don't think so. I did try to find her, once. The picture on the license was real, but the name and address were fake." She put her fork down and pushed her hair back. "Oh, my God, this sounds like such a soap opera."

"So it was your father's father you lived with?"

She nodded. "He lived in a secluded area surrounded by trees. I used to sleep with the window by my bed open, even in the winter. The wolves singing to the moon were my biggest comfort."

"I love that sound, too," he murmured. "Is that why you ended up here? Working with them."

"It's just home to me. And let's face it, I do better in places where I don't have to be anything other than what I am."

"A behaviorist."

"Someone who doesn't belong anywhere." She shrugged a little. "Here, in this small town, where there aren't a lot of people? It doesn't bother me as much. And then there are the wolves . . . they're such beautiful creatures, and they need to be protected. Even predators can be hunted, and humans are the biggest threat to everything."

This was why she wasn't going to stop him from leaving, Daniel thought. She was used to being alone.

"There are other places you could live," he said. "Other jobs."

"I know." She took a deep breath. "And I will have to find one . . . God, this was not how I imagined everything coming to an end."

"You said Candy left, too? Did she just quit?"

"She decided to take the afternoon off. After everything, why wouldn't she. But whether or not she comes back tomorrow morning is anyone's guess."

He nodded. "I realize I've said this before, but I wish things were different."

Lydia pointed at him with her fork. "Truer words have never been spoken."

They fell silent for a while as she worked through what he'd made for her. When she was finished, he cleared her plate and fork and left her to drink the rest of her milk.

At the sink, he ran the water. "That package that was for Peter. Are you going to find out what's on those disks?"

"No. I think I just need to give it to the sheriff and let him sort it out. What am I going to do, you know?"

"Yeah, I know—"

"You're leaving tomorrow morning, aren't you."

◆ ◆ ◆

As Lydia let the words out, she was aware of her whole body tensing like she was about to be hit by a car. And yet what was that thing they always said?

Don't ask a question you didn't want the answer to.

In this case, it was true, she didn't want the answer. But she knew what it was.

"I'm going to be fine," she said. *Was that directed to him or herself?* she wondered. "One thing life has taught me is that I'll always be okay. One way or the other, I always have been."

Daniel opened his mouth. Closed it. Opened it again.

"It's all right." She smiled a little. Or tried to. "It's been a lot. I mean, I'm even committed to the Project, and I'm drowning in the drama. Someone just passing through like you are? I get it."

"I wish things were different. Jesus, I'm just saying that over and over, aren't I."

"It's okay." She put her hand over her heart. "And again, I'm inclined to agree."

There was another silence. Then he said, "You don't have to pay me."

414 J. R. WARD

"You worked the hours at the WSP, you deserve the money."

"Nah. I'm good."

Lydia looked to the window. Pulling back the mauve drape, she stared into the darkness—and wondered what was out there. And not in terms of a threat against herself. She wondered where he would go, where destiny would take him.

She already knew part of the answer to that.

Away from her was where destiny was taking him.

"It's late," she said to the window.

"It's only eight-thirty," he countered. "I believe it violates your nine p.m. rule to go to sleep now."

"Wow, feels like four in the morning—"

The floor creaked next to her and she looked up. Daniel was standing over her, staring down from his great height.

"Will I ever forget your eyes?" she murmured.

Another question she already knew the answer to.

"I'm nothing special." His shoulders lifted briefly. "Just a handyman."

"So much more than that."

Daniel put his hand out. "Come on. Let's go upstairs."

Letting the drape fall back into place, she got to her feet and slipped her hand in his. When they came to the steps to the second floor, he ushered her forward, all ladies-first. As she brushed by his body, she thought that the normal things that couples who lived together did were such a quiet joy. Brushing teeth at the same time over the sink. Changing into PJs together. Settling in and turning off the lights.

She wished she could have a lifetime of that with him.

Upstairs, they went to her room, not the guest room, but then he doubled back to go to the loo by himself. After she changed into PJs, he came back in and took the side of the bed closest to the door, plumping up the pillows and testing the mattress with his big palms. Leaving him to sort things of the bedding variety to his liking, she did her normal nightly routine down the hall at the sink—and when she returned to the room, she noticed that he'd moved his saddlebags in and put them right beside where he'd stretched out in the sheets.

That's where his gun is, she thought as she pulled the covers back on the far side and slid in with him.

It was the most natural thing in the world to move through the cool sheets and find his warm body. Relaxing in against his chest, he stretched his long arm out and clicked off the lamp.

Lydia stared out the open doorway. She'd left the bathroom light on, so the banister's supports cast shadows on the bare wood floor of the hallway.

I could do this forever, she thought.

Just regular stuff, like dinner, and laundry, and dental care. She supposed it was pathetic to have such simple life goals. Aspirations should be all about cars and fancy vacations—and this made her think about Peter Wynne.

How much of those renovations on that barn had been paid for by donations to the Wolf Study Project? Had he been buying that information about those horrific experiments? Or selling it?

And what the hell was she going to do with what she knew?

"Try to get some sleep," Daniel murmured. "Morning is coming."

Just like a freight train.

And she supposed it was a testament to Daniel that, with the long list of things weighing on her, he was the only part of it all that mattered. How else could their relationship have ended, though. Seriously. What other end could they have?

Besides, if he was gone?

She knew that he was safe.

There was peace to be had in that.

FORTY-ONE

LYDIA WOKE UP to the sounds of spring bird-songs and the warmth of a patch of sunlight on her face. As her eyes blinked open, she found herself looking across at the window seat with its cozy pillows and its throw blanket and its never-had-a-cat-but-really-should-have cushions.

With an ache behind her sternum, she edited her alcove fantasy. Instead of the solo flight with the book and the tea and that cat, she imagined two people propped against opposite ends, their legs intertwined in the middle under the blanket. As they traded news-paper sections, and tossed those that had been jointly read on the floor, a TV table in between them held a pair of mugs of coffee and a shared plate dotted with muffin crumbs.

Rolling over, she looked at the empty place where Daniel had slept. He'd made sure she was tucked in after he'd gotten up, and the head print on the pillows was proof of the hours they had passed, side by side, in her bed.

Down the hall, the shower was running.

Glancing at the clock, she saw that it was a little after seven a.m. Time was running out.

With a sense of urgency, she threw the covers off herself and rushed for the closed bathroom door. But as she came up to it, she paused at the panels. Then she knocked.

"Lydia?" came the muffled answer.

Opening the way in, she was hit with a rolling, warm mist. Across the narrow space, Daniel had opened the glass enclosure and was looking around it, his broad chest glistening from the water, a bar of soap in his hand, suds drifting down his abs and onto his thighs.

As she stared at his sex, she watched it thicken. Harden. Become erect.

Lydia stepped in and closed the door behind herself. Ditching her PJs, she joined him under the warm spray, and with hands that trembled with anticipation, she ran her fingertips down his pecs and onto his six-pack.

Sinking onto her knees, she touched the sweeping wings of his pelvis and zeroed in on his arousal. Just as he groaned and fell back into the corner of the tub stall, she wrapped her hand around his thick shaft and stroked—

"Oh, *fuck*," he groaned.

Opening her mouth, she teased his head with her tongue, licking at him before sucking him in deep.

She wasn't sure exactly what she was doing, but with the way his hips jerked and he threw out both arms to hold himself up, she figured her efforts were good enough. And she loved it. He was so big that he stretched her lips, and the feel of taking his full length made her sex run hot for him.

As she fell into a rhythm, one of his hands went down to her head, and he urged her along. With every surge forward, she opened her throat to accept as much of his length as she could. And with every retreat, she stroked him with her palm—

Looking up, she got an erotic show of his undulating abs, and his straining pecs and shoulders, and the underside of his chin as he thrashed his head back.

Just as she was sure he was about to find his release, she pulled back and opened her mouth—

Daniel moved so fast, she couldn't track him. One second she was on her knees with the warm spray on her back and her head, and his sex in her mouth, and her breasts swaying back and forth as she sucked him—the next, she was up and spun around, her hands planted on the edge of the tub as he bent her over.

The probing at her core was quick—and then he sank into her deep, her head and shoulders pushing forward into the shower door. Shoving the glass out of her way, she held on to the lip of the tub as he began to move inside of her.

Faster. Faster still.

As she felt his big hands hook on to her hips, she looked up. Next to the sink, there was a full-length mirror on the wall, and the sight of him bowing over her, his magnificent torso rippling with muscle as he pumped into her sex, his eyes closed, his teeth bared—

It was more than she could handle.

Lydia came hard—and as his name left her lips, she knew she was praying for him to stay. Some way, somehow.

She just didn't want to lose him.

◆　◆　◆

As Lydia began to orgasm, Daniel couldn't hold on any longer. Letting himself go, his erection kicked inside of her, his ejaculations filling her up, the pleasure making his head swim and his balance get fucked up.

God, he'd never had a problem with so-called stamina before. With Lydia? He was a sixteen-year-old kid, all hormones and no control—

The sound that came out of his throat was a growl and he switched his hold on her, running his arm up between her breasts and locking on to her collarbone and shoulder. Then he braced his legs and kept going, as if his body knew this was his last shot to be with her.

His final chance to feel this way.

He had no sense of time as they kept going, riding the pleasure, skimming the eternal with their bodies . . . but as all things started, so, too, they had to end, and when he finally slowed to a stop and threw out a hand to the tub edge to hold his torso up, he felt like a folding table with loose joints.

Total collapse was not far.

Daniel was gentle as he helped her straighten, and then he was holding her body against his own under the warm spray, the softness of her breasts on his hard chest, the sweetness of her mouth still tempting even though it was going to be a little while before he could do anything about the lust that never seemed to leave him.

Or never left him when she was around, that was.

As the shower's rain fell on them, he swept his hands down her soaked hair and then rested his palms on her narrow shoulders.

The knowing look in her eyes made him want to stay, made him want to find a solution that allowed that which was, to use her term, irreconcilable, somehow fit together. He was desperate to negotiate, but come on. Like destiny was ever inclined to take a seat at the bargaining table?

Because it was all he could do, he reached down for the shampoo bottle. Squeezing some into his palm, he washed her hair for her, sudsing up the strands, being careful not to get any into her eyes. Then he made sure all the soap was out, his broad palm moving over her head again and again.

There was an almost-new bar of Ivory soap in a dish, the edges still sharp as he rolled it over in his hands. He washed her body with the same care, and watching the suds slip down onto her glistening breasts and drip off her nipples was nearly enough to get him going again. But they were out of time, the hourglass having been turned over the second they'd met, all the sand now gone from the top half.

It was time to leave.

When he was sure her smooth, beautiful skin was clean, he kissed her chastely. "I'll get you a towel."

He cut the faucet as he stepped out and stretched for the rod across the way. When he turned back, he had to stop and just stare at the woman in the mist. She was as ancient as time in her naked glory, and some romantic notion in his fucking pea brain turned her into the pinnacle of all that had come before.

She was the apex.

At least for him.

And that was the way it worked, didn't it. Perfection was relative, not any singular characteristic, or even a group of them, but rather how the composite fit together for the person who was regarding the whole.

Could you fall in love in a matter of days? he wondered.

Fuck that. When it came to Lydia, he'd fallen in

seconds, standing in the doorway of her office for that interview.

Daniel dried her off and helped her out of the enclosure. Then he wrapped her up.

"What about you?" she said as he opened the door to the hall. "You'll get cold."

It's nothing compared to the center of my chest, he thought.

"Don't worry about me."

As she lowered her head, he tipped her chin back up. And kissed her softly.

Lydia left the bathroom, turning away from him, going alone to where they'd slept side by side. Her wet feet left prints on the wood, and as she disappeared into her bedroom, he watched the moisture marks recede.

Closing the door, he opened the saddlebags he'd brought in with him. He used the T-shirt he'd slept in to dry off, and he threw some clothes on. Back out in the hall, he glanced to her open bedroom. He could hear her moving around, the creaking of the floor and the rustling of cloth making him picture her standing in front of her bureau, snapping on her bra, pulling on her panties, drawing up pants, tugging on a shirt over her still-wet hair.

Shaking his head, he hit the stairs with his stuff. If he went in there?

He was never going to leave her.

Down in the kitchen, he set his bags by the door and hustled into the cellar. During dinner, he'd run a load of wash through her machines, and as he pulled out his boxers, alternate pair of jeans, and three T-shirts from her dryer, he pressed them to his nose because they smelled like her.

He was ascending the rough-hewn steps, halfway back up, when he heard the knocking on the front door.

Instantly alert, he put his hand to the small of his back—

Damn it, he'd been distracted and hadn't tucked.

Hurrying up to the kitchen, he leaned around the open cellar door, using it as a cover to look to the front of the house. Overhead, Lydia was jogging down the stairs.

"It's okay," she called out. "It's just Eastwind."

"Lydia, don't answer the door before I—"

"I've got it."

Just as she reached for the knob, Daniel dove for his saddlebags and got out a gun. As he wheeled around, he got a look at the sheriff standing in the entry. The man took off his hat and held it in front of himself with both hands.

"Is there something wrong?" Lydia asked the guy.

A pair of dark brown eyes shifted past her and locked on Daniel's face. The other man's expression hardened to the point of granite.

"Sheriff?" she said.

"I gave you a chance," Eastwind said to Daniel. "To do what was right on your own. But you didn't."

"What are you talking about?" Lydia glanced over her shoulder. "What's going on here?"

Daniel closed his eyes.

"He's not who you think he is." Eastwind took a folder out from behind his hat. "Daniel Joseph is an alias. He never worked at any of the businesses he provided you as references—"

"Hold on." She put her hands up and shook her head. "I don't know what you're—"

"Candy gave me his résumé yesterday morning. She wasn't sure she had done the background check right, and she was worried because he was . . . getting close to you. When I went deeper than she did? Nothing exists."

As the folder was pushed forward, she took it with a shaking hand. Then she looked back into the kitchen. "Daniel?"

Eastwind spoke up. "I'm not going to tell you how to run your life, Ms. Susi, but whatever this man has said about himself, whatever he's done for you . . . you can't trust it. I can't even find his true identity. He's literally a ghost."

There was a tense silence. And then Daniel gave her the only answer he could.

He bent down and picked up his saddlebags. Slipping them onto his shoulder, he thought about the night he'd spent beside her, staring up at the ceiling, looking for a way out that included her not hating him.

There hadn't been one.

"I don't understand. Daniel . . . what is he saying."

Except she was catching on. Even without looking at whatever the sheriff had put in that folder, she was coming to understand the truth—her heart was just having trouble getting on board with what her brain was evolving to.

"I called," she said insistently, looking back and forth between him and Eastwind. "I spoke to the apartment building and they told me they loved the work you did—"

"Who exactly did you talk to?" the sheriff asked. "Because I also called the numbers and every one of them gave him a glowing report. But then I checked the websites and the numbers listed were different. And when I sent a friend of mine to some of the addresses? Sure, they were apartment buildings and schools—just with other names. And none of them had ever had a Daniel Joseph working for them."

Lydia stared down at the folder. And then her eyes returned. "Daniel?"

With a grim stride, he walked forward, and he met her stare the whole time. Because he deserved every bit of the disbelief and dawning anger that was coming over her face.

"I'm sorry," he said.

"So he's right?" She opened the folder, but didn't look at the report. "You lied to me?"

Daniel narrowed his eyes at the sheriff. "I was leaving this morning."

"You're still here," the man said. "So you'll excuse me for not believing—"

"*Why.*" As Lydia spoke up, she stepped into Daniel's path, blocking his way out. "Why did you come to the Project in the first place."

"I never intended to hurt you—"

"Why are you really here? It clearly wasn't about a job for a drifter."

"I protected you. Back at that deer stand. With the locator—"

"That is *not* an answer to my question." She put up her hand. "Actually, don't bother. I'm not going to believe anything you say and you are not going to tell me the truth, anyway. Are you."

"Lydia—"

"Get out of my house." She moved aside, so that she stood next to the sheriff. "And I will say this in front of law enforcement, I don't want to ever see you again. If you come anywhere near me, I will protect myself in any way I have to and to hell with the legal consequences."

"You won't see me again," he told her.

"Good."

Daniel left out of the front door. And after he

walked over to his Harley, he off-shoulder'd his saddle-bags and made quick work of strapping them on the back of the bike.

This was not how he'd pictured going out.

Then again, he did feel like he'd been shot in the chest—and he'd always seen that kind of injury in his future.

It had just been literally, of course. Not because he was leaving a woman.

FORTY-TWO

LYDIA REMAINED STANDING as long as Daniel was on the property. But the instant his bike disappeared down her driveway, she weaved on her feet.

"Here, you should sit."

Eastwind took her over to the couch just as her knees went out from under her. With a wave of dizziness making her eyesight fuzzy, the folder fell from her hand, and as the three or four pieces of paper flew across the rug, he chased after them.

"You want some water?" the sheriff asked as he put the sheets back where they'd been and laid the folder aside.

"No." Actually, she was pretty sure she was going to throw up. "I'm fine."

As she went to push her hair back—which was still damp from the shower she'd taken with Daniel—her hands shook so badly they were a blur.

But she was not tearing up.

No, she was not doing that.

She would not give him any more weakness. She'd already let him have way too much of that.

"I am a fool," she mumbled.

"No." The sheriff sat down next to her. "You are not that."

Well, there was no reason to debate the point. Besides, she didn't really care about the why's of it all—

No, that wasn't right. There was one "why" she was very interested in, but she wasn't going to go into it with Eastwind.

"Ah . . ." She cleared her throat. "Have you found Peter? And please, let's not have the whole ongoing-investigation thing, okay? I don't have the energy for that right now."

Eastwind shook his head, and, thank God, didn't beat around the bush. "We haven't found him, no. We've reached out to his known relatives. They haven't heard from him in months. There's nothing on social media—and his cell phone was in the house. The last time he used it was the night before you called me, when you were stalked to that deer stand. After that . . . nothing."

She stared across the room without seeing a damn thing. "I don't know if the Wolf Study Project is going to survive this."

"It will. And you're going to keep working there."

She looked him square in the eye. "At this point, fifty percent of us are dead."

"You're here for a reason." He slapped his thighs

and stood up. "And anyway, I'm not going to let anything happen to you—even though you doctored that camera feed you gave me."

Lydia blinked in honest confusion. "What are you talking about."

"I know you altered the footage of the hiker attack on North Granite Ridge. I'm not going to take this any further than this conversation, but don't ever pull a stunt like that again, okay?"

The sheriff nodded to her and put his hat back on.

As he approached the open front door, she said, "How did you know."

The man cranked his head around, and as she looked into his face, a warning shiver went down her spine.

In a low voice, he replied, "This is my land. I know everything that takes place on it."

She got to her feet. "It was the bite marks on the hiker. Of course the coroner would recognize them as an animal's. So you're just testing me to see what I say."

Eastwind slowly shook his head. "No. It's because I was up on the mountain, and I saw it happen."

Lydia grew utterly still.

"I took a sacred oath to protect the things on my mountain, Lydia Susi, and I have been doing it for a very long time." He touched the brim of his hat and inclined his head. "You have a good day there, and be safe."

As he walked out over to his SUV and got in behind the wheel, she watched until he, too, was gone. Then she went across, shut the door, and stared into her house.

In a fit of paranoia—which maybe wasn't so paranoid—she stalked down to the kitchen. When she and Daniel had gotten back the night before, he'd hung out on the front porch and had a smoke— and she'd used that time to stash the floppy disks she'd been carrying around in her purse.

Jesus, to think she'd felt guilty about deceiving him.

On the counter by her refrigerator, there was a lineup of metal canisters reading Flour, Sugar, Rice, and Salt, and she went to the first in the row, the biggest one. Whipping off the lid, she yanked up the Gold Medal bag she'd encased in a Ziploc—

They were all there.

But she counted them. Twice.

"Okay," she said. "It's . . . all right."

The hell it was, but under the fake-it-til-you-make-it theory, maybe if she kept trying to sell the optimistic bullcrap to the universe, the tide would turn.

Taking the disks, she put them back in her bag— and realized that not only didn't she have a car, she didn't really have the need to go into work.

One step at a time, her grandfather had always said. That was all she needed to do.

The trouble was, she didn't have a clue what direction to go in. Oh, and then there was the pesky detail that her heart had broken into a million pieces.

For godsakes, she was still sore in intimate places from having slept with that liar.

◆ ◆ ◆

Lydia was still in the kitchen, and back-and-forthing about what to do with what little she had to go on, when her cell phone rang.

As she jerked to attention, she looked at the clock on the stove—

Forty-five minutes had passed. Jesus, she needed to pull herself together.

Taking her phone out of her bag, she looked at the screen. It was a local number, but not something in her contacts list.

As she accepted the call, her heart started pounding. "Hello?"

"Hey, so I'm finished."

"I'm sorry, what—wait, Paul?"

"Yeah," came the gruff response from the owner of Paul's Garage. "I'm done, so you can pick her up whenever you want."

Lydia sagged. "Oh, thank God."

"I told ya it'd be ready. You think I'd lie?"

It's not about the car, she thought.

"Thank you so much. I'll walk down to you now."

"Suit yourself."

As Paul ended the call by slamming down the

receiver, she thought it was a good thing he was a terrific mechanic with no competition for his business—

Lydia let out a shriek and jumped back.

In the front of the house, in the windows of the door, Candy was peering inside. As their eyes met, the woman lifted her hand.

"Sorry," the receptionist said through the panels. "Didn't mean to startle you."

With a curse, Lydia covered her pounding heart with her hand and went to open things up. "I didn't know you were here—"

"You want a ride into work?" Candy glanced around casually, but not because she was assessing the furniture. "You know, I thought . . . you might like a ride."

How much does she know about Daniel? Lydia wondered. *Had Eastwind closed the loop with her?*

As the woman's eyes returned to Lydia's, her expression grew annoyed. "Look, I'm not going to apologize."

"For what?"

"Lying to you yesterday."

Lydia frowned. "About what exactly."

Candy checked behind herself. "I'm coming in and shutting this door."

The woman stepped over the threshold, closed things, and leaned back against the panels. Then she crossed her arms on her chest and played with her left earring. The pink flamingo matched the tropical theme of her sweater, all the palm trees and their beach scene with a sun like a postcard made out of yarn.

"You're right," she said abruptly. "I did know . . . some things."

Lydia sat down on her sofa. "Tell me."

There was a pause, as if the WSP's receptionist were ordering her thoughts. "I knew the money was leaving the accounts because I could see it coming and going. There were wire transfers in from what I assumed were legitimate sources, but I couldn't figure out where the withdrawals were headed." She shook her head. "Peter was definitely in on it because when I brought it to his attention, he wasn't surprised and he told me it was none of my business. He reminded me that I'm just a secretary and that I needed to worry about answering the phone."

Candy shrugged. "So fine. I answered the phone. I opened mail. I ordered supplies—but I kept track." She went into her purse and took out a spiral-bound steno notebook. "It started about a year ago. Money coming, I'm guessing from the trustees, and then leaving, on these wires."

She flipped open the cover. "And that wasn't all. Rick was ordering these slides, glass slides—you know for tissue samples?"

"Yes, we use them during the exams to check blood and—"

"But why was he ordering them by the thousands?"

Lydia sat forward. "I'm sorry, what?"

"Thousands and thousands of slides. For samples."

"That can't be right." Lydia shook her head. "I worked side by side with him in the clinic and I never saw him do anything out of the ordinary or unnecessary with testing—"

"And that wasn't all he was ordering." Candy looked back down at her notes. "He ordered a shit ton of something called bromadiolone?"

Lydia's brows popped. "I'm sorry—what did you say?"

"Maybe I'm pronouncing it wrong?" Candy turned the pad around and pointed to the word. That was repeated eight times with dates. "Brodiy—"

Dropping her head in her hands, Lydia started to tremble. Thinking back over the months, she remembered Rick's irritability and the obvious signs of stress he'd exhibited. Now that she considered it, he had lost some weight and been agitated. But she'd assumed it was because of the hotel across the valley and the threat that Corrington was presenting to the wolf population.

She might have been so wrong about that.

"What's wrong?" Candy asked. "You okay?"

Snapping back to attention, Lydia cleared her throat.

"That's . . . the poison." As she glanced at the other woman, she was certain she was in a nightmare. "Out in the field. That's what's been used on my wolves."

Candy blanched. "What the hell was Rick doing?"

"I don't know." She thought of the wolf she had found, near death, in the veil. "How could he hurt the very thing he was supposed to protect."

"He was coming in a lot after hours." Candy refocused and flipped to a different section in the notebook. "The security system reports whenever it's turned on or off and from which keypad. About a month after the first of the payments came in from the board, Rick started entering through the clinic door at night. It wasn't a regular thing at first. Only a couple times every once in a while. But since this past fall? It was every week, like clockwork on Thursday nights."

"How long would he be in there?"

"Hours."

"What the hell was he doing?" Lydia thought of the data on those disks and felt a raw rage. "He better not have been experimenting on those animals."

Bursting up, she paced around. Then she stopped. "What if it wasn't the hotel all along. What if Rick had poisoned those wolves, every one of them."

"But why?" Candy what-the-hell'd her free hand. "I don't get it."

"To bring them in for the tissue sampling. God, what was he doing to them when we brought them in for health screening? He must have introduced agents into their blood and then brought them in for autopsies . . ." Lydia rubbed her forehead, like that would somehow help. "Why would he violate all his professional standards and beliefs, though?"

"Well, I'm not supposed to tell you this, because it's confidential and only in his HR file." Candy leaned to the side and looked out the window over the sofa. "But he had a gambling problem."

"What? No, he didn't—"

"Right before you were hired, he voluntarily went to a treatment place for it. He was gone for a month and I had to suspend his paychecks, which was the only reason I was told. Apparently, it was a real problem—but when he came back, he seemed so much better. That was when he started working out all the time. Those triathlons, the running, the swim races. I thought his addiction was under control, though."

"He was a gambler?" Lydia thought of the sports sections he'd always had around. "I can't see it. I just . . ."

Except how much did she know anybody who she worked with?

As she fell silent, Candy closed the cover on the spiral notebook and held it out. "You asked me for what I know and here it is. It's all yours—oh, and that UPS package? You're right. I did reroute it from Peter's house. About ten days ago, he started bugging me about where it was, giving me the tracking number over and over again, calling three or four times a day. They did lose the damn thing—and when they finally located it at the processing center, I made them deliver it to the WSP building by forging Peter's permission. I figured it had to do with . . . whatever was going on. And it was delivered two nights ago, but I don't know who signed for it or where it is."

Lydia took the pad. "Thank you so much for this."

"I figure it's the least I could do. And listen, yesterday, when you called me out, I didn't know how to handle it. I also didn't know whether I could trust you." Candy held up her hand. "Oh, and really and honestly, I didn't kill Peter Wynne. But I have a feeling . . . Rick might have."

FORTY-THREE

As CANDY PUT the accusation out there, Lydia flipped through the pages of the woman's notebook. There were sections about the security system, mail, supply ordering, missed days—including, yup, those two days Lydia had been in Plattsburgh for the root canal. The entries were all in the same neat handwriting, but made with different colored pens and even pencil.

"So what do we do?" Candy asked.

"I don't know."

Where can I go with this, Lydia wondered. C.P. Phalen? Eastwind and the state police?

"Where's your handyman, by the way?" Candy shook her head. "And no, I'm not asking for Susan. Or Bessie."

Lydia controlled her expression. Or tried to. "He's quit. And I know you gave his résumé to Eastwind."

"I was worried about you."

"Thank you for that." She couldn't bear to go into what Eastwind had found. "What can I say."

"I'm sorry. You liked him."

"I didn't know him." She cleared her throat. "He was a stranger. It's just water under the bridge—and speaking of bridges, he did fix all three of them."

"And our toilet."

Lydia glanced at the notebook. "Can you do me a favor?"

"Maybe." Candy narrowed her blue lids. "If I do whatever it is, I am off the hook for lying to you yesterday, okay. No guilt."

"Well, I'm not sure I can be a party to that bargain. I'm not in charge of your conscience."

The woman put up a stop-sign hand. "I'm just laying out the landscape. That's where I'm at. Now, what do you need?"

"Take me to Paul's so I can get my car?"

"You got it." The nod was forceful. "Such a fair exchange."

Lydia grabbed her bag, double-checked that the back door was dead-bolted, and then walked out with Candy. After she locked the front, they got in the SweeTarts-smelling car and were off.

As they got on the county road, Lydia watched the riverbed go by. "Why would Rick want to bomb the hotel if he was behind the poisonings? I don't get it."

"I think I do. I had four different phone calls from members of his family, making sure we knew where the funeral was and when. I couldn't get the uncle off the phone." Candy shrugged. "All of them were so proud of him, so deferential. If you knew you were checking out? Like, if you were going to do yourself in 'cuz you'd been working nasty shit at your job? It's a better legacy to leave for the people who love you, isn't it. A warrior against a corporation hurting the wildlife. As opposed to a common criminal motivated by a gambling problem."

"I swear I never saw him do anything out of the norm in the clinic."

"If you were doing something wrong, wouldn't you work hard to hide it? It's like brooming up a mess before your parents come home. You make sure everything is where it needs to be."

They fell silent, and soon enough, the grungy layout of Paul's Garage presented itself, the business not much more than a smudge of motor oil and a debris field of rusting car parts at the side of the road. Turning in, Candy nosed her grill right up to the filthy glass wall of the office.

Getting out, Lydia followed the sounds of a power tool to a three-bay setup of lifts.

"Paul?" she called out.

"Yeah," came the response from a service pit underneath a Toyota that looked seven hundred years old.

"It's Lydia—"

"I know," he groused. "Your car's on the row."

"Yes, thank you." The whirring sounds started up again so she raised her voice once more. "Um, how much do I owe you."

"Nothing," was the impatient response.

She glanced back at Candy, who shrugged. "Ah . . . nothing?"

The grizzled old man dropped something on the concrete floor and walked up the four steps from the pit. He was in a pair of overalls that were so stained, they could probably stand up on their own, and his cap was so smudged, the logo was unreadable. Finishing the look was a gray beard the same consistency as the long hair that grew out at his nape—to the point where it was hard to tell where one left off and the other started.

"No charge." His watery pale eyes were bored. "Your friend killed hisself. That's enough."

Lydia felt the crazy need to hug the man. But she had a feeling he would spontaneously combust.

"Thank you," she said roughly.

"Yeah." Then he turned away to descend again. "Keys are in it."

"Okay—"

"And that stuff he left you."

Lydia did a double take. "What did you say?"

Paul looked up from the darkness. "The stuff he left for you. It's inna trunk."

The mechanic disappeared as if everything was explained—and therefore, off his plate.

As a sense of total disassociation came over her, Lydia scrambled out to where the cars were parked. Hers was the last in the lineup and her hands were shaking as she went to the trunk. Popping the latch, the top floated upward.

Inside, there was a black nylon duffel.

Candy peered in as well. "Okaaaaaaaaaay. At least there's no bad smell so Peter Wynne's not in it."

Lydia shot the woman a stare. Then glanced around. "I can't open it here. Where?"

"Let's go back to the WSP. Scene of the crime. Where else."

◆　◆　◆

"You know, in an Agatha Christie novel," Candy was saying, "this would be a grand manor house."

As she closed the door to Lydia's office, Lydia put the duffel on her desk—which was still swiped-clean from the night before. When she and Daniel had lost control on it. As if she needed the reminder of that? Ever.

Yet here she was with Candy . . . and whatever Rick had left her.

Please let it not be a bomb, she thought.

"I want to just say," Candy announced, "that if this is a bunch of vacuum-packed freezer bags full of Peter Wynne, I'm quitting. No paycheck is worth seeing, like, a hand and foot. Maybe an eyeball or two. Part of a leg—"

"Okay, can you quit it with the descriptions? I'm already nauseous."

Taking a deep breath, Lydia drew back the zipper and parted the nylon folds. Inside . . . a five-inch-thick binder. That was it. Opening the unmarked cover, she was confronted with a table of contents that detailed each of the twenty or so tabs. As well as two USB drives in a plastic pouch.

"Looks like I'm keeping my job," Candy muttered. "Until this ship goes under. Now what the hell is all that paperwork."

Lydia started to work her way through the pages. And when her back ached from leaning over—she was *not* thinking about the sex with Daniel again, no, really—she shifted around to her chair. When the scent of fresh coffee permeated the air, she had a thought she could use some—

Candy put a mug down in front of her. "Just the way you like it. I'm going to close this door on you, and you're going to do—whatever the hell you're doing in here—while I go out and pretend today is a nice, normal day. When you're done, I expect a report and I deserve that shit. I'm in this with you whether we like it or not. Got it?"

With an absent nod, Lydia took a sip. Then looked up.

"Candy, this is perfect."

The other woman snorted. "About time something around here went right."

Four hours later, Lydia got to the last page of what

Rick had prepared. Humping the binder's back cover over, she sunk into her chair and stared into space.

No, she thought. Back at the hotel site, Rick hadn't intended to blow himself up.

He was just going to make it look that way. So he could disappear and start a new identity—and these documents were his insurance policy. But when she and Daniel had come up on him at the fence line, he'd changed his mind. Maybe because he'd gone as far as he could take his conscience?

She guessed she'd like to believe that, but she doubted it. He was in so much deeper than she'd imagined, and it was hard to see any way out for him.

He had been doing experiments on the wolves. Genetic manipulation attempts to try to introduce human DNA into the animals through a virus host. He'd literally been trying to create a human/wolf hybrid. And the poison had been for those specimens who had been worked on so that no one else could mine the data or find out what was going on, and the traps were a plant to make it look like someone was threatening the whole pack. In fact, Rick had stalked specific wolves, tranq'd them, and presented the tampered meat right in front of them, ensuring the correct specimen was killed.

And Peter Wynne had been paying him to do it all.

The program was incredibly sophisticated, and only partially on-site. The samples had been sent somewhere else for processing, and the DNA/viral

load that had been injected had come from somewhere else, too.

The identity of that next layer up was not listed
anywhere.

She thought of the floppy disks.

"They were the past." She put her hands on the
binder. "This is the present."

And in the end, there was only one place to go with
it all.

FORTY-FOUR

AFTER NIGHT FELL and things got cold, Dan-iel lit a fire in the campsite's stone pit. He'd bought a bundle of dried hardwood at the gas station down by the highway—along with a six-pack of Coke, a bag of Doritos, and a carton of Marlboros. He'd paid cash for it all, as well as for the site rental, and by five o'clock, he'd settled in against the rock he planned on using for a pillow.

So much for his health kick.

So much for everything.

It was eight now. Eight-thirty tops.

Letting his head fall back, he listened to the crackling of the flames and watched the smoke drift up to the stars. He was about fifty miles away from the Canadian border, and he would have crossed, but he needed to arrange for another identity.

Disappearing was harder than it used to be.

Righting his eyes, he stared at the flickering orange and red flares around the logs. All he saw was Lydia, a slideshow of images of her passing before him, sure as if he were not just reliving the moments, but in them for the first time.

Lighting up another cigarette, he sipped his Coke and waited for clarity to come. Good thing he wasn't holding his breath.

As he coughed, he thought of when he'd sat down across from her desk that first day, the smell of antiseptic wipes getting into his nose, her frantic apology as she'd waved her hands to get things to dry faster. She'd looked at him like she'd never seen a male before.

Every time he got hay fever, she was going to be on his mind.

Fuck that, she was never going to leave his thoughts anyway—

The snap of a stick off to the left had him closing his eyes with exhaustion. "Really."

"Daniel Joseph, what the fuck are you doing."

The deep male voice from the darkness was the worst kind of surprise, one that was both expected and not enjoyable. And it was not Mr. Personality. It was the big boss.

"That's how you announce your presence," Daniel said as he ashed into his Coke bottle. "Not even a hi-how're-ya?"

"Would you prefer a bullet?"

"Actually, I'd like to never see you again, Blade."

"That's not going to happen. There's one way out, and only one way. You knew that from the beginning."

Daniel stared at the end of his cigarette. "You didn't come here for a debate on my pink slip, did you?"

"I shouldn't have to come find you at all."

"But you did."

"I'm talented. What can I say."

There was the temptation to palm up his gun and go to town, but that was going to get him only a delay. There were others beneath his visitor. Lots of others. And somebody in that group would take him alive, one way or another.

"So here's what we're going to do here, Daniel. You're going back and you're going to finish what you signed on to do—"

"Send someone else—"

"You refused to disclose the location of the hatch. So even if we were going to let you off, and we're not, you've left us with no choice but to force you—"

"So I'll tell you now."

"No, you'll talk some bullshit in hopes I'll let you go. And this is not a negotiation. You're going to go back and finish what you went there to do, or that roommate of yours is going to have a series of very bad nights. Because we'll keep her alive for a while. A long while."

Daniel sat up and jabbed his cigarette across the fire. "You fucking leave her out of this."

"Then go back there and do what you said you would do."

"You boys are a handy lot. If I can find it, so can you."

"True, but events have changed the landscape. You know this. Time is of the essence now."

Daniel thought of that vet at the chain-link fence. Then all the water coming down the stairs in that converted barn.

"You're overplaying your hand." Daniel shook his head as he spoke into the darkness. "I don't give a shit about that woman."

"Okay, then. She'll just be a honing stone for us. Training is so important, and you know that first-hand. And even though you say you don't care, from the moment we introduce ourselves to her to her last breath, we'll remind her that you put her in the position she's in. And when we hide her body so that no one ever finds it? We'll make sure that there's a memento of you with her."

"You're accountable for every crime you commit," Daniel spat.

"And so are you."

The slideshow of Lydia started up again, the mental pictures flipping by so fast, they were hard to track. What was easy to latch on to?

Riding a wave of emotion, Daniel jumped to his feet. "Listen, you sonofabitch, if you get anywhere near her—"

"You're going to do what? Kill me?" There was a soft chuckle. "You think there isn't someone right next to her this very moment? If I don't send a signal in the next four minutes, she's dead—after a while."

"You stay away from that house—"

"Oh, she's not at home right now, but we're with her. And don't worry—we'll keep her safe. Until we don't. Her life is in your hands. What are you going to do?"

As rage swelled, Daniel looked into the flames.

"We're watching you, too." There was a pause. And then Blade's voice came from farther away. "One more thing. The commitment you made continues after you stop breathing. So if you decide to solve this problem by taking yourself out? That's another choice, but we will still carry out our end of this. Lydia Susi will die slowly and painfully. The only way to save her is to finish what you fucking started."

◆   ◆   ◆

Lydia looked at the clock on the dashboard of her hatchback. From the security light streaming in through the windshield, it was easy to read the analog hands.

Eight-thirty.

She looked at the iron gates to C.P. Phalen's estate. She'd been parked right in front of them, directly in the eye of the security camera, for hours now. There was no way the woman didn't know she was on the property, and no matter how long it took, she was going to—

Off in the distance, the howl of a wolf had her closing her eyes. It was such a lonely sound, and her breath caught as she waited to hear if the entreaty was answered. When it wasn't, it felt like a commentary on her whole life. Always alone, always separate, even when she was around others.

Daniel had crossed that divide, though. But God, the damage he had done.

Trying to stay out of that abyss, she refocused on the gates. She had been so sure of what she was doing when she'd come here, and the hours of waiting hadn't changed anything. Even if it took until the morning, she was going to—

All at once, the gates began to open slowly, sound-lessly, everything well-oiled.

"Party time," Lydia muttered as she started her engine.

Proceeding into the estate, the hedge of bushes locking her in, her heart started to beat hard. But there was no question about fight or flight. She wasn't going to run.

No matter how this went down.

Just as she was pulling up to the well-lit house, that sound of rotor blades chopped its way through the quiet of the night.

Over the roofline, the blinking lights of the heli-copter cast shadows and then a spotlight was trained down onto the ground. The aircraft landed where it had the other day, on the grass.

Lydia stayed right where she was. Those dogs were no doubt on the property somewhere, and in the darkness, she wouldn't know which direction they were coming from. Although did the compass point really matter when it came to all those teeth?

C.P. Phalen once again emerged as the steps unfurled from the body of the helicopter, and as she descended and walked toward the car, Lydia replayed what she'd rehearsed so many times during the wait.

As the woman came into the headlights, Lydia killed the engine and got out.

"Well, if it isn't my favorite lupine behaviorist." C.P. Phalen smiled in that icy way of hers. "Sorry to have kept you waiting. I was in Manhattan."

I don't give a shit where you were, lady. "We need to talk."

"Then by all means, come in." The woman turned away and started walking. "I haven't had dinner. Perhaps you'll join me."

Lydia looked across the front of the mansion. Lights were on in every room, it seemed, and more illumination was shining up from the bushes that lined the massive footprint. But she still couldn't see inside, the diffused glow in each of the windows the result of that odd treatment over the glass.

She had a thought that there was a good chance she would never see the light of day again. She had no idea who she was dealing with anymore—and that included Eastwind. The only one she felt like she could trust was Candy.

And that woman knew what her job was tonight.

C.P. Phalen unlocked the door with that thumb of

hers and walked into all that marble. "See, I told you the furniture was coming."

Stepping inside, Lydia found that, yup, there were furnishings now, and surprise, everything was white. Just like Peter Wynne's house. Well, not exactly. The sofas and chairs were silk here, the glowing sheen on the tufted cushions and camel-back contours a testament to everything an unlimited budget could get you.

"I'm not going any farther," Lydia announced as the heavy door shut behind her. "We're going to do this right here."

C.P. Phalen pivoted around on her high heel. She was wearing yet another black suit with slacks, only the lapels and the detailing different. Clearly she subscribed to the Steve Jobs theory of wardrobes, a uniform that never varied.

The woman cocked a brow. "All right. Talk to me."

"I know you were paying Peter Wynne. All those millions were never for the Wolf Study Project. It was for what you and he were doing together with Rick's help. The WSP was used to launder the money, and you got yourself elected chair so you could hide the payments."

The smile on that perfectly made-up face was the most chilling thing Lydia had ever seen: It was cold as a diamond—and just as indestructible.

"Go on."

From out of the corner of Lydia's eye, a figure stepped into view and she snapped her head in that direction. It was a man. Dressed in a camouflage uniform.

Between one blink and the next, she saw Daniel jumping on the back of that "soldier" out in the woods.

But Lydia was not going to be intimidated. It was so too late for that.

"You and Peter Wynne and Rick are doing genetic experiments," Lydia said. "And Rick was the one poisoning the wolves because they were your subjects, and he had to both track the results and control the exposure of the program. Too many out in the preserve, and you all ran the risk of one of them falling into the hands of somebody else. A hunter. A truck driver who hit one. They were beginning to show genetic shifts and none of you were exactly sure whether they were going to lead to physical or behavioral changes—you hoped they would, but you knew that you couldn't control nature, even though you were the ones who let the proverbial cat out of the bag."

Lydia put her palm forward. "And before you deny this, I have everything thanks to Rick. A full dossier that includes the funds flow, the experiment details, the monitoring data. I've got it all, and your name is all over the documents. He'd decided to take his money and run, and to protect himself, he wrote everything down—it was his bargaining chip to stay alive and he didn't trust either of you. Before he staged his own death, he killed Peter because he knew he himself was at risk and Peter was the weak link he could get to and eliminate easier." She nodded toward the guard. "You, on the other hand, are never without protection. So he took care of Peter, and set about faking his own death. In the end, he really died, though. He killed himself—and his death, like Peter's, is on your hands."

C.P. Phalen's composure was complete. There wasn't a flush on that face, a flicker of an expression, a twitch or a stiffening.

She was utterly relaxed. Utterly in control.

"And now I'm probably going to die, too," Lydia said. "That's okay. I don't mind laying down my life for my wolves. Just know that whether I walk out of here or my body is carried out, you're totally done. I've made sure that everything is in the right hands. Your trying to create a hybrid species of wolf and human is fucking done tonight."

Now came the jerk of that platinum head. "What did you say?"

Lydia rolled her eyes. "Oh, come on. You're more sophisticated than to play it stupid—"

"Hybrid species? There is no hybrid species."

"Like I'm going to believe you."

The woman stood up even higher on her spine. If that was possible. "You're right. We were experimenting, but not to create anything that didn't exist. The research was on the immune system and cell division as it relates to longevity. The wolves were used because the packs on the preserve are isolated and from a single line of ancestors courtesy of the re-introduction of the species that took place in the nineteen hundreds. Further, their life cycles are short enough so that we could measure whether the drugs were working to keep them alive longer. It was not to synthesize—werewolves or something."

Lydia shook her head. "Like I said, I don't believe a word you—"

"I don't care whether you believe me. The truth is what it is without regard to you blessing it with your opinion."

And then the woman just shrugged as she stared Lydia right in the face with a bored expression.

"You have your proof," C.P. Phalen said. "And I have mine. Come, I'll show you."

FORTY-FIVE

I BOUGHT THIS HOUSE more because of what was under it than anything above ground."

As C.P. Phalen's narration started, Lydia walked along with her and decided this was like some kind of fucked-up museum tour, where the exhibits were unbelievable and the docent a madwoman capable of anything.

The two of them were descending a set of steel stairs that were shiny and new, positively sparkling, and when they came to the bottom, Lydia got a load of all sorts of whitewashed concrete walls.

Even though they were well underground, the air smelled fresh, like it was being blown in from the surface.

"Back in the seventies and eighties," the woman said as they walked forward down a well-lit corridor wide as a living room and long as—well, the damned thing seemed to go on forever—"there was word of experiments being done on things that didn't exist.

Things that had no evolutionary basis and supposedly no existence outside of Halloween myth."

The floppy disks, Lydia thought. The vampires.

"As I told you, I've been in the pharmaceutical sector for my whole career, investing in companies, promoting their research and development. I heard the whispered talk. I didn't believe it. It was just too fanciful, something out of a novel."

Lydia glanced around. There were no doors, no cameras, no offshoots from the main drag. No sounds other than the soles of her boots and C.P. Phalen's stilettoes over the concrete floor, either.

"I brushed the stories off as gossip told by drunks at annual meetings, nothing but drama created by businessmen who had to believe they were more powerful than Charles Darwin. But then something changed in my own life and I decided to look into it further. That's when I discovered it was true, all true. There were facilities, hidden out of sight, protected, defended, doing groundbreaking work that could change the landscape of human life. Over time, however, many of them had been abandoned, either from lack of funding or from incompetence. Or accidents."

No reason to ask about the "accidents," Lydia thought.

Finally, a corner, up ahead.

And then a door.

C.P. Phalen put her thumb on a reader and there was a loud, hollow *thunk!* The stainless steel panel seemed to open on its own, and on the other side . . .

"Holy shit," Lydia breathed.

"Welcome to my laboratory."

Lydia forgot all about the other woman as she stepped over the threshold. The open area was easily as big as a sports arena, and it was filled with people in white coats at stations full of equipment. No one looked up or paid any attention to her or the lab's owner. No one was nervous or afraid. It seemed like . . . a legitimate operation.

"The FDA and the regulatory systems of this country strangle innovation," C.P. Phalen said. "I got sick of it. I decided to just do it on my own and deal with the consequences if the breakthrough I expect comes through—and it will. Maybe it already has. Immunotherapy is in its infancy, and the medical community is thinking too small. It's not just about curing cancer, it's about prolonging life. The immune system is so much more than merely the guardian of the human body's health. It's part of the expiration date for life. But it doesn't have to be."

The woman turned to Lydia. "You're right. I did pay Peter Wynne and he did what he had to at the Wolf Study Project with Rick to get me what I needed. But this hybrid thing you're talking about? That was never part of it. Yes, I broke the law, and I'm not going to apologize for that. But it was about the work I wanted to do here, that is now being done here after I renovated this old facility and staffed it. My relationship with Peter and Rick was coming to an end.

They'd fulfilled what they'd promised to do for me, so we'd completed our business. And immune system work was all I was a part of. That's as far as I went. I don't have a goddamn clue what you're talking about with humanoid experiments. That is not my field of interest at all."

Lydia walked forward, not sure how much to believe of that speech. "This laboratory is . . ."

"Magic in test tubes," C.P. Phalen said. "That's what we're doing here. Come on, let's keep going."

As they proceeded along the periphery of the stations, the woman kept talking. "We're so close. I can feel it. I just need a little more time—which is what we all need, right? Just more time to be alive, stay alive. And be healthy while we're here."

She opened the door into a conference room with a long table and projection screens at both ends. A couple of sideboards set with water bottles and soft drinks created an odd—and misplaced—sense of security. Because the boardroom was a spot of normal in a sea of not-normal-at-all.

With the door closing them in, the sounds of the laboratory drifted off, but through the glass wall, Lydia could continue to watch the scientists striding back and forth to each other's work areas.

"I already run a company that does DNA sequencing," C.P. Phalen said as she sat down. "As well as one that does ancestry profiling. I have mined the data of millions and millions of people—"

Lydia glanced over her shoulder. "You can't do that."

The woman held up her forefinger. "Oh, but I can. It's in the disclosures that every single person who paid for the services had to sign. It's not my fault if they don't read what they're getting into, and besides, all the data is blinded. No names or addresses, just demographic information. It's entirely legal, trust me."

As Lydia looked back out, the woman said, "When you were standing in my foyer, you honestly expected to be killed on my premises. I can assure you, you're free to go. You can walk out and drive away anytime you want. And I'm not going to try to stop you from going to the authorities—if you haven't already. You're not going to get far with all that, though. I've set things up so that the legitimate businesses are a full cover for what we're doing here, and I've already had challenges, even from the U.S. government. Like you, though, they're free to sniff around. I have unlimited resources, the very best lawyers money can buy, and you'd be amazed what things people will look away from, under the right circumstances."

Lydia blinked and saw the wolf lying on its side, suffering. "Did you know they were poisoning the animals." She looked over her shoulder. "Did you?"

C.P. Phalen's brows went together. "No, I did not. Which is why I believed you when you said it was the hotel."

"You're lying," Lydia snapped. "Rick ordered the poison and administered it, and he was doing it for you."

"No, he wasn't." The woman leaned forward in her leather seat. "That was never part of the agreement. What we injected into those wolves was intended to strengthen their immune systems. It was otherwise harmless—"

"Bullshit!"

C.P. Phalen shook her head. "I did *not* have a program that involved poisoning the wolves."

The woman's eyes were so direct, so steady, she was either the best liar on the planet or—

"So who else were they working with?" C.P. Phalen said softly. "Who the *fuck* else was paying them."

◆   ◆   ◆

Hours and hours later, dawn light came across C.P. Phalen's backyard and illuminated the newly created brick walkways, the pool that was in the process of being dug, the rear terrace. As Lydia sat in a window and stared across the vista, a plate of eggs, bacon, and toast was placed in front of her by a butler.

On the other side of the circular table, C.P. Phalen was likewise staring out over the landscape.

"It's a ghost. A goddamn ghost," C.P. said.

Lydia looked back at the laptop she'd been working on for the last two hours. She couldn't say she exactly trusted the other woman. But she did trust the facts as she knew them: None of the science being done in that underground lab had anything to do with trying to create another species. She'd spent all night reviewing the data, which had, in fact, been generated out of Rick's clinic at the WSP. She knew this, because identical reports had been in his binder.

Along with others that were clearly unrelated to what C.P. was doing.

"I know what I saw in Rick's documents," Lydia murmured. "Your experiments were in there. But there was so much more."

"I believe you."

Glancing across the table, she started eating. "Why are you trusting me with all this?"

C.P. sipped coffee out of a porcelain cup. "I told you, I'm not scared of anything. Trust only comes into play when somebody else can hurt you. No offense, but you can't touch me."

Lydia thought it over. Then shrugged. "Fair enough."

The food didn't taste like anything, but then the whole world felt like it was a dream. Maybe it was the exhaustion. The heartache. The disbelief.

The deaths.

"It all started for me six years ago," C.P. said remotely.

"What did?"

"This whole . . . wild goose chase." The woman pushed her own full plate away. "I was diagnosed with leukemia. I'd never thought about death—

ironic, right, for somebody in the pharmaceutical business. I just decided . . . I had to save myself. The kind I have is going to come back. It's inevitable. So if I find a way of prolonging life, I may have a chance at a future."

"You're sick?"

"Not at the moment. But I will be at some point. All the money in the world, and I've still got a grave waiting for me." C.P. jogged her coffee cup to punctuate her point. "But I'm going down with a fight. That's my nature, and who knows, maybe I can save some others and win a Nobel Prize in the process."

"But what about the illegalities?"

"Details. Just details. You're telling me the robber barons were legal? The steel industry? Big Tech in the present? Please. Don't be naive. And don't get me started with the U.S. government."

Lydia fell silent and finished what was on her plate.

"Hybrids," C.P. murmured as if she were deep in thought. "I wonder if that's even possible. A human and a wolf."

"I think you're working on enough, don't you?" Lydia said dryly.

"Yes." C.P. smiled a little. "You're probably right."

Did she know about the vampire experiments? Lydia wondered.

"We're going to find out who the fuck else they were doing business with," C.P. announced. "One way or the other, we're going to get to the bottom of all this. Are you in?"

Lydia stared out at the dawn light. And thought about the wolves that had been killed.

"Yes," she answered grimly. "I am."

FORTY-SIX

DANIEL WORKED HIS way through the trees of the preserve, moving as silently as he could, staying behind trunks when he was able. The pack on his back was weighted down with tools for the job, as well as explosives, and his body was strung with weapons. In spite of his grim purpose, however, his feet were heavy in a way that had nothing to do with what he'd strapped on to himself. Fucking hell, he felt like he was pulling a car behind him.

And yet he kept going across the mountain, currently on a slight decline.

Overhead, the sky was cloudy, and soon enough, rain started to fall, but it was the lazy kind, just drops floating down that he ignored even when they got in his eyes. He just really didn't give a crap about anything.

Which made him a bad bet, didn't it.

People with nothing to lose were very unreliable. Then again, he did have one thing to care about, didn't he.

Sad as fuck that he'd already lost her.

As he continued along, the path he followed was a trail of deliberation that purposely made no sense, his forward progress full of double backs and random turns. With his thousand-pound boots, he was adhering to good tracking protocol for no other reason than habit—and as he took his own sweet time getting to his final destination, he really wasn't in a hurry.

With "final" being the operant word.

He was going to take a page out of Rick's book, just without the chain-link fence—or the interruptions.

And there was one, and only one, thing he could count on. Just like they would kill Lydia if he didn't do this . . . if he followed through as he planned, she would, in fact, be safe. Fuck Blade's honor bullshit. The more dead bodies, the more possibility for exposure, and with what Daniel was about to do, he was going to cast a whole lot of attention on exactly what they were trying to deal with discreetly. After his little boom-boom firework show here? There was going to be so much follow-up by the regular authorities that when it came to Lydia Susi, it was going to be in Blade's best interest to leave her alone. Otherwise, the man would be risking too much scrutiny and a loss of anonymity and autonomy.

Lydia would be safe because actions had ramifications, even for those existing outside of the law.

God, he was ready for this to be over.

Pausing, he looked through the trees. He was half-

way up the mountain, and if his memory was correct—
and it never failed him—he didn't have far to go.

Goddamn, he was so close.

As his legs started up again, his body went along
for the ride and took his mind with it, the latter nes-
tled in the stagecoach of his skull. And it wasn't much
farther until the line of "No Trespassing" signs made
an appearance, everything exactly as he remembered—

There it was, up ahead. The hatch—although it
was no longer flashing any of its metal. So Eastwind
must have moved the pine needles back into place.
The downed tree, however, had been left as is, and
that was how Daniel knew he was in the right place.

Closing in on all the "No Trespassing" missives,
he took a last look around, and then didn't hesitate
as he crossed over onto the property. As he kept hiking onward, he stayed aware of his surroundings.
The worst-case scenario? He got plugged by someone on the final goal approach and Lydia died not
because he was noncompliant, but because he was
sloppy and exhausted and got shot because of it.

Destiny had a sick-ass sense of humor, though,
didn't it.

And then he was at the hatch.

His boots stopped and he glanced to the left. To
the right. All was clear that he knew or could sense.

Bending down, he brushed the ground cover away,
exposing the hatch's face. There were supposed to
be four of them in total; that was what the building

plans for the underground facility had provided. But they only required one to get inside.

That stupid woman Phalen should have left the shit well enough alone.

But noooooooooo, she had to go get some bright ideas and try to resurrect the past. This was all her fucking fault, and if innocent people were collateral damage? It was on her.

Stripping off his pack, he opened the thing up. The acetylene torch with its tanks was heavy as fuck; the explosives had not been the weight issue.

Kicking more of the pine needles away, he knelt down, got out the red Bic that Susan had sold him along with his guilt-branded packs of cigarettes. With a crank of the gas and a flick of his thumb, he had himself a handy-dandy yellow flame.

He went to work on the seal of the hatch, the steel heating up to a glow, the going slow. But like he gave a fuck.

He was going to burn through this bitch, get down under, set the charges around the facility—and then have a last Marlboro before everything went Fourth of July.

The cleanup was going to be a bitch, and he wasn't talking about the damage to the landscape. But the spin, at least as far as the outside world, was already in place.

Animal activists. Protesting that hotel for what they were supposedly doing to the wolves. The headlines wrote themselves, and he could just picture the social media hashtags. And that was another reason Lydia Susi was going to be okay. She had no history of activism, no arrests, no criminal record of any kind. People who blew shit up did it either as a pattern of behavior or in a moment of psychosis, and she fit neither of those descriptors.

If they killed her, and tried to pin the explosion on her? It wasn't going to pass editorial review.

Besides, Blade had his own problems internally. Always had.

Daniel was hollow as he stared at the hissing flame. Dead, though he lived—except he was going to take care of the last part of that tag. Really fucking soon—

The bullet was soundless as it came at him. And the hit in the center of his chest was nothing but a *pfft*.

The impact, however, was like a cannonball, pitching him backwards off his crouch, the torch going flying, his visual field swinging from the hatch seal, to the pines, to the gray sky above as he flew back and took his sight with him.

As he landed on his back and gasped, his legs churned in the pine needles and his hands flopped on his pecs to find the lead slug's entry wound. But like that was going to help?

The footsteps coming toward him were muffled, although maybe that was because his hearing was failing already. And when he coughed and tasted blood, his brain struggled to come up with a plan to save himself—

The face that entered his visual field was not a surprise.

"Hi, honey, I'm home," Mr. Personality drawled.

FORTY-SEVEN

LYDIA JOGGED THROUGH the mountain's forest, dodging trees, jumping over rocks, hopping across streams. She'd been careful to enter the preserve not through a trailhead, but on a convoluted course from the WSP headquarters. And in spite of all the sleep she hadn't been getting, adrenaline made her hyperaware and fast on her feet.

Breathing hard, she hit a decline and then doubled back up. She was close, she was so close . . .

And then she slowed. Stopped.

Scrambled over to lock in behind a pine tree.

The main trail was up ahead, the broad concourse empty of hikers. But she waited, just to make sure she was alone and in the correct place.

Satisfied with both, she crossed the packed dirt and kept on going into the preserve, fifteen feet. Twenty. Thirty—

"Oh, God," she gasped. "Oh . . . God."

As she tripped on her own boots, she couldn't believe she'd been correct: The body was stretched out face up, the arms and legs tied to stakes that had been driven into the ground. The clothes were unmistakable. Gray flannel slacks. Blue blazer.

"*Peter.*"

She approached the remains slowly. The dead man's eyes were open in his pasty face, and as she stared down at him, it was unclear what he had died of.

Well, murder. Yes. But what had killed him? And who?

Looking him up and down—she saw no clues to the former. But the latter was answered. Words had been scratched deeply into a cleared stretch of dirt in the bed of pine needles.

You always Do the Right Thing

Scribbled, messy, cap'd in some places. Like it mattered.

Rick had done the killing on purpose here. Right in the place where she had found that wolf and called the WSP's vet in the veil. This was the exact spot— she was certain because of the orientation of trees, everything burned into her memory from lying nose-to-nose with the animal as he'd suffered.

Crouching down, she saw a trail of blood out of one of Peter's ears. And that was when it clicked.

Now she knew why the water had been running back at the barn.

Like a rat who had eaten RatX, Kaput, or d-Con, Peter had been seeking water. Before he had collapsed.

From the poison.

Lydia rubbed her face.

And when she dropped her hand and looked up—
"Grandfather?"

In the shadows between the pines, standing in the darkness, the ghostly apparition of her *isoisä* was staring at her, his mouth moving as if he were trying to speak across the dimensions that separated them.

Lydia rose to her feet and took a step forward. "I need you, Grandfather. What do I do? Where do I go?"

She put her hands out as her eyes flooded with tears. "Please . . . don't go. For once, stay and help me."

◆   ◆   ◆

Daniel coughed so hard, his eyes watered—and as a result, Mr. Personality's hard face, as it dominated his diminishing corridor of vision, became wavy and indistinct. But Daniel had bigger problems to worry about. He was struggling to breathe, gasping and gurgling for air, so he heaved himself over onto his side and tried to clear his mouth out of the blood that seemed to be golf-sprinkling up his esophagus.

When he was finally able to catch some oxygen, he opened eyes that he'd been unaware of closing—

And there was his former roommate, still right up close.

The man smiled from his crouching position. "You know, I'm usually a good shot, but I think I didn't take my emotions into account as I pulled my trigger." That expression faded. "I didn't want to play it like this, not with you. I got a little loyalty to you, my guy. I really do. Did. Whatever."

Daniel moaned. "Lydia . . ."

"What? Oh, the woman?"

"Save . . . Lydia."

Mr. Personality frowned. "She's too far into this, mate. Sorry."

"Kill me now. Do . . . whatever. Just . . . save . . . her. You owe me."

Eyes so pale, they were almost all white, moved away. "I didn't ask you to do what you did all those years ago."

"Owe. Me."

"I can't protect her against Blade. I'm sorry."

Daniel struggled to get up. Tried to breathe. Willed himself to stay alive so he could—

"And Lydia's got to go." Mr. Personality pointed the barrel of his gun into Daniel's face. "Yes, you did your part. You brought me here. But only because I followed you. More important, she knows waaaaaaaay too much to let live—"

The attack was so fast and so powerful, the other man didn't see it coming—and all Daniel caught was a blur of gray and brown fur.

Confused, he managed to lift his head.

A gray wolf with a silver stripe down its back had tackled Daniel's former roommate and was ripping into his throat. The man was fighting back as much as he could, struggling to get his gun up, punching and kicking. But the vicious animal was too much for him, those fangs flashing, the growling and snarling the kind of thing nightmares were made of.

And it didn't take long. Blood spurted from that jugular, speckling the wolf's jowls, chest, front paws—and as soon as that red rush started, there was no question who was going to win.

As the gun got thrown, and the human started to lose strength, the wolf straddled the body and went to town: Clothes shredded, skin ripped free of muscles, muscles torn off of bones, bones snapped and spit out or swallowed.

Daniel watched it all. And when it was over, when the wolf stepped off and licked its chops—and then looked at Daniel, all he could do was laugh inside.

After all this, after everything he'd done in secret for the U.S. government . . . he was going to die as Alpo. Out in the woods.

The wolf took a step toward him. And another.

"Have at me," he said hoarsely. "Have—"

The wolf let out a howl of pain and listed to the side. Then fell over.

What happened next . . . Daniel couldn't comprehend. And not just because he was bleeding to death internally.

As the guard in the black uniform returned—the same one Daniel had killed once and then seen the sheriff take out, with the same features and eyes and weapons—the wolf started to convulse.

And then it writhed in the pine needles, clawing at the earth, paws thrashing, hind legs kicking—

But that wasn't all it did.

The transformation was inexplicable. The fur began to recede into the pores it came out of, and then paws morphed, becoming hands, becoming feet, human hands, human feet. The chest and lupine stomach likewise distended, extended . . . changed . . . becoming a human chest, a human abdominal cavity . . . a human pelvis.

And finally, the muzzle retracted, forming a chin and a nose, as the ear flaps pulled up into the skull that was rounding, changing . . . the whole of it revealing a face that he knew.

A face that he loved.

"Lydia . . . ?" he croaked in confusion and disbelief.

Of all the things to learn as he died.

"Lydia!" he shouted.

In slow motion, in another facet of this horrible dream, the black-uniformed soldier stepped forward and stood over her naked body.

The gun muzzle lifted, but not by much, as it was pointed at her naked chest.

There was a lot of blood on her skin, but it was hard to know where she'd been hit—and what was just from what she'd done to Daniel's old roommate.

"No . . ." Daniel flopped onto his stomach and tried to drag himself over. "Don't . . . hurt her . . ."

Lydia's eyes fluttered open. As she focused on

him, tears fell onto her cheeks. "I'm sorry," she whispered.

"I love you, Lydia." He didn't understand anything, but he knew that one thing for sure. "I love you, it's okay . . . I'm going to . . ."

He was pulling himself forward, thinking that maybe, even though he was about three heartbeats away from passing out, even though she was one trigger finger away from being killed, there was something he could do to save her.

"I love you, too . . . Daniel . . ."

Those were her last words. And as her eyes rolled back and then fluttered shut, he let out a cry of pain—

Growling now. From all directions.

Forcing his head up, Daniel saw the wolves come out from the pines. A dozen of them. Maybe more.

The guard likewise snapped back to attention, as if even he'd been transfixed by Lydia's unbelievable shifting from one species to another.

That guard barely had time to redirect his weapon.

The wolves came at him from all sides, and as the frenzy took the man down, Daniel looked at Lydia.

The last thing he did before he died was reach forward . . . and take her still-warm hand in his.

Look at me, he thought at her. *See me.*

But it was too late for her.

And ultimately, too late for him.

FORTY-EIGHT

As Lydia died, her consciousness receded to a pinpoint in her mind, no longer a universe of sensations and thought, no longer a planet of them, not even a plot of land or a stone or a grain of sand.

Just a pinpoint.

But she felt Daniel's hand in her own, and knew he was holding what he could of her, and she heard the words he spoke.

Both the ones about her to the man who had shot him—and the ones to her after he had seen what had to have shocked him to his core: He loved her. And he had been true to her in the end, in spite of what he had lied to her about before, in spite of all that she didn't understand and yet couldn't question.

When Daniel had had nothing to lose, and hadn't known she was there, he had tried to protect her in his mission, whatever it had been. He had done his best.

So he had been true to them and what they had had.

That was all she could ask for really.

Lydia tried to squeeze his palm back. And as she

listened to the preserve's wolves attack to protect her, protect him, she began to cry . . .

Sometime later, it felt like years, there was only the scent of blood and the silence of the forest.

Opening her eyes for the last time, she looked into the face of the male wolf she and Daniel had released back into the wild.

Thank you, she thought at the animal.

He snuffled and lowered his head, giving her a nuzzle, as if he were thinking of what else he might do to help—and wishing there was more he could do to repay that which she had done for him.

And that was when she heard the repeating sound, the thumping, overhead.

As the wolf looked up and then reared back, she focused on the sky . . . and couldn't understand how C.P. Phalen's helicopter was coming in for a landing in a clearing a couple hundred yards away. How had the woman known . . .

The pack scattered into the trees, the wolves disappearing into the shadows beneath and between the pines. And then Lydia had a trippy vision of men in camo coming through the forest, with stretchers.

The woman with the short cap of white hair was unmistakable, and for once, C.P. Phalen was not in a business suit. She was wearing camo as well.

"I don't have a heartbeat over here."

At the male voice's grim pronouncement, Lydia moaned and turned her head to Daniel. It was hard to see him because the men were crowding around him, and opening medical kits.

"IV in," someone said.

"Paddles on and charged."

As Daniel's body jerked, she looked at their hands.

He had let go of hers. She was the one hanging on to him now.

C.P.'s face entered Lydia's vision. "We'll get you, too. Don't worry."

"Save him," was all Lydia could say before she passed out. "Just save him—"

FORTY-NINE

"D ANIEL!"

As Lydia shot upright and yelled, the pain that answered the callout was the kind that turned the stomach and made your vision go checkerboard.

With a groan, she collapsed back against something that was pillow soft—oh, it was a pillow. Actually, she was in a bed—a hospital bed—and hooked up to an IV and all kinds of monitors. Across the way, a TV was mounted on the wall, and there were no windows. A wooden door, which didn't seem to have a lock on it, was closed.

It didn't stay that way.

The thing was pushed opened. "You're awake. How are you doing?"

C.P. Phalen was still in the camo she'd been wearing when she'd arrived with her—

"Is he alive," Lydia croaked. "Is Daniel alive."

The woman nodded and urged the door closed even though it was shutting on its own. "He's in surgery still. But they expect him to pull through."

Tears speared into Lydia's eyes and she didn't bother to hold them back. And as the attendant weeping made her shoulder scream with agony, she realized she was bandaged up on that whole side, even on her arm.

"It's okay." C.P. came over to the bedside and sat down. "You've had a helluva scare. Just let it go."

"I thought he'd died. I thought I was . . . dead, too."

When the worst of the emotional breakdown had passed, Lydia wiped her eyes with the hand towel C.P. held out to her, and then took a shuddering breath.

"You're in my private clinic." C.P. indicated the bed and the monitors. "The standard of care down here is world-class."

"How did you know . . . we were there?"

"You're not the only person with cameras on the mountain."

Lydia's breath stopped in her chest. "So you saw me . . ."

C.P.'s eyes dropped to the floor, something that Lydia was very sure the woman very rarely did. Ever.

"I saw, yes. It was . . . unparalleled." Abruptly, the woman glanced over. "Guess we don't need to develop what already exists, huh."

Lydia tried to push herself up and failed. "I don't know what to say."

"You don't have to say anything—and no, I haven't said anything to your friends."

"Friends?"

There was a knock on the door. And then Candy put her head in.

"Oh, thank fuck," the receptionist said as she shoved her way into the room. "I look horrible in black, but I woulda worn it for your damn funeral. For an hour or two."

Right behind her, Sheriff Eastwind was a tall, quiet presence, his uniform's hat held between two hands, his strong face worried.

Lydia covered her eyes with the arm she could move as the tears came back.

"Don't start." Candy cleared her throat. "I really— oh, shit. Who's got Kleenex."

✦   ✦   ✦

About twenty minutes later, when the sheriff and Candy left, Lydia reflected that it was so strange ... the way strangers became family.

And she was glad to see even Eastwind, although she had questions she was far too tired to ask, like what exactly had happened when Candy had done what Lydia had asked and gone to him with Rick's binder and Peter's disks ... and what his response was ... and what all that would mean. But she had a feeling, given that they were here with C.P.?

Well, the woman had reach, didn't she. And money. And power.

And really, Lydia didn't care about the outside world. She just didn't.

"Where is Daniel?" she asked. "When can I see him?"

And that was when there was a subtle shift in C.P.'s expression.

"What." Lydia pushed herself up high on the pillows even though it hurt like a bitch. "You need to tell me. Right now."

C.P. flared out her manicured nails and inspected the gel tips that were done in a French mani.

"What," Lydia breathed. "You told me he was going to live. You told—"

"He'll survive the operation."

"Is he paralyzed? Blinded? Was he hit somewhere—"

"It's not a wound that's the problem."

After a long moment, C.P. turned her head. The fact that her cold, calculating eyes were watery made Lydia's heart stop.

"He has cancer."

"What?" Lydia sat all the way up, in spite of the pain. "I'm sorry, what did you—"

"He's riddled with it. It's in his lungs and his liver. The fact that he was able to go on at all is a miracle. We found the tumors because of the chest X-rays that were done before he was operated on for the internal bleeding. It's clearly stage four, although the primary site hasn't been determined yet."

"What . . . are you . . . is he . . ."

C.P. rubbed her eyes and cleared her throat. As she stood up off the bed, she put her hands on her hips and stared at the door.

The stillness of the woman as she spoke was so scary. "We're going to move him to a recovery room up in the house. He's welcome to stay as long as he wants, as long as he needs to. You, too. You're part of the family now, with all your baggage. Both of you."

"When can I see him?"

"As soon as he's medically stable and awake." C.P. went to the door. Then looked back. "Good thing we don't worry about HIPAA here, isn't it."

"Is he terminal?"

As Lydia let the words fly, she held on to a hope that in her mind she knew she couldn't justify. Still, miracles happened with cancer, right? Miracles happened all the time . . .

. . . right?

FIFTY

IN THE DREAM, *Daniel was running, running through the night, running through the moonlight, across a field of wildflowers. On his heels, tight as could be, a beautiful female gray wolf was galloping after him.*

Every time he looked over his shoulder, she was there, the light in her golden eyes one of love and adoration, happiness and loyalty.

He was laughing.

Taking great breaths of clean, fresh spring air, he was laughing—

Daniel's eyes flipped open. Overhead . . . there was no moonlit night sky. Across the way . . . there was no meadow, but a blank wall.

Next to him, though. Slumped in a chair. With her chin on her chest . . .

Was his wolf.

As if Lydia sensed his attention, her eyes flipped open and that was when the light came from somewhere: The illumination was so bright and blinding that he had to try to put his arm up.

"What's wrong?" she asked.

"The light—so bright. Can't see you in it?"

"There's no . . . oh, God, you're having a stroke—"

Instantly, it started to fade and he shook his head a little. "No, no . . . stroke. That was . . . weird. Just a bright illumination you came through."

As Lydia leaned over him, her eyes were rimmed with tears. "Did I . . . come through?"

"Yes . . . you did."

Their eyes clung to each other's, and Daniel found that all his pain drifted away. Then again, love was a drug that healed, wasn't it.

"I'm glad it's not nighttime," she said.

"Why?"

"Because then I'd be your past. Instead of your future. It's the veil. It's early in the morning."

He took her hand—or maybe she took his. "I want to be . . . your everything."

"You are."

"Are you okay?" he asked.

"Yes. I am." She cleared her throat. "And we're in C.P. Phalen's laboratory and clinic. It's a long story."

At that, her eyes ducked away and she lowered her head. A squeeze from his hand brought her focus back.

"You're beautiful," he whispered. "To me. Exactly how you are."

The tears that trembled on her lashes were like crystals, and as they drifted down her pale cheeks, he wanted to wipe them away, but didn't have the strength.

"Are you sure?" she asked hoarsely.

"I don't have to understand anything. I just know that I love you. Exactly how you are."

When he repeated the words, her tears fell faster and faster. And then she dropped her forehead to their linked hands.

"I love you, too, Daniel."

In the quiet that followed, the silence was broken only by the subtle beeping of monitors, but the air was warm and peaceful—and not because of the morphine drip he was on. He was just so happy to stare at her—because with every breath she took, and expression she made, and shift of her body . . . he was reassuring himself that she was alive.

And holy shit, so was he.

"You saved my life." He smiled a little. "*Susi*. Finnish for 'wolf.' "

"Yes. My grandfather."

He took a deep breath and rode a surge of strength that came from somewhere deep inside of him.

"I work for the government, Lydia. For a shadow agency that protects the genetic composition and integrity of the *Homo sapiens* species. It was established as the result of experiments being conducted in the seventies and eighties. I came here to stop what— well, what C.P. Phalen is doing. Kind of ironic where I ended up, huh. And yes, I know all about this lab and her clinic."

He coughed a little, and as her face paled, he

swiped his hand through the air. "Don't worry. This isn't the first time I've been operated on. I'll come through this—although it looks like I owe that woman with the white hair a big debt."

"So you're a government agent?"

"Eastwind was right. Daniel Joseph is not my real name, but I've been him for so long, it's my name now. And I did know what your last name meant— although I thought the latter was just a cute coincidence." He took a deep breath and tried not to give in to the coughing fit that was just under his surface. "Someday, will you tell me? Your whole story?"

It was a while before she answered. "Yes. Someday I will."

"I like the sound of that." As she glanced over again, he smiled. "Someday means we have a future."

The tears that came to her eyes put a stake in his heart. "What. What's wrong?"

At the sight of her crying again, he knew that even morphine wasn't going to help with the ache that flared behind his sternum. He didn't want her ever to be upset.

And then he guessed what might be wrong.

"Look," he said, "if you think things aren't going to work out because of . . . what I saw . . . I'll do whatever it takes. I'll swear to whatever I need to swear to. You have to believe, your secret is safe with me, and I will always protect you."

Fuck, and then there were the others in the Federal Bureau of Genetics.

Who were going to be after him for not blowing up C.P. Phalen's lab.

Who were going to be after Lydia for the same reason.

The implications of the reality they were both in were going through his mind as a look of incredible sadness changed the color of Lydia's eyes.

A stillness came over him.

"It's not any of that, is it," he said in a low voice.

The way she slowly shook her head back and forth chilled him to the bone.

"What did they find," he asked in a dead tone. "When they opened me up, what did they find?"

◆　◆　◆

He knew, Lydia thought.

As she sat on the side of Daniel's hospital bed, and tried not to break down completely, she had a feeling he was not going to be surprised.

Who'd have thought that her being a wolven half-breed was the least shocking thing they'd have to deal with?

"Why don't I go get the doctor," she said.

When she went to stand up, he grabbed her arm with a surprisingly strong hold. "No. I want to hear it from you."

As she hesitated, he whispered, "I'm scared, Lydia."

Easing back down on the hospital bed, she took both his hands. In a choked voice, she said, "I love you. I want to tell you that again before . . ."

His lopsided smile was heartbreaking. "Because I'm not going to hear anything after you lay it on me, huh. Well, I'm glad to hear the words." His eyes traveled around her face. "Do you remember when you once asked me why I stayed? What the word was?"

When she nodded, he squeezed her hand. "It's love. That's why I stayed. I think I fell in love with you from the moment I first saw you in person."

"Me, too." She let out a soft sob. "I knew when I saw you . . . nothing was going to be the same again."

Daniel winked. "Even if I don't have a sense of humor?"

"I still think you're blind to your potential in that department."

"So let's spend the next fifty years arguing about it, sound good? Great. Let's book it."

Lydia's face fell, and she couldn't hide it from him. Then again, she wanted to be honest with him. She had to be.

Daniel took a deep breath. "Okay, spit it out. Just let it fly, whatever it is, we'll figure something out. Although given that I need to quit my job, I'm going to lose my health benefits so . . ."

As his voice drifted off, she felt a tear slip out of

her eye. Brushing it off with impatience, she wanted to be strong. *Had* to be.

"It's your lungs, Daniel."

He put a hand lightly on his chest, on top of the white surgical bindings. "I have pneumonia?"

When she shook her head slowly, he cursed. Looked away. Cursed again.

"Sonofabitch. That fucking cough."

"It's in your liver, too, Daniel."

As he closed his eyes, he went quiet for a moment. And then his lids popped open and he looked at the ceiling and he nodded.

"I started coughing blood maybe six months ago. I powered through it, told myself it wasn't a big deal because it wasn't an all-the-time kind of thing. And I've been fucking exhausted and nauseous. Losing weight. I just thought it was . . . well, now I know what it is."

"I'm so sorry." She stroked his arm. "I don't . . . it's just what you said. We'll handle it together, okay? We can handle it together."

The silence became so loud in the room, it felt like a scream. Or maybe that was the sound in her head, the howling pain at the unfairness of it all supersonic in its volume.

To have met the love of her life, who knew the impossible truth about her and still accepted her . . . only to lose him before they began? Come on, destiny.

"I need to know more," he said finally. "I want to

know what kind and ... everything. Maybe we'll get a miracle. Or good news or ...'"

"That's right." Lydia nodded and all but crawled onto his chest. "That's what we're going to hope for. That's what I'm going to pray for. And you're going to do the same."

She reached up to the nape of her neck. "Here. Take my grandfather's St. Christopher medal. You're going to wear it."

When he struggled to lift his head, she helped him, and the delicate gold chain barely fit around his neck. But as he relaxed back against the pillows, she arranged what her grandfather had given her.

"He would approve of you having it," she said. "He was the one who guided me to you out in the woods. He appeared before me ... and he took me to you to save you."

"And now we're here," Daniel mumbled in a dull voice.

"We just need to pray for good news. And a path forward."

FIFTY-ONE

BACK IN CALDWELL, at the Brotherhood's mansion, Xhex was chilling on one of the sofas in the billiards room, watching John Matthew, Qhuinn, V, and Butch squabble over who was playing in the first twosome at everybody's favorite pool table. Even though there were a couple of others, the center one was, like, some kind of good luck talisman or some shit.

She didn't know. She didn't play games with balls.

Okay, not those kind of balls.

When John Matthew looked over and wagged his brows, it was clear he and Qhuinn were going to go at it first. No doubt, the winner of the match would play the next person in line, and so on and so on. Until dawn came and Fritz put on a massive Last Meal with enough pieces of cooked meat to feed a den of lions.

Natch.

Meanwhile, all around the house, other people were talking. Laughing. Relaxing.

It was rare that everyone had a night off at the same time, but Wrath had started the tradition a couple of months ago, and it seemed to be sticking. And as this month's free time happened to hit on a Sunday, Xhex didn't have to go in to any of the clubs.

So here she was. On the couch. Totally determined not to think about everything she'd been ignoring—

A glass of grapefruit juice appeared in front of her and she looked up at Rehvenge with a jump. Accepting the vitamin C, she said, "How the hell did you get Lassiter to let you use his juicer thing?"

The king of the *symphaths* sat down beside her with his own ginger ale. "What he doesn't know won't hurt him."

"Spoken like a true member of the Colony."

"Come now, is that any way to say thank you."

She toasted him. "Thank you."

Underneath the folds of his full-length mink coat, which he was wearing even though the room was a balmy seventy degrees, Rehv crossed his legs at the knees and made sure the two halves covered his lower body completely—which was kind of a pity. He was wearing a perfectly cut dark gray suit that would have been appreciated by Butch, the other clotheshorse in the room.

"Speaking of *symphaths*," Rehv drawled, "do you know what's really annoying about them?"

Glancing over at him, she met his amethyst eyes. He'd recently had the sides of his Mohawk reshaved by V, and the top had been trimmed as well, the stand-up strip only about two inches high. Lounging back on the leather sofa like he was, he looked like a dangerous animal, even in his at-ease pose.

"You think I've forgotten?" She sipped more of the juice, the tart sweetness waking her up. Bonus. "Or is it just because you're king of all us sociopaths and you—"

"*Symphaths* see what others hide." Those glowing eyes went to the pool table and settled on John Matthew, who was leaning over with his cue, about to strike the rack of balls. "We know what others wish no one else did."

Xhex stiffened. "It's rude to read my grid."

"So read mine back and we'll be even. I'll honestly tell you what you'll find in me first, though. Unlike you. If I were to ask you how *you* are, you'd lie and give me some bullshit about how you're sleeping fine and perfectly alert and—" Those purple eyes swung back in her direction. "—perfectly. Fucking. Fine."

Shaking her head, Xhex smiled coldly. "You're a fucking—"

"No, the asshole is your brother."

"Yeah, okay, I'm not talking about Blade right now. And I was having a nice night until you came around—"

"Your grid's collapsing."

Xhex blinked. Then started to get up. "Well, on that note, I'll just take this grapefruit juice—"

Rehv clapped a hold on her arm. "I'm not fucking around here, female. Your grid is collapsing. Do you understand what that means."

When she pulled at her wrist, he let her go. "I've had a little trouble sleeping," she said. "No big deal."

Try, she hadn't slept since she went onto Deer Mountain and talked to that . . . whatever that was.

Wolven.

As the word ricocheted around her mind, she tried to ignore it. Tried to ignore . . . the obvious concern in Rehv's normally harsh and unforgiving face—

At that moment, her phone rang and she jumped again, splashing grapefruit juice everywhere.

"You're going to want to answer that," Rehv said grimly.

"Why."

"I was the one who told them to call you."

"Who is it."

"Answer. The. Phone."

If it had been anyone else, anybody else on the planet—except for John Matthew—she would have fucked off the order. But as a strange feeling came over her, she took out the vibrating cell phone—

And answered. The. Phone.

"Hello?" Out of the corner of her eye, she saw John Matthew look up from his third shot, like he was debating whether to come over and see what was wrong.

"Hello," she said with more force. "Well, say something, goddamn it."

"Is this Alex Hess," a deep male voice replied.

"Yes."

"I need to talk to you. About the labs. And yes, the ones you and I both know about."

Xhex swung her eyes over to Rehv. Her old friend, her fellow *symphath*, her other king, was staring at her with something she had never seen on his face before.

It was stark terror. For her.

Between one blink and the next, she heard that ghostly entity's voice in her mind, sure as if it had been inserted there deliberately: *That is not your question, child.*

"Who the fuck is this," she demanded.

"You don't know who I am. But I need to talk to you."

As a feeling of premonition came over her, she shifted her eyes to John Matthew. He'd flubbed his shot and was standing off to one side, staring at her.

He was the love she would never have dared believe in, the one, pure thing in her life, uncontaminated by both her bad side . . . and what had been done to her all those years ago.

There is a path before you, my child. It will be long and dangerous, and the resolution of your quest is not clear at this time. But if you do not start . . . you will never, ever finish.

"I don't know what you have to do," Rehv said softly, "but you need to take care of your business. You don't have a lot of time left."

"Alex Hess?" the voice over the connection repeated.

"If your grid collapses," Rehv announced, "psychosis is going to own you and everyone who loves you is going to lose you even as you live and breathe in front of us."

With a feeling of dread, she stared at John Matthew. And all she thought of was how much she loved him.

"Yeah," she heard herself say. "I'll meet you. Just say when and where."

EPILOGUE

THREE WEEKS LATER, the night was unseasonably warm, and as Lydia walked out of C.P.'s mansion onto the terrace, she decided she wasn't going to need her sweater after all.

When Daniel didn't immediately follow, she glanced back into the professional kitchen.

Through the open sliding-glass door, she saw him over at a counter, laughing and saying something to the cook. Then he was turning to her. Walking to her. Smiling at her.

He was as he had always been, tall and strong and powerful.

It was hard to believe that he was dying. That under his smooth skin and still-heavy muscles there were rogue tumor cells multiplying millions of times over, and developing reliable blood supplies, and spreading far and wide.

It was hard to believe that their time was so short.

Today, at around three twenty-one p.m.—not that

she was counting—they'd discovered that, yes, it was confirmed, the lung cancer was in his brain, too.

Before long, his quality of life was going to nose-dive . . . because he had turned down treatment. After a team of C.P. Phalen's doctors had looked at all the scans, and then talked with other experts in the nation, and gotten together a semblance of a plan . . .

He had said no, thank you.

No chemo. No radiation. Nothing but comfort measures.

She didn't blame him. Six pretty good months without, nine miserable months with. Why ruin the time he had? The time they had—

"Penny for your thoughts?" he said as he stepped out and slid the door shut behind himself. "Or would you rather keep them private?"

"Just remembering what we did upstairs in the Jacuzzi."

"Ahhh . . . I like those thoughts." He took a sip of his Jack and soda—and as he coughed, he covered it up quick, then talked through the tail end of the fit—as if, as long as he ignored it, it didn't exist. "I like them very much."

As he wrapped his arm around and pulled her in close, she molded her body to his and welcomed his kiss. In the lee of the setting sun, and in the pleasant cuddle of the warm spring air, she drank in the eternity they grabbed at every moment they were together.

When he eased back, she ran her hands over his face.

"I'm sorry," he whispered.

"What for?"

"For bringing the end so damned soon."

"Oh, my God, like it's your fault." She shook her head. "Daniel. It's not your fault."

"I just want you to know that the last three weeks have been the best weeks of my life. And whatever time we have ahead of us, it's more than I could have expected or deserved. You're the best thing that's ever happened to me."

"I feel the same." When his expression grew remote, she frowned. "What is it?"

Taking her hand, he led her over to an arrangement of wrought iron furniture. It went without saying that they sat together on the love seat. She wanted to be close to him as much as possible, and he felt the same.

Daniel swirled his Jack around in the rocks glass. "There's something I want to do before I go."

Lydia took a deep breath. "Okay. Let's do it. Whatever it is—"

"We're going to find your family, your people."

She lifted her brow. "I told you, my grandfather's passed—"

"Not that family."

". . . oh."

Daniel took her hand and rubbed the center of her

palm with his thumb. "I'm not leaving you alone in this world. There are more of you here. Somewhere. And I have a contact that can help us find—"

"Come on, Daniel. This isn't a Stephen King novel. What do you think—that there's, like, a lair of the wolven somewhere in the woods?"

"We're going to find your people, so you're not alone. After I'm gone."

Lydia looked up at the backside of C.P. Phalen's enormous house. And thought of Candy and Sheriff Eastwind, both of whom had been by regularly as soon as they had heard of Daniel's cancer.

The story of everything at the WSP was an illusion sold to the press and the state law enforcement officials: Rick had killed Peter, and then himself, over a simple embezzlement scheme miraculously untied to anything that had to do with genetic experiments. Past or present. It had been big news for a short while—after which the nation's twenty-four-hour shock-information cycle had moved on to something else.

And Lydia was still working at the WSP. At least on paper.

In reality, she hadn't left C.P.'s estate since she'd been flown in and treated for her gunshot wound. And she wasn't going to leave. Daniel had been invited to stay for comfort measures and he'd accepted the offer.

So no, they weren't going anywhere.

"But I thought you said it wasn't safe for me out there." She focused on the horizon. "That because of the way things went, your agency was still coming after me. Still coming after C.P."

With a grim curse, he put his glass aside. "I really can't leave here . . . without knowing you're with people who understand and can protect you."

She thought of the wolves in the preserve, the way they had come and surrounded them. Protected them. Saved them both.

"That's why you refused treatment, isn't it." She tilted his chin when he looked away. "That's why."

"I don't have a lot of time left, Lydia. And I've found someone who I think can help. I used some back channels to get the contact. It's a woman by the name of Alex Hess. I've never met her, but somebody I know and trust has. Word has it, she's got some familiarity with the experiments on those floppy disks."

"Did she work at the labs?"

"I don't know, but my source tells me that she is a gatekeeper. That she will help, if she wants to."

Lydia shook her head. "Listen, I don't want to waste what little time we have—"

"Please. This is my last mission. I want to complete . . . my last mission. For you."

With a sigh of resignation, she settled down onto his chest and—

"I wish things were different," he said roughly.

Funny, that was just what she was thinking.

Lydia looked up to his face. "Love is immortal. It survives all things." She thought of when she had seen him in the veil. And when the same had happened for him. "You're my future, no matter how little time we have."

"And you're my everything."

They kissed. And kissed again.

"And okay, if it's that important to you," she said as she stroked his face some more, "I'll meet with the woman. But my main focus is on you. You're all that matters to me right now."

"It'll help me . . . let go, when it's time."

Lydia closed her eyes as tears threatened. Over the last couple of weeks, she'd been so careful not to let the dam break—because if she gave in, she was going to sob until there was no breath in her lungs.

And there was going to come a time when she was going to have to breathe for the both of them.

"It's okay," Daniel said sadly. "I'm here now. I'm holding you . . . now—"

There was the sound of the sliding door opening, and then high heels on the terrace.

Lydia took a deep breath and smiled up at C.P. "Well, if it isn't our hostess with the mostest—" She frowned. "Are you okay?"

C.P. Phalen was not a pacer. She was never hesitant. And she never, ever had to choose her words.

And yet the woman started to walk back and forth in front of the sunset, her profile cast in grim lines.

"Okay," Daniel said dryly, "I think I've proven over the previous weeks that I can handle bad news. Or have you missed all the pathology reports and PET scan results I've been getting?"

As C.P. turned to them both, she hesitated some more.

And then she spoke the words that would change everything:

"What if I told you there was another option for you."

"As opposed to outright croaking?" Daniel drawled as he lifted Lydia's hand and kissed the back of it. "No offense, but I don't have a lot of interest in getting stuffed and propped up in the corner—"

C.P.'s eyes locked on Daniel. "What if I could give you ... a new life. Through a cure."

Don't miss the next installment
of Lydia and Daniel's love story:

FOREVER

Coming Summer 2022!

ACKNOWLEDGMENTS

WITH SO MANY thanks to the readers of the Black Dagger Brotherhood books! This has been a long, marvelous, exciting journey, and I can't wait to see what happens next in this big world we all love. I'd also like to thank Meg Ruley, Rebecca Scherer and everyone at JRA, and Hannah Braaten, Andrew Nguyen, Jennifer Bergstrom, and the entire family at Gallery Books and Simon & Schuster.

Thank you as well to the incredible Robin Covington for all her help and support around Sheriff Eastwind!

To Team Waud, I love you all. Truly. And as always, everything I do is with love to, and adoration for, both my family of origin and of adoption.

Oh, and thank you to Naamah, my Writer Dog II, who works as hard as I do on my books!

Do you love fiction with a supernatural twist?

Want the chance to hear news about your favourite authors (and the chance to win free books)?

Christine Feehan
J.R. Ward
Sherrilyn Kenyon
Charlaine Harris
Jayne Ann Krentz and Jayne Castle
P.C. Cast
Maria Lewis
Darynda Jones
Hayley Edwards
Kristen Callihan
Keri Arthur
Amanda Bouchet
Jacquelyn Frank
Larissa Ione

Then visit the *With Love* website and sign up to our romance newsletter:
www.yourswithlove.co.uk

And follow us on Facebook for book giveaways, exclusive romance news and more:
www.facebook.com/yourswithlovex

PIATKUS